Sara Jo Whitlock

To **Love**
and to
promise

To **Love** and to. **promise**

a novel

Rachel Ann Nunes

Covenant Communications, Inc.

Published by Covenant Communications, Inc.
American Fork, Utah

Printed in the United States of America
First Printing: September 1999

06 05 04 03 02 01 00 99   10 9 8 7 6 5 4 3 2 1

ISBN 1-57734-536-3

For Kristy, Diane, and Fátima, who each fought a tremendous battle and won despite losing. And to all of the other women in the world who, in the face of great adversity, have given and are giving everything to make their eternal marriages work. The Lord knows your struggles and He loves you.

Also to Lisa, Wendy, Donna, Jodi, and so many others who jointly with their faithful partners have suffered a unique kind of loss. Your courage, strength, faith, and love have been a lifeline in a time of great trial. Thank you. I pray that this book may reach out and help others in the way that you have helped me.

PROLOGUE

Brionney's heart was breaking. She looked at Marc, feeling the tears overflow and slip down her cheeks.

"Don't, Bri," he said. His voice was rough and full of remorse.

She loved him—there was no other way of describing the feeling in her heart. His friendship during the past summer had made Brionney understand herself and had also boosted her self-confidence. Marc hadn't cared that she had been overweight and shy, unsure of herself. He had enjoyed her company and appreciated her opinions. He had loved her.

In the end, it wasn't enough. Brionney had wanted more from their relationship, and Marc had wanted more, but they eventually discovered that the magic between them was only destined to go as far as friendship.

"I'm going to miss you," she said, speaking in French as they always did.

His eyebrows drew together tightly, and for a minute she thought he was going to cry. "You've been the best thing in my life in a long time, Brionney. I would give anything if this could be different."

She nodded, not trusting her voice.

He leaned over and kissed her gently on the lips. The action brought no stars, no quickening of her heartbeat, just that wrenching sadness that ate away at her soul. Brionney wanted to pull his face back to her and try again, but she knew the feelings wouldn't change.

"I've tried to put her out of my mind," Marc said miserably.

But Brionney knew the older woman who had first captured Marc's heart when he was fifteen was only a part of the problem. If Marc loved Brionney as a woman, and if she loved him as a man, their relationship would have conquered his obsession with Danielle. Brionney thought his love for the unattainable, happily married woman was like a security blanket he held onto as he waited for true love.

True love. What was it really? Would she ever know?

Not with Marc.

But her heart was still breaking. She wished desperately that she could love Marc more. Her love alone might carry them through. But she had learned enough with him in the past months to know that she could never settle for anything less than a whole relationship.

Yet it hurt to let go. It hurt desperately. He was closer than a brother, but now that was ending. The knowledge hung over them like a dark shadow.

"You'll miss your plane," he said.

A little sob escaped her throat. He pulled her to him tightly, as though he wouldn't let her go. "If you ever need me, call."

Those closest to them hoped they would still get together someday, and Brionney herself entertained this thought when the pain of losing him was too much to bear. But they both knew that this moment was it. Once she returned to America and began her studies at Brigham Young University, there could be nothing more for them except letters and sporadic phone calls as they gradually grew apart on their separate continents. Their time together had come to an end.

"I love you," she whispered.

This time it was Marc's turn to nod in agreement, too close to tears to speak. He gave her a gentle shove in the direction of the entrance. She lifted a hand to wave, but he was already leaving. She watched him go. He didn't turn around and she was glad. To see his face again would hurt too much.

Resolutely, Brionney picked up her bags and turned away. Now all she had were the memories of the long, lazy days in France and the hope of the future BYU would bring. *I will be happy,* she vowed. *I will find my true love.*

* * * * *

Behind her, Marc stopped and watched her go, happy that she couldn't see the tears streaming down his face. He couldn't give her what she deserved, though he badly wanted to be the one who could.

Brionney was innocent, trusting, and so beautiful. She was a woman to be loved and cared for. She was a woman who could give her whole heart. He envied the man who would receive it.

I love you, he thought. *Good-bye.*

* * * * *

Brionney awoke with the sound of the alarm. She was tempted to slap it into silence and return to her warm covers, but a thought of the chunky, awkward girl she had been before visiting France forced her to her feet. No way! She would not be fat again—ever. She certainly didn't want to listen to any snide BYU coed jokes. No, a rigorous morning jog kept the pounds away and also kept Brionney in her new jeans. But, oh, how she hated exercising!

When she returned from the morning torture, she showered and went into the kitchen, where her mother met her at the door with a smile. The delicious aroma of cooking bacon filled Brionney's nose. She groaned silently. Even after almost six weeks of being home from France, her mother was still not used to her new eating habits.

"I have breakfast ready."

"No bacon for me, Mom. But thanks."

"Well, okay," she said uncertainly. "Do you have a date tonight?"

"No, there's a dance. I'm going with Becky and Kim." Brionney couldn't keep the excitement from her voice. How different dances were for her now that she didn't hold up the wall for the entire duration!

"How fun! Are you going to wear those new jeans? They make you look—what was the term you always use?—hot."

Brionney laughed. "Yeah, I am." She slid a piece of omelet between two slices of whole wheat bread and made her way to the door. "See you later."

On campus, Brionney watched the students pouring past her. She loved the life, the vitality, the heart of BYU. A man she didn't know smiled at her, and Brionney smiled back. Not until he passed did she realize how much he looked like Marc. Her smile faded, and the old pain returned. *I still miss him.*

Her sadness didn't remain long. She arrived in class and was immediately swept into the discussion. French was her favorite subject, and she knew she was good at it—better even than most of the returned missionaries.

"Are you going to that dance tonight?" whispered Curt, who usually sat next to her.

Brionney nodded, anticipating his next words.

"Then save me a dance, eh?"

"Okay."

They had been out a few times, and he was good for her lonely heart, but she didn't know if the relationship would amount to anything. Maybe tonight she would find out. She had the feeling something big was going to happen.

* * * * *

"Man, I've only had one date this whole month," groaned Becky above the blare of the music.

Kim rolled her eyes. "Yeah, well, if it weren't for Gunther, I'd have had no dates at all."

"That's only because you still go out with him," Becky said. "If guys knew you were free, they'd ask you."

"Well, probably." Kim was gorgeous and always had a boyfriend *and* a slew of admirers.

Brionney laughed. She had been on six dates in the last month, and had enjoyed herself immensely. She wasn't about to admit to these new friends that before her summer days with Marc, she had never been on even one date. BYU was a whole new world, and she was making up for lost time.

"If someone would ask us to dance, we could try out that new step we learned in class," Becky said, eyeing the crowd around them.

Kim moaned. "Oh, Becky, maybe you'd better not." The girls shared a dance class, but Becky couldn't seem to get any of the moves right without falling or tripping her partner.

"May I have this dance?" someone said in Brionney's ear. She looked up to see a handsome man staring down at her—not hard, since she was so short.

"Sure."

Brionney danced almost every dance, until finally she leaned against the wall for a rest. Becky joined her. "Looks like Kim has found a new friend. Between you and me, I don't think Gunther is going to last long."

"Me neither," Brionney said with a laugh.

Feeling unseen eyes, Brionney turned and saw a man watching her. He stood with a crowd of friends, talking and laughing. His piercing blue eyes and white-blond hair, the same color as Brionney's, separated him from the other strangers. He was the most handsome man she had ever seen. She tried to tear her gaze away, because surely he wouldn't be interested in her. Just then he smiled, and a chill rippled through her body. She wanted to stare at him forever, but felt a blush stain her cheeks, and dropped her gaze quickly. Thank heavens it was fairly dark in the ballroom; he shouldn't be able to see her red face. From the corner of her eye, she saw the man separate himself from his friends and approach. Her hands grew sweaty, and she wiped them on her jeans.

"Would you like to dance?"

"Sure," she said casually, trying to match his air of ease. His hand touched her arm as he led her onto the floor.

"I'm Derek Roathe," he said loudly enough to carry over the music.

Her heart was pounding so loudly she almost couldn't speak. He was so incredibly good-looking! "I'm Brionney Fields," she managed.

"So what's your major?"

"French." Since Brionney's brother had first been called to serve a mission in France, the language had fascinated her. Her relationship with Marc during the summer had only helped her talent along. "I'm a freshman." She didn't add that her French classes were already three-hundred-level courses. Bragging wasn't her style.

"I'm in business management," he told her. "I'm a senior."

The music changed to a slow dance, and Derek put his arms around her. Brionney's heart did crazy things inside her chest. She'd always thought the descriptions in the occasional romance novel she had read were corny. They had always seemed to make the heroine's heart seem like it had a life of its own. But that was exactly how her heart felt when Derek touched her. Marc had never given her that feeling.

Their conversation came easily, and flowed even more smoothly as the dances progressed. He didn't seem to want to leave her side. After a few dances, he took her over to his group of friends and introduced her.

"This is Brionney." He went around the group, putting a name to each face, and everyone nodded and smiled—except one girl with long dark hair. Brionney felt her unfriendliness like a bucket of cold water on a warm day.

While Derek was deep in a conversation with a friend, she came up to Brionney's side. "Just watch it," she said. "He only likes skinny girls. You gain an ounce and you're out."

Brionney stared at her, surprised, not knowing what to say. Derek turned to her at that moment, and the girl faded into the crowd. "Want to dance again?" he asked. Another slow song was playing, and Brionney definitely did want to dance.

Her own friends, Becky and Kim, were suddenly scarce, but she caught sight of them behind a pillar, peeping out and giving her the thumbs-up signal. Much later, when it was time to go home, they were nowhere to be seen.

"Would you like a ride?" Derek asked. "My apartment's near here. We can walk there and pick up my car, if you live far."

"I live off campus," she said. Then in a lower voice she added, "With my parents." If that bothered him, he gave no indication.

The October night was clear and unusually warm, with bright stars overhead, as if signaling the beginning of something beautiful. He reached out and firmly took her hand, causing her heart to beat like thunder in her ears and making it difficult for her to breathe. Both reactions scared and thrilled her simultaneously. She couldn't believe it was happening to her! Not even the romance novels had prepared her for this!

The walk to his apartment was over too soon. His car was a sleek, dark green convertible, a sporty model. "Nice car," she said, trying not to gape.

He grinned. "Thanks. It's a pre-graduation present from my father."

"Wow!" Brionney's father worked hard at his real estate office, but she didn't think he would ever be able to buy her such a gift.

"Don't let it fool you," Derek said. His voice took on an odd note. "He's trying to buy his way into my life. He and Mom recently got divorced, and I haven't seen him much. He's a good guy, but—" He shrugged and opened the door for her to slide in.

"Is it working?" she asked when he was seated beside her.

"What?" He started the engine with a single fluid movement.

"Is he getting into your life?"

Strong shoulders lifted in a shrug. "Yeah, why not?"

"Are they members, your parents?"

"Not active. They set their sights on other things. I hope they'll come back one day. I learned on my mission that anyone can change if they want to."

"Any brothers and sisters?"

"A half-sister. My father is remarried now. But I've never seen her. My sister, I mean."

"How old is she?"

"I really don't know. I go and see him sometimes, but he keeps that part of his life pretty separate from his relationship with me." He paused. "So how about you?"

"Three sisters and one brother. All older than me, and married. They have six kids between them and three more on the way. Zack, my brother, and his wife live in France. They just had a baby a while ago." She laughed and Derek smiled. "Other than the French connection, I guess we're just your average Mormon family."

When he pulled up at her house, Brionney was glad her mother spent so much time in the yard. While they didn't live in one of the largest homes in the neighborhood, they did have an incredible landscape to set off their stylish residence. A white light shone on the sculpted bushes and evergreens, making them more remarkable at night. She watched as Derek glanced around in appreciation. "Beautiful," he said. He motioned toward the house, but looked at her as he spoke. She felt a blush on her cheeks and was grateful for the darkness.

"Come on," she said quickly to hide her embarrassment. Derek laughed, as if all too aware of her feelings.

Derek won her parents over in minutes, impressing them with his politeness and confidence. Before long they were talking with him as if they had known him forever. Then came the moment Brionney dreaded. "Would you like to see some family pictures?" her mother asked.

Brionney shook her head vigorously behind Derek's head. "No!" she mouthed, trying to silence her mother with her eyes. She jumped from the couch. "I'm sure Derek doesn't have time for that, Mom." Brionney got him out of the house as quickly as possible.

"I'm sorry," she apologized as the door shut behind them. "Acres and acres of baby pictures—I don't know what they were thinking! Were parents ever young?"

He laughed. "Thanks for rescuing me."

Standing by his car in the brisk air, they talked for a long time about everything and nothing. Then suddenly Derek stepped closer and put his arms about her. His face lowered, and Brionney held her breath. Should she let him kiss her on this first night? She hadn't planned on it, but she felt powerless as their lips met. A million fireworks went off in her head. For a moment, she felt she was drowning and didn't want to be saved.

Derek drew back after a long moment. "I'll call you," he said gruffly.

"You have my number." She took a few steps up the walk and then paused to watch him drive away.

She went inside the house, feeling as though she were walking on air. Her parents were still in the living room. "I can't believe you were going to show him my fat pictures!" she said. "I don't want him to know what I was like."

"You were still you, Brionney," her mother said with a trace of amusement.

"No, that life's gone now. I'm a new person." Brionney looked at her mother urgently. "Please don't show them to him." *If he ever comes back,* she added silently.

"All right. I won't."

Brionney kissed her parents and said good night. It wasn't until she arrived in her room and saw the picture of Marc on her dresser that she realized she hadn't thought about him all evening. Even now, the sadness that normally accompanied thoughts of him was absent. She took the picture and placed it under some clothes in her top drawer where she wouldn't see it every day. "I think I may have found him, Marc," she whispered. "And it was worth waiting for."

Now if he would only call!

* * * * *

Brionney waited for two days before Derek finally called. He took her out to a movie and dinner. There was still magic between them, sparking like electricity. When he kissed her good night, she never wanted it to end.

After that night, Derek became a constant visitor. Brionney knew her grades were slipping, but Derek made the world so exciting. They went to movies, plays, fine restaurants, and occasionally walking in the park.

"Don't you think you should slow down a bit?" her mother asked one evening. "I mean, I know you were pretty shaken up about Marc. Maybe you should give yourself time to heal."

"Marc?" Brionney asked absently as she thumbed through her latest issue of *Bride Magazine*. "Marc was just a friend, Mom. That's all he ever was. But Derek, he's different. I love being with him."

"But you never go roller blading anymore. You don't go hiking or do anything that you used to love."

Brionney smiled gently. "I'm just growing up, Mom. Get used to it." She hugged her to show that she wasn't trying to be mean.

"Just be careful," her mother said in her ear. "Don't settle for anything less than a temple marriage."

"Of course not."

There was a honk outside and Brionney ran to meet Derek, who waited for her in the car.

* * * * *

Irene Fields watched her daughter slip into the green sports car and drive away. She felt her husband come into the room behind her. "What's wrong?" he asked.

"It's Brionney and that boy. I just worry. At first I really liked him, but now I've noticed that he seems so intent on having fun and spending money. And have you noticed that every time I bring up his family he changes the subject? I don't know. Maybe it's the way youth is today, but I get the feeling our daughter's heading into a dark tunnel, and I am helpless to stop her."

Terrell put his arms around his wife. "I know the feeling," he said. "But I don't know if it's real or because she's our last child at home. It'll be lonely without her."

Irene sighed. "Well, there's really nothing more we can do now but be here for her . . . and pray."

* * * * *

Christmas was in the air, and Brionney felt her excitement build. She hadn't been out with anyone besides Derek since the night of the dance. To her knowledge, neither had he. "He is so right for you," Becky said enviously at their dance class. "You two look like a couple out of a magazine or something. Do you think he might ask you to marry him?"

Brionney hoped so. Every night she prayed that he would. She had the wedding practically planned in her mind. They would get married in the Provo Temple in early May, after Derek graduated. Her brother Zack and his wife, Josette, would come from France to attend, bringing the baby no one in America had yet seen. Everything would be perfect as she and Derek promised their eternal love. Afterwards, they would live together in warm Arizona where Derek had already accepted a job, pending his graduation. They would have children and live the perfect Mormon fairy tale.

"Brionney, are you listening? I want to know what you'll say if he asks you to marry him."

"Derek makes me feel like no one ever has," she replied with a faraway smile.

"Not even that Marc guy you used to always talk about?"

"Not even him."

A few days before school let out, Brionney met Derek at the Cougar Eat. After collecting their food, he led her to their usual place. "No, sit on this side," he said.

"Why—" she began. Then she saw the banner covering the entire back wall.

BRIONNEY, WILL YOU MARRY ME?

She was stunned into silence, but her tears came readily.

"Is that a yes or a no?" he asked, pulling a ring box from the inner pocket in his coat.

"Y—yes," she managed.

Derek whooped and opened the box to reveal the biggest diamond she had ever seen, surrounded by clusters of smaller diamonds. He put it on Brionney's trembling finger.

Suddenly they were swarmed by a group of Derek's friends, slapping them on the back and hollering congratulations. Someone took pictures. Brionney would rather have been alone with Derek to revel in her new status, but she had never been happier. *I found him,* she thought. *At last.*

"We are going to be so happy," Derek promised in her ear, sending chills up her spine. "We'll have every comfort life has to offer. Everything!"

Brionney believed him—then.

PART ONE
twenty months later

CHAPTER ONE

It was the Internet and a simple online chat that first began the corrosion of Brionney's perfect life. For months afterward, memories would haunt her whenever she closed her eyes, as vividly as though she were reliving that fateful day, so inextricably woven with miracle and deceit.

A steady breeze came from the hall cooler and into her room where she rested on the bed. Through the window she could see the shade trees in the yard, reflecting the sun in varying shades of green. Not even a gentle breeze stirred the branches, though several small sparrows flitted there, seemingly tireless even in this stifling Arizona weather.

"Brionney, I just heard!" Debbie burst into the bedroom unannounced, her short dark hair tousled. "How dare you go and have your baby on the one day I'm not home! I can't believe it. One night! One night I take the kids to see their grandparents, and you go into labor. I should have let them drive by themselves. Well? Where is she? Let me take a look!" She slipped off her sandals and settled onto Brionney's bed.

Brionney pulled the thin baby blanket back to reveal a tiny face. The baby's eyes were closed and she slept contentedly, though at times she gurgled or sighed in her sleep. With a finger, Brionney traced her soft cheek.

"She's beautiful!" Debbie exclaimed. "I think she looks a lot like you."

Brionney snorted. "Me without the fat, you mean." The weight was the only thing that marred her new happiness—her weight and the odd remoteness she had been feeling from Derek. But she hoped that was over now that the baby was here and she would soon be back to normal.

"You just had a baby. You're *supposed* to be fat."

"Yeah, but I've always been fat my whole life, except for when I lost it all in France two summers ago." Brionney grimaced. "Now I've got to start all over, before Derek decides to trade me in. Oh, if only I weren't so short!"

"Would you give her back?" Debbie asked in a slightly mocking tone.

Brionney grinned and shook her head. Debbie certainly knew how to put things in perspective.

"Oh yeah, I almost forgot. I brought you a present." Debbie pulled a sack onto the bed. Brionney already guessed what was inside.

Debbie was a master quilt maker. She made at least two or three a week, using mostly discarded material her sister picked up at the Coleman factory. The flannel, designed to make sleeping bags, was checkered either blue and black or red and black. There were sometimes a few plaids, but those seemed few and far between. Debbie now had her whole basement filled with food storage and hundreds of quilts. She was planning to feed and shelter an army in the Last Days. There wasn't any room left to stuff any more quilts in the basement, but that didn't stop Debbie. Checkered blue and black or red and black quilts were slowly spreading to all the less-fortunates who lived in Phoenix and Mesa. Brionney already had three of them.

As Debbie handed her the present, Brionney wondered what color the checks would be. Certainly not blue and black; she knew the baby was going to be a girl. But red and black didn't seem right either. Slowly, Brionney pulled back the wrapping paper and revealed a quilt with pink and white checks on one side and little animals on the other. Debbie had tied the quilt as usual, but had included a pink ruffled border. "It's beautiful!"

"Of course," her friend said. "What did you expect, red checks?"

"Uh . . ."

Brionney was glad Derek chose that moment to bring in her lunch. "Here we are," he said, setting the tray on the bed. He smiled and reached out to take her hand, squeezing it. "Brionney sure does a good job having babies, Debbie. You should have seen her, like an old pro."

Brionney laughed. "I hardly had a choice. She was coming whether I wanted her to or not."

"That's for sure." He briefly studied the baby, his blue eyes inscrutable. "They sure do sleep a lot."

"They do that for a few weeks," Debbie said. "Enjoy it while you can."

He sighed. "Well, I guess I'll leave you alone to visit. I've got some calls to make. Work, you know." He kissed Brionney's cheek. "Call me if you need anything."

As he left, Brionney looked at the food on the tray and sighed. Steamed vegetables surrounded a broiled chicken breast. In the corner there was a small bowl filled with fresh fruit salad and a glass of orange juice. Her stomach rumbled, but she knew that every bite she took would be one more she'd have to work off later. She had quit running months ago, but now the torture would have to begin again.

"Eat," Debbie urged. "You'll need strength to nurse the baby. And to get up during the night. Hey, it's not that fat thing, is it? Don't worry about it. There's fruit, chicken, a little juice. Packed with vitamins and hardly any fat. Eat."

Brionney frowned. The food showed too clearly that Derek was bothered by her weight.

"Are you still naming her Savannah?" Debbie asked.

"Yes." Brionney took a bite of chicken.

"Can I hold her? No, forget it. I should know better than to ask a new mother that. I remember I could barely stand even Max to hold our first baby. I felt so strange when he wasn't near me. To think of him all grown and on a mission now."

"Go ahead. Hold her," Brionney said before Debbie could turn sentimental. Debbie was normally a person who rarely said anything very serious, but where her son Chad was concerned, she was still feeling the recent separation.

"Okay, but only for a minute." She scooped Savannah expertly into her arms, hardly disturbing the baby's sleep. "She is truly beautiful. How's Derek taking to being a father?"

Brionney finished drinking her juice before answering. "Well, he seems nervous around her. He doesn't try to hold her much, just stares at her."

Debbie looked at her sharply. "Don't worry about that. It's normal for some men to feel awkward around a new baby. Guys usually start enjoying the process when babies can crawl and sit up. That's when the play begins."

"Oh, I'm not worried," Brionney said. "Well, okay, maybe I was. But what you said makes sense. Besides, Derek wanted to have a baby, though I admit it was probably more because he thought it would help him get promoted at work." She set aside the chicken and settled back into the mound of pillows behind her, watching Debbie with little Savannah. Brionney was so glad the baby was finally here. Maybe now she could spend more time with Derek.

"Look, she's waking up."

Sure enough, Savannah's eyes fluttered and then opened. They were a dark blue, large in her flawless face. Brionney leaned over and kissed her head, feeling the soft fuzz of blonde hair against her lips.

Debbie handed her the baby. "So is Derek staying home again with you tomorrow?"

"He said he has to work. I never knew that being an advertising manager would be so demanding. At least we'll be able to move out of this apartment soon. I just wish my mother could have come like we'd planned."

"How's her hip mending?"

"Good. But she's pretty upset about missing her first granddaughter. Nine boys . . . then finally someone in the family has a girl, and she misses it!"

"What did Derek's mom say about the baby?"

"He called her and she seemed excited, but I don't think she'll be visiting soon. She's got a new boyfriend or something. She never really wanted us to have children right away. She told me at the reception that I should wait until I was sure the marriage would work out. Can you imagine?"

Debbie clucked sympathetically. "Well, at least you've got me. I'll come over and stay with you for a while."

"You could work on a quilt," Brionney suggested. "And we can probably eat leftovers for lunch. My visiting teachers are bringing dinner tonight and tomorrow night as well." Since Debbie hated to cook, and burned nearly everything she put in the oven, this would be the perfect bribe.

"I'll be there," she said. "With bells on."

Brionney laughed. "I thought so."

Debbie stayed for a few minutes, then stood to go. "Better see how my gang's getting along." Her short brown hair rippled in the breeze from the air conditioner. "I'll let Derek know I'm going. Where is he?"

"In the den, probably. On the Internet. I don't know what he finds so fascinating about it. He'll stay in some of those chat rooms for hours."

"There's some neat stuff on the Internet," Debbie said.

"Yeah, but I haven't gotten into it yet. Derek had to because of his job, and now . . ." She shrugged. "One Internet addict in this family is enough."

"Well, we'll see you tomorrow." Debbie turned and marched down the hall.

The apartment had only two bedrooms and a small kitchen linked to the living room. On the far side of the living room was a large alcove Derek had sectioned off with a Japanese screen. His computer equipment fit in the space perfectly, with plenty of room for his books on business management. Brionney rarely intruded on him there, as he was always so intent on whatever he was doing. But he wouldn't mind Debbie interrupting him to offer to stay with her tomorrow.

Savannah made soft slurping noises, drawing Brionney's attention. She had her fist near her mouth and was trying to suck on it. "That won't give you any milk," Brionney cooed. She brought the baby to her breast like the nurses had shown her in the hospital. Savannah latched on almost immediately, sucking with surprising strength for such a tiny creature.

Brionney stared at the miracle of her daughter, feeling the exquisite wonder of having a new baby. The feelings she had for Savannah went beyond any emotion she had ever experienced. It was as strong and deep as what she felt for Derek, only different somehow.

True love. That was what she and Derek shared.

Brionney admitted to herself that there had been loneliness in the past sixteen months since her marriage, but that was because Derek had been so involved with learning his job and how to best use the Internet. His pressures were already easing. And now with Savannah, life was complete. Brionney felt sure that whatever appeal work or the Internet had for him, it would be diminished by the baby's addition to the family.

Savannah must not have been really hungry, because after a few swallows she fell asleep, completely innocent and perfect. Brionney set her on the bed, away from the direct breeze of the cooler, and began to eat her fruit. She looked up when Debbie came into the room, curiously silent. "I thought you were leaving," Brionney said.

She shook her head slowly. "Uh, I . . . Derek was on the Internet like you said. I waited a few minutes, but he seemed pretty involved and I didn't want to disturb him. Look, I've got to go check on the girls and make sure they haven't burned down the house or something. Is it all right if I bring them over after dinner? They want to see the baby."

"Sure. But why are you acting so strange?" Brionney was sure something had happened—something Debbie considered important.

Debbie sat on the bed, and her eyes bore into Brionney's. "It's probably nothing. Don't mind me." There was a long pause as she seemed to search for words. "Just remember that I'm your friend, okay? You let me know if you ever need anything. Anything at all." She smiled, but her eyes seemed more worried than anything else. Standing, she walked to the door, her shoulders slightly hunched. With a half-hearted wave of her fingers, she left.

What had Debbie seen? Why had she acted so strangely?

An overwhelming urge to see Derek made Brionney slide out of bed and walk awkwardly down the hall, slowly and silently. Her abdomen ached, and she had to hold the loose stomach skin up to ease the strain.

She stopped in the bathroom and briefly studied herself in the mirror. Her face was white and tired-looking, her thick hair disheveled and looking like a white-blonde rat's nest. She ran a brush through it, bracing her sore midsection against the counter. Feeling more presentable, she continued down the hall.

"Yes, I'll have it done by Sunday night," she heard Derek saying. "Don't worry. Everyone will pull the extra hours. It has to be done."

Her spirits plunged. One more Sunday without him. During the entire time they had been in Arizona, he had worked two or three Sundays each month.

Derek hung up the phone, and she could hear him moving papers about behind the Japanese screen. She circled the screen, and what she saw made her blood freeze.

Several pictures of a woman filled the computer monitor. She had dark hair and eyes, and a figure many women dream about having— one not given by nature but rather in a doctor's office. In one picture the woman wore jeans and stood up against a tree; in another she looked tanned and radiant in a bikini on the beach. The last one was a soft focus close-up of her fine-boned face. She was beautiful.

Tears sprang to Brionney's eyes. She wanted to scream and break the monitor. Who was this woman, and what did she have to do with Derek? A sound must have escaped her throat because Derek's head jerked around. "Brionney!"

"Who's that?" she managed to ask.

He glanced at the screen as though he hadn't realized it was there. His finger pushed the suspend button on the keyboard and the image turned black.

"That's just Melinda," he said. "A girl I ran into in one of the chat rooms. I don't know why she sent me the pictures. She lives in New York, so I guess she wanted to show me what she looks like."

Could it be as innocent as he made it sound? "Does she know you're married?"

"Yes. In fact, I was just going to see if she and some of the others were in the chat room, and I was going to announce about Savannah. Don't worry about it, Bri. She's just a friend. Someone I'll never even meet. She's had a hard life. Abuse, you know, when she was young. Some of us are trying to help her."

Brionney's heartbeat slowed. She put a hand on the back of his chair, steadying herself. Her legs felt weak.

"You shouldn't be up out of bed," Derek said. "You look pale. Here, let me help you back to bed."

He put his arm around her and led her down the hall. Brionney glanced back at the computer, almost expecting to see the woman's eyes following them, but the screen was still blank. She clung to Derek, loving the feel of his arms around her.

Brionney settled in bed and lay back against the pillows. She saw Derek staring at the baby. He reached out to touch her soft cheek. "Where did Debbie go?" he asked idly.

"She went home. But it was really strange. She went out to tell you that she was leaving, and came back acting really weird."

Derek's eyes met hers, showing his sudden interest. "What did she say?"

"Nothing." Then an idea came to her. "Maybe she saw the pictures."

"Oh." Derek's eyes dilated and he seemed far away. "Well, you'll have to explain to her then," he said. "About Melinda."

"Was she really abused?"

"I think so. It seems to be real. You want me to help her, don't you? I mean, I would just hate myself if she ended up killing herself or something because she didn't have anyone to talk to."

Brionney wanted to say no, but felt mean and small inside. What could she say when he put it like that? Wasn't she sure enough of his love to let him help a daughter of God? "I guess it would be okay," she said. She had to trust him. Besides, New York was a long way from Arizona.

He seemed relieved. "Are you going to be all right tomorrow?"

"Debbie said she'd come and stay with me. Will you be home on Sunday?" she asked, already knowing the answer.

"No, we have a deadline Monday morning." He saw the disappointment in her eyes. "But I'm sure it's the last one for a long time. I'll get that promotion, especially now that we have Savannah. They promote men with families before any others. More stable, I guess."

Brionney managed a smile. "One last pull before a long rest. I guess it's worth it."

"It will be." He glanced at Savannah again.

"Do you want to hold her?"

He gave a quick shake of his head. "No. She looks pretty comfortable right where she is."

They watched her together for a few minutes, a feeling of unity seeping into the room. Brionney could almost believe she hadn't seen the pictures.

Finally, Derek stood. "I'm going back on the Internet to finish my work. Why don't you rest? I'll let you know when they come with dinner."

"Thanks." As he left, Brionney remembered Debbie's strangeness, the way she had proclaimed her friendship. Had she seen the pictures, or something else that was even worse? Was Derek hiding something more from her?

No, he told me all about that girl. It's nothing. But why did she send such suggestive pictures in the first place?

Brionney shook the thoughts away. She was the one married to Derek, and he loved her and only her. They were a perfect couple, living the perfect live. A Mormon fairy tale.

Outside the sun suddenly darkened, obscured by the onslaught of a monsoon wind carrying tiny grains of sand and dust throughout the city, followed by heavy rainfall. She could see the unrelenting wind whip through the young trees, tossing the leaves and branches wildly.

Brionney had grown accustomed to the suddenness of the storms and the layers of fine grit left behind to mark their passing. She laughed, but the laughter seemed to reverberate softly from the walls and come back to her. It sounded hollow and afraid.

CHAPTER TWO

"My dad's coming to visit tomorrow," Derek's voice said over the phone. In the background, Brionney could hear the faint voices of his co-workers.

"Now?" Two weeks had passed since Brionney had given birth to Savannah. "Where are they going to stay?"

"It'll only be for one night," Derek said. "You can make up the couch bed. And something nice for dinner. It'll be fun."

Brionney didn't think it would be fun. She had met Derek's father briefly at the reception. He was an older version of Derek and deadly handsome, the life of the party. Alice, his second wife, was a very pretty brunette with green eyes, much younger than he, and in obvious awe of her husband. Their daughter was ten, older than Brionney had expected. She had thought they had only been married a few years.

"They want to see Savannah," Derek added. "Hey, gotta run. We've got some important stuff in the works. We're pretty sure we're going to be merging with another company soon, and we're busy tying down the ends." The phone went dead.

"I love you, too," Brionney said softly. She looked around at the mess in the kitchen. Things had certainly been out of her control lately. It was time that ended.

Why did she feel so uncomfortable about having Derek's father visit? She should get to know him. After all, he was Savannah's grandfather. *It won't be bad,* she thought. *It might even be fun.* Whistling a song, she started loading the dishwasher.

* * * * *

An hour later, Debbie found Brionney on her hands and knees, scrubbing the kitchen floor. "Brionney, what are you doing?"

Brionney looked up. "Cleaning. Uh, you know . . . that terrible, hateful thing everyone has to do."

"Not when they've just given birth two weeks ago."

"I feel fine," Brionney said.

"And why on earth are you doing it on your hands and knees? Where's your mop?"

Brionney grinned self-consciously. "I guess I was feeling a little tired. I think Savannah was up all night. It's easier to clean sitting down."

"Do you want to get sick? You need to rest. Go sit down on the couch right now." Debbie took the rags from Brionney's hand and helped her to her feet. Brionney headed toward the adjoining room, stopping to check on Savannah, who slept peacefully on a blanket in front of the green floral couch.

"You should have called me," Debbie said. "I would have come over. And why are you doing this, anyway?"

Brionney groaned. "Derek's father and stepmother are coming tomorrow for a visit. Oh, that reminds me. I have to change the sheets on the mattress in the couch."

"They're staying here? When you just had a baby? Who are these people, anyway?" Debbie made no pretense of hiding her anger. In her view, Brionney was just a little too much of a push-over.

"It'll be good for them to see Savannah. And for Derek to see his father. They haven't had much contact since his parents divorced. As far as I know, they haven't even talked since the wedding."

Debbie grumbled under her breath. As she cleaned, she thought about what she had heard Derek saying on the phone that first day she had come to see Savannah. And those pictures! Poor Brionney!

Debbie cleaned vigorously for the next two hours. She wished she could clean the knowledge of Derek from her mind. "Well, that about does it." She looked around in satisfaction.

"Thanks, Debbie. I don't know what I would do without you."

"It's nothing." She sat on the couch next to Brionney. "How are things going with you and Derek?"

"Good. Only he works so much. Sometimes I wish we could go

back to our BYU days. We had a lot of time for each other then. But it'll get better."

"Do you know anyone named Melinda?" Debbie asked.

Brionney froze. Then she turned her face slowly to Debbie. "She's a woman Derek met on the Internet. Seems she was abused as a child. He and some of the others are trying to help her."

Debbie saw that Brionney desperately wanted to believe what she was saying.

"You saw the pictures of her, didn't you?" Brionnney asked.

"Yes."

Brionney sighed. "She's very good-looking. And skinny."

"Too skinny," Debbie said. "And that figure is definitely not natural."

Brionney shrugged. "Oh, well. Derek hasn't said anything about her for a while. It could be they've lost contact."

"You could get on the computer and see," Debbie said. She knew she should keep her nose out of Brionney's business, but as a lawyer's wife she had seen too many nasty situations where men had taken advantage of their trusting spouses.

"I don't know anything about computers."

"I could teach you."

Savannah awoke and began crying. Brionney picked her up. "I love Derek," she said, "and I trust him."

"Well, if you ever want to, let me know," Debbie said, deciding she'd better keep quiet about the phone call she had overheard. She couldn't open Brionney's eyes by forcing her. Besides, maybe she was right. "Well, I guess I'd better get going. I'm going to the grocery store. Do you need anything for your company?"

"No, I've got food in the freezer," Brionney said. Abruptly she looked down at her body. "Oh my gosh, I just thought of something! What am I going to wear tomorrow when they come? It'll have to be maternity clothes. Yuck!"

"You need to go shopping for something," Debbie said. "Or send Derek."

"What I need is to lose this weight!" Brionney pinched the fat on her leg.

"You are beautiful as you are," Debbie said. And she meant it. Brionney was a little overweight right now, but she had the kind of features that shone at any weight. A classic beauty.

Brionney sighed. "Well, I guess I'll have to make do."

* * * * *

Derek seemed more nervous than usual as he waited for his father to arrive. "Are there fresh towels in the bathroom?"

"Yes, I put them there this morning. Don't worry; everything is ready." Brionney already felt exhausted, and the night hadn't even begun.

Derek stopped pacing and stared at her, an odd look in his eyes. "Don't you have anything better to wear?"

Brionney grimaced. "Nothing that fits."

"What about those black jeans? They were always loose on you."

"Nope. I tried."

"I didn't realize you were so—" he broke off.

Hurt enveloped Brionney, and she turned away so he couldn't see. Derek hadn't meant to be mean. He was right; she was fat. Tomorrow she would start exercising, even if she could only walk, pushing the stroller the women in her ward had given her at the baby shower.

Derek paced toward the window. "Hey, they're here!" He shot to the door, opened it and bounded up the few stairs. Brionney followed more slowly with Savannah in her arms.

Derek was giving his father a hug. "You look great, son," said Logan. "You must be working out."

"Three days a week at the gym," Derek said, flexing his arm muscles.

Logan laughed. "That's my boy."

Derek nodded coolly at his stepmother before turning and leading Logan toward the apartment. "Let me see this grandbaby," Logan said. "I can't believe I'm a grandfather. I don't feel that old."

Derek took Savannah from Brionney and handed him to his father. "She's a pretty one," Logan said. "Too bad she's not a boy, but at least she's good-looking, eh?" He nudged Derek and they laughed. Brionney didn't find the comment amusing. She watched them go into the house.

"Hi Brionney," a voice said.

Startled, she turned to see Alice. In the wake of Logan's grand entrance, Brionney had forgotten his wife's presence.

"Hi, Alice. Nice to see you again."

"I'm sorry for barging in on you when you've just had the baby. But Logan got it in his head to see Derek, and here we are. I tried to get him to stay at a hotel, but he said he wanted to spend as much time as possible with his son."

"It's okay, really," Brionney said. "Come on in. Are you hungry? I made dinner."

"Yes," Alice said. "But I could have made something. Or we could have gone out to eat."

"We could have gone out. I wonder why Derek didn't think of that." Alice shrugged. "He's a lot like his father."

Brionney didn't think so. From what she had seen, Derek was nothing like Logan. But telling Alice so wouldn't be polite. Besides, what would she have worn if they had eaten out?

The men were deep in conversation and scarcely noticed Brionney and Alice when they entered. "It's not bad for a four-plex," Derek was saying. "It's cheap, and since I got the promotion, we should be able to move up soon."

"You got the promotion?" Brionney said. "That's wonderful! Why didn't you tell me?"

"I thought I did," he said. Brionney crossed to the couch where the men sat and gave Derek a hug and kiss. He looked embarrassed. She wished she had something better to wear. "It's nothing, Bri."

"So tell me about this merger you were talking about on the phone," Logan said.

"Okay, but are you hungry? Brionney almost has dinner ready." Derek looked at her expectantly.

Brionney went into the kitchen, feeling oddly out of place. "It's better to just let them talk," Alice said in a low voice.

"Well, I guess they have a lot of catching up to do."

Alice helped her ready things in the kitchen. She didn't say much, but glanced at her husband often, as though waiting for a signal.

Brionney kept a casual ear on the conversation. Suddenly something Derek was saying made her listen more closely. ". . . New York. It's a big company with some important clients, but we've got the building and equipment. By merging, it'll help both companies. Melinda says that everyone in her company is really excited about the merger. Stock has already begun to rise, and I think it will go right through the roof when we actually join the companies. I have to go to New York next week to start settling things. The great thing is that it was all my idea."

Brionney carefully put down the plate she held in her hands. Melinda? Derek in New York? Had she heard right?

Derek glanced at her. "Oh, look, dinner's ready." He took the baby from Logan and settled her in the swing.

"You're going to New York?" Brionney asked.

Derek sat down at the bulky new table that nearly filled their small kitchen. "Yes, I just found out about it today."

"You just have to live with business trips," Logan said. "That's what I always tell Alice. It's part of a man's life." Alice didn't say anything, but stared at her plate.

The rest of the meal was torture for Brionney. She remembered the pictures on the computer monitor and how thin and beautiful Melinda was. There was no way she wanted that woman anywhere near Derek! As soon as they were alone, they were going to have a talk about this trip.

The meal was no sooner finished than Logan pulled out a cigarette. Brionney took Derek aside. "I don't want him smoking in here around the baby."

"He's my father. What do you want me to say?"

"To go outside." The request seemed reasonable to her.

Derek went reluctantly to his father, his eyebrows drawn slightly. "Hey, Dad, this kitchen's kind of small for all that smoke. What do you say we take a walk?"

Logan gave Brionney an icy stare. "Better yet, son, why don't you show me where you work? Then maybe we can stop for a small drink to celebrate your promotion. The ladies won't mind our leaving, will you?"

"No," Alice said faintly.

Derek smiled at Brionney as he reached for his car keys. "I'll drive."

Brionney was relieved to see them go. She and Alice cleaned up the dinner dishes together. "Where's your daughter?" Brionney asked to fill the silence.

"I left her with my mother. Logan's not very good traveling with children. If she had been a boy, it might have been different."

"So how did you meet Logan?" Brionney was reluctant to pry, but her curiosity was too great.

Alice put a plate in the dishwasher. "I worked with him," she said. "We've only been married three years."

Suddenly Alice sat at the table and stared into space. "I think I'm going to leave him." She laid her head on the table and began to cry.

Brionney left the dishes and sat across from her, not knowing what to do.

Alice mopped at her face. "I'm sorry, I shouldn't put this on you. I just . . . I just can't stand it anymore. He used to make me so happy, but now all I am is ignored. I hate the way he treats me. If only I didn't love him so much!"

Her sobs grew louder, and Brionney patted her back lamely. "Maybe you'd be happier without him."

Alice stopped crying. "I know. And that's part of why it hurts."

Just then Savannah clenched her tiny fists, screwed her eyes shut, and let out an indignant scream. Brionney took her out of the swing. "I think that means she's hungry."

Alice approached and touched Savannah's cheek. "She is really a beautiful baby," she said. "There's so much hope in her, isn't there?"

Brionney met Alice's eyes. "Maybe you need to fight, to give it everything you can."

Alice nodded, then added quietly, "But what if you're the only one who wants to save the relationship? What if you fight until there's nothing at all left inside?"

Brionney had no answer.

The two women busied themselves bringing in the luggage and setting up the couch bed. Derek and Logan didn't come home until nearly midnight, both smelling like cigarette smoke from wherever they had been. Brionney thought Logan had been drinking.

Alone in the bedroom, ready for bed, Brionney confronted Derek. "What's this about you going to New York? I don't like that idea!"

He sat on the bed. "I have to, Bri. I don't have a choice! With this promotion, I'm going to be in charge of all the advertising for our agency and the other business. I have to be a part of the planning."

Brionney stood in front of him, hands on her hips. "Will you see Melinda? And what does she have to do with the merger, anyway?"

He put his hands on her arms. "Is that what's worrying you? Well, don't get so uptight. She works for the company and I'm bound to see her, but it's not like we'll be working together. Really, though, we owe her a lot. If I hadn't met her and become aware of her company, I wouldn't have had the idea for the merger. It was fate."

Brionney frowned. "Well, I still don't like it!" In fact, she hated the helplessness of her position.

Derek stood and put his arms about her. She tried to trust him, but Alice's tearful face kept coming to her mind. "I think Alice and your father are having trouble," she said, wanting to focus on anything but her own dilemma.

"Yeah, he told me. They might be separating."

Remembering Alice's declaration of love, Brionney felt sorry for the woman. "I think that's terrible."

"Well, he's been feeling trapped. Maybe it's for the best." Derek pulled her to the bed. Brionney snuggled next to him, thinking how grateful she was that Derek was nothing like his father. She didn't like the idea of him going to New York, but it was only for a week.

"Let's say a prayer," she said after a while. But Derek was already asleep—or at least he didn't answer. Brionney slipped to her knees and said a long prayer. *Please Father,* she begged. *Please don't let Derek go to New York. Let something else happen.*

She nursed Savannah again and put her in her bassinet next to the bed. Then she slipped wearily under the thin blanket. Every bone in her body seemed to ache. She expected to fall asleep the minute her head touched the pillow, but instead visions of a beautiful brunette came to her mind. Maybe Brionney should get on the Internet and see for herself that nothing was going on. At least it would make her feel better. Debbie had said that . . .

A thought came, piercing the darkness with its forcefulness. When Debbie had asked about Melinda, she had said her name. How had Debbie known? What else had she seen that day?

CHAPTER THREE

The next morning before she left, Alice hugged Brionney and whispered, "Thanks for listening. And good luck."

Brionney watched them go with relief. Then she lay down on the couch. Derek looked at her. "I thought you were going to exercise."

Brionney groaned. "I feel as though I already ran a marathon. I'll have to rest a little while."

"Okay," Derek said. He made a face by blowing air into his cheeks. "If that's the way you want to be."

Brionney threw a baby diaper at him. "Give me a break. I just had a baby two weeks ago. Now go to work, would you? And try to find out if you can get out of the New York trip, okay?"

Derek rolled his eyes. "It's not going to happen."

Brionney watched him leave. Sliding to her knees, she prayed again, more fervently than before. Afterwards, she walked with Savannah in the stroller. She managed only half an hour before returning home to collapse on the couch. She decided that was enough for one day.

In the afternoon, she went to Derek's computer and turned it on. It went directly into Windows. Brionney found the icon to access the Internet, but once there, she didn't know where to begin. "I'll have to ask for Debbie's help," she told Savannah.

But when Derek came home, he brought a marvelous surprise. "I'm not going to New York after all." He hurled his briefcase carelessly onto the couch.

Brionney hugged him. "That's wonderful!"

"I don't think so." His face darkened. "They're all a bunch of idiots running that company. If I was in charge, this merger would

already be a done deal." He kicked the couch for emphasis and swept
a few books from the cushion to the floor so he could sit.

Brionney picked them up. "What exactly happened?" She had
seen Derek in one of his angry fits before and knew that the best way
to deal with it was to let him talk.

"There's been a delay, so they've decided to come here next month
instead of us going there. I guess it makes sense, since they're the ones
moving here to merge with us. But I hate delays. I have the advertising plans for everything ready to go, and I'm irritated that a bunch of
idiots are getting in the way." He fell into silence, staring darkly at the
blank TV screen.

"That's too bad," Brionney said, not meaning it. "But I'm sure
when it finally happens, your advertising will get a lot of attention.
Profits will probably shoot through the roof."

Derek relaxed noticeably. "That's dang right. And I'll probably get
another raise."

"I knew you would go far."

Derek actually smiled.

"So," she asked casually, "does that mean you won't have to work
this weekend?"

"Nope, I'll be home." He grabbed the remote and turned on the
television.

Brionney smiled so hard that her cheeks ached. She left Derek in
the living room with Savannah, went into the bedroom, and quickly
knelt. *Thank you, Father, for answering my prayer!* "Now if only I could
get this weight off," she muttered, coming to her feet.

She quickly made the bed and straightened their room. When she
returned to the living room, Savannah was in the swing and the TV
was blaring. Derek was nowhere to be seen. Brionney hurried around
the Japanese screen, dreading what she would see. Why couldn't she
trust Derek? He had never lied to her before. Or had he?

He was typing something onto the screen. When he saw Brionney,
he added the words: *My wife sends her regards.* Then he exited.

"Who was that?"

"Melinda," Derek said. "I was just telling her what was going on."

"Won't she hear it from her work?"

"Yes, but I thought with us being friends, it would be better coming from me." He pulled her onto his lap. "You know, you're cute when you're jealous."

Brionney shook her head slowly. She wished he would promise not to talk to Melinda anymore. She knew if she brought it up, he would talk about Melinda's potential for suicide. Or maybe get angry. Perhaps it was better not to make a big deal out of it. She sighed. "I don't feel cute."

"Well, you will once you are back to your old self. But there's nothing going on. Trust me." He sniffed the air. "What are you making for dinner? It smells good."

* * * * *

Derek's moods alternated between depression and agitation for the next few days. On Saturday afternoon, Brionney was almost glad to see him off to the gym. He returned in a better mood and on Sunday went to church with her. She was still too large for her best dresses, but made do with a blue one that had an elastic waist. The fit was tight and uncomfortable, but manageable for three hours. Derek, as usual, looked great in a striped shirt and gray pants.

"That blue makes your eyes really stand out," he said, pulling her close and kissing her. Warmth spread to her heart. It was the first compliment she could remember from him since she had been pregnant. *My husband loves me,* she thought. *Everything is all right.* Derek carried Savannah into the meetings and even held her most of the time on his lap. Brionney almost forgot about Melinda.

* * * * *

"Are you sure you're not overdoing it?" Debbie asked Brionney as they rounded the last curb toward home. "I mean, you've been out walking every day, pushing this stroller for more than an hour. I know you want to get off the weight, but—"

"I've already lost five pounds," Brionney said. She was slightly flushed, and small beads of sweat dotted her brow. "That leaves only twenty more to go. I have to keep pushing." A shadow seemed to flit over her face.

"Is there anything you're not telling me?" Debbie asked. She had the feeling something was dreadfully wrong, but she didn't know how to help her friend. "Is Derek treating you right?"

"The problem isn't Derek. It's my weight. You just don't understand, Debbie. You've always been thin."

"I know enough to know that what you weigh doesn't change what's in your heart."

"But it does," Brionney said. "There's fear, and loneliness, and . . . never mind. Do you want to go once more around the block?"

"Okay," Debbie agreed.

* * * * *

Brionney arrived home out of breath. She immediately sat down to nurse Savannah, who had just awakened. From where she sat on the couch, she could see a box of Twinkies Derek had bought sitting on the table. Her stomach growled. "No, it's fruit for you—at least for the next few months," she said.

Savannah stopped nursing and grinned up at her. She had been smiling for the last week now, and Brionney remembered that it was time to get her one-month pictures taken.

The phone rang, and Brionney picked up the portable on the small table next to the couch. "Hello?"

No answer. But someone was still on the line, listening.

"Who is this?"

A dreadful suspicion fell over her. "Melinda?" she asked.

The line went dead.

Brionney laid the sleeping Savannah on a blanket near the couch. Who had been on the phone? Then she remembered the TV commercial that said she could find out who called by dialing star six nine. Without debating Brionney dialed, but to her disappointment, the number was unavailable.

She sighed deeply. Her eyes went again to the Twinkies on the table. *Just one wouldn't hurt.* But she didn't stop until she had finished the rest of the box. Then she lay down on the couch and cried.

CHAPTER FOUR

Six weeks after Savannah's birth, Brionney waited under the grapefruit tree in the small backyard they shared with the three other tenants in the four-plex. It was still warm for early October, even this late in the afternoon. Inside, dinner was ready, waiting for Derek to come home from work. It was a clear Friday night, promising to be serene—perfect for a date. In the next few weeks they would have much to celebrate: first her birthday, then the two-year anniversary of the day they had met.

Brionney found herself thinking of home. While she missed the snow-capped mountains and beautiful streams of Utah, she had found in Arizona's year-round warmth an even exchange for the piercing cold that filled her childhood memories. And of course Derek and Savannah made up for the occasional homesickness.

Savannah rested in her lap, blinking her eyes at the brightness. Her cheeks had filled out, giving her a chipmunk sort of look, but she was as beautiful as ever.

Brionney smiled at nothing in particular, thinking how wonderful life could be. She had lost two more pounds, and was feeling prettier. Derek had still been spending long hours at work and on the Internet, but after today the merger would be complete and he would be able to rest. She had heard nothing of Melinda.

A quiet rumble announced Derek's arrival in the parking lot. His hands were empty, and Brionney knew he wouldn't be working the weekend. "Hi!" She stood and walked toward him.

His eyebrows rose in surprise. "What are you doing out here?"

"It's better than being stuck in the apartment. Do you realize that we haven't gone out since Savannah was born? I thought we could go somewhere tonight."

"What about her?" He pointed to Savannah.

"We can take her. She won't be a problem."

His mouth fell into a doubtful frown. "Well, I wish you had told me before," he said, turning to the house. "I have a banquet for work tonight. I have to be there. It's to celebrate the merger."

"A banquet?" Brionney hurried after him. He had already reached the stairs and was descending the five steps to the apartment. "You didn't mention any banquet. But that's okay. Those banquets aren't too bad. We'll have fun." The last one they had attended had been when Brionney was five months pregnant. "Savannah will be good, or Debbie will watch her for a few hours. She's always asking. I'll wear my blue dress. I can fit into it perfectly now."

Derek stopped at the door, his hand on the doorknob. "I didn't plan on you coming," he said slowly.

"What?"

"I didn't think you'd feel up to it, with the baby and all, so I didn't order a dinner for you. This thing is prepaid, and . . ." His voice trailed off.

"Why didn't you ask me?" Brionney was both hurt and amazed.

He shrugged. "You've been so tired. And complaining about the weight. I just didn't think you were ready."

Brionney glared at him. "Is it my weight that's bothering you? Don't worry, it's coming off. I just had a baby, remember?"

Derek turned his head, sighing. "Brionney, let it go."

"You're ashamed to be with me, aren't you!" Brionney hoped he would deny it, but he didn't meet her gaze.

"I'm sorry," he said, "but I liked you the way you were."

"I can't believe you'd say that!" She thought of all the torturous hours she had worked to lose weight. Hadn't he seen any improvement? Somewhere above them a window shut, and her anguish increased. Not only had he admitted her weight bothered him, but he had said it where others could hear.

"Would you rather I lie?" he asked tersely.

"I'd rather you love me no matter what."

"I do love you."

"Well, you have a funny way of showing it."

"Brionney, what's done is done." His voice was that of a stranger. He opened the door and entered the apartment.

Brionney followed with dragging steps. The delicious aroma of roast rolled over her in a wave. It was Derek's favorite, and she had gone out of her way to make it just the way he liked, with little onion rings layered over sliced potatoes and carrots, the meat in the middle, basted carefully with prepackaged sauce and spices. She even had his favorite potato rolls from the bakery, after walking over a mile to the store to get them. The special dinner was meant as a prelude to their first evening out since the baby had come. Now her plans lay in ruins.

He sniffed. "Smells good."

"It's your favorite." She stared at the ground, her tears hot on her cheeks.

He stiffened. "I'm sorry, Brionney. I should have told you. We can have it tomorrow. As he spoke, he was loosening his tie. "I've got to shower before I go. My clothes are stuck to me."

She watched him walk down the hall toward the bathroom. Dabbing at her tears furiously, she scooped up the house keys and headed out the door. *Let him wonder where I went,* she thought. But would he even care?

Brionney walked down the road, feeling conspicuously alone despite Savannah's presence. For the first time, she wished they had a second car. Along the street, she could see other people arriving home from work, embracing their families and laughing together. Derek hadn't even kissed her. How long had it been since he had stopped kissing her when he came home? It was all Brionney could do not to sit on the sidewalk and cry.

She passed the place where the four-plexes gave way to large houses. Across the street, she could see three cars in Debbie's driveway, signaling that the whole family was at home. She wiped her face with Savannah's receiving blanket and forged up the steps. At least here she would be welcome.

"Brionney. Hi. Come in." Kelli, Debbie's thirteen-year-old daughter, opened the door and ushered her into an expansive entryway paved with ceramic tiles. "Hello, Savannah," she cooed at the baby, tossing her long, dark hair to one side with a flip of her hand. "Can I hold her, pleeeaaase?"

Brionney was relieved that the girl seemed too intent on the baby to notice the mascara that must be smeared down her face. She handed over the baby and followed Kelli into the living room to wait for Debbie.

As she waited, Brionney felt oddly uncomfortable in the nice room. Debbie had worked hard to achieve just the right blend of sophistication and comfort. Solid wood furniture and the elegant paintings combined perfectly with the partly papered walls. The gray marble carpet was of the highest grade and matched the curtains and upholstery. Full-sized plants decorated the open space in front of the large window. Brionney had been living in the small apartment so long that she had almost forgotten what it was like to have the space and furnishings of a house like her parents. Would she and Derek ever reach that point?

"Brionney." Debbie looked as though she had come from the kitchen at the back of the house. Her thin face was flushed, and she was fanning herself with a cookbook. "I heard you come in. What's up?"

"Are you cooking?" Brionney asked, trying to laugh. A sob escaped instead.

Debbie looked at her sharply. "Come with me." She took Brionney's arm and led her to the end of the entryway where it joined the kitchen on one side and her bedroom on the other. Inside her room, she shut and locked the door. "What happened?" she asked.

Brionney began to sob again, with more emotion than before. "It's nothing, really. I just cooked a nice dinner, and then Derek comes home and tells me he has a work banquet—and I'm not invited."

"Why not?" Debbie's face looked red and angry.

"He didn't think I'd be up to it." She shook her head. "I'm so mad at him, I want to kill him. I can't believe he'd do this." She wished she could tell Debbie what Derek said about her weight, but pride stopped her. But she did add, "I feel so hurt. He was never this way before. I don't know what happened."

She cried for a long time in Debbie's arms. At last the sobs grew less intense, and she said in a low voice, "I knew if I didn't get out of the apartment, I'd go crazy!"

"Have dinner with us," Debbie invited. "And afterwards you and I can go out for an ice cream or something."

"What about your family?"

"The kids have their own plans—even Kelli, who's going to a sleep-over. Max is preparing a case he has to present on Monday and won't be leaving his office upstairs until late Saturday night. Thank heaven we have Sunday to keep him from working himself to death!"

"Does he always work so much?"

"Normally he keeps it at the office, but occasionally before big cases he has to work at home."

Knowing that Max sometimes worked late made Brionney feel better. "Is that why you make so many quilts?"

Debbie laughed. "Probably. But I don't mind his work as long as he keeps his priorities straight."

"Derek has only been to church once in the last few months," Brionney said softly. "He keeps saying 'just one more week.' I'm afraid he'll never go back. I—I think he's losing his testimony. It's like he doesn't need the Lord anymore to help in his decisions. Or me." Brionney sniffed, trying not to cry again.

"That can happen," Debbie said. "But who knows? Maybe things will look better in the morning."

Brionney shook herself. "You're right. I mean, it's not as if today is the last day of the world."

"That's the spirit. Now, I'm going back to the kitchen before dinner burns. I already have enough complaints about my cooking as it is. Go ahead and wash your face or whatever in the bathroom." She pointed at a closed door at the far end of her room. "Use my makeup if you need it. And I'll check on Savannah for you. They may even let me hold her. I tell you, there's nothing more baby-hungry than my three teenage girls." She left the room, humming to herself.

Brionney went into the bathroom and stared into the mirror. Her face looked red and puffy. What was it Derek saw when he looked at her? Biting her lip to stifle the tears that were still close to the surface, she turned on the water and splashed her face.

Later at dinner, there was much laughter and talking. Debbie was the loudest, making jokes about her own cooking. "I have to say them first," she confided in a whisper. "That way I won't get my feelings hurt." She smiled to show she was kidding.

The overwhelming feeling was peaceful, and Brionney relaxed. But homesickness for her parents and sisters, whom she hadn't seen since last Christmas, also intensified. Dinner had always been a time for talking, a time for unity. She especially missed Zack, but he was still in France. Josette was expecting their second baby now.

After dinner, the girls scattered. Max unfolded his long frame and stretched slowly. "Well, back to work," he said. He paused long enough to kiss Debbie tenderly and whisper something in her ear. Brionney averted her gaze, remembering how Derek hadn't kissed her when he had come home.

"So, shall we go out for dessert?" Debbie asked when Max left. "I know a great frozen yogurt place. They even have nonfat, and pretty good, too. What do you say? I'll pay."

Brionney smiled. "Can't refuse an offer like that." Then she wrinkled her nose. "But we have to go home for diapers and the car seat. I didn't come prepared."

"No problem." Debbie took a set of keys from a hook below the telephone and ushered her out the door and into her white minivan.

The moment Brionney opened the apartment door, she smelled smoke. "Oh, no!" She quickly laid Savannah in her car seat, stored near the door, and ran to the oven. Black smoke billowed out when she opened it, setting off the smoke alarm. She turned the oven off, picked up the potholders, and moved the roast to the sink. Cold water poured over the mess, dousing the tiny flames that still hovered around the thin layer of fat covering the meat.

Debbie was already opening windows and waving the smoke away from the alarm with one of the kitchen towels. Savannah began to scream, and Brionney herself was near tears. "How could I have forgotten!" she wailed, trying to comfort her daughter.

The alarm abruptly shut off, and in the sudden silence, Debbie said, "What? Is this the first time? Why, I burn something at least every week. Max has to replace the batteries in the alarms each month to make sure they warn me in time." She spoke with a straight face, blinking innocently.

Slumping to a chair, Brionney laughed until tears blocked her vision. Debbie joined her at the table, sulking. "You're as bad as my children." Brionney didn't point out that she was only two years older than Debbie's missionary son. Age had never made a difference in their friendship.

"Let's turn on the cooler and get this place aired out," Debbie said. "We've frozen yogurt awaiting us."

"You do it while I change Savannah."

Within half an hour they were on their way, leaving the apartment smelling more like a campsite than a house. The roads were crowded for a Friday night, but Debbie didn't mind. She darted in and around cars as if she were in some kind of a race. To Brionney's surprise, she didn't drive to the nearest yogurt shop, but to a nice hotel. "They have a quaint little yogurt shop off their main restaurant," Debbie said. "I discovered it when Max brought me here for my birthday last year. I've been back at least four times since. It's a little more expensive, but well worth it. You'll see."

Everything in the yogurt place was decorated in dark green and burgundy. Old-fashioned black and white pictures of movie stars, political figures, and antique cars hung on the wall, giving it an air from the past. The wood tables lining the walls were nearly full, and the people around them talked and laughed contentedly.

Brionney was surprised at what came with her nonfat strawberry yogurt. Chocolate-covered wafers were stuck into one side, with dainty sugar cookies on the other, and freshly cut strawberries sprinkled on top. The yogurt was in a glass dish, and a long metal spoon with a small head completed the array. Brionney was delighted. She couldn't wait to bring Derek here. Thoughts of him brought pain, but Brionney shoved it to the back of her mind. She couldn't deal with that. Not yet.

Brionney enjoyed herself thoroughly. Debbie entertained her by making up stories about the people around them. "Now that girl over there is not interested in what her companion is saying," Debbie said. "See how she keeps looking at that table in the corner? Well, the man she's watching there is her old boyfriend, whom she knew in Russia as a child. They were promised, but the girl rebelled and ran away to college in America. Now he's come to search for her—not to marry her, you see, but to kill her because she stained his honor. But things got complicated when immigration found him first. He had to find an American girl and marry her so he could stay in the country long enough to find and kill the woman who was promised to him. Only his wife accidentally found out about it, and she's a black belt in karate—see how strong her arms look?—and says she'll kill him if he leaves her."

"What about the man who's with the first woman?" Brionney asked.

"He's actually her son from the future, trying to save her life so she can somehow get married and have him." Debbie grinned triumphantly.

Brionney laughed, holding her stomach. "Very funny."

"Shhh, the waitress is going to ask us to leave if you keep making so much noise!" Debbie said.

But it was Savannah who brought the night to an end. She wanted to eat, and Brionney didn't feel comfortable nursing her in public or in the rest room. Debbie understood. "But you'll get less self-conscious the more children you have," she said.

As they left the yogurt parlor, Brionney paused at the door to the main restaurant and looked in. The place was full, and everyone seemed to be enjoying the night away from home.

"Let's walk through," Debbie suggested. "They won't mind. The decorations are wonderful. That is, if Savannah will behave." The baby was fine now that they were walking, and since Brionney didn't feel like facing an empty apartment, she nodded and followed Debbie through the door.

Most of the diners were dressed in their Sunday best, although some of the ladies' clothing would never be worn to a Mormon church. Brionney felt out of place in her jeans and thin blouse, but no one seemed to notice. Waiters in black tuxedos brought out an array of delicious-smelling foods, some even flaming. It reminded Brionney of a scene from a movie. The decor was definitely modern, featuring flowing lines and faceless sculptures.

They had reached the end and were about to leave the restaurant by the parking lot door when Brionney noticed a set of double doors connecting another room to the restaurant. Waiters were coming out of it, and she could see inside. Abruptly, she froze. Sitting on the left of the room was someone she recognized, a man from Derek's work. Anxiously, she scanned the rest of the people and recognized several more. She stepped closer to the door. The waiter there moved out of her way, as if expecting her to enter.

"What is it?" Debbie asked, pausing in mid-stride.

Brionney's eyes finally came to rest on Derek. He looked great in his deep blue suit and matching tie. The outfit set off his marvelous eyes and blond hair. He looked trim and vibrant. How good they would have looked together with their matching features! Only Brionney's extra pounds separated them.

Then Brionney saw her. She was wearing a black, spaghetti-strap dress that inadequately covered her ample cleavage. The low-cut gown had drawn the eyes of half the men in the room. The woman's dark brown hair was set in the latest style, and Brionney could see the deep red lipstick from where she stood in the doorway. The woman was incredible.

As Brionney watched, Derek put his hand over the woman's in an oddly intimate gesture. She laughed and whispered something in his ear. He lowered his head and whispered back.

Brionney couldn't breathe. She felt as though her heart had been ripped from her chest. "Melinda," she whispered.

"Silicone implants, I bet," Debbie muttered.

Brionney clutched at Savannah, wild thoughts racing through her mind. She couldn't believe what she was seeing. It couldn't be true!

The beautiful Melinda had a cigarette in her mouth and seemed to be asking Derek for a light. Smiling, she blew the smoke in his direction. He didn't flinch.

"Yuck. Cancer sticks," Debbie said. Others in the room were also lighting up, and the ceiling fans worked overtime to suck the fumes away.

With a little cry, Brionney leaned up against the wall. The action took Derek from sight. She clung to Savannah. What had gone wrong with her marriage? She attended church faithfully, had honored her temple covenants and other church obligations. How could this be happening to her? And all because of a woman who, to her knowledge, Derek had never met in person before this week.

Brionney slid to the floor, sobbing.

"Do you need some help?" the waiter asked coldly.

Debbie glared at him and put her arms around Brionney. "Come on, let's get out of here."

She half-dragged Brionney to her feet and away from the door—but not before Brionney saw Melinda inch closer and incline herself into the crook of Derek's arm.

Somehow they made it to the van, with Debbie nearly carrying Brionney, who still held Savannah as though the baby were her life raft. In the car Savannah began to fuss, and mechanically Brionney nursed her. They waited in the dark, with only the baby's tiny swallows and Brionney's sobs breaking the silence.

"I'm so sorry," Debbie said finally. She sounded miserable. "I wish we'd never come here."

"What do I do now?" Brionney asked.

"You could leave him."

"Leave him?" The thought made Brionney's heart ache worse. "We were married in the temple—sealed. I promised to be there forever."

"Not through something like this, you didn't. The promise works both ways."

"I love him!" Brionney said, and knew it was true. "Oh, dear Lord," she prayed, "why is this happening?"

"He hasn't been treating you right," Debbie said. "Even I can see that."

"But that doesn't mean I give up!" Brionney exclaimed, a swift anger quelling her tears. "I don't know that anything's happened between them, not really. Maybe—"

"Don't you think you're fooling yourself?"

Brionney remembered then that Debbie had known Melinda's name since the day she had visited after Savannah's birth. She turned to her friend urgently. "I need to know what it was you saw or heard that day when Derek was on the Internet. How did you know Melinda's name?"

"I don't want—"

"Please." Brionney's voice was harsh. "I need to know."

"I heard him on the phone. He said her name—Melinda." Her voice was hesitant.

"What aren't you telling me?"

Debbie looked at Brionney, her gaze desperate. "There were the pictures on the screen, but you knew about those. And then at the end of the conversation, Derek said, 'Love you too.'" Debbie paused and then rushed on, "But it could have been my imagination, or even a joke. You know, my kids are always saying sarcastic things to each other and then saying, 'I love you too,' as sort of an ironic thing. Nothing serious. Please, Brionney, don't look at me like that!"

"You should have told me!"

"I wanted to, but you wouldn't hear. You believe anything Derek says!"

Brionney wondered if things could get any worse. It was bad

enough thinking that Derek had turned to Melinda for companionship, but what if he loved her? The thought made Brionney want to die. If only she hadn't gained so much weight!

She had the wild urge to run back to the restaurant and confront Derek in front of everyone. She wanted to announce that she was leaving him, wanted to hurt him as he had hurt her. But even as the thought came, a vision of herself in Debbie's mirror appeared in her mind. Red, puffy eyes, bloated face and body. And people laughing at the pathetic girl who couldn't satisfy her own man.

Savannah had fallen asleep. Brionney held her gently, closing her eyes and letting the pain wash over her. *Dear Father, what do I do now?*

"Do you really love him?" Debbie asked after a long time.

"Yes," Brionney said. "At least I love the Derek I married. But I don't know who he is anymore."

"Then you fight for him."

"But what if he's . . ."

"Cheated on you?"

Brionney nodded numbly. Her heart screamed that it couldn't be true. Derek had married her! They had been sealed in the temple of God! He had promised to be faithful! The idea of him sharing with another woman what he had promised only to her was too much to bear. She felt helpless with hurt and betrayal.

"You still need to decide what you want to do. Either way, it isn't going to be easy." Debbie paused, and her voice took on a faraway tone. "Max and I had problems like this once. We felt separated and alone. There were outside influences, but the fact was that things weren't right at home. We talked about it and decided we would do everything in our power to bring our love back, including praying nightly and begging the Lord to bless our relationship."

"And it worked?"

"Very much so—after a few hard months. But then, neither of us went so far as to stray from our covenants."

Staring into the dark, Brionney said nothing. "Can you take me home?" she asked weakly. "I need to go home." What she needed was to be alone to sort out her feelings.

Debbie patted Brionney's arm. "I'm here for you no matter what. I hope you know that."

Brionney nodded, not trusting her voice.

They didn't talk on the way home. Other cars' headlights made shadows dance inside the van, where Brionney sat clutching her thoughts to her heart. Never in a million years had she expected something like this to happen to her. Six weeks ago, she had thought she was living the perfect Mormon fairy tale. But now the book was torn in shreds around her.

CHAPTER FIVE

At home, Brionney put Savannah in her bassinet and then lay on the bed, thinking. Visions of Derek at the hotel brought renewed anguish to her heart, as well as unending tears. *What do I do now?* she kept asking herself. She loved Derek and had promised to love him forever—no matter how difficult, painful, or humiliating.

I must fight! she thought at last. Only then could the promise be fulfilled. Deep down, she knew the covenants she had made with Derek were more important than her pride. Besides, she didn't want to live without him.

But, oh, it hurt! Could she really do it?

After a while, she slid to her knees and said the longest prayer she had ever said in her life. She needed a miracle. "I'll do my part, but I need your help, Father." In the Book of Mormon, Alma the younger had changed his life after his father's prayers had evoked a miracle. The Lord had done it in Brionney's own life when Derek's New York trip had been canceled. And the Lord could do it again. Only He could heal the breach between them.

She ended her prayer on a more hopeful note. Though she still felt devastated, she would vanquish the phantoms that threatened her marriage. She would make Derek fall in love with her all over again—beginning tonight.

With determination, Brionney wiped her eyes and washed her face. Then she eradicated the last hints of burned roast from the house with scented candles and scrubbed the pan until she could detect no remains of the charred dinner. She changed into a long, feminine nightgown, brushed her hair till it shone, and added a little makeup.

After feeding Savannah and leaving the sleeping baby in her bassinet, she went to wait for Derek on the couch. To her extreme relief, he came home before ten.

Should she confront him about Melinda? A part of Brionney wanted to drag every bit of sordid detail into the open, but the other part of her couldn't face the whole truth. *Not tonight,* she decided. *Tonight will be for us to start mending. I'll deal with the rest another night.*

Derek came in whistling and obviously in a good mood. Brionney's heart pounded nervously. "Hi, honey." She rose from the couch to greet him. In a few steps she crossed the brown carpet and stood with him on the cold linoleum.

He smiled, eyeing her silk nightgown. Brionney lifted her lips to his. She could smell the smoke that had permeated his clothes. A vision of the lovely Melinda blowing it in his direction made her want to hit him rather than kiss him.

"I missed you," she said instead, leading him to the couch. "The late show is on." She didn't ask him if he wanted to watch the old black and white movie, not wanting to give him a chance to refuse. These types of films were his favorites, and she knew he'd be hooked immediately. Sure enough, his eyes were already glued to the TV. He didn't see her grin as she cuddled up next to him on the couch. There would be no Internet surfing tonight. If Melinda was waiting for him to sign into a chat room, she'd be waiting all night.

"How did the banquet go?"

"All right. The usual boring speeches."

"Were all the new employees there?"

"You mean the ones from the merger? Yes, they were. All who have moved here."

"What about Melinda? I would have liked to meet her." Brionney tried to keep her voice steady.

"She was there. She's been transferred to my department, you know. I can't help seeing her every day."

Brionney grasped at her ever-thinning hopes. She told herself that even though the scene between Derek and Melinda had been intimate, maybe it hadn't gone as far as she imagined. Regardless, there was still time to save her marriage.

Later, when they went to bed, wrapped in each other's arms,

Brionney knew she was on the right track. No matter what, she would fight for the kind of happiness they had left behind.

* * * * *

On Saturday morning, Brionney got up early and made Derek's favorite pancakes for breakfast. By the time he awoke, she had Savannah taken care of and in her swing so that she could pay attention to him. He seemed content and friendly. "What's the special occasion?" he asked.

"There isn't any. I just love you."

He smiled and filled his plate.

"We could start looking for a house," Brionney said as she flipped a pancake. "Wouldn't it be great to have our own place?"

He smiled. "I'll say. To be able to hang pictures wherever we want or to change the paint or wallpaper. Or even to tear down a wall if we feel the urge!" They both laughed.

Derek didn't have to work, but after his usual Saturday afternoon visit to the gym, he sat down at the computer and began to surf the Internet. Brionney stifled her objections and tried to act supportive, but she stayed in the small alcove with him as much as she dared to make sure he wasn't talking with Melinda via the terminal. She didn't want to make too much of what she saw as his Internet addiction, for fear it would cause a black mood to come upon him.

The day passed in a tense sort of peace. But despite all her trying, they still had an argument. Brionney put Savannah to bed, and they were about to sleep themselves when the baby awoke and wanted to eat. "Be quiet," Derek growled at her. Hearing the tone in his voice, Savannah screamed louder.

"She's just hungry," Brionney said.

"Well, I'm tired of her waking us up at night. Just leave her there and let her cry. She'll learn soon enough to sleep through the night. My dad never let me eat at night."

"The doctor says I'm supposed to feed her when she wakes," Brionney said. "She's too little to go without night feedings."

"It's a bad habit," Derek insisted.

Brionney had always tried to be agreeable to Derek's wishes, but Savannah's care was too important to compromise. She wouldn't stand by and listen to her daughter cry for food and comfort when it was such an easy thing to give. Brionney had been learning only too well during the past weeks how it was to crave such comfort and receive nothing. Besides, Savannah was beginning to move around more, and Brionney was worried that she would soon be too big for the bassinet altogether, making it unsafe. She would have to approach Derek about buying a crib.

"It'll only take a second." Brionney went over to the bassinet and picked up Savannah. "There, there, little one." Savannah immediately stopped crying. If only Derek could reassure Brionney of his love so easily!

Derek frowned and buried his face in the pillow. Brionney fed Savannah quickly and put her back in bed. Then she turned out the light and scooted closer to Derek under the covers. She desperately ached to ask him to hold her, to explain her insecurity away. How would he react if she did?

She had to try.

"Derek?" she whispered.

"Huh?"

"Hold me?"

He said nothing, and in a few minutes she heard his snores in the darkness. She shook her head in sorrow, pulling the blankets up to ward off the coolness in her heart. Her face was wet before she knew she was crying, and she hugged her pillow to stifle the sound. So close, yet so very far away. She began to pray silently. *Please make everything all right again. Please.*

* * * * *

When they awoke on Sunday, Derek groaned when she got up early to dress for church. "I have a terrible headache," he said. "I don't think I'm going to make it to church today."

"Want some Tylenol?" Brionney asked, not wanting to leave him alone.

"No, this is too big for Tylenol. I just need some sleep." He rolled over and shut his eyes.

Brionney debated what she should do. She felt an overwhelming desire to take the sacrament and renew her covenants with the Lord, yet she wanted to stay with Derek.

To make sure he behaves, said a mocking voice in her head.

Brionney decided she would go to church. She would keep her part of the bargain she had made with the Lord, and the Lord would certainly uphold His. Derek would be in His hands.

Brionney attended sacrament meeting and Sunday School, but then she felt an urge to go home. She found Derek at the computer. He shut it down as she walked in, but not before she saw some disturbing images on the screen.

"What are you looking at?"

"Just ran into some dirty pictures by accident." He chuckled, looking completely cured of his headache. "Sometimes you find stuff you aren't looking for."

Brionney wondered how many years of practice a person needed on the Internet before he wouldn't stumble onto questionable material. She remembered only too well how at the last General Conference several of the General Authorities had talked about avoiding pornography in all its stages. Derek had been at work that day, as usual, and hadn't heard the counsel. Could he have a serious problem she wasn't aware of?

Derek left the computer, taking Savannah from her and going into the living room. Brionney stared at the computer. What else had he been doing? Maybe it was time she asked Debbie to teach her about the computer.

* * * * *

The next three mornings Brionney exercised faithfully. After doing aerobics with Richard Simmons, she pushed Savannah around the block several times. She completely avoided sweets and fatty foods. After the third morning, another pound had disappeared. At this rate she would be thin again in two months! That was liveable.

On Thursday, while Derek was at work, she went shopping with Debbie. Today was her birthday, and buying new clothes would be the perfect way to celebrate.

"This would look great on you," Debbie said, pointing to a teal-colored dress.

When Brionney put it on, her eyes seemed even bluer. Though more expensive than her usual purchases, she bought it anyway, as well as a pair of jeans. She needed something to look and feel good in during this in-between stage; and as she planned to have more children in the future, the clothes would be a good investment.

She was eager to show her new clothes to Derek, but he didn't come home until nearly eight. When he arrived, she ran to him, smiling. "Hi," she said, proffering her face for a kiss. He tasted oddly stale, in spite of the mints she could also smell on his breath. His suit smelled of smoke, and though it often did when he came home, Brionney wondered if he had been working with Melinda. "How was work?"

He yawned. "It's been a long day. I think I'll relax at the computer." He started for the alcove, barely responding to Brionney's questions. His interest flickered when she mentioned dinner, but there wasn't a word about her birthday.

Derek loosened his tie and turned on the computer. He didn't sit in his chair, and it occurred to her that he was waiting for her to leave. Brionney had expected a present, or at least some sign that he was aware this day was special. The year before, he had brought her roses and taken her to a fine restaurant. Today it looked like there would be nothing.

Brionney wouldn't let his lapse in memory bring her down. People forgot birthdays, especially husbands. She had always thought it a stupid thing to get depressed about. Of course, it had never happened to her before.

"Just wait till you see what I bought today!" she said, wanting to make it all better. *When he sees me in that dress,* she thought, *he'll never be able to even look at another woman!*

But when Brionney brought out the clothes, his eyes narrowed and his smile disappeared. "That's a lot of money."

"I need another dress that fits me. And some jeans. After all, it's my bir—"

"But is there any sense in buying stuff that isn't going to fit when you've lost all your weight? I mean, it's not a good incentive to lose, is it?" His words were reasonable, but his voice sounded hard.

"Well, it's not as if Savannah is the only child we're going to have. I need something to feel good in while I get back in shape."

He pursed his lips. "I think it's a waste of money. And every bit of waste makes us further away from buying a house."

"But you always buy the best. Your clothes, our dining table."
They were still paying monthly on that.

"Those are investments," he said. "Now if you had a job, expensive clothes for you would be a different story."

"I do have a job. And it's every bit as important as yours!"

"It doesn't bring in money."

"Money isn't the only important thing!" Brionney cried. When had he become so hung up on money? Little snatches of memories came rushing to her mind—how he had insisted on only the best at the wedding reception, but had not given her a wedding present; and the weekend at her parents' cabin instead of the honeymoon on the beach she had always dreamed of.

No! No! Those were coincidences!

Brionney wanted to yell her hurt at him, but she was also desperate to keep his love. She clenched her fists until the nails dug into the soft flesh of her palms. Looking away from him, she forced herself to say softly, "You're right. I'll take them back tomorrow."

He touched her chin, pulling it up so he could look into her eyes. She tried to blink back the tears. His face softened. "Good. When you lose the rest of the weight, we'll buy you something nice. I just want you to be happy in the long run."

"Maybe I should get a job," she joked with a trace of bitterness.

"That might be a good idea. Do you think Debbie would watch Savannah?"

Brionney's heart dropped to the floor. For a moment, she wanted to run away where the nightmare was over. Where she could be safe from hurt and betrayal. She was too tired to fight, but for Savannah's well-being, she had to speak. "You make enough to take care of this family," she said slowly and carefully. "I'm not leaving Savannah. She's little, and she needs me."

Derek stared at her for a long moment. "Fine." His voice was remote, as though speaking from far away. He left the waiting computer and began to search the cupboards. "Do you know where those Twinkies are that I bought last week?"

"Uh . . ." Brionney knew her face showed her guilt.

Derek shook his head, disgust plain on his face. "This is exactly why you shouldn't have those clothes," he said spitefully. "You ate them all, didn't you? Every last one. Obviously you can't control your-self. You must *like* being fat. Well, I don't like it. And there are other fish in the sea, you know!"

With that last thrust of the knife, he went to the phone. "Melinda," he said brusquely into the receiver, "I need to do some work on the Stewart account. Scott hasn't got it finished and I need your help. Could you come back to work tonight?"

"Is anyone else going to be there?" Brionney asked as he hung up the phone. "I mean, I've always heard that it's best to avoid the appearance of evil—not that anything would happen," she added hurriedly. "They just say that at church."

He stared at Brionney as if seeing her for the first time. "Brionney, you are such a baby. When are you going to realize that the Church doesn't hold all the answers? I work in the real world, and that means with women as well. If you worked, you'd understand. If something is going to happen between Melinda and me, it would happen whether or not we're alone tonight at the office." He snorted in disgust. "Don't worry, I have things under control." He left without another word.

But could he handle it? In his face she saw a flicker of . . . guilt? Desire? She couldn't be sure, but it told her that something was dreadfully wrong with her marriage.

Derek raced off in his car. Brionney slumped to the chair at the table and laid her head on her hands. Her inner turmoil had grown tenfold. "Other fish in the sea," Derek had said. Other women.

The words were ominous. When she made her vows with Derek, other men had ceased to exist for her. But apparently not so for him. He hated her being overweight and dependent upon him. He was keeping his options open.

Suddenly, Derek's word wasn't enough. Her own hopes weren't enough. She had to know the truth!

Brionney grabbed Savannah and ran to Debbie's house, clutching her small bundle. "I want you to show me how to get into the Internet and Der—the files on the computer."

"May I ask why?" Debbie asked.

Brionney dropped her gaze to the floor. "I have to know," she whispered quietly. "I just have to know."

Debbie gave a sympathetic grunt and took her immediately to her own computer and began showing Brionney how to find her way. "It'll probably be a little different on your computer, depending on the programs you have installed," Debbie said. "But you'll figure it out."

Brionney wrote everything down carefully. She constantly fought tears.

"Uh, Brionney," Debbie said as they walked to the door. "I'm sorry for saying this—it's the lawyer's wife in me—but look, make a copy of everything you find, would you? It might come in handy."

Brionney nodded dumbly and went back to her apartment. She almost hoped Derek had come home and would thwart her attempt at the computer. But he was nowhere to be seen. She nursed Savannah again and put her in bed.

The computer waited for her as though it had a life of its own. When he had stormed out of the apartment, Derek had forgotten to turn it off. Brionney clicked the icon for the Internet and then clicked on the place Debbie had shown her that would reveal the last addresses Derek had visited on the Internet. She could tell by the names that many of the web sites supported pornography. Maybe this was his only problem. As damaging as such an addiction was, to her it was better than the alternative.

She checked out several of the other addresses and found chat rooms, but she didn't bother to enter. Derek wouldn't be there now so she couldn't spy on him, even if she knew what pseudonym he used. Next she went to the e-mail files. She had to search a bit, but soon found what she was looking for in a folder named *My Relief.*

My dearest Melinda. I am counting the hours until the merger is complete and I can see you again. Your brief visit here last month wasn't enough to satisfy the ache in my soul. I wish they hadn't canceled the meeting this week. I long to see you and . . .

On Brionney read, unable to stop. *No! No! Dear God in Heaven, make it not so!* she cried silently in anguish.

She continued through the rest of the e-mails and Melinda's replies, feeling a disbelieving numbness fall over her. The earliest were dated from Brionney's fifth month of pregnancy. Derek had lied to her—not once but many, many times. This was proof. No more could she tell herself that he was innocent, and that if anyone was to blame, it was the husband-stealer Melinda. Not only had Derek lied repeatedly, but he had broken their temple covenants. No wonder he didn't want to go to church with Brionney! No wonder he had begun to hate her!

Mockingly, Brionney thought back to when Savannah was born and everything had seemed perfect. How could she have fooled herself so thoroughly? How could things have slipped away? She stared hatefully at the computer, wishing she dared to throw it out in the street. But she knew that it wasn't the reason for the failure. *They* were.

She stumbled away from the computer, barely making it to the couch before she collapsed. Tears overwhelmed her. As she sobbed, she beat her hands against the couch until she was exhausted. Then she fell on the floor and prayed with all her might. She had vowed to fight for Derek. She had vowed to stay with him no matter what. Could she? It hurt too terribly.

"Dear Father," she prayed with all the faith in her heart. "Please help me!"

Savannah awoke and began to cry. Brionney went into the bedroom and nursed her back to sleep, feeling completely inadequate as a woman, wife, or mother. Where was Derek at this moment? Was he with Melinda? Did he love her?

The idea of seeing Derek with someone else ripped Brionney's heart in two. She loved the way he looked, the way he touched her, how at times he could be so charming and gallant. When it had been good between them, it was a slice of heaven. Why couldn't they keep that slice continually?

"What is wrong with me, that he can't love me?" Brionney asked the baby. Savannah had no answer, only reproach in her wise eyes.

Derek never came home that night and Brionney went to bed alone, feeling a small part of herself die. But it was only the beginning of what was to come.

CHAPTER SIX

Friday morning, Brionney told Debbie about the e-mails and that Derek hadn't come home all night. "You have to confront him," her friend said. "This won't go away by itself."

Brionney knew Debbie was right, but she feared the cutting words and the agony that would surface once she faced Derek. Only the love she held for him in her bruised heart and the memories of past happiness gave her the resolve to print the e-mails to show him. On Debbie's insistence, she made two copies of the many letters and gave one to her friend for safekeeping.

Before lunch, the phone rang. Could it be Derek apologizing? Or was it *her*? Brionney grabbed the phone.

"Hi, it's Mom," said a familiar voice.

"Mom! How wonderful you called!" Homesickness ate at Brionney. "How are you?"

"My hip is mending well. What if I come out soon for a few weeks? It's about time I saw my only granddaughter. All your sisters seem to do is give us boys." There was a squeal of protest in the background. "Not that little boys aren't wonderful," she added hastily.

"That'd be great!" It would be so wonderful to see her mother, to depend on her again, even if only for a short time. Brionney wanted to cry out all her problems, but she was too embarrassed and too ashamed of Derek. Then too, there was the little voice inside that said if only she could do more, Derek would come back to her fully. Brionney hated that voice, even knowing it was her own.

She hung up the phone, feeling better than she had earlier. She could do this, she could. The fight had only begun. *Just shut out any thoughts of that woman*, she told herself.

The day went smoothly as Brionney exercised, cleaned the house, and washed the clothes. She piled Derek's dress shirts on the couch, then she set up the ironing board. She could work and watch Savannah at the same time, stopping to feed or hold her as needed.

Hours later, the thirty finished shirts nearly filled Derek's half of the closet. Brionney couldn't believe he had so many, or that she had waited so long to iron them. But then, Debbie *never* ironed shirts for her husband. "He's got two hands," she always said. "And he never burns himself, either. Why should I suffer, when he doesn't mind doing one at a time as he needs them?"

Derek did mind. He'd rather go out and buy a new shirt than iron one. Brionney thought of the clothes she had bought yesterday, and how he told her to take them back. She bit her lip so as not to cry again.

Derek came home from work as usual that evening, as though he hadn't been out all night. Brionney was relieved to see him, but also worried about the fight she knew they would have once she brought up the letters. She was tempted not to talk about it at all, but she knew the healing couldn't begin until the cancer was cut out. More than anything, she wanted to have things back to the way they had been. She wanted Derek to love her. Oh, how much easier it would be if she could hate him!

He sat on the floor and played with Savannah until she started to cry. "She's just tired," Brionney said. "If you rock her, she'll go right to sleep."

Derek put her none-too-gently in the swing. "I don't have time to baby her. Can't we eat yet? I have work to do."

Brionney stifled her irritation at his treatment of Savannah and took a deep breath. "We have to talk first." She pulled out the papers and handed them to him. He glanced at them, then took a second look, his face paling. She felt glad that his first reaction was so obvious.

"Where did you get these?"

"I think you know where."

"Did *she* give them to you? This type of thing can be forged, you know."

"I got them from your computer." Brionney knew he had never thought she would look for them herself.

He slumped to the couch, saying nothing.

"So it's true?" she asked. "Will you finally tell me the truth?"

"Yes. It's true."

"No 'I'm sorry'? Just 'Yes, it's true'?"

He shrugged and held up his hands. "You were busy. We drifted apart."

"Oh, no," Brionney said, shaking her head. "Don't you dare put this off on me! I wasn't the one out with someone else while my wife was having my baby."

"I—but," he began. Then anger grew in his face. He jumped to his feet. "Okay, so I'm human," he said. "What do you want from me? Do you want a divorce?"

"No, I don't want a divorce." She began to cry. "I hate what you've done, I hate the way you've treated me, and I'd give anything to go back and have it not happen. But we can't do that!"

Derek's face lost some of its anger. "I'll give you a divorce."

"I don't want a divorce," she nearly screamed. "I want you to keep your promise to me. I want to make our marriage work. But I can't do it alone!"

Leaving would definitely be easier, but Brionney knew their marriage was meant to be eternal and without Derek, it couldn't be. Like a drowning woman, she tried desperately to hold on to the future. She would do anything so Savannah wouldn't have to grow up without her father.

"You'll have to find a new job," Brionney said. "Or she will."

Derek was silent a long time. Then he went into the bedroom and began putting a few things in his briefcase. She stared at him. "What are you doing?"

"What I should have done a long time ago—leaving." Snapping the case shut, he went to their room and collected a few suits from the closet.

"You're leaving? What do you mean, leaving?"

"I'm so tired of all the sneaking around," he said calmly. "You don't know what a relief it is to finally have it in the open. Now I don't have to pretend. I'm finally free. I think we should get a divorce."

"A divorce?" Her voice squeaked. This had never been a part of all her imaginings. She had thought he might cry and beg for forgiveness, that he might proclaim his love, that he might even yell and be angry and embarrassed. But never would he leave her!

"Look, Brionney, don't make a scene. Let's be adult about this."

"Adult about this!" Brionney said. "I'm the one who's been hurt here, Derek! I'm the one who's going through hell. Not you. You say you are finally free. Well, look at what your freedom costs me! I'm still willing to make this work. We can do it. But you have to talk to the bishop and stop seeing her!"

"I'm not going to talk to some overzealous do-gooder about my sins."

"I know it's embarrassing—how do you think I feel? But we can get counseling. We can make it work!"

"I don't want to try to make it work anymore," he said. "We're just too different. We don't agree on anything. And I don't want to watch life pass me by."

"But we've had good times. We can have them again!" Brionney knew she was begging, but she was beyond caring. Somehow this was all wrong. He should be the one on his knees, begging for her to forgive him. "I love you, Derek. I'll do anything to make it work! Anything!"

He averted his gaze from the pleading in her eyes. "I can't stop seeing her," he said softly. "I tried."

Brionney's chest heaved with the ache of this revelation. She touched his sleeve. "We're sealed in the temple, Derek. We made promises to each other, and I for one meant them. I'm not saying things will be perfect, but with the Lord's help, we can get through this." She closed her eyes and took a deep breath against the pain that seemed too large for a human heart. "I know it won't be easy, but I believe in the covenants we made. You can get through it, too. You just have to be willing to try!"

For a moment she thought she had won him, but then his jaw set resolutely. "I love her," he said. "I want to be with her. I want to have a life with her. No obligations or guilt. Freedom. I—I don't think I believe in the Church anymore. It can't be right if it stops us from being happy. I can't take the pressure. I should never have tried to be the perfect Mormon boy. That's what I thought I could be—with you. But now I can't fool myself anymore. I'm just like my dad. It'll be better for both of us if I leave now."

Tears fell from her eyes, and Brionney understood everything. As long as his transgression was unrevealed, part of him could still pretend to be what she needed. But now that she knew everything, there was no reason to keep up the pretense. She realized that if he had lost his faith, all the love in the world wouldn't keep him from leaving. Nor would their temple sealing. There was only one chance left.

"What about Savannah?"

"You'll keep custody, of course."

"That's not what I meant. Don't we owe it to her to try? This is her eternal family we're talking about."

"I can't let my life be ruled by a child," he said stonily. "My father stayed with my mother because of me. It didn't do any good. They fought, and he was never happy. And he kept seeing Alice on the side. Is that what you want? Well, I won't live my life like that."

"But we can be happy. We can love each other. You won't need anyone else. You loved me once." Brionney couldn't stop the desperate words.

He looked at her in disgust. "I've tried enough." His voice was final. He picked up his briefcase and laid the suits over his arm. "Look. I'll send someone to get the rest of my things in a day or so. I'll give them a list. There's enough money in the account to pay another month's rent. By then you'll have decided what you want to do. I'll have my lawyer contact you." Without waiting for a reply, he turned and left.

Brionney was too shocked to move. All her fears and suspicions had become reality, and now he was gone. He had left, and her eternal family had vanished as if it had never existed.

For long, wrenching moments, tears fell from her eyes, obscuring her vision. They came from deep inside, where her soul shrank from the pain. Strangely, they weren't hot tears, but cold. So cold that Brionney wondered why they didn't turn into icicles or freeze to the warm flesh of her cheeks. She shivered in the warmth of the room, feeling her heart heavy in her breast like a block of ice. With that feeling came some relief, seeming to stem the all-consuming anguish. She stared out the kitchen window, hoping he would come back and wipe away the cold, cold tears. And beg for forgiveness. And say he loved her.

He didn't return. Brionney knew then that he was never coming back, not ever. With this blinding perception, her icy heart burst into a million razor-edged shards of frozen hopes, sending shudders of torment through her. The pain in her soul was more excruciating than any she had ever imagined. Her hands reached out and clutched the counter top for support.

A strong cry from the bedroom told her Savannah was awake. Brionney felt a momentary fear of facing her. *How can I tell her I've lost her father?*

This vein of thought brought a fresh surge of tears to her eyes. This time they were hot and guilty, and full of blame. The protecting cold had deserted her, just like Derek.

She forced herself down the hall and picked up Savannah. The baby stared up at her with wide blue eyes, so serious and wise. Brionney hugged her and cried until she couldn't cry any more. The cold crept back; she welcomed it. She wanted the pain frozen away forever.

CHAPTER SEVEN

Much later, she dialed Debbie's number on the phone in the living room. Debbie would know what to do, especially with Max being a lawyer. In the glass of the entertainment center Derek had bought for them last Christmas, Brionney could see her eyes, swollen and red against the stark white of her face. She clenched her jaw and turned away.

"Hello?"

"Debbie," she croaked through a throat raw from crying.

"What's wrong?"

"Can you come over?"

"I'll be right there." She heard a click. Setting the receiver down with one hand and clinging to Savannah with the other, Brionney went to wait by the door. Already it was very late. She wasn't surprised; it seemed an eternity since Derek had left.

"He wants a divorce," she said as she opened the door to Debbie's knock a few moments later. "He's already gone."

Debbie looked shocked but said nothing, putting her arms around Brionney. The embrace was warm and comforting. "I'm so sorry," Debbie murmured after a while.

No more tears came, and Brionney was glad. She pulled away. "What should I do? He's getting a lawyer already."

"Did he take any financial papers and such?"

"No. He said he'd send someone for his things." She paused, and for the first time since Debbie came, her voice broke. "He's not himself, not the Derek I love. I don't know who he is."

Debbie went to hug her again, but Brionney shook her head. "I'm okay, just tell me what to do. I'll need some money to take care of Savannah until . . ."

She nodded. "First let's search his papers and find anything regarding your bank accounts. We'll give it to Max and let him figure it out. You won't even have to see Derek again, if you don't want to."

Brionney did want to see Derek again. She wanted to throw herself at his feet and beg for another chance, and promise to be the wife he needed. Inside, she hated herself for wanting to grovel. Why couldn't she hate him?

"And you need to make an inventory of everything he takes. Everything. And what you keep as well," Debbie was saying, seemingly unaware of Brionney's inner turmoil.

"I don't have any money to pay Max."

Debbie snorted. "It doesn't matter. What's important is that you get what you need for Savannah."

She was right, and for Savannah, Brionney was strong. Methodically, she searched Derek's small den. She found the bank papers Debbie wanted, and others that detailed their joint purchases. There were other papers also from the bank, dated from before Savannah's birth, only they weren't accounts Brionney recognized and her name wasn't on any of them. With amazement, she saw that Derek had sixteen thousand dollars in the two savings accounts. Sixteen thousand dollars, plus the few thousand they had in their joint account—and he kept saying they didn't have enough to put down on a small house! Brionney's hand trembled. Something didn't add up. Was she so blind that he could squirrel this much money away from his paychecks? Was there no end to his deception?

"I think he planned to leave me all along," she said.

Debbie looked at the papers. "You didn't know this existed?"

"No." Brionney's voice was a whisper.

"May I keep them for Max?"

Brionney nodded almost violently. "Yes, if they'll help."

"They will, especially in a custody hearing."

"He said I would retain custody."

"He says that *now,*" Debbie said, "but you never know about tomorrow. It's best to get the custody settled as soon as possible."

Next, Debbie helped her make an inventory of everything they owned. When they got to the bedroom, Brionney broke down. "The shirts. I just ironed all his shirts."

Debbie was quiet for a moment, as if uncertain how to react. "At least he could have left before you went to all that work," she said. "The worm!"

Brionney couldn't smile. How could she, when inside she was dying?

"Do you want me to throw them on the ground and wrinkle them up again?" Debbie asked hesitantly. "I'm good at wrinkling things. Just ask Max."

She grabbed the shirts and threw them to the brown carpet. With strong hands on Brionney's shoulders, she pulled her onto the pile and began to jump up and down. Tears flooded Brionney's eyes, but didn't fall, as she stomped on the shirts, pretending they were Derek.

"Doesn't that feel better?" Debbie asked.

Brionney slumped to the bed and stared at the pile, wrinkled and dirty from their feet, battered and broken like her marriage. It was a minor triumph. "Yes. It does," Brionney said, her voice cold. "But they would look better out in the street with tire marks on them."

Debbie looked at her with approval, but shook her head. "No. Now that could be taken out of your half of the settlement, or at least I think so. It's better if we just stuff them into some grocery sacks and leave them for Derek."

"Are you going to be all right tonight?" Debbie asked when they were finished. "I'll talk to Max and tell him everything. He'll talk to Derek and his lawyer."

Brionney's hand closed over her friend's arm. "I won't give Derek a divorce. I want to fight it in any way I can. Please tell Max that."

Debbie shook her head. "Look, Brionney, I know it may seem like the end of the world to you now, but Derek's walking out may be the best thing that ever happened to you. Oh, I know it makes you angry when I say that, but I'm your friend, and I've seen the way he treats you. You deserve better than that."

"We made promises," Brionney said. She didn't cry, but her heart ached so badly she thought it must really be torn in two. "It was supposed to last forever. That was what we promised. I really believed it."

Debbie's eyes watered. She blinked back the tears. "I know. It just doesn't seem fair. But I'll be here for you whenever you need me. And the Lord will never desert you. I know you can't think beyond this moment right now, but someday I promise, everything will be okay."

Brionney let Debbie hug her, but derived small comfort from the embrace. When she was gone, she opened the couch bed in the living room and found one of the red-and-black checked quilts Debbie had made. She couldn't bear to sleep in the same bed she had shared with Derek. Not when she didn't know where he was sleeping at that moment. She nursed Savannah until she fell asleep. Her own stomach growled, but she had no desire to eat. With the light out, the silence was complete, except for the soft breathing of the baby.

An eternal family. The phrase now left a bitter aftertaste on her tongue. What had gone wrong? Where was God when she needed Him? How could He desert her when she had done everything He asked?

"Why, Father? Why?" she moaned. "Why didn't You answer my prayer?"

In a blinding flash, she knew the answer. Debbie had been wrong when she had said the Lord was with her. He wasn't. He could have answered her prayers and prevented the collapse of her marriage. Such a thing would have been so easy for Him. But He did nothing. And she knew why. He hadn't helped simply because He didn't care. He didn't love her at all.

This revelation hurt as much as Derek's leaving. Ever since Brionney could remember, she had depended upon her Father in Heaven. Only now, he had failed her. The long months of praying and striving to strengthen her marriage had ended in bitter failure.

God let it happen, she thought. *He doesn't love me enough to interfere.*

Her whole body trembled with this terrible knowledge. What's more, she knew that nothing she could do would change the fact that God didn't love her. Any prayers she said for herself would be in vain. But maybe, just maybe, He still loved Savannah, so recently come from His presence.

She slipped to her knees. "Father," she said. "I know You don't love me. I accept that." For a long moment she paused, feeling a tempest of emotion in her breast. "But please, please, don't hold Your lack of feelings for me against Savannah. Surely You love her, even if You don't love me. She's innocent. A baby. Please watch over her."

She slipped into bed, feeling the icy cold of earlier become even stronger in her breast. She knew the Lord wouldn't bother to send His spirit to warm her. Instead, she cuddled to Savannah for warmth, but nothing relieved the frozen feeling.

Sleep didn't come for a long time. It was a day Brionney would always remember for the rest of her life. Not only had she lost her husband, but she had lost her faith in God. She didn't know which was worse.

CHAPTER EIGHT

The next day, Brionney awoke to a pounding headache and an empty stomach. Savannah was crabby and hungry, and Brionney wondered if she unconsciously knew how their lives had changed, or if it was simply that Brionney's unplanned fast had decreased her milk supply. Suspecting the latter, Brionney forced herself to eat a good breakfast. Savannah was still too young for baby cereals and wouldn't take a bottle at all.

"You can't depend on my milk forever," Brionney said. She felt guilty the minute she said it. "Don't worry," she added, hugging Savannah tightly. "I'll never leave you. Not ever."

Outside the day promised to be warm, but the warmth didn't extend to Brionney's heart. She paced in the apartment, wondering what she was going to do. She couldn't stay here, haunted by so many memories. Even if she wanted to, she couldn't pay the rent. She could try to get a job, but what about Savannah? The child had lost a father; she didn't need to lose a mother as well, if only during the day. Besides, Brionney's one year of college wouldn't give her a job that paid enough to support them and pay childcare. She would have to have help, either from family or the government. Anger welled up inside her—anger at Derek, and at the Lord for letting this happen.

The heat from the anger threatened to melt the cold in her heart and free the pain, so she fought it down. "Come on, Savannah. Let's go for a walk."

The day was beautiful and warm, so unlike many late Octobers she had known in Utah. Brionney found herself missing the austere mountain peaks, capped with snow, white Christmases in front of the fire, and snowmen in the yard. *Maybe I should go home,* she thought. *I could have a white Christmas.* But what would her parents say when they knew she had made a wreck of her marriage? Her temple marriage. How could she face them as a failure, a woman whose husband had left her? *Why wasn't I enough? What is wrong with me?*

Another voice added in her mind, *Not even Heavenly Father loves you.* She tried to push the thoughts away.

As she walked back down the street to her apartment, Brionney saw a small moving truck in the parking lot behind the apartments. She hurried around to see what was going on.

Debbie stood in front of the back door with her arms folded firmly across her chest, staring defiantly at two tall men. One of them Brionney recognized from Derek's work, a man called Jason. The other she had never seen before.

"I tell you, we have permission, lady. We're not here to steal anything, only to take what's on this list. Look, we even have a key." Jason waved the key in front of Debbie's nose.

"I'll take that," Brionney said. She was angry that Derek had given his key to a person she barely knew. Now she wouldn't feel safe at night until she moved or had the locks changed.

Jason held onto the key until he recognized Brionney. "It was only in case you weren't home. Look, I don't want any trouble, I just came to get Derek's things. I owe him a favor." Brionney knew that meant Derek was over Jason at work, and that Jason was doing his share of boot-licking to worm his way to a promotion. "This here's my brother-in-law, Ralph. He's a mover and agreed to let me use his equipment."

Debbie turned to Brionney. "I was on my way over to see you and I saw them drive up. I wasn't about to let them take things without you knowing."

"Thanks, Debbie." Brionney looked at the men. "He certainly didn't wait to send you." This was too fast. Only last night he had left her.

"Hey, it's Saturday," Jason said. "And I couldn't do it tomorrow."

"Let me see your list."

Face relaxing in relief, Jason handed her the paper. Brionney scanned it quickly. "He wants the table *and* the entertainment center," she said in amazement.

"Wasn't the entertainment center your Christmas present to each other last year?" Debbie asked.

"Yes. I would have preferred something more just for me, but I'm not giving it up now. I don't care about the table, though. I think it's ugly. I never knew what Derek saw in it."

"Yeah, it's too short and bulky," agreed Debbie. She leaned over her shoulder and peered at the list. "He wants the Japanese screens, the coffee tables, and the couches? Isn't that going a bit overboard, even for Derek?"

Brionney snorted. "Obviously not. And my parents gave me the couches for our wedding. They're mine." Brionney couldn't believe Derek's selfishness. Besides his clothing, the list only mentioned the furniture items that were new or made of solid wood. He didn't want the bed or fake wood dressers, which were hand-me-downs.

"It's a good thing I didn't let them in," Debbie said.

Jason shifted his feet restlessly. "So can we start loading up?"

"No," Brionney said. "I'm not letting anything go. If Derek wants his stuff, he'll have to come get it himself."

Debbie looked alarmed. "Brionney, just let them take the stuff you agree to. It's better to let him—"

"I'm going to fight this!" Brionney said through gritted teeth.

"Then fight it, but not this way. He'll just get a court order or come back himself. Denying him his stuff isn't going to make him agree to stay married."

Jason and his brother-in-law turned their faces to the truck, pretending not to hear. Their embarrassment deepened Brionney's own discomfort. "Tell Derek," she said clearly, "that if he wants his stuff then he needs to come back for it. I won't have strangers in my apartment." The men looked at each other helplessly before turning toward their truck.

"Oh, wait," Brionney called, "there is one thing he can have." She ran inside and came back with the garbage bags full of Derek's wrinkled shirts.

Debbie laughed out loud when she saw them.

"Here," Brionney said, pushing the bags at the men.

At the top of one bag, she saw what had always been her favorite of Derek's shirts. The thick cloth was subtly striped with varying shades of green. Impulsively, she took it out and held it to her heart.

Jason looked at her for a moment, and it seemed his expression softened. "For what it's worth, I'm really sorry," he said. He didn't ask for the shirt back, but turned to Ralph. "Let's go."

"And tell Derek if he wants the couches, he'll have to pay for them!" Debbie shouted after the men as they got into the truck. Jason waved and slammed the door behind him.

Debbie mumbled under her breath. She seemed more upset than Brionney about the items Derek had tried to take. "So what now?" she asked. She obviously didn't agree with Brionney's decision not to let the men take Derek's things, but would support her.

Brionney shrugged. "I don't know. I have a week left here and enough money to pay the rent for another month. But I won't want to stay here forever. I'll have to break the lease . . ." Her voice trailed off. The truth was, she had no idea what she would do. Deep inside, she still hoped Derek would come crawling back on his hands and knees to say it had all been a terrible mistake. As painful as it would be to forgive him, she would try. She wanted him back.

* * * * *

When Debbie left sometime that afternoon, Brionney opened the couch bed again and spent the rest of the day in bed. The apartment seemed empty, even with Savannah's gurgling. She watched TV until her head ached and ate whatever came to hand when she was hungry.

Once she spied her scriptures on the bookshelf. She gave a bitter laugh. No, she wouldn't read them as she had nearly every day since childhood. What difference did it make? The scriptures couldn't help her now. Before sleeping, she repeated the prayer of the previous night. Savannah was innocent and deserved protection; the Lord *had* to love her. For herself, Brionney was already lost.

She didn't go to church the next day, nor did she answer the phone. It rang often, but she wasn't even curious as to who it was. There was only the slim hope it was Derek, and she knew him well enough to know that he wouldn't be calling.

Sitting there in bed, she thought of all the things she needed to do. There were bills to pay, the apartment lease to take care of, and food to buy. Most of the financial things Derek had always taken care of, and Brionney didn't know where to begin. Nor did she have the will to try.

In the evening, Debbie came over. "I've been calling you all day," she said, her sharp eyes taking in Brionney's pajamas and unkempt appearance. "Are you sick?"

"Just tired."

"We missed you at church."

Brionney shrugged, not wanting to tell her friend that she wouldn't ever be going back. She couldn't face the knowing looks and the pity she knew would be in the members' faces. Besides, how could she worship a God who didn't love her? Better that He didn't exist at all. Better that she didn't exist at all.

Brionney went back to the couch bed and sat in misery while Debbie made small talk. Finally, her friend gave an exasperated sigh. "You can't run away from this, Brionney. You're fighting depression right now, I understand that. But this isn't the way to face it. Eventually, you'll need to get on with your life."

"Derek was my life," Brionney retorted.

"And he's gone. Now I'm not saying that's forever, but you have to be okay inside of you before you can have a relationship, especially with Derek."

"I am okay with me."

"Is that why you've been taking the crap Derek's thrown at you these past months? Don't think I haven't noticed you bending over backwards to make him happy. And you've given every excuse in the book for him. He's taken everything you've offered and not once given you something in return."

"He didn't used to be that way," she stammered.

"Would you stop defending him? The real person is the one who left you. He's the one in the wrong here. You did everything you could to save your marriage. I tell you, I would have walked out on him months ago! You would have eventually had to leave him yourself. He's done you a favor."

Brionney felt angry at Debbie. She was making things more difficult.

"It's all easy for you to say. You still have Max and *your* eternal family." Silently she added, *And the Lord loves you.*

Debbie was quiet for a long moment. "Okay, you're right. I can't begin to imagine how you must feel. But I do know your life is just beginning. You can't give up now."

"You think he might come back?" Brionney asked hopefully.

Debbie looked disappointed. "Maybe he'll come crawling back. I don't know." She played idly with Savannah for a few moments before standing up to leave. "I'll be back tomorrow. In fact, why don't we go out to lunch?"

Brionney shook her head.

"Okay then, I'll bring something in. Expect me about noon."

Before Brionney could protest, Debbie was gone. Brionney locked the door behind her and slipped back into the couch bed, staring up at the ceiling. The apartment was silent and still. Gradually the room darkened, and Brionney drifted off to sleep next to Savannah.

A loud knocking woke her from a restless slumber. Glancing at the clock, she saw that it was after ten p.m. "Who—" She bounded to the door. Could it be that Derek was returning? She imagined he would be on his knees and carrying a dozen red roses. How should she act? He'd have to be really sorry for her to even begin to forgive him.

She opened the door, holding her breath. The person at the door wasn't Derek. "Mom!"

Irene gathered Brionney into her arms. "Oh, Brionney, why didn't you tell me what was going on? Honey, this isn't something you should face yourself. You need your family."

"How did you know?"

"Your friend Debbie called me yesterday. I came as soon as I could. I'm so sorry."

Relief flooded through Brionney. The tears came, and for the first time since just after Derek left, she cried. Not just a few tears, but so many that her mother's shirt grew wet where she held her.

Irene took control at once. The next day she went through the bills and talked to the landlord. "It's all arranged," she said. "You can move out when you want. He won't hold you to the lease. He says he has several people already interested in the apartment. He said to tell you he was sorry about what has happened."

Brionney felt some of her burden lighten. But now what?

"You sit right here," Irene said. "I'm going to the grocery store.

And while I'm gone, I want you to think about going back with me to Utah."

"I can't leave here," Brionney said. *That would be too final.*

"I just said to think about it."

Debbie showed up as Irene left, making Brionney wonder if they had the exchange planned. "I see you've showered and changed," Debbie said approvingly.

"Thanks for calling my mom."

"You should have done it," she said, toying with one of the hamburgers she had brought for their lunch. "But since you couldn't, I did."

"You're a great friend. Thank you."

"Well, I hope you still think so after I tell you that I talked to the bishop yesterday. He'd like to see you after he gets off work today."

"Why?"

"I don't know. I think it's customary when something like this happens." Her eyes pleaded. "Well, will you go? He'll probably call you soon."

"Maybe."

"Good. He'll be able to help."

Will he bring me back my husband? Brionney wanted to ask. *Can he make things like they were?* "I'd like to talk with Derek," she said instead. "Maybe he'll come with me to see the bishop. Only, I don't know where to reach him. Do you think I should call him at work?"

Debbie looked away. "No, Brionney. I think you should let the bishop call him. I gave him the number."

Brionney hugged her friend. "Thank you," she whispered.

"I don't know that he'll come," Debbie said.

"He might."

* * * * *

Bishop Clark was a thin, balding old man who reminded Brionney of Santa Claus without the rolls of fat. With always a kind word and a rosy smile for everyone, he embodied the perfect ward father. Even so, Brionney was rather embarrassed to explain her trouble to him, and she was grateful Debbie had already told him the story. Some part of Brionney ached for him to heal her spirit, if not her marriage. The other part mocked the fragile hope. She was unloved by the Lord; His servant could not help her now.

After a few words about the weather and the ward, Bishop Clark kindly told her what he had heard. Brionney confirmed the story with a nod. She felt too distressed to say anything.

"I think I should begin by telling you that I took the liberty of going to see Derek at work today," he said.

Brionney sat up and looked at him intently. "And?"

"I want you to know that I really tried. I talked to him for over an hour. But he refused to come in to counseling and told me he was having serious doubts about the truthfulness of the gospel. He asked me not to come see him again. I had to ask for his temple recommend. He gave it to me."

Brionney watched her hands twisting in her lap. She wanted to scream, but it took all her strength to mutter, "I should have done something more!"

Bishop Clark shook his head. "It is not your fault," he said firmly.

"But I saw the pornography. I saw the pictures of that woman. But I didn't want to believe! He stopped going to church and I let him. I should have brought him in before it was too late. I saw it all happening. But I thought he loved me. I—" She started to cry. "I thought he loved me!"

Bishop Clark handed her a tissue. "Brionney, hear what I am saying. Derek lost his testimony because he put other things before his membership. He left you for the same reason he lost his testimony. He put the world first. He stopped asking the Lord for help, and trusted in his own strength. I've seen it happen over and over again. Sometimes it can be reversed, if the person is willing. If not, it usually takes years before they realize why they are so unhappy. Eventually, most do return. Derek is one of those who aren't yet willing to face the truth. You can't make him change. It has to come from within himself."

"So what am I supposed to do? Wait years for him? He's with *her* now. How can I bear knowing that?" *Oh, how that hurt!*

"I'm not sure waiting is the answer," said Bishop Clark. "I'm convinced you have done all Derek will allow you to do in regards to helping him and saving your marriage. I think he feels a lot of guilt because he knows he's in the wrong, but he's trying to run away from the feeling. His heart has been hardened, and he wants it that way. You must go on with your life. If he comes back and is willing to try, then that's another story. But you need to consider your daughter, as well as your own happiness. You need to stay close to the Lord so He can guide you. It's very difficult being a single parent. Reading the scriptures and attending your meetings is very important—vital, even."

"What's the point?"

The bishop examined her with his wise eyes. "What do you mean?" he asked. "Do you doubt the Lord exists and that this is His church?"

"Oh, no," Brionney said, not hiding her bitterness. "I know this is the Lord's church. And I know He lives." She paused and Bishop Clark watched her, waiting.

"I know He lives," she repeated, not meeting his gaze. "But I also know He doesn't love me." The tears came, and she angrily blinked them back. Bishop Clark still didn't speak. She raised her head and saw him watching her. Tears wet his cheeks, gathering in the deep wrinkles of his aged face.

He stood, walked slowly around the large desk, and settled gracefully in one of the black upholstered chairs near her. Brionney felt his eyes trying to penetrate her soul. "Why do you think He doesn't love you?"

She looked away again. "All my life, I've worshiped Him. And now, when I needed Him to help me with something so simple for Him to fix, He's not there. I've prayed as I've never prayed before, yet Derek still left me and has fallen away from the Church. I've done everything the Lord's ever asked me to do. I obey the commandments, I married in the temple, I'm trying to have a family, I pay my tithing, I serve in church callings, I go to the temple. You name it, I've been doing it. And now, when I just asked for one thing, something He could easily give, He doesn't do anything." She began to sob. "Derek's gone, my eternal family is gone, and there's only one reason: the Lord doesn't love me. He doesn't hate me. He just doesn't care."

She cried loudly now, feeling betrayed by everything she held dear. Bishop Clark sat silently. What was he thinking? How did he feel, knowing the Lord didn't love everyone? Would the revelation pierce the depths of his soul as it had hers?

The silence grew until it seemed concentrated enough to touch, so impenetrable that Brionney considered running from the room. The door was closed, but already she could see herself opening it and darting away. The bishop would stare after her, blindly, deep in his thoughts, his own faith destroyed.

Her muscles bunched, but before she could flee, the bishop's thin hand reached out to touch her arm. His flesh was cool and papery, but demanding as well. Almost unwillingly, she looked into his eyes. Instead of confusion, she saw compassion and love. Not for a moment was the bishop considering the truth of her claim.

"It may seem that way to you now," Bishop Clark said. His voice was neither loud nor soft, but firm and penetrating. "But now, more than ever, you need the Lord. You need the scriptures, and you need the Church."

"Why?" The word felt as if it had been ripped from her throat. "What does it matter? Why should I read the scriptures? Why should I go to church? I've lost my eternal family and the Lord doesn't love me, so there's no point in trying to live commandments that aren't going to get me anywhere." She stood to leave. Misery lay about her like a cloak, and she held her arms crossed over her chest as if to ward off the dark, cold feeling.

Bishop Clark also stood. "Why?" he asked. "I'll tell you why, Brionney. Because if you don't read the scriptures and follow the commandments, you will lose your daughter. You will lose your parents and siblings, and you will lose your chance at eternal life. They will go on and progress, but you won't. You'll be stopped right here and be separated from them forever. But that's not all. You have to try because *you are wrong.* The Lord does loves you, more than you can ever imagine. Hasn't He always been there, even though your will isn't always done? Perhaps you need to go back and count the times He was there for you."

"But what about *now?*" Brionney said with an anguished cry she hardly recognized as her own.

"Once, many years ago, I was laid off my job," Bishop Clark said. "But I immediately found a place that was hiring and applied for work. I knew the new job would support my family, and I would be happy doing the work. There was an added urgency because at the time my wife had been diagnosed with some serious medical problems, and our insurance was about to run out. We needed the extra money the job would provide. It could mean the difference between her life and death. I prayed hard and since I was qualified, I felt it would be no problem getting the job. When I didn't, I was bitter, and struggled with my testimony, especially during the months my wife suffered and my children had to go without because I wasn't working. I questioned the Lord's love, but my wife remained strong. She reminded me to trust in the Lord. Of course, she was right. Eventually something else came along, something better. Our new health insurance required us to go to a few certain doctors, and they had just begun to use some new techniques for people with my wife's condition—procedures a lot less intrusive. I realized then that the Lord really did know the future and had my best interests in mind when He didn't help me get that first job."

The bishop's story was good, but Brionney didn't see how it applied to her situation. "Is that what you think is going to happen to me?" she asked incredulously. "That I'm going to find something better to replace Derek?" To even suggest it seemed immoral.

"Not exactly. But I do know the Lord knows the future, and He will help you find happiness. I don't know why you have to go through this, but you will grow and be stronger for it, whatever the outcome. It's too easy to say the Lord doesn't love you because He didn't make Derek stay. But Derek has his agency, remember. The Lord will not take that away from him, no matter how much He loves you. He cannot. And who knows? Maybe this separation will save you and Savannah greater pain later on."

Brionney kept her lips tightly together, wishing she were anywhere but there in that small office. What Bishop Clark said made a strange kind of sense, but it threatened the frosty layers she had built around her heart.

"You'll think about it?" he asked.

She nodded. But as she left, she felt her own heart harden. *Maybe Derek is right*, she thought as she drove to the apartment in her mother's car. *Maybe the Church isn't true.* Maybe she should go out and try the world's way of life. Maybe that would ease her pain.

She wondered what Derek would say if she told him she had lost her testimony. Would he be satisfied? Or would he not care at all? Maybe she would never get the chance to ask.

But Brionney's chance came sooner than expected. Derek's green convertible was parked in front of the apartment with the top up and windows shut, as he always left it when he wasn't inside. When she drove around back to the parking lot, she saw Derek pacing by the back stairs. Her heart jumped. He wasn't carrying roses, but at least he was there. What did he want? Brionney started to pray, but then stopped. The Lord didn't care, so why pray to Him?

She got out of the car, and Derek stopped pacing to watch her. Neither spoke. Brionney noticed how handsome he was, and her heart longed to hold him and have everything be all right.

"Hi," she said tentatively.

His face had been expressionless, but now twisted angrily. "That's all you have to say? Why didn't you let them have my stuff? You can't keep it from me. It's mine. I need the rest of my clothes, my papers, my furniture. It's only fair."

"It's just so soon. I—I wanted to talk."

Derek slammed his fist into his other hand. "The time for talking has past, Brionney. It's over. Don't you understand that? I want out."

"No!" she said. "I know we could make it work. I'm just asking for a little time. Don't think I'm going to make this divorce easy for you—forget it! I'm going to fight it every step of the way! We're meant to be together!"

Derek's face turned a deep red. She recognized the anger that would send him into a yelling fit. Never before had it been so fully directly toward her, and she nearly cringed. "I don't love you!" he said cruelly. "Don't you understand that? I don't love you. I never did! You were pretty and attractive, and that was it. Do you understand now? It's over! Get it through that fat brain of yours."

Brionney began to cry. She wished now that she had let Derek's friend take everything. Better that than to suffer such humiliation.

"You leave her alone!" Irene came from the apartment, her fists clenched.

He glared and stalked past her. "I'm getting a few of my things."

Irene flew to Brionney's side. "What a jerk! Come on, we'd better make sure he doesn't take something he shouldn't."

"It doesn't matter," Brionney said. "It doesn't matter anymore." She couldn't face another confrontation.

"Well, Savannah's acting like she needs to eat. I put her in bed, but—"

"Savannah!" Brionney ran past her mother and down the few stairs into the apartment. She went to the bedroom, expecting to see Derek piling his stuff on the bed, but he was gone.

Savannah's bassinet was empty.

CHAPTER NINE

"My baby, my baby!" Brionney screamed it repeatedly as she ran back through the house, passing her mother in the hall.

"Isn't she in bed?" Irene questioned.

Brionney didn't answer. She ran out the front door and saw Derek climbing into his car. "Stop!" she yelled.

His smile mocked her. "Maybe you should give me what I want. Or maybe you can think about who will have custody of Savannah."

Could this be the same man she had married? Brionney ran for the car. "She's hungry! She needs to nurse!" Her milk let down as she said it, soaking the front of her shirt.

Derek disappeared inside the car, revving the engine. Brionney tried to open the passenger door, where she saw Savannah lying on the seat. It was locked. She could hear the baby crying. Brionney pounded on the window, wishing she had a knife to cut through the white convertible top. "Okay, okay! Anything you want!"

Derek grinned at her and waved before driving calmly away. Brionney followed the car, screaming at him to stop. "My baby, my baby! Anything you want, just give me my baby!"

At last she was exhausted and had to stop. She slumped to the pavement, crying uncontrollably as she watched the green car fade from sight.

How she got back to the house, Brionney couldn't remember. Her mother was hovering around her. And Debbie was on the phone, speaking rapidly. When had she arrived?

Debbie's words flowed around Brionney with no meaning as she clutched the quilt that had been in Savannah's bed. She thought Derek had taken everything with him last Friday, but he had left something worth living for, something priceless: Savannah. Now he had taken even that. *I hate him!* she thought fiercely. *I hate him!* At that moment, the hate was stronger than her love had ever been.

She could imagine Savannah crying for her. The baby had never taken a bottle. What would Derek feed her? "He has to bring her back," she moaned. "He has to."

But the minutes passed and he didn't return. How long would it take for Savannah to learn to eat from a bottle? She was only two months old and would soon forget her mother. *No!* The agony in her heart surpassed all that had gone before.

"Of course he'll bring her back," Irene said. "How can he take care of a baby?" Brionney clung to her and sobbed.

Debbie came to sit with them on the couch. "Look, he hasn't gone far. I mean, he works here. It's not like he's kidnaping her. He's just trying to prove a point, right?"

"He deserves to be shot!" Irene said. "Taking a baby to prove a point. That certainly shows what kind of man he is."

"Well, I've got Max talking to his lawyer right now. He actually contacted Max this morning about the divorce."

"Tell him he can have everything. I just want Savannah," Brionney said.

"Don't worry, Max will handle it."

"What about the police?" Irene asked.

"Well, as far as they are concerned, you two are still married and both have custody. If Derek wants to take his daughter for a ride, it's his right. He's done nothing illegal—yet."

Brionney jumped to her feet. "I can't just sit here. I have to find her!"

"Where?" Debbie asked. "Do you know if he has an apartment somewhere?"

"No. He could be staying with friends." *Or Melinda,* she thought bitterly.

"Well, Max has his secretaries working late, and they're calling to check phone listings in all of the surrounding cities. If we find a number for Derek, we'll be on the right track. Meanwhile, I'm going to go see if I can find someone at his work. They have to have a way to reach him."

"They're closed now," Brionney said.

"Well, someone might be working there. Otherwise, I'll contact the owners. I don't care. I'll find out something!"

"What can I do?"

Debbie squeezed Brionney's shoulder. "Just wait right here in case he comes back."

"What if he—if he hurts her?" Brionney asked softly.

Debbie shook her head. "Derek may be a lot of things, but I doubt he'd hurt a baby."

"I mean by accident." Brionney stared at the other woman anxiously, her panic increasing. "He doesn't know her. He hardly ever takes care of her. He doesn't know that she's nearly rolling over. I know it's early, but she's determined to try. What if she rolls off something? What if he puts her on a pillow? What if she smothers? Or what if he stops suddenly in the car? He didn't even have the car seat! And he's so angry at me. What if he shakes her too hard because she's crying? So many things could happen!"

The others were silent. They knew only too well that what Brionney was saying was true. Irene folded her arms calmly. "We'll have to trust the Lord in that respect, Brionney. We can't teach Derek to be a decent father, but the Lord can. We must pray for Savannah's safety."

"Pray?" Brionney spat out the word. "He doesn't listen to me. God hates me!"

Debbie's mouth opened in astonishment. "No, Brionney," she said. "No. He loves you."

"Oh, is that why all this is happening to me? Because He *loves* me? Ha!" She snorted. "I can do without that kind of love!"

Debbie was about to say more, but Irene put a restraining hand on her arm. "Stop right there, Brionney. I won't let you say another foul thing about our Heavenly Father. Not one more word."

Brionney said nothing, but glared at her.

"Is that what I taught you?" Irene asked. "To turn against the Lord when things don't go your way? Is that what kind of a child I've raised? Shame on you, Brionney. Shame on you! I'll tell you right now that if you ever want to see your daughter again, you'd better get on your knees and start repenting." Her voice resounded in the small apartment like a prophecy. "You are wrong here. Wrong! And your daughter's welfare is at stake." Her face softened. "Brionney, I'm your mother, and I love you every bit as much as you love your daughter. And like it or not, I couldn't stop all of this from happening to you."

"The Lord could!"

"He could stop famines and wars, too. But He won't, because we have our agency. Don't you see? We must learn for ourselves. We are free. Derek is free."

"It worked when Alma's father prayed!"

"But Alma was still free. He chose to be good!"

Brionney held her trembling lips closed tightly. She felt so helpless, so angry. And now her own mother had turned against her. She glanced at Debbie. "Please go find out something!" Debbie nodded, touched her hand briefly, and left. Irene opened her mouth to speak, but Brionney turned from her. Alone in her bedroom, she locked the door.

"I'm taking my car and driving up and down the streets," Irene said, her voice muffled by the door between them. "I know it's not much, but I might spot his car. Please, honey. Just think about what I said."

Brionney said nothing. She hugged Savannah's quilt, feeling lost and alone. Would she ever see her daughter again?

* * * * *

Derek parked his car at the run-down apartment building, the only place he'd found available on such short notice. The atmosphere of the place annoyed him, but he had taken it sight unseen Saturday morning. After all, it was only for a month until the new condo he had signed for last week was ready.

"Would you shut up?" he said to Savannah, who had been screaming since he had left Brionney at the apartment. He felt uncomfortable to hear his own father in the words. His anger increased.

That first night, after leaving Brionney, he had stayed at the new apartment Melinda was renting. But as she shared it with several other female employees who had transferred from New York, it had been awkward. And a hotel for such a long time had been out of the question. A few early-morning phone calls on Saturday had found him this dump.

When he had seen the condition of the apartment, he had hired a cleaning service and had Jason go to pick up his things from Brionney.

He would at least live in some comfort. Or would have if Brionney had complied with his desire.

He swore, letting off the tension. This was all Brionney's fault. If she would just be reasonable and let him live his life, he wouldn't have to teach her this lesson.

The baby yelled loudly. Cursing again, he picked her up, and she stopped crying. Her tiny mouth opened, as though searching for something to eat. Brionney had said something about her being hungry. Well, he had some milk in the refrigerator. That might do in a pinch.

When he didn't feed her immediately, Savannah started crying again. "Shush," Derek told her.

A large, unkempt woman from one of the downstairs apartments stared at him as he began to walk up the stairs. Derek ignored her, but she approached. "What a cute baby."

The woman smelled of something he couldn't identify, something putrid. "Thanks," he said coldly.

"Is she yours?"

"Yes, she's just visiting. If you'll excuse me, she's hungry." Derek climbed several stairs to get out of smelling range.

"I have a sort of playpen. If you want to use it," the lady said. "My dad made it for me when I was little. It just goes on the floor and folds up real nice like."

"Thanks, I can manage," Derek said. Without another word, he took the stairs two at a time.

Savannah was still screaming. "No!" he said, flicking her cheek with his finger. "Stop that."

But she screamed on, no matter how many times he flicked her cheeks. He put her on the middle of the new queen-sized bed that had been delivered today, and went to the kitchen for the milk. But how to give it to her? What about a spoon? Maybe that would work.

The doorbell rang. Since the door didn't have a peephole, he had to open it to reveal the old woman from downstairs. She smiled at him and thrust something heavy into his hands. "Use it for as long as you like," she said. Her round eyes took in the living room, furnished only with a new big-screen TV and a leather easy chair, both of which Derek had delivered with the bed. "Just make sure you give it back."

"But I—"

"No thanks necessary. That's what neighbors are for." She left before he could refuse.

Derek eyed the thing in his hands. It was made of thin bars four or five inches apart, with no top or bottom. Obviously, this was the homemade playpen the woman's father had built. But such a thing was useless to Derek. Savannah couldn't even crawl. He put it outside in the hall, hoping the old bat would take the hint.

It took a visit to the store, three different types of bottles, and numerous attempts to feed Savannah before Derek admitted defeat. "Forget this," he said, tossing the bottle onto the floor. "You'll eat when you get hungry enough."

He left her on the bed and fixed himself a sandwich. When he checked back on her later, she had finally stopped crying and was asleep. She was still on her back but seemed to be closer to the edge than before. Impossible? He didn't think she knew how to turn over. She had probably just worked herself near the edge during her tantrum. That was easily solved. He went to retrieve the playpen from the hall and put it over the baby without moving her. "There, now you won't roll off."

Derek glanced at his watch. Had he already wasted two hours trying to feed that stubborn child? Melinda would be wondering why he was late for dinner. He wished now he had left the baby with Brionney. She was more trouble than she was worth.

He headed for the door, reveling in the freedom he felt. Too long he had lived a double life. He was glad Brionney had found out his secret. Now he didn't have to lie and sneak around. He was free to find happiness wherever he wanted. Later, if he felt the need, he could always go back to the Church.

He paused briefly at the door. Surely Savannah would be all right for the short time he would be gone. Even if she woke up, there was no way she could hurt herself or roll off the bed. After all, she had been fine alone while he had run to the store. And this way if she started crying, he wouldn't have to hear her. It was high time she learned to sleep through the night.

* * * * *

An hour after Derek left, Savannah awoke. She screamed until her face was red and wet. Her stomach was empty and her diaper uncomfortable. Why didn't anyone hear her? She struggled on the bed, searching, crying, and finding nothing. One tiny foot slipped between the bars of the playpen on the side closest to the edge of the bed. As she struggled, she worked herself farther between the bars meant for a child much older and larger than herself.

Savannah balled her fists and screamed louder. But no one heard her cries.

CHAPTER TEN

Five hours had passed and there was still no news. Brionney was exhausted from the tension. Her breasts were full and aching. What was Savannah eating? Was she all right? Brionney had already asked herself the questions a million times.

As if in accompaniment to the painful images in her mind, Bishop Clark's words came back to her in faint echoes. "You will lose your daughter. You will lose your parents and siblings, and you will lose your chance at eternal life. They will go on and progress, but you won't. You'll be stopped right here and be separated from them forever."

Forever.

Lose Savannah?

Brionney hadn't comprehended that pain until Derek had taken her daughter. This separation had been more excruciating than she could have imagined, but what would it be like to be separated from her for eternity?

Savannah was all Brionney had left. She loved her daughter more than her own life. More than her pride, and, yes, she admitted it to herself, more than she loved Derek.

Had she been acting like a spoiled child, angry at the Lord because she hadn't gotten her way? Was she throwing a tantrum because her Godly parent had refused her a toy?

But Derek was hardly a toy. And temple marriage was the most important bond Brionney knew. The Lord could have so easily changed Derek's heart. He could have forced him to see . . .

Force.

Through her agony, Brionney realized abruptly that her situation wasn't like the story of Alma the Younger, who was visited by an angel in response to his father's prayer. Alma had felt remorse and had repented. Brionney had to admit that perhaps Derek would not repent, regardless of what happened. Heaven knew she had given him enough opportunities. She recalled now that Laman and Lemuel had also seen an angel of the Lord, yet had never been converted to the gospel. It was the person who made the difference, not simply the experience.

And Brionney knew better than to doubt the Lord. She had known it all along. Memories flooded her mind of the time she had been lost in the mountains as a child, and had prayed and been found; of when her father had been in the hospital near death, and how the Lord had healed him; of her grandmother who lay dying painfully, with her family praying at her bedside for her release. There were more memories, running together like a silent movie in the deep recesses of her mind. Brionney couldn't doubt that the Lord had been a part of those days, that He had acted solely because He loved her.

Like the Nephites of old, she had received an ample witness to His love. And also like the Nephites, she had turned her back on Him when she needed Him the most.

Shame washed over Brionney in accusing waves. Never had she asked the Lord if Derek's leaving was His will; she had only asked Him to save her marriage. She had been so afraid His will wouldn't coincide with hers. She was a hypocrite, and without faith. True faith included the courage and desire to accept the Lord's will, no matter what it brought into her life—or took out of it—with the knowledge that she would not pass through the trials alone, but with the Lord as a buffer.

She had forgotten Debbie's loyalty and her mother's support. How could she not have seen that they had been sent from the Lord? Even the bishop had used the right words to help her understand.

"Oh, dear Father, what have I done?"

Brionney bowed her head and prayed. First she begged for forgiveness, humbling herself in the depths of her soul. Then she asked for guidance, for help to find Savannah, and protection for her as well.

As she finished, she paused, thinking deeply before she said the words. "But Thy will be done. I've tried it the other way, and I know it won't work. Please, I beg Thee to help bring my baby back, but I will accept Thy will."

At once, she felt the cloak of misery that had been her constant companion lift from her shoulders as if taken by invisible hands. Her eyes flew open, but she saw no one. Nevertheless, she was not alone. Heat enveloped her, and a tingling sensation began around her heart. The iciness was abruptly gone, and she felt the trauma of Derek's betrayal more deeply than she had on the day he left; but there with the pain was the all-encompassing love of her Father. The love tempered her sorrow, soothed the ache, until she could endure it.

She knew then that her Father and her Savior suffered with her. Both understood the grief that was hers and the hardships she had yet to face. No matter what the future held, she would never be alone again.

What's more, she knew how to find her baby.

* * * * *

Brionney came out of the room at nearly midnight, the tears drying on her face. Her mother had returned and was in the kitchen staring into space. Her face showed that she had been weeping. Debbie was with her at the table, busy on the portable phone. She looked up in frustration. "Nothing," she said. "Only answering machines and people who refuse to tell me anything. The person over the records says she has received no change of address. Several people say Derek has a new cell phone, but nobody knows the number. I even found where that girl Melinda is staying, but she's out. I'm sorry . . . I don't know what else to do."

Brionney waved her words aside. "Jason," she said. "Remember the man who came to pick up Derek's things? He had to know where to take them!"

"Yes! I'll have to wake up that secretary again," Debbie said. "But, boy, is she not going to be happy."

"Or call the brother-in-law and get his number. I remember the name of the business. The moving truck said Tompkins Fast Move." Brionney could see the sign clearly in her mind. "Better yet, look up his name. Ralph, wasn't it? How many Ralph Tompkinses do you think there are?"

They looked up the company quickly and found a listing in Mesa. No one answered there, but they also found a home number in Mesa for a Ralph Tompkins. "Cross your fingers," Debbie said.

Brionney knew it had to be the right one. It was. And though Ralph Tompkins had no idea where they had been going to deliver Derek's things, he willingly gave them Jason's phone number. Debbie thanked him and punched in the new digits. "It's ringing."

Brionney held out her hand for the phone. "Let me talk to him."

"Hello?" said a groggy voice.

"Jason?"

"Yes, who's this?"

"It's Brionney Roathe, Derek's wife. Look, this is really important. I need to know where Derek is staying. Where were you going to take his stuff?"

"Why are you calling this late?"

"It's an emergency. Please don't hang up!"

"I promised not to tell anyone where he was staying."

Brionney gave a little sob. "Please, Jason. He's got my baby! He came and took her from me almost six hours ago. She doesn't take a bottle, and it's been about eight hours since she's eaten. She's going to be crying like crazy and I'm afraid of what Derek will do. His temper—"

"I know about his temper," he said. "But I still can't . . . just a minute, my wife is saying something."

Brionney prayed with all her heart.

A woman's voice came on the phone. "I have the address right here. When Jason told me what Derek—oooo, it makes me so mad! Taking a nursing baby from its mother! Do you have a pen?"

"Yes." Brionney wrote down the address. "Thank you very much," she said gratefully.

"Good luck. I'll be praying for you."

"Thanks." Brionney hung up the phone. "Let's go!"

"Let me call Max," Debbie said. "We can pick him up on the way. My kids are old enough to stay alone, and we might need a man with us. Max is no fighter, but he can throw out legal mumbo-jumbo like there's no tomorrow."

Brionney felt she could tear Derek apart with her own hands, but Max might come in handy. She was relieved to find him waiting outside his house; she didn't want to waste a minute. "We'd better call the police, too," he said, pulling out his cell phone. "Just in case."

Brionney thought that was wise. She was going to Derek's, and she wasn't going to leave until she had Savannah—no matter what he threw at her. She only hoped it wasn't too late.

* * * * *

Derek came home and turned on his new TV. He needed to get to bed soon. He peeked into the dark bedroom and was relieved to hear no crying, only the baby's soft breaths. *See, nothing to it,* he thought.

He reclined in his comfortable leather chair. Probably better if he slept here tonight, so as to not wake the baby. If she awoke, he would let her cry until morning, when she would probably be hungry enough to take the bottle. Before work, he could drop her at Brionney's. No, better than that, he could drop her off at a day-care center. He would send Jason again for his things, and if Brionney gave them to him, he would call her and tell her where Savannah was.

Feeling pleased with his decision, Derek set the timer on the TV to turn off in half an hour, and pulled a blanket over him.

* * * * *

Savannah awoke at the sound of the door. She lay on her back and cried, weakly at first and then louder, her tiny voice hoarse. She wriggled a few inches further through the bars, her feet pumping wildly in the air. Straining, she tried to turn over. All at once the portion of her body dangling over the edge outweighed the upper part, and her body turned as she slid off the bed. She was saved a rough tumble to the ground by the bars that were far enough spaced to allow her body through, but not her head. She hung there, face pressed against the blanket, struggling for breath. It was not a fight she could win.

* * * * *

For once, Brionney was glad Debbie drove like a maniac. Still, it seemed to take forever to arrive at the address. They ran up the stairs and found the apartment almost immediately. As Max pounded on the door, Brionney wondered how long it would be before the police arrived.

A sleepy-eyed Derek opened the door. When he saw who they were, he tried to slam it shut. But Brionney put her foot in and pushed her way inside, followed closely by the others. "Where is she?" Brionney demanded.

"She's not here," Derek said. But he glanced toward a door on the other side of the room.

Brionney started for it. Derek pushed her back. She tried again, but he held her back. Max and Debbie stepped forward. "Let her go!" Max said.

"You slime!" Debbie added.

Brionney jerked away and darted behind Derek toward the door. She opened it and flipped on the light. "Savannah!" she screamed. "Oh, dear Father, no!"

Savannah's body hung off the bed, her neck caught between two bars on a wooden contraption Derek had rigged around her. She wasn't moving.

Brionney raced to the bed and shakily rescued her daughter's dangling body. The infant's face was blue and her chest unmoving. At Brionney's frantic cry, the others had stopped their yelling and come into the room. Everyone stared with horror. Max pulled out his phone to dial the paramedics. Irene and Debbie rushed to Brionney's side.

Brionney laid Savannah on the floor. "Breathe, honey, breathe!" she cried. But Savannah didn't move. Brionney put her hand under the baby's neck and held the tiny pathway open while she breathed a small puff of air into her daughter's lungs, trying to remember the exact method she had learned in her prenatal classes.

"She has a pulse," Irene said. "Don't give her too much air. Just little breaths."

"Max went outside to wait for help," Debbie said. "Those cops should be here by now."

As she spoke, Max entered the room with two police officers. Immediately they knelt by Brionney and took over. "Come on, Savannah, come on!" Brionney pleaded, her body beginning to shake all over. "You can do it. Mommy's here. I'm not leaving you. Please try!"

Then she heard a faint cry and a tiny gasp of breath. "She's breathing," one of the officers said.

Thank you, Father! Brionney's relief was as keen as had been her despair. The paramedics arrived and after stabilizing the baby, rushed her to the hospital. Brionney went with her in the ambulance while the others stayed behind to answer questions from the police. "We'll meet you there as soon as we can," Irene said, squeezing her daughter's arm. "The Lord will go with you."

"I know," Brionney said, her voice full of tears.

Brionney stayed with Savannah while the doctor examined her. The baby wasn't crying, but she seemed dazed. Toward the end she began to suck on her fist, making soft moaning sounds.

"Your daughter is a very lucky little girl," the doctor said finally, his face grave. "Another minute, and she most likely would have suffered irreparable brain damage. And the minute after that she would have been dead. As it is, she has some damage on her neck and will have some bruising. She is also likely to have some minor brain damage, though we'll have to do a few more tests to see what effect if any that will mean to her in the long run. But her spine and esophagus are fine, and she's alert. That's a good sign. In fact, she looks very hungry."

"Can I nurse her?" Brionney's arms ached to hold her baby.

"Yes, I think that'll be all right. But let the nurse know immediately if there is anything odd about the way she's swallowing. She'll be a little sluggish at first. That's normal, so don't worry." He smiled and walked to the door. "We'll still want to keep her under observation tonight, but if all goes well, you can take her home tomorrow."

"Thank you," Brionney said.

The doctor paused. "We will need a complete report on what happened. This is a very serious injury resulting from neglect. There may be charges filed against your husband."

Brionney nodded, too numb to think beyond the moment. "May I?" she said, motioning to Savannah. One of the nurses nodded, and Brionney gently lifted Savannah to her chest. "Mama's here," she said. "I'm not going to let anything ever happen to you again!" Savannah looked in the direction of her voice and let out a soft cry, then began nursing weakly. Brionney was a little self-conscious in front of the nurses, but they kept back, allowing her to have some time with her daughter.

Love welled in Brionney's heart. "I love you, Savannah," she murmured. Feeling her baby alive and tugging at her breast was the most intense and inexplicable feeling Brionney had experienced. Her daughter was alive! And she knew that her Father in Heaven was responsible.

Another nurse came into the room. "The father is here," she said, "with some others. He wants to see the baby."

Brionney clenched her jaw. But not even Derek's presence would shatter her new peace.

CHAPTER ELEVEN

When Savannah had had her fill of milk, Brionney asked Max and the newly arrived bishop to give her daughter a blessing. Afterward, Max gently touched Savannah on the cheek as she slept. "She's going to be just fine."

Brionney smiled and her tears began again. "I know," she whispered. "The doctor says there may be some brain damage, but I know she's going to be okay." She looked at Debbie. "Thank you for driving like a maniac."

Debbie sniffed and wiped the tears from her cheek. "Any time," she said. "It's one of the things I do best."

Bishop Clark squeezed Brionney's shoulder. "Welcome back," he said. Brionney knew what he meant and she wanted to thank him, but she had to bite her lip so she wouldn't cry again. The bishop understood without the words. He smiled. "We'll talk later."

"I'll come back tomorrow morning after I get the kids off to school," Debbie said.

"And I'm going to find something in this hospital for you to eat." Irene picked up her purse. "I'll be right back."

They all left together, and Brionney was alone with Savannah and one nurse. "I guess you can let him come in now," she said, steeling herself for a confrontation.

Derek's face was pale and drawn. "Well?"

Brionney knew he had already been told everything about Savannah's condition. "You need to hear it from me?" she asked. "Well, *my* daughter is going to be fine, no thanks to you."

"Brionney, I'm sorry." He ran a hand through his blond hair, looking at the baby in her arms so anxiously that she almost felt sorry for him.

Almost.

"You nearly killed her, and that's all you have to say?" Brionney shook her head.

"I never meant for something like this to happen! I swear it! If I could take it back, I would!"

"And since when can I believe you? Look, you wanted the divorce. Fine. You can have it. Whatever you want. I won't fight it. You don't want to be married to me, and I don't want you around Savannah. But I get full custody. Otherwise, I'll make your life as miserable as you've made mine these last few months!"

Derek blinked at her in surprise. But Brionney also saw something else she hadn't seen in him before: respect. *Oh, so that's how I get your respect.*

"That is, if you stay out of jail," she added angrily.

Derek put his hands in his pockets. "I've talked to my lawyer. He says as long as they can't prove a history of neglect, I'll be fine. It's not as if I went out and left her alone! Believe it or not, I was trying to protect her by putting that playpen on the bed."

"And I'm supposed to be grateful? If you hadn't stolen her in the first place, nothing would have happened!"

"She's my daughter, too."

"Is she?" Brionney asked with venom in her voice. "Didn't you lose that right when you decided to have an affair? When you decided to desert us?" She gave a disgusted grunt. "Forget it. I don't want to fight with you. I don't even want to talk to you."

"We can be adult about this." He lifted his chin, showing more of his former arrogance.

"I am being adult," she sneered. "If I weren't, I'd tear your eyes out! You almost murdered our baby because you wanted to teach me a lesson. Well, fine. I learned. I'll give you what you want. And I'll tell you something else. I don't want you back! How does that feel? I don't want to see you at all. Now, will you please leave!"

His face darkened, and Brionney knew he was angry. And her heart ached, because though she said the words everyone would expect her to say, she didn't mean them. She wanted to hate Derek. But try as she might, she still loved him. If he would only humble himself and come back on her terms, she would find a way to forgive him as the Lord had always forgiven her. They would turn to each other and find greater understanding and strength within their relationship. They would be faithful and happy and good parents. This near-tragedy would strengthen them. But all that was impossible as long as Derek wasn't repentant.

"I'll have my lawyer contact yours," Derek said stiffly.

Brionney held her head erect as he left, feeling some satisfaction in not letting him see her real feelings.

Savannah moved in her sleep and Brionney watched her. There was nothing she would rather do.

* * * * *

Brionney took Savannah home the next day. "Mom," she said on the way, "I think I'm ready to go back to Utah with you. Maybe some distance is what I need right now."

Irene hugged her. "I'm so glad, honey. You'll feel much better when this is behind you."

This. It was what everybody was calling the remains of her marriage. *This.* No longer did it have even the dignity of a name. Perhaps that was only fitting. All that she and Savannah had left were each other and a lot of shattered dreams. No, that wasn't true. They also had Brionney's family and the Lord. And hope. What did the Lord have planned for them?

* * * * *

A few days later, Jason and his brother-in-law Ralph showed up again to collect Derek's belongings. Brionney let them have everything she didn't want to keep. To save her the trouble of getting rid of it, she made them take the ancient bed, though she knew Derek had bought a new one. It was impossible for her to sleep in it now. At the last moment, she put in his green-striped shirt, the one she had kept earlier. The reminder was too painful.

The following days passed in a blur of activity. Irene was at the center of it all, taking care of the many details of moving. She and Debbie became great friends, and Brionney's small kitchen grew alive with chatter and laughter. After a few cranky days, Savannah seemed to recover from her ordeal and returned to the happy baby she had been. Healing wasn't as easy for Brionney. She often had nightmares of finding Savannah too late, her face black and lifeless.

Nights were the hardest for Brionney, because it was then she couldn't seem to drive Derek from her thoughts. She tortured herself endlessly by wondering what he might be doing, and who he was with.

By the first week in November everything was packed in boxes, large and small, and stacked in the living room. Since Brionney wouldn't be picking up the moving truck until the next morning when Max and several other men in her ward would come to load the heavy items, she found herself with nothing to do.

"Let's get our hair done," suggested Debbie. Her oldest daughter Alicia worked at a beauty college, and Debbie was always going to get her hair cut in the latest style.

"I could really use it," Irene said. She fluffed her white-blonde locks. It was her own color, white-gray blending in perfectly with the blonde strands. Brionney hoped her hair would look like that one day.

"Okay," Brionney agreed. "But I'll just watch." Her hair was straight and in one length just below her shoulder blades, the same style she had worn since high school.

Debbie shrugged and winked at Irene. "She may change her mind."

They took Debbie's minivan to the beauty college. The reception room had a large wooden booth in front, and a small row of padded chairs lined the walls. Two small tables held a variety of beauty magazines. Worn carpet, a faded gray, and posters of ladies with perfectly styled hair completed the decor. The air was heavy with the smell of perming and coloring solutions.

"I'd like my daughter to do the cutting, if she's not busy," Debbie said to the girl in the booth.

"Oh, Mom, thank you!" Alicia said when she came to the front. "You saved me from having to give a permanent to a wig. I owe you big time!" Her eyes focused on Brionney. "Oh, I know the best hair cut for you. Come on, I'll show you a picture."

Before Brionney could protest, Irene took the car seat with Savannah and Alicia led them to a stall in the back room. "Sit here, Brionney," she said, and placed a big book on her lap.

Alicia kept up a constant chatter as she searched through the pages of beautiful models sporting the latest haircuts. "There." Alicia pointed. "That's the one. When I saw that, I thought to myself, Brionney would look so great in that."

Brionney stared. The model's hair was a white-blonde like her own. The front was layered to make it look soft and full, the back still long enough to reach her shoulders. It looked elegant, sexy, and completely modern. *But it's not really me,* Brionney thought. She was about to say no and leave the chair when she caught sight of the model on the opposite page. Her hair was dark red and she bore no real resemblance to Melinda, except that her hair was cut in the same style as the woman who had caused such havoc in Brionney's life. The haircut Alicia wanted to give Brionney looked nothing like Melinda's, but was just as exquisite. Maybe it was time for a change. "Okay," she said. "Let's do it. Just like you want."

Alicia squealed her delight. She immediately called over another student to work on Debbie's long nails. "And cut my hair too," Debbie grumbled, "since my daughter's going to be busy. We don't have all day." She winked at Brionney.

When they left the shop, Brionney couldn't believe how different she felt. Alicia had put a little extra makeup on her face and insisted on doing her nails. She almost didn't recognize herself when she looked in the mirror.

"You've always been pretty," Irene said, "but today you look spectacular."

Brionney knew people had always thought she had a pretty face, though it had often been overlooked because of her weight. In the stressful past weeks she had lost ten more pounds and was feeling much better about herself. She could even fit into some of her old clothes. She felt like celebrating. "Let's go out and do something," she suggested.

"Okay, but first let's go home and change into something nice." Debbie pulled her keys out of her purse. "And I need to tell Max and the kids that I won't be home tonight."

"They'll sure be glad to get rid of me," Brionney said. "I keep taking you away from them."

"Right. Then they'll go back to dodging me. Before you moved here and we became friends, I was always trying to get them to go places with me. Children never like to be seen with their mother, you know, and Max is basically a homebody. Now that you're leaving, it'll be back to the same old thing."

"I'll visit," Brionney promised as they reached the van.

Debbie turned her head to Irene, her key in the lock. "Irene, I've been meaning to ask you. Do you need any quilts? Or do you have any people near you that might be in need? They're nothing too elaborate, just red and black or blue and black checks. You see I make them from . . ."

Brionney smiled, rolling her eyes heavenward and flipping her new hairdo in the slight breeze. She would certainly miss Debbie and her odd fetish.

* * * * *

None of them were prepared for what awaited them at Brionney's apartment.

"Who's that?" Debbie asked.

Brionney turned to see a woman pacing up and down the sidewalk near Brionney's front door, glancing every so often at her wristwatch. She had dark blonde hair and a plain figure.

"I don't know," Brionney said. But the woman seemed oddly familiar. Then she remembered. "It's Derek's mother! She said she might stop by sometime when she was in town, but I thought it was just talk. I don't really know her. I only met her once at our reception."

Debbie turned off the engine and hopped out of the van, a curious smile on her face. "Come on," she said eagerly. "Let's go meet her."

Brionney lagged behind with Savannah. She wasn't anxious to face the nondescript woman who had practically ignored her at her reception. She had hinted that Brionney's marriage might not work out, and it had bothered her then; but it angered her even more now that Derek had left her. She didn't want to face the woman's gloating.

"Kris, hello," Brionney said reluctantly.

"Brionney, is that you?" The bright blue eyes that reminded Brionney of Derek's widened in surprise. "It is, isn't it? Why, you've cut your hair or something. You look wonderful!" Her voice was warm and took Brionney completely off guard.

"Uh, Kris, this is my mother, Irene Fields. You probably remember her from the reception. And this is my good friend, Debbie

Crandall." Brionney didn't introduce Kris by her last name because she wasn't sure which one she was using.

"Sure, I remember your mother," Kris said. "Nice to see you again, and to meet you, Debbie." The others murmured appropriate greetings. "And this must be Savannah," Kris said. "Oh, she is so adorable. Hello, little one. I'm your other grandmother."

Once again Brionney was astonished. This didn't seem to be the woman she remembered from the reception. There, she had been uptight and remote, and the tension between her and Derek's father and his new wife had been—

Brionney's thoughts cut off abruptly. Had the reception been painful for her? Even after years, it must have cost Kris to see her ex-husband with Alice.

"Will you come in?" Brionney asked softly, seeing Kris in a new light.

"Thank you."

There was almost total silence as they entered. Kris immediately noticed the boxes stacked in rows against the living room walls. "Are you moving?"

"I'm going back to Utah for now."

"Derek didn't mention this when I talked to him last month."

"I—uh, he doesn't live here anymore. He left me."

The startling eyes in the plain face showed a mixture of dismay and surprise. "I didn't know."

"You didn't? I thought perhaps that's why you had come."

"No. A friend of mine had a convention here, and I came along for the ride. That's her car out front. You see, I talked to Alice briefly and she mentioned seeing you and the baby. I wanted to come and see her for myself. I was a little worried about just showing up, but there wasn't time to call. It was sort of a last-minute decision. I'm really sorry I didn't call first. This is so awkward."

"It's okay, really."

"When did he leave?"

"A few weeks ago." Brionney clenched her jaw emotionlessly. "He's been seeing someone else."

Kris shook her head, as if doing so could make it untrue. "I'm so sorry, Brionney."

"So am I." A large lump seemed to block her throat, no matter how she tried to swallow it.

"Well, are we still going out or what?" Debbie asked into the silence that followed.

"Kris, we were just about to go out for dinner," Irene said. "Will you join us?"

Kris hesitated. "Are you sure I won't be in the way?"

"No," Brionney said quickly. "And it will give you time to get to know Savannah."

The woman's smile echoed in her eyes, making them stand out even more in her plain face. "Thanks, I'd love to."

* * * * *

Brionney had a wonderful time at the restaurant. Debbie flirted outrageously with the waiter, though he was about the same age as her missionary son, making everyone helpless with laughter. She made the words so conspicuous that no one would ever misconstrue them as real. The boy was good-natured and laughed right along with them.

Brionney couldn't remember laughing so hard since their family outings in Utah. She and her siblings had always enjoyed being together, and took special pleasure in embarrassing their parents. She looked forward to going home. It would feel good to be in a family again.

Her thoughts shook her. Hadn't she been in a family with Derek and Savannah? Flashes of the last months of struggle entered her mind. No, that was not what a family should be. But that didn't mean it couldn't work out in the end, did it?

Toward the end of the evening, Debbie and Irene went to the rest room to change Savannah's diaper, leaving Kris and Brionney staring awkwardly at each other. "I'm glad you came," Brionney finally said. "I'm glad I got to know you better."

"I'm sorry I haven't been very friendly," Kris replied. She swirled the ice in her near-empty cup, eyes fixed on the pattern the cubes left on the glass. "You know, Derek was always so much like his father that it scared me. I tried to tell you at the reception, but, well, I didn't know for sure anything like this would happen. I just knew Derek the way he was before his mission. He had several serious transgressions that I feel he didn't ever take care of properly. I was afraid you'd get hurt. And truthfully, I didn't want to like you in case . . . well, you know." There were tears in her eyes. "I'm so sorry, Brionney. You know, looking at you reminds me of myself. Derek's father left me for the first time after we'd been married a year. But I kept seeing him, and eventually he came back because of Derek, but it never lasted for more than a few months. I finally got tired of it and divorced him. Alice was waiting with open arms and a five-year-old daughter, but now even she's wised up to him. They're getting divorced."

"Do you think Derek will try to come back?"

"I don't know." She looked at Brionney earnestly. "Do you want him to?"

Brionney frowned. "I told him I didn't at the hospital. I was so angry at what he had done. But the truth is, I miss him. I hate being alone."

"I know the feeling. But you know, even if he does try to come back, maybe you should think twice about it. Oh, I can't believe I'm saying that about my own son, but it's what I feel. If he's not really repentant, it won't work. Believe me, I know. You really have to be careful—especially for Savannah's sake."

"Thanks for the advice," Brionney said. But it hurt. Every word reminded her of Derek's broken promises.

"I hope no matter what happens between the two of you, we can be friends. I'd like to get to know Savannah. Just a few visits, maybe. At your house in Utah or wherever."

That didn't seem too threatening. "Sure. She can use all the love we can give her."

"I'd like to see Derek before I go back to California," she said. "Do you know where I can reach him?"

"I have a number at work, and I know where he was staying two weeks ago. I'll write it down for you when we get back to the apartment." Brionney wanted to ask Kris to report back, to tell her how he was doing, but she bit her lip before the words slipped out. She had to remember that this was the man who had nearly killed her daughter out of spite.

It was an accident, she told herself.

Kris left that night. Brionney had the odd feeling she would be seeing her again. Shaking off the sensation, she went into her apartment to sleep on the couch bed for the last time.

Near midnight, a soft knock on the back door awoke Brionney. Who could it be? Probably Debbie, with some last-minute news or a few more quilts for Irene to distribute. But wouldn't she have waited until morning?

"Who is it?" Brionney called nervously.

"Derek."

Brionney's heartbeat quickened. Why was he here? What did he want? She glanced at Savannah, sleeping next to her on the couch bed. Had he come to try and take her again? Fear made her breath come quickly. She couldn't allow him near Savannah. "What do you want?" she asked.

"To talk. Just to talk for a few minutes."

Brionney wasn't taking any chances. "Wait a second," she called. She picked up Savannah and took her to the bedroom, where Irene slept on a borrowed cot. "Mom, wake up."

"What is it?" came a groggy voice.

"Derek's here. He wants to talk."

"Now?"

"I guess so. Look, could you watch Savannah in here? And maybe lock the door? I'm going outside to talk with him."

"Okay, but be careful."

Brionney heard the concern in her voice. "Don't worry, Mom. He has never physically hurt me."

Irene's eyes looked at her sadly. "It's not the physical hurt I'm worried about."

"I'll be okay."

Brionney slipped into her jeans and a sweater for the November night. She didn't bother with socks, but wore her most comfortable loafers. She put the apartment keys in her pocket, checked her hair in the glass of the entertainment center, and went to the door. Derek stood on the other side, looking cold. He took a step forward, but she shook her head. "Let's talk outside."

"It's cold," he said.

"Not compared to Utah, it's not."

"I heard you were going back."

"Is that why you're here?"

He shuffled his feet. "Look, can we at least talk in my car?"

"Okay." She followed him to his car. He turned on the engine and put the heat on. In a few minutes the car was warm, and he turned it off.

"I saw my mom," he said. "She told me you were going back to Utah."

"Nothing keeping me here."

He had the grace to look away. After a long, silent moment he said, "You look really good. Fit. And I like your hair like that."

The unexpected compliment filled Brionney with a bittersweet pleasure, but she wasn't about to let him know that. "I've lost most of the weight," she said without emotion. "It takes time after having a baby. But I told you that before."

"I didn't come here to fight."

"Then why did you come?" Her voice showed the anger she still felt toward him. "I'm still waiting to find out." She thought he might have come to ask her forgiveness again for Savannah's accident. She didn't dare hope that he had learned his lesson and was ready to make the long journey back to her and the Lord. In her angry state, she wasn't even sure she could begin to discuss that possibility.

"When I was talking to my mom, she told me what a good time she had tonight and how nice you were to her." He gave a dry laugh. "You know mothers. She gave me a long lecture. And after she left, I got to thinking what a good time we used to have when we were dating. Don't you remember?"

"Yes," she said, her voice barely a whisper. The memories hurt and threatened to cool her anger. "It was just you and me then. No one else." *No Melinda.*

"Well, I thought maybe we should date. You know, like in the old times. Have some fun."

Brionney stared at him. This was beyond belief. "You want to *date?*"

"Yes. Bring back the good times."

"What about Melinda?"

He was silent for a long minute. "Now that we're broken up, she wants a commitment."

"Of course she does," Brionney said. "Every woman wants a commitment from the man she loves."

"Well, I don't want a commitment."

"You want to *date.*" There was irony in Brionney's voice, but Derek didn't seem to notice.

"Do you still love me?" he asked.

"After all you've done to me and Savannah, you have the nerve to ask that?" The anger Brionney felt came back all at once. "I told you how I felt in the hospital!"

"You didn't mean that. You were angry." Abruptly, he leaned over and put a hand on the back of her head, pulling her close and kissing her. It was a deep, searching kiss that seared Brionney's soul. She wanted to fight him, but couldn't find the strength. Another part of her wanted it to go on forever. He was right. She still loved him.

Furious at herself, she deliberately thought of the beautiful Melinda. Had he kissed her this same way? The thought gave her strength, and Brionney pushed on his chest with both hands. "You want to date," she said, breaking away.

He grinned at her, sure he had won. "Yes. Will you stay in Arizona?"

"Are you still going through with the divorce?" she countered. "Are you still working with Melinda? Are you 'dating' her?"

"That has nothing to do with us."

Brionney's anger grew, and she struggled to contain it. "Yes, it has *everything* to do with us. Giving you time is one thing, but you have to give something, too! You always talk about what you want, but what about me? I need a father for Savannah. I need someone I can trust. You want to date. Well, okay, let's date. You can have all the time you want. But you'll have to give up this job and meet me halfway. I'm going to Utah tomorrow. If you want any future with me, you'll find a new job there and leave everything here behind. And I mean everything and everyone."

Derek stared at her. "Brionney, be reasonable."

"I am being reasonable. I have to do what is best for my daughter, and that is going where I can have a place to live and not worry about having to leave her to get a job."

"You're asking too much."

"No. I never asked more than you promised to give." With that she got out of the car. "If you want to contact me, you know where I am." Then in a softer voice she added, "It would be a long road, Derek, but you could come back."

She turned quickly and ran to the house, glad the tears had waited until she was away from him. That kiss! Why had he kissed her? Did he love her after all? Perhaps. But he didn't love her enough to be faithful.

Irene met her at the door. "Brionney, what happened?" she asked. "No, don't worry about Savannah. She's asleep in the bassinet. I left the door to the bedroom open so I could hear her. I know you wanted me to stay inside with the door locked, but you were gone so long I started to get worried."

Brionney slumped to the couch bed. "Derek says he wants to date," she said. "He still wants to go through with the divorce, but he wants to date. On top of that, he's not willing to change his lifestyle. I don't understand it. Why come here with such a ridiculous offer?"

"I'll bet he misses the security you represent," Irene said. "And he wants that security, but not the commitment. I've seen it happen before."

"I don't think he knows what he wants," Brionney muttered. "But I won't share him. It's not right."

"Of course it's not. And Derek's old enough to learn that he can't have his cake and eat it too."

"He didn't even mention Savannah, not even when I brought her up. It's as though for him she really did die that night—or maybe never existed at all."

Irene put an arm around her. "Come on, let's get you to bed. I'll go get Savannah. I know you'll sleep better with her right here where you can see her."

"Mom?"

Irene stopped. "Yes, honey?"

"Do you think he'll come back if I give him enough time? I mean, part of me is so angry at him that I want to strangle him. But the other part . . . I still love him. I miss him." The tears fell more readily. "But it hurts so much knowing he's with someone else, that he's choosing not to be with me."

Irene sat next to her. "I don't know what the future holds, but I know you'll be okay. The Lord loves you so much. For now, I think you just have to live your life and leave Derek to make his own decisions."

Brionney nodded and lay back on the bed. After her mother left to get Savannah, she said a prayer. She didn't ask for Derek to come back or for her marriage to be saved, she simply asked for the strength to endure.

* * * * *

The next morning, an array of different people from the ward assembled in front of the apartment. Within a few hours, Brionney's meager belongings were loaded on the small truck. She said good-bye to everyone as a group, then turned to Debbie. "Thanks for everything."

"We'll keep in touch," she promised.

"Of course. Besides, Max is handling the divorce."

"You still hoping Derek changes his mind?"

Brionney blinked away the tears. She hadn't known her feelings were so obvious to others. "Yes. But it has to be on my terms, and I don't know if he could do that. And I'm not going to try to force him." She had learned that much.

"Well, drive carefully. Here's a lunch for you on the road." She shoved a basket into Brionney's hands. "There's a red and black tablecloth in there so you won't have to eat on those sticky tables at the rest stops."

Brionney knew that the cloth was Debbie's way of saying how much she loved her. "Thanks." They hugged each other tightly.

Savannah was already strapped in her car seat in the front of the truck, and Irene was walking toward her car. There was nothing to do but leave. Brionney took one last glance at the apartment where she had so many memories, both bad and good. Hot tears threatened, but only in the truck did she let them fall, away from Debbie's sharp eyes. Brionney started the engine and waved one last time.

The rental truck was small but unfamiliar. When they had moved to Arizona, Derek had done all the driving, towing his car behind the moving truck. Now Brionney was in charge. She put the truck in gear and pushed on the gas. Determinedly, she began to sing *The Lord Is My Shepherd*, with musical variations she had learned as a child.

The Lord is my Shepherd; no want shall I know.
I feed in green pastures; safe-folded I rest.
He leadeth my soul where the still waters flow,
Restores me when wand'ring, redeems when oppressed.

Thru the valley and shadow of death though I stray,
Since thou art my Guardian, no evil I fear.
Thy rod shall defend me, thy staff be my stay.
No harm can befall with my Comforter near.

"We're on our way, Savannah," Brionney stopped singing long enough to say. She didn't know exactly where they would end up, but at least they had each other.

PART TWO

CHAPTER TWELVE

The November weather in Utah was much colder than in Arizona. But the air was pure and the looming mountains familiar and comfortable. Brionney's father had prepared her old room, complete with the twin bed and dresser she had used as a child. His face grimaced slightly with effort as they moved the new crib he had bought for Savannah into the room, but his blue eyes twinkled above the dark wood.

Terrell Fields was older than Irene by ten years, but his face and body didn't show his age. He was average height, but very strong. In hardly any time at all, he and Brionney's brothers-in-law had moved the rest of her furniture into her parents' empty basement, hidden away as though it had never existed. When they were done, Brionney felt strangely as though she had gone back in time. Had her marriage and Arizona been only a dream? The odd sensation left her empty and sad, longing for what wasn't. The only visible reminder of her time with Derek was Savannah.

Brionney's three sisters and their families were there to welcome her home and to celebrate her arrival with an impromptu family dinner. Her nephews had grown almost beyond recognition, and Lauren and Mickelle, the second and third sisters, were both expecting again. It would be Lauren's fourth child and Mickelle's second, both due in August, a week or so before Savannah's birthday. Talia, the oldest, had four boys. All of the sisters had married at nineteen, except for Mickelle, who had been twenty-two. None had ever been separated from their husbands.

As she watched the easy interaction between her sisters and their husbands, Brionney felt a keen sense of envy. It was all she could do to keep from embarrassing everyone. If Derek had been there, he would be the center of attention. She would have felt loved.

After dinner they gathered in the large family room, Brionney's favorite part of the house. Terrell had started a roaring fire, and they watched the latest Walt Disney release while eating popcorn from Irene's oversized aluminum bowls. The children were glued to the TV, mouths gaping in wonder.

"So what are you going to do now?" Talia asked. She sat next to Brionney on the couch with her youngest, seventeen-month-old Roger, on her lap. Talia had shoulder-length hair, still blonde but darkened almost to a light brown. Her eyes were more of a hazel color instead of the dark blue the rest of the family shared, and she was short like Brionney.

Lauren and Mickelle looked over with interest as Talia posed her question. Both were taller than Brionney and thin. Their hair color was also blonde, though not as white as hers.

Brionney gazed at Talia with a feeling of helplessness. *Why does she have to put me on display?* She wished Zack were home. He would jump in and fill the silence. "I don't know," she said. "I've never planned for something like this. I just wanted to be a wife and mother."

"I know what you mean," Talia said. "But you can really take advantage of the opportunity and go back to school or something. Both BYU and Utah Valley State College have great programs to get you started. You could go part-time, and I'd love to help out with Savannah. A little girl would be fun after four boys."

Brionney stroked Savannah's halo of blonde hair. "I don't want to leave her. She needs me."

"I know exactly how you feel," Talia said. "I had the same dilemma when I went back to get my nursing degree. But while I loved my kids, they also drove me crazy at times. I found it was great to get out of the house a couple times a week for a few hours. Don't you remember baby-sitting them?"

"But that's different."

"How? They had more fun with you in those few hours than they would have had with me, and I was a lot more able to cope with them after the time away. Savannah needs you right now, you're right about that. But she needs all of us, too. We *want* to be involved."

Brionney forced a smile. After all, her family was the reason she had come back to Utah. "You're right. I guess I've just been depending on myself for so long that I forgot I had family I could trust."

Talia tried to stop the flash of pity that came to her face, but Brionney saw it anyway. *It's okay,* she told herself. *Going back to school is a good idea, and even Derek would be the first to agree. In fact, it might help him decide to come back to his family.*

She didn't reveal any of these thoughts to Talia. As far as she and the others were concerned, Derek wasn't a part of their circle anymore. Brionney wished she could feel the same way. Why did she continue to love him?

Savannah was difficult to put to sleep that night. She seemed anxious and irritable, and Brionney understood exactly how she felt. Nothing was as it should be. Long after her parents were asleep, Brionney held the infant to her chest, rocking her in the family room and singing softly. At last, the baby's soft snores declared that she had succumbed to sleep.

"Dream with the angels," Brionney whispered, kissing her little cheeks. She stood and crept quietly to her room, trying not to notice how alone she felt, despite the weight of Savannah in her arms.

* * * * *

The first weeks at home passed by in agonizing slowness. Brionney tried to keep busy, and her parents and sisters helped a great deal. They shopped, ate out, attended movies and plays. Everyone went out of their way to be kind. But everything seemed to emphasize that Brionney didn't have a husband, or even a real home.

Irene especially tried to help Brionney feel like an adult, but no matter how she looked at it, she was still a child in her parents' home. She was dependent upon them for food, clothing, baby diapers—everything. Brionney began to dream of having her own apartment, but she wasn't prepared to leave the tiny, still nursing Savannah to get a full-time job. Anger at Derek increased inside her, further dampening the love which had once consumed her. He was the one who had broken the promise, the one who had destroyed the dream. Bitterness and despair often filled her inner thoughts, and only in her prayers did she feel safe and loved.

As though sensing her despair, Zack called her from France and cried with her on the phone. "I'm so sorry, Bri," he said. "I would give anything for this not to be happening to you."

"I know." Her brother's obvious love gave her great comfort. "So how are Josette and little Emery?" she asked, steering away from the painful subject.

"Doing really great. But she's pretty uncomfortable with this new pregnancy. Sometimes it's a lot for her to take. Emery's a big handful of energy. You'll have to come and visit and get to know him."

"Maybe," she said. But she knew she wouldn't. Things had been complicated enough with Marc the last time, though now those emotions seemed trivial with what she had since endured.

As if reading her mind, Zack said, "Marc's asked about you. I didn't tell him much—just that you were having some problems. But you wouldn't have to worry about him if you visited, because he's been dating a returned sister missionary pretty regularly. I don't know if anything'll come of it, but they're together a lot. We're all hoping she's the one. Except little Rebekka, of course."

Brionney laughed. "Rebekka wouldn't be happy about it. She's had a crush on him for ten years." Brionney knew Marc had never seen the fifteen-year-old's feelings as anything but a silly childhood crush. And he probably never would see beyond Danielle, the woman he secretly loved—the woman who was also Rebekka's mother.

"Well, I've got to hang up now, Bri," Zack said. "But if you ever need me, I'm here. Josette and Emery and I could even come and visit."

"Thanks, Zack. But I'm going to be fine."

Despite her assertion, Zack called her every Saturday for the first few weeks, and Brionney loved him for it. He was the brother who should have been her twin, like Marc and Josette were twins. They looked alike, they thought alike, and their hearts were one. During their conversations, Brionney almost felt like her old self.

Zack also convinced her to return to BYU. Brionney registered for two night classes that would begin in January. Finally she was doing something positive toward her future. And Savannah's.

But the one phone call she awaited never came. *He just needs time,* she thought. Still, she couldn't help thinking that each second between them was one more lost portion of forever. At least she heard nothing about the divorce. Perhaps no news was good news.

* * * * *

"It's like she's afraid of offending anyone," Irene said to Talia the week before Christmas. Little Roger played at their feet in the kitchen. "She cleans constantly, slinks around like a shadow, and refuses to approach me when I'm busy, even if she needs something. She hushes Savannah and whisks her away at the first sign of tears. It's like she's afraid I'm going to get upset with her if Savannah interrupts what I'm doing. I thought at first I was imagining things, but the other night she made dinner and it was really good. We told her so, and she seemed to go into shock because we had thanked her. She was nervous, jumped up for any little thing we might need, and literally worked herself to exhaustion. Your father even commented on it later. And you know that for him to notice something like that, it had to have been obvious."

Roger's play-acting with his airplane rose to a crescendo. "Shh, Roger! Not so loud." Talia looked at her mother. "Maybe she's just trying to make sure she's not a burden on you two. After all, this is your home. And it's got to be hard for her to lose her independence."

"That's what I thought in the beginning, but this goes way beyond courtesy." Irene remembered how devastated Brionney had been when Derek had first left her. Nothing was so painful as seeing a beloved child suffer so deeply. But these other signs were just as difficult to take. "I think Derek put a lot of pressure on her before he left. It's a subtle form of abuse, but abuse all the same. It's not fair she had to live like that. It makes me so angry. He put on such a nice face in front of us, but who knows how he'd been treating Brionney? I want to strangle him when I think about it."

"Well, it's over now, and she'll come around."

"Is it over? How do we know that for sure? What if he comes back? I know she's praying for it. She's hurt and she's angry, but she's also very vulnerable where Derek's concerned."

"We'll just have to pray that he doesn't," Talia said. "I can't bear to think of what she has gone through—especially almost losing Savannah like that. I don't know that I would forgive him."

Irene smiled slightly. "You don't love him. It's easy for us to say. But the heart doesn't always act like we want it to."

"Well, I for one hope he never comes back," Talia said.

There was a gasp from the hallway, and Brionney suddenly emerged, her face red and angry. "Well, I want him to come back!" she said. "He can change, if he wants to."

Irene looked at Brionney in dismay. "Honey, we—"

"Derek has some problems with his testimony, I know," Brionney interrupted. "But that doesn't mean the covenants we made in the temple are any less important. I love him, and I would help him if he'd let me. Now all I can do is pray. And if I'm acting a little strangely, it's because I'm hurting. I've been betrayed, not abused."

"Of course," Irene said. "We're sorry, Brionney. We just worry about you."

Brionney's expression softened. "I know. And I'll get things together soon, I promise. I just need a little time."

Irene hugged her. "You take all the time you need."

* * * * *

As much as Brionney tried not to let the overheard conversation affect her, it did bring a lot of questions to her mind. Had what she endured really been emotional abuse? Daily life certainly seemed less stressful without Derek and his demands. The constant tension in her body had diminished. But then again, so had the love and companionship. Was it even possible to have one without the other? Did stress and love go hand in hand? What if Derek did come back, but they never had the relationship she craved? Was that fair to her? Or even to him? To Savannah? What Brionney wanted suddenly wasn't clear anymore, and it seemed even harder to forgive Derek.

* * * * *

Church became a very important part of Brionney's life in those months of limbo as she waited to see where the future would take her. She was called as a Valiant Ten teacher and adored every minute. Savannah also loved to see the girls and to be the center of attention. She began to sleep well at night.

Christmas passed and there was still no word from Derek, not even a card. Snow fell and covered the world with its white blanket, but

Brionney could find little joy in the customary holiday celebrations.

In January she began classes at BYU, and was surprised at how much she loved the atmosphere. Many of the students in the night class were her age or older, so she didn't feel out of place. At the end of the month, one of her fellow students asked her out.

"I—I can't," she stuttered. "I'm married."

He looked down at her hand, where she still wore her wedding ring. "Oh, I didn't know. I'm sorry. I should have noticed your ring."

"Well, we're separated right now, and sometimes when I'm feeling particularly mad at him, I don't wear it. And truthfully, I don't know what's going to happen. We have a baby . . ."

"Well, good luck," he said hastily, and vanished into the flow of students. Brionney stared in the direction he had taken, feeling lonely. Would it have hurt to go out and enjoy herself for one evening? Even as she thought it, she knew that it *would* hurt. No matter what Derek was doing, she was still married to him.

* * * * *

The months passed quickly, and the hope in Brionney began to die. The bomb fell in April, when Debbie called. "Max wants you to come out and take care of the final divorce papers," she said without preamble.

"I thought maybe Derek had put it on hold," Brionney said. Her hand shook, and an impossible lump appeared in her throat. After so many months of hearing nothing, now Derek was making a move. She had given him time, waited, and this was how it was all going to end. She felt the knife in her heart twisting. Strangely, through the agony, there was relief that something was finally happening.

"Well, he didn't have anything done on them for a while, but they're in now. His lawyer told Max that Derek is anxious to get it taken care of."

"Will Derek be there?" Brionney asked.

"Yes."

"When should I come?" She numbly wrote down the details, unable to believe the finality. "I'm out of class then, so that will work for me."

"Let me know when your flight's coming, and I'll pick you up. It'd be great if you could stay a week or so. I miss you and Savannah. I bet she's grown a foot."

Brionney tried to respond naturally. "She's crawling all over. She's eight months now." That meant it had been nearly two years since she and Derek had married, and six months since their separation. It seemed like an eternity.

Debbie said something more and at last hung up the phone. Brionney sighed wearily and sank onto a kitchen chair, her mind churning. Now she would see Derek only one last time. She wondered if he would still want to "date." She put her head in her hands and cried.

The next Tuesday on the plane, Brionney studied the college class schedules. She had registered for one summer class, but was thinking about trying to add another. No matter how she tried, she couldn't concentrate. Here she was, on her way to sign papers that would cancel her marriage, at least in the eyes of the law. That she would still be sealed to Derek confused her. Would she be married or not?

The flight seemed amazingly short, not at all enough time for her to work out what she would say to Derek. None of her rehearsed speeches seemed appropriate.

"Brionney! Over here!" Debbie stood outside the gate, waving her arms vigorously. Her three daughters, Alicia, Chelsie, and Kelli, were with her.

Brionney hugged them. "Oh, it's good to see you!"

"Hello, Savannah," Debbie crooned. "Do you remember your Aunt Debbie?"

"And me too?" asked Kelli in the same ridiculous voice. She scrunched her face in an exaggerated smile, waiting for the baby's reaction.

Little Savannah's eyes opened wide as she stared at Debbie and the girls without recognition. Debbie tried to hold her, but Savannah clung to Brionney. "I'll win you over, just wait and see," Debbie threatened.

Savannah peeked out from where her head was buried in Brionney's neck and grinned. They laughed and made their way to the baggage pick-up. It was like old times, with Debbie chattering up a storm and everyone else laughing. For a moment, Brionney almost forgot why she was back in Arizona.

"I see you've kept your hairstyle," Alicia said as they arrived at the house.

"I really love it," Brionney said. "But it's grown out a bit since the last time I had it trimmed."

"I'll cut it tonight if you want," Alicia said.

"Could you?" Brionney had hoped Alicia would have time to trim it before she saw Derek.

"I'll make you so beautiful that he'll bite his tongue," she said. "I even have my own nail kit now."

"What will you wear?" Kelli was obviously not too young to understand the importance of the meeting with Derek.

"A teal dress I bought last week," Brionney said. "It cost way too much."

Debbie chuckled. "Good for you." From the way she said it, Brionney knew she remembered the other teal dress Brionney had returned after Derek left her.

"My mom was the one who bought it," Brionney admitted. "It's really pretty. And at least it hides those five extra pounds I still haven't lost."

"You look great," Debbie said. "And I'm not just saying that. What Max wouldn't give for a little flesh to squeeze."

"Gross, Mom!" the girls groaned together.

Debbie threw Brionney a quizzical look. "Kids," she said. "They beg you to be frank, and when you are . . ." She shrugged and sighed.

* * * * *

"I want you to understand what you're going to sign this afternoon before we go before the judge," Max said to Brionney the next morning at breakfast. Debbie had made pancakes and her two youngest were eating with gusto, despite the slightly burned flavor. Alicia was nowhere to be seen, and Brionney assumed she had left for work or was sleeping in. "That way if you have any questions, I can answer them now."

"No surprises, huh?"

"Exactly." Max bent his gray-flecked head over the papers he retrieved from his briefcase. "Let's see, now. You are, of course, awarded full custody. That means he has no say in her upbringing, including any medical decisions. Derek will have the opportunity to visit Savannah, but only in the state in which you reside. If he chooses to exercise that right, he will be liable for child support. Alimony will be paid until such time as you remarry."

"I guess he didn't want to pay for the rest of his life for one little mistake," Brionney said bitterly. There was silence around the large oval table, and she immediately regretted her words.

"Well, that's the way alimony is usually done," Max said mildly. "And I've arranged for the payments to be deducted directly from his check. It's not much money, mind you, but getting it directly will make sure you get it at all."

Brionney didn't really want Derek's money, but she couldn't deny that the few hundred dollars would ease the pressure. Asking her mother to buy personal items after being on her own for so long had been embarrassing and made her feel like a child. At least she could now have a semblance of independence, though most of the money would probably go for Savannah and school books.

"You could ask for child support as well," Max said. "You would win it in any court."

Brionney shook her head. "No. I don't want him having any rights to Savannah. Since he has agreed to give up custody and visitation if I don't ask for child support, I think it's best this way." Truth was, she remembered all too well how Derek's neglect had nearly killed Savannah. She couldn't live with that fear.

"Very well. That's just about it," Max said. "There's the divorce settlement itself, which divides the assets you had at the time of separation. His lawyer's done some fancy bookkeeping, but I've managed to get your share at nearly eight thousand dollars plus the furniture you kept, less a few court fees."

"Eight thousand! I never dreamed he had so much money! I mean, I saw those papers in his desk, but . . . oh, thank you, Max! I've been so worried. My parents have done so much, but I—"

"It's okay," Max said gruffly, waving aside her thanks.

"You have to take a fee," Brionney said. "Since I'll have the money."

"No. I want to help you, Brionney. And you're going to need much more money than that. It'll go very fast."

Debbie leaned over and kissed him. "Ain't he the best?"

"Yeah," Brionney agreed.

Debbie and Max exchanged tender looks until their children's disgusted sighs brought Max to his feet. "We'll sign at four-thirty," he said. He slid the papers back into his briefcase and shut it with a decisive click. "If you'll bring her to the office, Deb, we've arranged to meet with the judge in the same building. She can ride back with me, since I'll be coming home right after."

"You'd better," Debbie said. "I've got plans for dinner tonight." She stared hard at Max.

"What is it?" Brionney asked skeptically.

"Oh, I'm just having a special dinner tonight. In your honor. I've invited a few of the ward members."

"Are you sure she'll be up to it?" Max's glance showed sympathy.

"Of course. It'll be exactly what she needs—to relax in the company of old and new friends. Right, Brionney?" The old friends part of it sounded great, but the other part about the new friends rang suspiciously in Brionney's ears, and the twinkle of mischief in Debbie's eyes did nothing to reassure her. Before Brionney could ask any questions, however, Debbie bent her head and stared at her watch, her jaw dropping in mock horror.

"Goodness, Max, you'll be late for the office! And children," she focused on Kelli and Chelsie, "I'm not taking you to school if you miss the bus. You'll have to walk the whole two miles. And that's nothing compared—"

"To what you had to do as a child," Chelsie and Kelli said together.

"Yeah, we've heard it before. Five miles. Uphill, both ways, in a snowstorm," Chelsie said.

"Waist-deep snow," added Kelli. "With no shoes."

"Or coat." Chelsie ducked her mom's pretend blow and scampered out the back door.

"See you tonight, Brionney!" Kelli called as she followed her sister.

"What was all that about?" Brionney asked. "I thought you grew up in New Mexico."

Max grinned. "She did. But they had snow there back then, didn't you know?" He gave Debbie another kiss and sauntered to the door, whistling.

Debbie shrugged. "I haven't had to give them a ride to school since I came up with that story."

"Came up with it? My dad tells one very similar."

"Don't we all? Someday you'll tell Savannah, too."

Brionney laughed. She was right. Who knew how awful riding the school bus would sound to whatever way Savannah would get to school? Technology moved faster than they dreamed. The thoughts reminded Brionney of the Internet. Would Derek still be hers if it hadn't existed?

The afternoon passed quickly. Savannah lost her fear of Debbie, and when Brionney left them in the minivan outside Max's law office, she knew the baby would be all right without her. At first she had thought to bring Savannah, to force Derek to at least acknowledge his daughter, but decided against it on the way to the office. What they had to say was between them, and Brionney didn't want Savannah in the middle. Besides, what would she do if he changed his mind about giving her full custody?

Slightly ahead of schedule, she made her way slowly up to the third floor. The building was air conditioned, contrasting with the breezeless warmth of the outside. Brionney wore the short-sleeved teal dress that went to just above her knees. Its fine lines and petite cut made her look and feel great. She had the sensation of being flushed from the heat outside—or was it from the way her heart pounded?— and she ducked into a bathroom to check her makeup. Her face was slightly red, but as she powdered her nose the color vanished, leaving her face a light tan color, the result of her long walks in Utah's sunshine. She took a deep breath, fluffed her newly trimmed hair one last time, and headed for the door.

A glance at her watch told her that she was now on the verge of being late, but she refused to quicken her pace. No matter what, she wouldn't arrive at the judge's office in disarray. She wanted to make an impression on Derek—one he would never forget.

The receptionist on the third floor directed her to a waiting room. She slowly rounded the corner and saw Derek sitting on one of the leather couches. He was impeccably dressed, as usual, with a new pinstriped suit. On his wrist was the watch Brionney had given him for their wedding, the only piece of jewelry he ever wore. He looked incredibly handsome, as always, though his hair was longer than she remembered. Brionney wanted to rush into his arms and kiss him, to convince him they were right for each other. She knew that if he would only hold her, she would be safe. Above all, she still believed in her temple vows, that somehow they would help patch things up the way they were meant to be. Even if the divorce went through, they could begin again.

The room spun slightly, and she reminded herself to breathe. Lifting her head, she went to meet him. She took one step, two, and then she was brought up short by a silky voice. Her hopes plunged; Derek was not alone.

CHAPTER THIRTEEN

"Have a cigarette," Melinda said from the couch beside Derek. With her presence, all of Brionney's hopes seemed impossible. Why had she expected him to be alone? Derek had never done anything alone. He hadn't even proposed to her without an audience.

Melinda wore a see-through long-sleeved white blouse and a tight linen skirt. A discarded jacket lay over her lap. In her slender hand, she held a cigarette.

"I don't want one," Derek said sharply. But Melinda put hers to his mouth and he inhaled. Now Brionney knew why he had tasted so stale during their last months together; he had taken up smoking.

"Really, darling. What do you care if she sees you smoking?"

"I don't." But Derek pushed her hand and the cigarette away. "I just want to sign and be done with it."

Brionney took a deep breath and walked into their sight. "It won't be long now, Derek."

He started, then stood to greet her. Melinda also rose, but watched Brionney with a wary expression. Brionney felt Derek's eyes run over her, and for a moment she saw approval. He smiled, almost like in the old days.

"Why is it taking so long?" Melinda complained.

He turned to her. "That's the way it is. Lawyers are busy people." The words were an obvious insult to her intelligence, not simply a comment. Her eyes narrowed with hurt, but she covered it quickly.

"Of course, but so are we," she said in pretended nonchalance. Her hand went out to Derek's arm possessively, a thin smile pasted on her striking face.

Brionney felt a rush of pity for the beautiful Melinda. Derek's words had been unnecessary. Perhaps he hadn't intended to hurt and demean, but the results were the same. Had he treated Brionney with such thoughtlessness in front of others? She couldn't seem to remember, but she thought he must have. Even now she was rehearsing words in her mind before saying them, words he couldn't belittle. She pushed them aside with a vengeance.

"You look good," Derek said.

"Thank you." Brionney didn't return the compliment, though he looked great. She was finished fawning over a man who didn't want her. This brought triumph to her heart, a little sweetness mixing in with so much bitter.

He waited as if expecting her to speak, but she crossed to the opposite couch and settled comfortably, noting the rich leather upholstery, a light-brown to match the new-looking carpet. She picked up a magazine, feeling Derek's eyes on her. "So how's Utah?"

"Great. It's nice being home. I'm staying with my parents for a time."

"That's good."

His words made her angry. "Good? Well, I'm lucky to have a family I can depend on. But it hasn't been very fun."

He had the decency to look guilty. "Look, there's no reason we can't separate amicably. It's better for both of us."

"Maybe it is, maybe it isn't. One thing's for sure: it's not better for your daughter. Or had you forgotten her?"

His lips squeezed together. "Leave her out of this."

"As if she never existed?" Brionney shrugged delicately. "Well, sure. She's not *your* problem anymore."

Derek sat abruptly on the couch, brooding. Melinda again offered him a cigarette, but he scowled at her. Laughter bubbled in Brionney's throat, but it had a tinge of bile in it as well. Things were not going at all as she had planned.

"Just tell me one thing," she said. "Are you sure about this?"

Melinda gasped and glared at her. "Of course he's sure," she said. "He wants nothing more to do with you or your church!" For once, Derek seemed content to let Melinda do the talking. He averted his gaze, giving his answer as clearly as if he had spoken. Brionney stared back into the magazine, steeling her face not to show her pain. Six months apart, and she still suffered like it had been yesterday.

As if on cue, Max appeared and ushered them into the office where the family judge awaited. Derek's lawyer stood to the side, and the judge sat behind the desk with his hand on a sheaf of papers. Everyone was silent as he briefly went over the papers, then placed them on the desk to be signed. Brionney didn't want to sign . . . and yet . . . seeing Derek had brought up not only the emotions of love she had expected, but also anger, betrayal, hurt, and fear. Despite her months of dreaming and planning for his return, maybe she didn't really want him back at all. This revelation hurt, and bitter tears stung her eyes. She lifted her head and met Derek's gaze. He clenched his jaw and firmly signed the papers. "There," he said.

Brionney signed, feeling a loss she couldn't describe. Then it was over. Derek shook hands with the judge and the lawyers before going with Melinda to the door. He didn't look back. Melinda did, and her expression was triumphant. Brionney wanted to hate her, to hate them both, but she couldn't feel anything. She had the distinct feeling that Melinda might someday be in her position. Like Derek's stepmother, Alice, had been. It was a continuous cycle of betrayal and abuse. How could she hate Melinda, knowing so well the pain of her future?

"Are you all right?" Max's voice was kind. He held on to her arm as they went from the office.

Brionney stared up at him, clutching her copy of the papers. "I thought we might talk, that we might say something, anything important. That's why I agreed to do it this way."

"Usually people are past talking when they get to this point," Max said lightly.

Brionney gave a dry laugh, but there was no mirth in her heart. "I guess you're right." Then she added, "You know, the strangest thing is that I'm not sure I even want him back. I kept thinking I did, that life could be good again for us, but I'm not sure now that he'll ever change. The temple vows we made mean nothing to him. How can I respect a man like that?"

Max settled into a chair in the waiting room and Brionney sat next to him. "You have a point, Brionney. Promises made in the temple are very important, and that doesn't change just because Derek didn't honor them. Believe me, I know that anything can be overcome if two people love the Lord and are willing to obey His commandments completely. This includes doing everything in your power to make your partner happy. Of course, it's a two-way street. If one isn't committed, it won't work."

His words made Brionney feel worse. "And what now? The vows I made are gone, broken by Derek, but I feel they're still there. I'm still married to him in the eyes of the Church."

"You can be remarried in the temple one day," Max said.

Brionney shook her head. "I think I'd be afraid to try."

"That's a natural feeling. But give it time." He glanced at his watch and bounded to his feet. "Oh, no! Debbie'll make me sleep on the couch for a week if we're late for dinner. If we leave right now, we can still be on time. Come on."

Brionney hurried out the door after Max, grateful for the moment to put aside her worries. Signing the papers had been difficult, but now that it was over she didn't feel any different. She was still so lonely. But how could she even look at another man while she still felt married to Derek?

She had thought her emotional battles were over for the day. She certainly wasn't prepared to find Derek waiting for her outside. Melinda was nowhere to be seen. "Can I talk to Brionney for a moment?" Derek said to Max.

Max looked at Brionney, his eyes questioning. She gave a short nod. "I'll wait for you in my car," he said. "It's the blue one down there in front of that big sign."

"Thanks." Brionney watched him go.

"I wanted to talk to you alone," Derek said.

"Where's Melinda?"

"In the car."

"Oh." Silence fell over them, and Brionney shifted uncomfortably. Derek touched her arm. "I just wanted to say that . . ."

"What?" she urged. She wondered if he was going to try to kiss her like he had that night in the car. Did she want him to? *I'm so lonely!*

"Just because we're divorced, it doesn't mean I don't love you. I still do."

His words made her feel worse. "And I'm supposed to be grateful?" she asked. "Are we supposed to date?"

"Well, we could have some fun. Like old times." He ran his finger down her arm, sparking goose bumps.

"What about Melinda?"

"What about her?"

His reply disgusted her. "Derek, we're divorced now. You left me. If you ask me, that's a strange way to show love. When are you going to stop playing these games?"

Without another word she walked away, her head held high. Tears blinded her, and she almost passed Max's car. "I'm here," he said, grabbing her elbow. Brionney was grateful he didn't ask any questions. *How could I ever have fallen for a man like Derek?* She took off her wedding ring and zipped it into a pocket in her purse. Later, she would put it away for Savannah.

The traffic was thick, but Max shared Debbie's ability to weave in and out of tight spaces. He pulled up at the house at fifteen to six. "Ah, made it," he said with a sigh.

"She wouldn't make you sleep on the couch."

"She has before."

"Well, I'm sure you deserved it."

He snorted. "Women, they're all alike!"

Brionney shrugged. *If we didn't stick together, who would protect us?* She didn't say the words aloud, not wanting to insult Max, who had been so kind.

Debbie met them at the door, hands on her hips. "Where have you been?"

"You said dinner was at six." Max raised his hands defensively. "We're early."

"Dinner is at six, but the guests came at five-thirty. What am I going to do with you?"

"Make him sleep on the couch," Brionney suggested.

Max threw her a disgusted glance. "Deb would never do something so petty."

"Don't be too sure." But Debbie gave him a kiss as Max's arms went around her.

Envy surged in Brionney's broken heart. How she wished her relationship with Derek could have been like theirs! To be able to tease and to love, to laugh together!

Her thoughts must have been plain on her face, because Debbie wriggled from Max's grasp and pushed him farther into the entryway.

"Everyone is waiting in the family room or out on the deck," she said. "Tell them Brionney's coming. But first I have to talk to her."

Max grumbled something, but walked off in the right direction. Debbie watched until he disappeared, then turned to Brionney. "How'd it go?"

Brionney shrugged. "Melinda was there. He didn't ask about Savannah, and we didn't talk." She leaned against the entryway wall.

"Are you all right?"

"Yes. I think I am." Brionney stared at the wall, tracing imaginary pictures in the deep texturing with her eyes, anything not to look at Debbie's face. "But I've spent all these months thinking he would change, sure that once he saw me he would remember our vows and the love we shared."

"But that didn't happen."

"And I didn't want it to!" Now Brionney met her eyes. "It was like I still loved him, but I don't like him very much. Is that possible? It sounds crazy."

"No, it sounds like you're getting over him, seeing things as they really are."

"Have I been so blind? Like the women you read about in the papers who are so willing to take abuse and do nothing? It doesn't make sense. I thought I was strong."

Debbie put her hand on Brionney's shoulder. "Many women would have abandoned all hope at the first sign of trouble. Believe me, I know. But you fought for the promises you made, despite everything. That takes real strength."

"Is that being strong or stupid?"

"Strong," she said firmly. "I mean, I can't say it was the best way, but you did what you had to do. And you've learned a lot."

"But what good was it all?" she said, feeling the words wrenched from her throat.

Debbie bit her lip, thinking. "Well, for one thing, when you look back, years from now, you'll know that there was nothing more you could have done. You'll have no regrets or what-ifs. You've proven that the covenants you made mean something to you. I respect you for that. I don't think I could have been so strong."

Brionney blinked back the tears. "So I wasn't weak because I wanted to keep my marriage—in spite of the way he treated me?"

"Heavens, no! If everyone, especially men, were so committed, there would be a lot less divorce."

"And a lot less pain." Brionney heaved a sigh. "Debbie, I don't know if I'm up to this dinner right now."

"But it's exactly what you need," Debbie insisted. "Besides, I have someone I want you to meet."

"What!" The way she said it, Brionney knew she meant a man.

"He's perfect for you. I just know it!"

"I'm not ready!"

"And when will you be? Months from now? Years? It's already been six months, and it's time to at least start meeting people."

"Isn't that for me to decide?"

Debbie's gaze dropped to the ceramic tile on the entryway floor. "Yes, it is." She lifted her face, and this time her eyes weren't teasing, they were serious. "But I know you're supposed to meet this guy, and this is the only chance. I know it's lousy timing, but heaven knows when you'll be back here to visit, and he's so great, he won't last long. He just came back from his mission."

"Then he's probably younger than I am, and certainly not interested in an older woman with a child."

"You don't turn twenty-two until October, and that makes you about the same age as most returned missionaries. Beside, this guy is different. He was baptized into the Church when he was twenty-one and didn't go on his mission until a year later. He just got back last month. That makes him about twenty-four. He's got three years of college behind him and only one more to go. He's in computers or something."

"He's still not going to be interested in me."

"But he is!"

Brionney scowled at her distrustfully. "What did you tell him? I don't want a pity date." In fact, the idea of dating frightened her terribly, but she wasn't going to admit that to Debbie. She had already heard enough lectures.

"Just who you are, and about Savannah," she said innocently. "He'll be good for you. Trust me." She paused and added softly, "Savannah just loves him."

"What? She doesn't even know him!"

"She does now. He came a little early. It seems I told him five o'clock. Oops." She gave a little laugh. "He didn't seem to mind."

Brionney pushed past her and nearly ran to the end of the entryway, where it met the kitchen. "Where is Savannah?" she demanded angrily. She had trusted her friend to be considerate of her feelings, but Debbie seemed to be stepping all over them.

"She was in the family room when I came out here," Debbie called after her. "Don't worry, she's in good hands."

In good hands! What was Debbie trying to pull? If she thought Brionney was going to fall for another man, she was, well, crazy. And certainly not the first man that came along! Especially not one she met on the day she signed divorce papers. On the day her husband had said he still loved her.

Why had he said that?

No, Brionney didn't need another man! And she certainly wouldn't be pawned off on someone just because Debbie thought it was a good idea. She and Savannah might not be the best catch in the world, but they were worth true love.

True love.

Brionney stopped for a moment in the kitchen and closed her eyes. True love was what she thought she had felt for Derek. She blinked back tears and tightened her jaw. Not anymore. That part of her life was over. Now she just needed to get to Savannah and book an earlier flight home. She had planned to stay until Monday morning, five days away, but it was too painful to be here on the same street where she had lived with Derek. Debbie pushing her toward another man, when the ink on her divorce papers wasn't even dry, only made things worse. *Boy, am I going to give her a piece of my mind when I feel bet—*

A gurgle of laughter brought her eyes wide open. Savannah! She was giggling with the same abandon Brionney had only heard when she played with her grandfather. A smile came unbidden to Brionney's lips, contrasting with her dark thoughts. Kelli or Chelsie must have found Savannah's ticklish spot. She walked quickly through the deserted kitchen and into the family room. The glass doors to the patio were wide open, and she could see people from her old ward, Bishop Clark and his wife among them. Max was already seated next to the grill, watching Alicia flip hamburgers. The conversations were punctuated with frequent laughter, and everyone seemed to be having a great time.

But it was not the patio or the people there that held Brionney's attention. In the family room, opposite the big-screen TV, Chelsie and Kelli were sitting on the couches watching Savannah, who was on the floor with a strange man. He had a baby blanket over his head, so Brionney couldn't see him clearly. Savannah clapped her chubby hands with pleasure and reached to pull the blanket from his head.

"Peek-a-boo!" said the man in sing-song.

Savannah giggled in triumph and threw the blanket back on his head. She missed and the man rolled on the ground, twisting to catch the blanket on his face so as not to disappoint the baby. His gaze caught Brionney's, growing wide-eyed, just as the blanket covered his face. Savannah laughed again and crawled near him to remove the blanket. This time, his eyes focused on Brionney's as he called out to Savannah. "Peek-a-boo! I see you." They both laughed, and the girls on the couch giggled as well. "Look who's here, Savannah," the man said, pointing at Brionney. "Is that someone you know?"

Savannah looked up and smiled happily. "Ma Ma," she gurgled. She held her arms out to Brionney, bobbing up and down on her bottom in a way that said she wanted to be picked up. Brionney crossed the room and lifted the baby into her arms. Savannah immediately presented her with a slobbery kiss.

"I missed you, cutie. What have you been doing?"

Of course it wasn't Savannah who answered. "Playing and waiting for you," Kelli said, getting to her feet. "Hey, the hamburgers smell ready. I'm starved. I get the first one!"

"No, you don't!" Chelsie was already making her way to the door, and Brionney was left alone with the strange man. She doubted their sudden desertion was coincidence; it reeked of Debbie.

The man shifted into a sitting position and climbed to his feet. Now that the blanket wasn't obscuring his features, Brionney could see laughing brown eyes and unruly dark brown hair, cut extremely short. He crossed the room, presenting his hand.

"Hi, you must be Brionney."

She shook his hand somewhat awkwardly, feeling a warmth rush up her arm and to her face. It reminded her strangely of the chill she had felt when meeting Derek, only it was warm instead of cold. She pulled her hand away.

"I'm sorry," he said, realizing her discomfort. "It's habit. Shaking hands, I mean."

"Who are you?" Brionney asked. Here was a man who played with her daughter more easily than her own father ever had, and instead of being afraid of him as she usually was with strangers, Savannah wanted more. Even now, she struggled to get down. The minute she landed, she crawled after the blanket and brought it to the man's knee.

He laughed and reached down and spread it on top of Savannah's head. In a fit of laughter, she let go of his leg and fell on her bottom.

"And I fall down go boom!" sang the stranger. Savannah tore off the blanket, giggling all the while, and stared up at him with shining eyes. She held the blanket out again. Brionney thought she must be the most persistent child alive.

"I'm Jesse. Jesse Hergarter," he said as he took the blanket, his eyes on Savannah. He grinned at the baby, and Brionney couldn't help smiling with him. He wasn't very tall—at least not as tall as Derek—but she still had to look up at him. His complexion was clear and tanned, as if he had spent a lot of time in the sun. He put the blanket over Savannah again before meeting Brionney's gaze. "I just got back from a mission to England. I was in the ward here before I left."

So he was the returned missionary Debbie had told her about! Brionney didn't know why she hadn't understood it the minute she had seen him. Another glance out the glass doors proved he was the only person from the ward she didn't know.

Brionney stiffened. She didn't care who he was; she wasn't ready for another relationship. And what kind of silly name was Hergarter, anyway? She reached down to get Savannah so they could escape from this new threat, but the baby was still under the blanket. Jesse pulled it off and tickled her stomach. The two burst into loud laughter. Despite her resolve, Brionney cast a grateful glance at him. Savannah's happiness was the most important thing to her now.

"Your hair is really blonde," he said abruptly, staring at her. "Is it natural?"

What an odd question. But it came so unexpectedly that she didn't have time to be offended. "Yes."

"What luck. My older sister dyes hers, and she constantly goes around with dark roots. She says it's the curse of her life. I'm glad you don't have to live with that."

"Why doesn't she use her natural color?"

He shrugged. "Blondes have more fun, I guess. I don't know. Maybe you can tell me. She's really pretty either way."

How peculiar to be talking to a stranger about hair color! One thing was certain, he was no ordinary man. Savannah was proof of that. He would make someone a very good catch. *Someone that isn't me,* she thought forcefully.

"Let's eat!" Kelli called from the patio. "Hurry, Jesse and Brionney. I'm starving!"

Jesse gave Savannah a last tickle and handed Brionney the blanket. "Shall we?" he asked politely.

Brionney shook her head. "You go ahead. I'll be right out."

"Okay."

She watched him leave, angry that he was so likeable. Or was she simply feeling admiration for a man who loved children? Her eyes followed his movements across the patio where he joined the other members. He was certainly a puzzle.

A light cough drew Brionney's attention to the kitchen door, where Debbie stood watching. She had a self-satisfied smile on her face, as if Max had brought home a diamond necklace.

Brionney glared at her. "Don't even think it!" she growled. "Now I'm going to change into some jeans and check Savannah's diaper. I'll be right down, or you can start without me!" Scooping Savannah from the floor, Brionney charged past her into the kitchen.

"We'll wait," Debbie called.

Brionney barely heard. Her mind churned with a mixture of anger, yearning, and regret. But there was no way she would fall for another man. She was through letting men push her around by her feelings.

"I still love you, Brionney," she said to herself in a mocking voice. "But not enough to stay faithful."

Besides, Jesse Hergarter—*where did he get that odd name?*—could have his choice among the many single girls in the area. What could he possibly want with a woman who had already been married and thrown away?

* * * * *

Jesse took his place at one of the two picnic tables. Inside, he felt shaken. When he had first looked at Brionney, he had seen a clear white light about her head, like a halo. The sight had startled him so much that he had opened his mouth and asked about hair. Of all the dumb things to ask such a beautiful angel!

When Debbie had told him about Brionney's life, he had felt sorry for her, and had even thought they might become friends so he could help her get on with her life. He enjoyed helping people. But that shining halo could mean only one thing. Could it really be true? Was she the woman he was supposed to marry?

Little Savannah had already won his heart. Jesse sighed inwardly. For so long he had been following the Spirit on his mission as he searched for and taught people ready to receive the truth. There was no denying the feeling he had when he saw this angel of a woman. But he also saw the pain and mistrust in her eyes. Any relationship he pursued with her would not come easily.

Was he ready for that?

She came outside, dressed in jeans and a short-sleeved shirt, and his doubts evaporated. Whatever would happen between them, he knew they were supposed to meet.

After the blessing on the food, Jesse busied himself getting hamburgers for Brionney and Savannah. "Just the bun for her," Brionney said. "She doesn't eat much. She has no teeth."

"How about some juice?" he asked. "Look, I found a sippy cup."

"Thank you," she said, looking surprised.

Jesse laughed, feeling so happy he couldn't keep it inside. When Brionney glanced at him, his face flushed as it always did when he felt great emotion or embarrassment. Would she mind a man whose thoughts were so apparent?

"When are you going back to Utah?" he asked to mask his feelings. He sat down next to her and Savannah at the picnic table.

"Monday," she replied.

"That's great! Would you, I mean, do you think you could let me look at your BYU class schedule? Debbie said you brought it. I've been thinking about going there for my last year. You know, to be with a lot of other Mormons and—"

"To find a wife," Max interjected from his end of the table. He and Debbie exchanged knowing looks.

Jesse felt his face turned red again as everyone laughed. "Yes, that too," he admitted. "I don't want to marry out of the temple. Just once is all I'm planning to do it."

"We all *plan* it that way," Brionney returned, her voice sharp. There was an abrupt silence, and Jesse felt himself go even redder than before.

"I'm sorry," he said. "I didn't mean . . . it's just . . . well . . ." He glanced helplessly at Max but found no rescue. "My parents and older sister aren't members, you see, and no one really understands how important—"

Debbie came up to him with a platter of brownies. "Would you like some dessert? Or would you like a shovel to dig yourself in deeper?"

Jesse gulped in relief. "A brownie," he said. Then he grinned. "That is, if *you* didn't make them."

Debbie nearly hit him over the head with the platter, and he held up his hands to ward her off. "I'm joking! I'm joking!"

"No, you're not," Alicia said. "We all know how Mother *loves* to cook. But you don't have to worry, Sister Clark made these."

Jesse reached for a brownie. The bishop's wife made the best desserts in the ward. The members always joked that her talent was why he had been made bishop in the first place. Jesse's hand touched Brionney's as she also reached for a brownie. She pulled her hand back and stared at him nervously.

"Go ahead," he said.

She helped herself and broke half of it for Savannah. "That's not fair," he said, taking two from the plate for himself and handing another to her. "You won't get any if you give it all to her. These deserve to be savored."

"As if I need the calories," she said in self-deprecation.

"None of us do." He pinched his waist, which still had a small but noticeable missionary spare tire. "But we're only on this earth once, and I'm not about to kill myself to look like one of those hunks in the magazines. Or is that the kind of guy you go for?"

He had meant it as a joke, but her eyes seemed to glaze over. Then Jesse remembered something Debbie had said about Brionney's ex-husband always working out at a gym, and how he had belittled her weight. Jesse knew his face was flushing again, but this time with anger at what she had suffered.

"You're a man," she said. "It's different for men."

"Not in my book. A person is who he is, and as long as he or she is happy and comfortable at the weight they are at, then that's all that matters."

He was rewarded with a smile that lit her whole face. He scooted closer to her on the picnic bench. "I'm sorry," he whispered. "I know your divorce wasn't your fault. I'm sorry if I hurt you by what I said earlier."

"It's okay. I know what you were trying to say."

"So do I still get to look at the class schedule?"

She smiled. "Yes, but are you sure you want to go to Utah?"

"No, but I'm not too excited about staying in Arizona."

"It's cold there. In the winter, I mean. And it gets hot, too, only a different hot than here. It's not very comfortable sometimes."

"Are you trying to talk me out of it?" he asked teasingly.

"No, of course not. I just wanted you to know what you were getting into."

"Then can I come tomorrow to see the schedule? Say about ten?"

"Sure. Or you can take it tonight and bring it back whenever."

Was it his imagination, or did she not want to spend any time with him at all? Well, he could understand that. "I might have some questions for you. Besides, I'm baby-sitting my sister's children tonight and won't have time for anything but games. I'm trying to get her indebted enough to me to accept hearing the discussions."

Savannah squirmed on Brionney's lap, dropping a piece of brownie on her knee and grinding it into her jeans. She sighed and flicked it off with a long fingernail Jesse suspected was Alicia's work. "That would do it for me," she said. "Free baby-sitting is worth taking the missionary discussions any day!"

Jesse laughed. "That's what I'm hoping." He gestured to Savannah. "May I?" He took the baby and bounced her on his knee. "She's a great kid."

"Thank you," Brionney said. The ice in her voice had melted considerably. Jesse wondered what it would be like to hear her laugh.

Half an hour later, Jesse excused himself with great reluctance to go to his sister's. "See you tomorrow," he said to Brionney.

Brionney nodded, but he wondered if she had heard. Already the sadness he had seen earlier was stealing over her face. For a moment, he wanted to grab her and tell her that he would make her happy, that her ex-husband wasn't worth the tears.

Just give me time, he told her silently. *I don't give up easily.*

CHAPTER FOURTEEN

When Brionney awoke in the morning, she forgot for a moment where she was. The bed cradling her body was large and comfortable. Near it, the window was flung open wide, and the white curtains blew carelessly in the breeze. Then she saw the blue and black checkered quilt and remembered Debbie.

Savannah snored softly beside her, looking like an angel. Love and tenderness filled Brionney's heart, and she marveled anew at the miracle of motherhood. Raising a child was never easy, but well worth any problems she had endured.

Even divorce?

Tears gathered in her eyes. In her mind, she could see the covenants she had made burning into tiny pieces that blackened and were blown away by the wind.

Oh, Derek! Why do I love you?

She wished she didn't, that when she had stopped wanting him back, she had also stopped loving him. But her heart didn't work that way. And Derek's final confession of love confused her more. He wouldn't give up Melinda or his new lifestyle, and yet he claimed to love her. Brionney knew she could chase after him, perhaps even get him to come back to her for a time, but that would never give her what she desperately needed.

Too bad Derek's not more like Jesse, she thought. She remembered with pleasure their time together at the barbeque, especially his constant laughter and the endearing way he had of turning red with the slightest embarrassment. But then again, Derek had also been charming at first.

Ding-dong! A bell sounded throughout the entire house. Brionney scrambled for her watch on the bedside dresser. Ten o'clock on the dot! She threw back the checkered quilt and slipped out of bed, only to trip over her feet and fall on the soft carpet. She made it to the door before she remembered Savannah. Glancing back at the double bed, Brionney saw the baby watching her quizzically.

"Ten o'clock!" Brionney muttered, returning for the baby. "Ten o'clock. You never let me sleep until ten o'clock! Why today?"

A brief buzzing noise from the small box near the door startled her. "Uh, Brionney, Jesse's here. If you're awake, just press talk to speak to me." Debbie's voice was slightly distorted by the intercom.

Brionney pushed the button. "I—I—I'll be right down," she stuttered. "I'm a little late getting ready."

Savannah was already investigating under Brionney's shirt to see if she could nurse. Brionney had cut down on the frequency with which she nursed Savannah, but it would be another two or three months before she stopped the feedings entirely.

Brionney nursed Savannah, then quickly showered and dressed. She grimaced at her hair in the mirror, wishing she had time to wash it. From where she sat on the bathroom floor, Savannah gazed up at Brionney, as if wondering why all the fuss. "It's just been so long since—" Brionney broke off. Since what? Since she was admired? But had it not been only yesterday when Derek had admired her in the teal dress, then turned and signed the final divorce papers?

Get over it! Brionney thought roughly. *Get a grip!* Holding back a sob, she whisked out of the bathroom, Savannah in one arm and the BYU class schedule in the other. How long would it be until she would quit thinking about Derek and the broken promises? How long would she hurt every time she thought of him? She suddenly wished Jesse would go home and leave her alone; being near him was a reminder of what she had lost.

Jesse waited for her at the kitchen table where Debbie had spread a variety of cereals and fruit. "I've never known a recently returned missionary to refuse food," she was saying to Jesse. "I knew you'd be hungry."

Jesse brought a peach to his mouth. "That's because it's our only physical pleasure, you see. No dancing, movies, or pretty girls, just food—and the spiritual side, of course. That makes it all worth it." He looked up at Brionney and smiled. "Hi, Brionney. How are you? And Savannah. Hi, baby. Want more peek-a-boo?"

Brionney muttered a hello, but Savannah babbled excitedly, her enthusiasm more than making up for Brionney's lack of welcome. When Jesse talked to the baby, she grinned and kicked to get to the floor, where she stalked him, slowly but surely.

Debbie laughed. "Oh, no you don't, Savvy. You're coming with me. Mommy has to help this nice young man, without you in the way." Before Brionney could protest, Debbie grabbed Savannah and a peach from the bowl on the table and disappeared, leaving her alone with Jesse.

"That's neat you're back in school," he said as he thumbed through the schedule. "I think every woman should get her degree, whether it's one or two classes at a time like you're planning to do, or full-time before she has children. There's so much to learn, and life is much more precious if you understand how the world works and why people do the things they do."

"It is a lot of fun," she said. "I know it sounds strange, but it's kind of like rediscovering myself." She wondered if she had said too much. Would he even understand that going to school had made her feel like Brionney Fields again, not just someone's wife and mother? Not just someone who ironed shirts and cleaned the house and hoped to be noticed. School had helped her see Derek's declaration of love yesterday as the garbage it was when once she might have believed him. School had helped her retain enough dignity not to throw herself at him again.

Jesse glanced at the schedule. "Even if I transfer, I think I can be finished in a year. See? I need this class and this one. And I still have a half credit of P.E. to get. Boy, am I dreading that. I like to exercise, but some of those guys get so serious about basketball!"

Brionney smiled at Jesse. Why did he always seem to affect her that way? He glanced at her, and his gaze seemed to soften. "You're really pretty when you smile like that." It didn't sound like one of Derek's lines.

"Uh, thank you."

"So what classes are you taking?" To her surprise, he actually seemed interested.

"French, mostly," she said. "But I'm still plugging away at the General Ed requirements. I also have a P.E. credit to get. I think I'll take dancing again."

"You know how to dance? That's great! Hey, you wouldn't go to a dance with me on Friday, would you? It's a singles' dance and I'm a little nervous. It's my first one since I've been released from the mission field. I won't know what to do with all those girls wanting to dance, but I'll bet we could have fun. What do you say?"

Brionney's heart seemed to skip a beat. Her eyes dropped to the table as she recalled all too well how she had met Derek at a dance. She wasn't ready for this, not yet. But, oh, how she wanted to go! Yet for all her brave thoughts of independence, she wasn't yet free from Derek. "I'm sorry, I can't." She made no attempt to explain.

Jesse watched her for a long time before reacting, as though trying to decipher her feelings. "Okay," he said finally. "I understand, I think. And it's not like it's the first time I've been turned down."

"I'm sorry."

He shook his head slowly, never letting his eyes fall from her face. "Don't ever be sorry for how you feel. When you're ready, you'll know." His voice seemed to imply he would be there to see that day, but she couldn't be sure. A promise like that was best left unuttered.

"I'd better find Savannah," she said, standing. "She nur—ate, but she'll be hungry again." She pointed to the schedule. "I hope this helped you. You really can take this one. I can get a new one when I get home."

He stood. "Thanks, but there's no need. I've written down what I need."

Disappointment shot through Brionney. That he didn't want to keep the schedule might mean his interest in BYU had never been serious. Like the song so aptly said, they were ships, passing in the night. "Well, see you around," she said casually. "Shall I walk you to the door?"

If he knew he was being dismissed, he showed no sign of it. "I'd like to say good-bye to Savannah and Debbie."

"Come on then. I think they were headed out back."

They made their way through the family room and out to the empty patio. They heard a splash in the pool and found Debbie and Savannah in the water. Debbie had on her suit, but Savannah wore only a diaper and shirt. A huge smile lit her face. She gazed at the water in fascination, trying to bring it up to her mouth. Finally, she scrunched down in Debbie's arms and took a large mouthful. She coughed it out and started to cry.

"Silly, the water isn't to drink." Debbie spun Savannah around, but there was no stopping the tears. "And we were having so much fun," Debbie grumbled, handing her to Brionney. At once, Savannah tried to put her hand down Brionney's shirt, and she reddened in embarrassment. It was one thing to be a nursing mother, and another to have it so thoroughly demonstrated in front of an attractive man who had just asked her out.

"It's her first time in a swimming pool," Brionney explained, drying Savannah's face with a white towel.

"Here's your peach, Savannah," Debbie said, noting Savannah's determination to nurse. "And I already took out the seed. I'm sorry about the nasty water, but you have to learn it's only to play in, not to drink." Savannah grabbed the peach in both hands and bit down with her gums. The peach juice ran out of both sides of her mouth. She struggled once more to get down, then crawled near the water, but not too close for Brionney's comfort.

Jesse stared at her. "Children sure are fascinating to watch."

"I'll say." Then Brionney remembered his sister. "So how did it go last night? Did your sister agree to hear the discussions? Or did you baby-sit for nothing?"

A bright grin lit his face, and tiny smile lines appeared around his dark eyes. "Oh, I'd baby-sit them any time. But she did say she'd listen."

"That's wonderful!" Debbie said.

"It sure is. I've been working on her since I was converted, but she has refused any overtures I've made. Until now."

"Slowly is the way to do it," Debbie said. "Sometimes all you can do is to love them."

Brionney knew first-hand that sometimes even love wasn't enough if it wasn't returned, but she wasn't about to spoil Jesse's moment. "And your parents?" she asked. "How do they feel about the Church? And where are they, anyway?"

"Here, in Phoenix. In fact, I'm living with them until I get settled. Before that, I haven't been at home since I left for college. It's a little too tense for comfort. You see, they threw me out when I first started investigating the Church. That was one reason it took me so long to accept baptism. Three whole years of study, even though I knew it was true after the second discussion. I didn't want to hurt them."

"Well, better late than never," Debbie consoled him. "And you haven't lost out. You're still young, with only one more year left in college. That's pretty good."

"Yeah. You'll be graduating before I finish my sophomore year," Brionney said.

Jesse opened his mouth, but a splash from the pool cut off anything he planned to say. The splash wasn't loud, but they could see Savannah's towel floating in the pool.

"Oh, no!" He ran to the pool before Brionney could do anything. A huge jump landed him, clothes and all, near the floating towel. He reached for it, face pale, and came up with a towel and a half-eaten peach.

Brionney walked over to the pool and picked up Savannah, who was comfortably settled on one of the lounge chairs near the water. The baby pointed at Jesse and clapped her hands.

Jesse grinned up at them sheepishly, his face redder than Brionney had ever seen it. "I thought it was Savannah."

Brionney clamped her mouth shut, but a strangled giggle escaped despite her efforts. "I tried to tell you, but . . . you're quick when you want to be."

"Yeah, sometimes." He pulled himself out, soggy and dripping. "I was afraid if something had happened, it'd be my fault for talking so much. How did you know it wasn't her?"

"I've been watching her, and I saw her wrap the peach and throw it into the water. You learn to do two things at a time when you're a parent. I know enough not to take my eyes off her, especially around a pool."

"I saw her, too," Debbie put in.

"I see," he said. He hunched down to Savannah's level. "You scared me, little girl. Try not to do that again, okay? I think I aged five years this time, not to mention the fact that I embarrassed myself in front of your mother. Now she'll never go out with me!" Savannah giggled and Debbie joined in, but Brionney stayed silent.

"Come with me," Debbie said to Jesse. "I'll give you something to change into, and I'll dry your clothes."

"No way," Jesse replied. "I'm finished embarrassing myself today, thank you very much. I'll just see myself out to my car and home. Besides, I've got to go up to my old college and check things out." Once again he looked at Savannah. "And you be a good girl, you hear? I'll come play peek-a-boo again before you go back to Utah, but no more jumping into pools." He emphasized his words by jabbing his finger gently into Savannah's ribs. She giggled with complete abandon, grabbing his finger and holding on tightly.

"You've had your laugh for the week, Savvy," Jesse continued. "There's only so much a guy can take from a blonde-haired, blue-eyed heartbreaker like you. But don't worry, I'll be back when you least expect me." The words were addressed to Savannah, but Brionney felt they were for her as well. Jesse's deep brown eyes met hers briefly before he swung on his heel and left, his wet tennis shoes squeaking as he crossed the cement.

Debbie and Brionney stared after him. "He's a good man," Debbie said. "And I told you he was interested in you."

Well, he had asked her out and seemed disappointed when she refused. But beyond that, Brionney had her doubts. After all, even Derek had wanted to date.

"Maybe. But I think we've seen the last of him." Brionney picked up Savannah. "Are you up for another swim, sweetie? Mommy brought her suit, and this weather is just too good to pass up."

* * * * *

The rest of Thursday and most of Friday dragged by. Every car that drove near Debbie's attracted Brionney's attention, but it was never Jesse. She grew irritated at herself for caring at all about him when she had sworn off men completely. What was she waiting for? For him to come over and tell her his decision about his schooling? For him to ask her out again? Ridiculous!

Then again, he had said he would return to play with Savannah.

And who cared if he didn't? *I'm through with running after men!* she told herself repeatedly.

She admitted to herself that Jesse seemed Derek's complete opposite. Never could she imagine Derek jumping into a pool to save even his own daughter; it might spoil his name-brand suit. He would lean over or use something to pull her out, but never take the plunge so wholeheartedly. Or would he? Maybe she really didn't know Derek at all.

Brionney also wondered if she liked Jesse because he reminded her of Marc in France. They were both dark and handsome and kind. But kissing Marc had been like kissing a brother—nothing at all like the passion she had shared with Derek. Too late she had learned that loyal friendship was a far better deal than passion. Loyal friendship at least could form a lasting relationship. Perhaps she should have stayed and fought for Marc.

What would it be like to kiss Jesse? She groaned and put her face in her hands. Now what was she thinking?

Late Friday afternoon, Brionney sat on the patio in the shade of the orange tree, watching Savannah in the little wading pool Max had bought her. The baby loved the water. She had a ball and never seemed to tire of throwing it out of the pool and waiting for Brionney to throw it back.

Debbie came out of the house, carrying tall glasses of lemonade and ice. "Thought you could use some refreshment." She set the glasses down on the table near her and pulled up a chair. "And tonight there's a new movie playing, a PG. I can't remember the name, but it's supposed to be good. Want to go?"

"Yes. Sure," Brionney said absently.

"The girls even want to come, can you believe it? It must be because of you and Savannah. They never want to be seen with me!"

"Oh, you're too sensitive. You're the hippest mother I know—besides myself, of course."

"Of course," she said with a smirk. "And guess what? Alicia is going to bring that boyfriend of hers. He's a nice guy, but a little serious. Between you and me, I don't think it's going to last. She's not ready for marriage. She wants to go on a mission."

"Well, she'll turn twenty-one about the time Chad comes home, won't she?"

"A few months after. At least I won't have two out at the same time. Even with Max's salary, it's expensive to support a missionary."

Savannah threw the ball, and this time Debbie went to get it. "What about Jesse?" she asked when she returned to her chair.

"What about him?"

"The other day he mentioned that he asked you out."

"Yes. To a dance. But I wasn't up to it—not yet."

"Wasn't it at a dance that you met Derek?"

Brionney's smile faded. "Yes."

"Well, he couldn't have known that. Just dumb luck."

Yet, how wonderful it would have been to go dancing! Brionney frowned. Jesse would go there tonight, and a crowd of single women would be after him. They would dance and have fun, and he would never miss her.

"We'll stop and get some burgers on the way," Debbie was saying.

"Huh?"

"On the way to the movies. One more night I won't have to make dinner. Oh, I love having guests!"

Everything went exactly as Debbie said. They ate hamburgers and french fries for dinner, then went straight to the movie theater. Savannah had always slept through movies when she was younger, so Brionney wasn't anticipating any trouble, just a good time. The feature turned out to be a love story, and as she was already emotional, she soon had tears in her eyes. The opening scene was a dance, and she couldn't help but think of Derek as he had looked that day. And of Jesse, surrounded by young girls.

Just then she noticed someone making his way across the row, and Debbie's family shifting seats. Brionney sat near Debbie on the end, with Savannah on her lap. Before Brionney realized what was happening, Debbie moved over a seat and Jesse sat down next to her. Her heart lurched as she stared at him. Why wasn't he at the dance? Then she spied Debbie's contented glance and knew her friend had planned everything. Brionney was nothing more than a charity case. Her initial excitement died, and she turned resentfully back to the movie.

"Sorry to disturb you," Jesse whispered. "Debbie told me you were all going to the movies, and I asked to come. I hope you don't mind. I couldn't stand the thought of going to the dance alone."

"It's a public theater," Brionney said icily.

He looked at her, surprised. "Yes, I guess it is."

Brionney felt guilty. Jesse didn't deserve the rude treatment, but she just didn't like being played like this. Still, at least he wasn't out dancing with someone—*Stop it already!* she thought.

Savannah started to fuss, biting her fist and making noises. Brionney hadn't brought anything to entertain her, and there was no way she was going to nurse her with Jesse sitting there next to her. She sighed and started to get up to carry the baby from the theater, but Jesse stopped her with a whisper. "I brought something for her." On his palm, he held a small box of dinosaur-shaped cereal. Savannah grabbed for it. She was completely satisfied until they were gone, but then, before she could complain too loudly, Jesse held out another treat of a few tiny bear cookies. When she finished, there was something new, always small and different, until finally she fell asleep with an unfinished sack of Cheerios in her hand.

"Where'd you learn that?" Brionney asked.

"My two nephews and niece. I take them to the movies a lot. The boys are older and actually watch the movie, but my niece is a handful unless I'm prepared. I just wanted to help you with Savannah. I'm glad it worked."

"Me too." Brionney smiled at him in the dark. Her heartbeat started that funny irregular pumping. "I'm sorry about how I acted before," she whispered. "It's just that Debbie can be overbearing sometimes with all her matchmaking."

"It's okay," he said. "I understand." His face was very close to hers, and came closer. Brionney began to panic. What would she do if he tried to . . .

People around them stood and began to file out of their seats. "That was a good movie," Debbie said.

What! It was over already? Brionney couldn't remember what had happened. "So did he get the girl?" she asked Jesse.

Their eyes met again. "I don't know. I guess I didn't pay much attention." His face was red, matching the color Brionney knew was on her own cheeks.

"Of course he got the girl," Debbie said, coming between them. "Didn't you see? It was beautiful!"

"Uh, we were a little busy with Savannah." Brionney tore her eyes away from Jesse's. The conflicting emotions inside her were too overwhelming, too confusing. Cuddling Savannah to her chest, she turned and fled up the aisle, wanting to be anywhere but where Jesse was at that moment.

* * * * *

Jesse watched Brionney charge up the aisle, wanting to kick himself for letting his emotions show so plainly. He had wanted so much to take her in his arms and tell her how strongly he was beginning to feel toward her. But the softness in her face and the fear in her eyes had given him mixed emotions. Should he have spoken? Well, perhaps it wasn't too late. He could still catch her.

Debbie's hand fell on his shoulder. "Give her a little space," she said. "She's just scared."

"I wouldn't hurt her."

"She doesn't know that—yet. It's too soon."

Jesse stared at the ground in frustration. "I know, I know. But I just wish she could trust me."

Debbie slapped him on the back. "Buck up, Sir Lancelot, Guinevere will come around soon enough. Boy, I love it when I'm right. I might just go into matchmaking as a profession. Do you think there's any money in it?" Debbie walked up the aisle with her daughters and Max. Jesse let them go. He watched from a distance as they met up with Brionney, who waited for them outside.

He saw her glance around, as though afraid of seeing him. He sighed. This was going to be even harder than he had thought. But as he watched her get into the minivan, he knew he wasn't giving up. If time was what she needed, so be it.

CHAPTER FIFTEEN

Brionney kept too busy on Saturday to wonder about Jesse. She and Debbie went shopping, had lunch, visited a craft fair, went shopping again, and then had a late dinner. Savannah was an angel through it all, and with Debbie and her daughters the conversation was never dull.

On Sunday afternoon, Brionney visited her old ward with trepidation, only to find that she was met with warm smiles and sincere greetings. The bishop, as he always did with returning members, publicly announced her visit and welcomed her. If they had heard about her divorce, no one made mention of it or asked awkward questions. She relaxed and began to enjoy the service.

Unlike in Brionney's Utah ward, sacrament meeting was last, and as the meeting progressed, Savannah became restless at so many hours of confinement. She slipped down to stand in the aisle, hands on the bench to support herself. Ignoring the outstretched hands of Debbie and her daughters, she launched herself in the opposite direction. Of course, she fell the instant she let go of the bench and started crawling faster than Brionney could make a grab for her. Swiveling, Brionney saw where Savannah was headed. Jesse!

He sat a few rows behind them, urging the baby on. Savannah finally reached her goal, and for the rest of the meeting she stayed with Jesse. Brionney knew that like at the movie, he had probably come prepared. She felt a little envious that Savannah took to him so readily. In fact, they had both taken to him. She remembered how she had felt staring into his eyes, and how she had run away from that feeling. *I don't want to like him!* The last thing she needed was another broken heart.

Don't be ridiculous. You don't even know him. But something warned Brionney away. Jesse was too good to be true—as Derek had been.

"She's adorable," Jesse said as he brought her back after the closing prayer. Savannah was sound asleep against his chest, her features looking cherubic and content, and her fist full of orange fish-shaped crackers.

"Thank you," Brionney said, reaching for her baby. It was impossible not to touch him as she gathered Savannah, and she felt her cheeks burn at the contact. Why did she react so to him?

"Hey, are you staying for the singles' fireside?" a young girl at Jesse's elbow asked. She looked at him the way all of the available girls in the ward did—with an anxious longing. Brionney recognized her as the bishop's daughter, Mandy.

"I hadn't heard about it," Jesse said.

"If you'd come to the singles' ward like you should, you'd know," Alicia said. "They told us weeks ago, and probably announced it again today, if we had been there to hear."

"They announced it just now, here in our ward," Debbie said.

Alicia grinned. "I guess I didn't hear. Anyway, it's for all singles over eighteen. It's supposed to be about Isaiah or something. I can't go because I promised I'd be to work early tomorrow, and I've still got some institute stuff to finish before bedtime. But why don't you stay for it, Brionney?"

"I'll take the baby," Debbie volunteered.

"But I've got an early flight home tomorrow. And I don't really feel comfortable with—"

"You have to stay," Jesse insisted. "And Savannah, too. I promised I'd play peek-a-boo with her before she left."

"I doubt she understood," Brionney said dryly.

Jesse's eyes flashed angrily. "I always keep my promises."

"Well, not this time," she said, matching his tone. "I'm going home tomorrow, and I'm tired. It's been a long week. But thank you for your concern over *my* daughter." She glanced at Debbie. "I'll wait for you in the car." Turning, Brionney left them, but not before she saw the look of satisfaction on Mandy's face. The girl wasn't being cruel. She was simply content to have Jesse to herself. After all, Brionney had once had her chance with a man—and blown it.

"Why were you so mean to Jesse?" Kelli asked her on the way home.

"I wasn't trying to be. I just felt pressured." *I don't want to be hurt,* she added silently. "So, I guess he's pretty angry, huh?" *At least now he'll stay away.*

"He wasn't angry at you," Debbie said. "He's just frustrated."

Brionney wasn't too sure about that. "It doesn't matter," she said, sighing wearily and feeling much older than she was. "I'll never see him again."

But she was wrong. Jesse was waiting for them at Debbie's. "Thanks for inviting me to dinner," he said to Debbie.

"Mandy wasn't too happy," Alicia said with a giggle. "I thought she was going to rip your eyes out, Mom."

"Oh, come on. Mandy's a nice girl." Debbie went into the house. "Hurry up, everyone. We're having pot roast—that is, if it didn't burn while we were gone."

Jesse grinned at Brionney. "I hope you don't mind."

"Of course not." *Just as long as you keep your distance.*

Seeing they were alone, Brionney hurried into the house. Upstairs, she laid the sleeping Savannah on a blanket on the floor bed and changed into a pair of jeans and a shirt more conducive to nursing. She stayed in her room until Debbie called her down to dinner.

The whole family and Jesse gathered at the table around several steaming pizzas. "What happened to the roast?" Brionney asked.

Debbie grimaced. "Need you ask? Anyway, we like frozen pizza, don't we, gang?"

Through the moans of dissent, Jesse asked, "Where's Savannah?"

"Asleep."

Jesse looked disappointed.

Brionney endured dinner, saying very little. Every time she looked up, she found Jesse watching her. Why did he insist on torturing her?

After she finished eating, Brionney arose and excused herself. "I have to pack. And I'd better check on Savannah."

"Could I say good-bye to her?" Jesse asked, jumping from his seat.

With everyone watching, Brionney didn't feel she could refuse. "Okay," she said reluctantly.

Jesse came with her to the room, but Savannah still slept peacefully. "Could we wake her?"

"She'll be so cranky." *Would you just go away?*

Jesse stared at her as though she had spoken aloud. Had she? In two large steps he closed the gap between them. Without a word he put his face next to hers. "Why are you so angry at me?"

Their faces were so close, Brionney thought he had been going to kiss her. "I'm not," she said, backing away.

He took another step forward and then another. "Yes you are. And I don't understand why."

Brionney's back was nearly against the wall. "What are you doing?" she asked, her voice rising.

"What I should have done Friday night." He kissed her, his touch at first tender and gentle, then more demanding. Fire shot through Brionney's heart, and she responded without meaning to.

Kissing Jesse was nothing like kissing a brother. The passion reminded her of what she had felt with Derek, and yet there was more tenderness, more promise. Time seemed to stop, and at the same time go on forever. She never wanted the moment to end, and yet . . . she burst into tears. Jesse was immediately repentant. "I'm sorry, Brionney. I shouldn't have. I won't do it again. Oh . . ." He grabbed her and held her as she sobbed against his chest. One strong arm wrapped around her and the other stroked her hair.

They stood in that embrace for a long time until Brionney calmed down enough to murmur, "I'm so embarrassed." She couldn't look at him.

"Don't be, it was my fault." He pulled back slightly and wiped at the tears on her face with his fingertips. "Are you going to be okay?"

"Yes." She drew completely away, at once missing the strength of his arms.

"I guess I ought to listen more to Debbie," Jesse said.

"What?"

"It doesn't matter, really. I've always been a bit impatient. Will you forgive me?"

Brionney wasn't sure what he meant. Their kiss had shaken her deeply. She had never expected to feel that way again. "There's nothing to forgive. Let's just forget it." Brionney turned her back to him and knelt by the bed, pulling out her suitcase.

"Well, give Savannah a kiss for me when she wakes up."

Brionney nodded, not trusting her voice. Not for all the treasures in the world could she have looked at him. She heard him leave, then turned to stare at the empty doorway. Her fingers went to lips that were still burning with his touch. He had awakened a part of her that she had thought was dead. Their kiss had been wonderful . . . and also scary. She shook her head slowly. Well, it was over now, and tomorrow she would be far away from here.

It was then she knew that she was running away from something she couldn't face. Was it Jesse? Derek? All men in general? Whatever it was, she would be safe in Utah.

* * * * *

Jesse trudged down the stairway, berating himself for his timing. Debbie had warned him repeatedly to take things very slowly. But he had received such a strong impression that they should be together, and then Brionney had made him furious by her indifference. Kissing her had proven that he was right. But at what price? He hadn't wanted to rush her; he hadn't wanted to make her cry. He had simply wanted to break through that stupid wall she had erected between them and let her know he really cared.

And now she must think of him as an insensitive jerk. Maybe he was.

Why did he feel so helpless around her? And why was his yearning to be with her so strong? Every time he looked into those sad blue eyes, the color of a clear sky, he wanted to take her in his arms and wipe the sadness away. He wanted to make her happy. He wanted to hear her laugh.

Well, he wouldn't let her go so easily. He would follow the Spirit that had prompted his feelings, but this time he would give her space—even if it killed him. What was important now was to gain her trust. But how?

CHAPTER SIXTEEN

Feeling rich with the divorce settlement money, Brionney began to look for an apartment as soon as she was back in Utah. The search discouraged her. The money she had wouldn't last long spent on high rent, and she still wasn't prepared to leave Savannah full-time to earn more. Her parents were supportive and encouraged her to do what she felt best, but it was hard to trust her own decisions. She had seen how a seemingly good decision could quickly turn into disaster and heartache.

Her father's real estate business was going well, and he offered her a part-time position answering phones. Since Savannah could come along, the job was ideal. Brionney continued in her college courses with the idea that once Savannah was old enough for school, Brionney would teach French.

In mid-May, three weeks after the divorce, Talia called Brionney at the office. "Guess what?" she said. "I know you've wanted some space of your own, and I found the perfect apartment for you!"

"Really, where?"

"At my new house!"

"What?"

"We're moving! Dad found us the perfect house yesterday! It's near Mom and Dad, and it has a separate mother-in-law apartment behind it. It's small, but almost new and has its own adorable front porch. We'd much rather rent it cheaply to you than have to worry about tenants. What do you say?"

Brionney knew they had been looking for a larger house because their current one was too small for four rambunctious young boys, but she never imagined they might find something to benefit her as well. "Great! When can I see it?"

"Any time you want. The owners have already moved to another state, and the house has been vacant for three months. They were trying to sell it themselves when Dad stumbled across it. He agreed to wave his realtor fee when he knew it was perfect for us. That's how we got it for such a good deal. And it helped the owners, too. They really needed to sell at a fair price. Now everyone's happy. I'm so excited to move in! I can't believe the boys will finally have more space! Four boys in one bedroom is really stretching things."

Brionney fingered a paperweight and stared out the glass doors directly opposite her desk. "So when do you move in?"

"Next week, but I'm starting in on the lawn and stuff immediately. Of course, we'll only be renting until the mortgage papers come through, but it'll soon be ours."

"Give me the address. Savannah and I will come right over after work." Brionney jotted down the numbers on a memo pad. "And thank you, Talia. Thanks so much."

Brionney hung up and turned to Savannah, who was in a playpen full of her toys. "We've found a home for just the two of us," Brionney said. "But with plenty of cousins nearby in case we get lonely." Savannah's chubby face cracked a grin, and she held out her arms. Brionney sighed. "In just a minute, honey. I'm almost finished." Hoping the baby wouldn't cry, she turned back to the paperwork on the desk.

The apartment turned out to be perfect and was Brionney's first step toward real independence. Already she felt better about herself. She still had to use her parents' car and went to Talia's more than she should for dinner and company, but just having her own furniture, dishes, and pictures around her once more made her feel like a real person. There was a gaping hole in her life—the place Derek had once filled—but she tried to ignore it. *At least I don't have to iron his shirts,* she told herself. Some lonely nights, it was meager comfort.

She also thought about Jesse, and about that momentous kiss. What was he doing now? Was he enrolled in school? Brionney was sure she would never see him again. She was glad things between them hadn't developed far. As it was, she was embarrassed when she thought about that last night and how she had burst into tears after he had kissed her. Not very romantic, to say the least.

The first part of June, Brionney walked to her parents' house for their customary bi-monthly Sunday dinner. All of the family would be there except Zack and Josette. Brionney normally loved these dinners and the closeness of her family, but today melancholy thoughts of Derek and Jesse filled her mind.

"Hi, Mom," she said as she walked into the kitchen where the family was gathering. Nine-month-old Savannah clapped her hands excitedly when she saw the familiar faces. She especially loved the tumble of boy cousins who treated her like a princess. Kicking to get down, she crawled over to where the children played with a huge bucket of Lego blocks in the corner.

Irene smiled. "Oh, Brionney, hi. Guess what? Zack called to say that Josette had her baby! Another boy. They're naming him Preston, after my father."

"That's great. I wish we could see them more."

"Me too." Irene blinked away her tears. "But as long as he is happy, that's what's important. Oh, that reminds me. There was a young man here for you a while ago."

"Who?"

"Oh, uh . . . I've forgotten his name. I'm sorry."

Did I leave any bills unpaid? Brionney thought. "What did he look like?"

"Short brown hair. Brown eyes. Not very tall, but nice looking. He drove an old gold-colored car with rust all over it."

"It was an old Ford Fiesta," Terrell said. "A four-door."

"Yeah, it was old, all right," said Joe Jr. Named after his father, he was Talia's oldest, and at nine knew more about cars than both his father and grandfather. "It looked like it was just hangin' together. Man, I would rather walk through a desert without water than be caught in a car like that!" He snickered.

His father shook his head disapprovingly. "I drove a car like that for years. It's much better to make do with an old car while saving for a good one than to pay more interest than the car is worth. Remember that, young man." Talia nodded and put her hand on her husband's shoulder in approval.

"You can't judge a man by his car," Terrell said. "It's better to have a Cadillac man in a rattletrap car, than a rattletrap man in a Cadillac car." These were the same words Brionney had heard since childhood.

Joe Jr. was silent for a moment as he puzzled it out.

"You can always change a car, but it's harder to change the man," Terrell elaborated.

"But why not go for a Cadillac man in a Cadillac car?" Joe Jr. said. Everyone laughed; it was an argument Brionney and her sisters had teased their father with for years.

"Because Cadillac men usually start with rattletrap cars," Terrell insisted. "Their priorities are straight."

Brionney thought of the green convertible Derek had owned when she met him. Maybe there was something to the old adage after all.

"So who is this guy?" Irene asked.

Brionney shrugged. "I don't know." The only man she knew who fit the description was hundreds of miles away in Phoenix, finishing up college.

"Well, that's okay," Irene said. "I told him to come back later. That you'd be here."

"You *what?* What if he's a lawyer or something, and Derek has decided to get custody of Savannah?" Brionney lived with that fear daily, in spite of the divorce settlement.

"In that car?" smirked Joe Jr. "Even I know lawyers don't drive rattletraps."

He had a point, but still Brionney waited, jumping at every sound until dinner was ready. The doorbell rang before Terrell could call on someone to pray over the food.

"I'll get it!" Joe Jr. was out of his seat before anyone else could move. He was back in less than a minute. "It's the man with the rattletrap," he announced.

"Shh," Talia said.

Brionney stood and left the dining room. Joe Jr. started to follow with a curious smile, but his parents called him back. Whoever the stranger was, Brionney would face him alone.

He sat stiffly on one of the green couches in the elegantly furnished living room, studying the gold shag carpet. He was dressed in a suit despite the heat, and trying to hide his discomfort.

"Jesse! What are you doing here?"

He stood and met Brionney's relieved smile with one of his own. "I always keep my promises. I've come to play peek-a-boo with Savannah, if that's okay with you. Debbie gave me this address."

"What! You came all the way from Arizona to play peek-a-boo?"

He grinned. "Well, not just that, but she was a deciding factor. I'm here for school, too. With some connections I have in Phoenix, I found a job fixing computers and putting them together, so I came out earlier than I expected. Meanwhile I'm taking some independent courses—religion and P.E." He chuckled. "No basketball competition for me!"

"But I thought you were going back to your old university. You said you were going there that day you jumped into Debbie's pool."

"I did go there, but just to find out about transferring. I'd long before decided to come to Utah."

"Oh." Brionney felt rather stupid. She should have just asked him. But then that would have meant she cared, and . . . "Well, it's nice to see you."

"And you, too. I've wanted to apologize again for that last night. I didn't mean to upset you."

"It's okay. I've forgotten it already." Brionney lied, but he didn't have to know that.

His face grew red, and he looked away from her, past the gold patterned curtain to the grass outside. "So can I see Savannah?"

"Well, we're about to eat. We always have family dinners here on the first and third Sundays of each month."

"Then I'll come back later. Or on another day," he said hastily, turning toward the door.

"Nonsense!" Irene came into the room. "Brionney, invite him in. We've plenty to go around. And any friend of yours is welcome."

"Well, thanks, but . . ." Jesse gazed at Brionney, waiting for her response. She could see that he wanted to stay but didn't want to force her into inviting him.

"Please stay, Jesse," she said, wanting him to more than she would admit to herself. "If you can, that is."

"Are you sure?"

"Yeah. Besides, you've got some peek-a-boo playing to do, remember?"

His grin was a mixture of relief and something else she couldn't place, something that made her stomach churn and sent warm shivers up her spine. Brionney wasn't sure she liked the feeling. "I'd like to stay," he said. "Thank you."

"It's right this way," Irene said with a smile. "Follow me." She cast Brionney an unreadable stare.

Jesse was immediately welcomed into the group. He was soon telling about his plunge into Debbie's pool and how he would have heroically saved Savannah. He made it seem as funny as it had been, and this time Brionney felt free to laugh openly.

After dinner, Jesse removed his suit jacket and played peek-a-boo with Savannah and the other toddlers who weren't too old for the game. He gave each a turn, but he favored Savannah, and by her giggles and hugs she made no secret of how much she adored him. Once he crossed the room, and giving a grunt of determination, she followed him, teetering as she balanced on her feet.

"Look! Savannah's walking!" the children shouted. Brionney turned to see her fall into Jesse's waiting arms, a smile of triumph on her face.

"More than five steps without falling," Talia said. "Yep, that's walking. Savannah is officially walking at—how old is she?"

"Nine months and two weeks," Brionney said, bending to kiss the baby's cheeks. She sat in Jesse's arms, and Brionney could smell his aftershave and the detergent on his white shirt. A rush of emotions came, reminding her of their kiss. She felt her face redden. Jesse stared at her, his eyes never leaving her face. Brionney thought that if they were alone he might try to kiss her again. And what's more, she wanted him to.

"That's the earliest yet," Talia said to Lauren and Mickelle, bringing Brionney back from the brink of distress. "None of the boys walked until eleven months, right?"

The evening continued with no more awkward moments. Brionney found herself enjoying Jesse's company. He seemed to fit in with her family in a comfortable way, as if he belonged. Not in the least like the way Derek had dazzled everyone with his presence, but more like a longtime friend of the family.

"A rattletrap, huh?" he said when Joe Jr. mentioned his car.

The boy blushed and crinkled his freckled face. "You heard me. Well, uh, that's what we call old cars around here."

"It's a good name. It does rattle." Jesse put his hand on Joe Jr.'s shoulder. "You see, I like to think of the Fiesta as a practice for the real thing."

"Oh, yeah? Well, what kind of a car do you want some day?" The two were off and talking. Joe Jr. was thrilled to find someone who actually recognized the names of the latest models. Already the boy had a touch of worship in his eyes.

When Terrell discovered Jesse was majoring in computer science, he interrupted to ask about a new system for his office. A little flare of jealousy sparked in Brionney's heart, and she wanted to go to Jesse's side and grab his attention. *Ridiculous,* she told herself. Secretly she could pretend they were together, but it wasn't really true.

"Hey, don't you have some pictures to show me?" Jesse asked. "I want to see what Brionney looked like when she was a kid."

The fat pictures, Brionney groaned to herself. Irene looked over at her expectantly. "Well, go ahead," Brionney said. Better that Jesse knew the truth.

He went through all the albums with relish. "You were always so cute," he said to her. "Look how your eyes stand out."

Brionney looked at the picture he pointed to. She didn't look as fat as she remembered. Jesse's hand touched hers. "Thanks for letting me see these. You have a great family."

Darkness fell, and Jesse walked Brionney and Savannah to their small apartment in back of Talia's. The warm night air was filled with the perfume of flowers from the landscaped yards, and despite the lights showing in most of the homes, Brionney felt as though they were completely alone.

"I had a really great time tonight," Jesse said. He stopped walking and Brionney tensed, not knowing what to expect, but he simply reached up to his shoulders where Savannah rode. He pulled her down and cradled her in his arms. Her eyes were shut. "I think she's almost asleep."

They continued walking. "I did too," Brionney said.

"What?"

"I had a good time, too. It was fun."

She felt more than saw his smile in the darkness. "I like your family. It's big and . . ."

"Loud?"

He chuckled. "Now that you mention it. But that wasn't what I was going to say. Your family is close. I like that. And they share the same values. I hope my family will reach that stage one day. We're close, but they aren't members, and well, it's different. You're very lucky." There was envy in his voice, and Brionney remembered that his own family didn't support his choice of religion. How hard that must be! A new admiration for Jesse entered her heart.

"Thank you, Jesse. You're right, I am lucky." Since she had lost Derek, she had not spent much time counting her blessings.

They walked the rest of the way in silence. At the door, Jesse waited until Brionney turned the key and opened her door. Then he gently laid Savannah in her arms. He hesitated, looking at Brionney for a long, guarded moment. Was he going to try and kiss her again? She didn't know whether to run or to urge him on. But it was Savannah whom he kissed good night before sauntering into the darkness. Without thinking, Brionney leaned down and kissed Savannah in the same place.

* * * * *

Jesse found himself whistling as he walked back to Brionney's parents' house to retrieve his car. He was grateful he had come. Seeing her had been worth the long wait. He had been desperate to get to Utah to see her, and had prayed long and hard to find a job so he could support himself. That things had fallen into place wasn't coincidence, he knew. He was supposed to be here.

Seeing her with her family had been a revelation to him. Within the arms of their security, she was free to be herself—funny, open, and intelligent. Tonight he had even heard her laugh. Their souls seemed to be able to communicate here the way their mouths couldn't. One thing was certain: he was more attracted to her than ever. Maybe now he could convince her that their relationship was worth the chance she would have to take.

* * * * *

Jesse began to appear at Brionney's apartment nearly every evening during the next few weeks. He played with Savannah outside in the yard, but rarely went inside. Being alone with her was too tempting, and he had vowed to take things slowly.

They often worked on their school assignments on the shaded porch as Savannah played. Jesse felt comfortable discussing anything with her, from religion to politics. He found she had a sharp mind, full of insights he had never thought about. Often, they would talk until the baby fell asleep in Brionney's arms. Jesse found himself more and more reluctant to leave her each night.

When it happened that work and school kept him away three nights in a row, he almost went over at midnight. He did drive by, hoping to see a light, but there was none. Did she miss him at all?

The next night he came over earlier than usual. Brionney and Savannah were just finishing their dinner. Brionney invited him inside. "Would you like something to eat?" she asked.

"No, thanks. I already ate." He picked up Savannah from her high chair. "But I sure did miss you, little one." Savannah threw her arms around him.

"She missed you, too," Brionney said. "She kept looking around like she was searching for you."

Jesse wanted to ask if Brionney had also missed him. Instead he said, "I've heard there's an aviary in Salt Lake. Have you ever been there?"

"Once when I was a kid. It's okay." She paused. "So what did you get on your test?"

For the last two weeks, Jesse had been dropping hints about places he would like to visit, but like today she would always deflect the subject. It was sort of a game between them, one that he enjoyed immensely. "I'll bet Savannah would like the birds," he said, giving her an indulgent smile.

"She likes water better," Brionney said firmly. "I bought her a wading pool today. Come on, I'll show you." She took him outside and onto the lawn, where Jesse saw a light-blue pool with bright-colored fishes covering the bottom. There was a little water in it and Savannah immediately kicked to get down.

"You're right," Jesse said, watching Savannah splash her hands into the water. Unknowingly, Brionney had played into his hands. "I think she does like water better. And that reminds me. Seven Peaks sounds like a fun place. We should go. I bet Savannah would love it."

Brionney looked surprised, and Jesse almost laughed at her expression. "You up for more rescuing, eh?" she asked.

Well, at least that wasn't a direct refusal. Jesse was encouraged. *Okay, no more beating around the bush. Let's try a direct approach.* "No, I mean it. Let's go. It'll be a real date. I'll come and pick you up in the rattletrap and pay for everything. We could pack a lunch if we want."

"No, Jesse. I can't. I—"

Jesse's hopes faded. He hadn't felt so frustrated since that last night with her in Arizona. "Is it because of Derek?" he asked, trying to keep the hurt and frustration from his voice.

For a moment, she stared away from him. When she spoke her voice was faint. "Yes, partly. I know it may seem strange, but I'm still sealed to him. And I—" She stopped, and Jesse's heart ached with her. Fear was so plainly written on her face that she might have added, "I'm afraid of being hurt again."

A heavy silence fell between them like an impenetrable wall. Jesse knew he had no choice but to tell her what he knew. She had to face it someday. "Derek's gone," he said gently. "He's not coming back."

"He said he loved me that day," she whispered. "After we signed the papers."

"Is that what you're waiting for?"

"No. I don't know." She sighed. "I just don't know. How could he say that? I feel so confused."

Jesse's mouth tightened. He knew all too well that Derek was playing with her emotions. The man didn't want to be married to Brionney, but he didn't want her to go on without him, either. Jesse wished he could strangle Derek for using her the way he had.

Tell her, he told himself. He took a deep breath. "He's married again." Jesse heard the note of pain in his own voice.

Her eyes widened. "He's what?"

Fumbling in his pocket, Jesse brought out a folded newspaper clipping and reluctantly handed it to her. "Debbie sent me this last week. She thought you should know. She thought it'd be better if I told you in person than if she sent it to you in the mail. But I couldn't give it to you before. I just couldn't."

He watched as she unfolded the worn clipping that he had kept in his pocket for a week. It looked as if it had been folded and refolded a hundred times. How many times had he opened it and stared at the beautiful faces?

Brionney gasped as she took in the happy-looking pair, adorned in their finest. Below the picture, the partially blurred words told of their marriage only a few weeks earlier.

Misery clung to Jesse as Brionney began to cry softly, her shoulders shaking. Jesse felt helpless. "I'm so sorry," he whispered. "I knew I shouldn't have shown you. Please forgive me. It wasn't my place. Should I leave?"

"No," Brionney mumbled. "I had to know someday. Better not alone. Better with a friend."

Jesse hugged her until her shoulders stopped shaking. She looked up at him gratefully. "Thank you for being here."

"Did you really—" He broke off, unsure how to continue without causing her further pain. But he had to know. "Expect him to come back?"

Brionney gave a short, bitter laugh. "You want to know the truth? I don't even want him back. But it still hurts. The covenants we made, all gone. I feel so betrayed. And poor Savannah without a father. I think I hurt because of all that could have been. Do you understand that? All the blessings that—"

"That will still be yours," Jesse interrupted. "Oh, Brionney, if you could only see through my eyes and know what kind of a person you are. You're smart, intelligent, a great mother, a wonderful person to be with. You're really special. The problems have come, but you're surviving. That's what's important now."

"But who will ever look beyond the surface?" she said, pushing away from him. "I'm used goods. A woman abandoned. Who can see beyond that?"

"I can," he said quietly. "Don't you know that yet? I knew I wanted to be with you from that very first day in Debbie's family room. There you stood, staring at me with those blue eyes, so determined not to like me."

Brionney looked at him in amazement. He touched her cheek, catching a stray tear. "You don't know me very well yet, but I can also be pretty determined, especially when I know I'm right. I promise you now that I'm not going anywhere. Whatever happened in the past with Derek was not your fault, and I'm not going to let you pay for it forever."

"I've been so afraid."

"I know. But you can't let that rule your life."

"Okay," she said, looking more determined than happy. "Saturday. We'll go Saturday. To Seven Peaks. But don't expect me to look skinny in a bathing suit."

"Yes!" Jesse whooped, jumping at least a foot. He leaned down and kissed her cheek, then spun around and hopped off the porch. "You won't regret it, you won't! I promise." He looked at her carefully to make sure she would be all right. Already she was smiling. Better he leave before she changed her mind.

He ran over to the pool. "Guess what, Savvy? You and I are going swimming. Just wait till you see all that water!" He kissed her good-bye and then started across the lawn. Things had turned out much better than he had expected. *Thank you, Father,* he prayed. Maybe the weeks of patience had been worth the torture after all.

* * * * *

Brionney stared after Jesse's retreating figure. "And you always keep your promises," she whispered after him. "You won't forget that, will you?"

She heard a car start somewhere in front, out of sight: Jesse's old Fiesta. It was too late to call him back and change her mind. The sun had started to set over the horizon, promising what? An ending? A new beginning? Or neither?

Brionney collected Savannah and went into the small house. She trembled, though the evening was warm. In her hand she felt the newspaper clipping, now crumbled in a tight ball. She stopped and put it in the trash.

CHAPTER SEVENTEEN

The week passed in a flurry of expectation. Jesse came over nearly every day, but never stayed long. At the first sign of serious conversation, he would kiss Savannah and leave. Brionney began to wonder if he was really as committed to finding out where their relationship would lead as he claimed, or if he was pulling away slowly so as not to hurt her feelings. Friday arrived before she realized that the real reason he kept leaving was that he feared she would cancel their Saturday date.

What he didn't know was that finding out about Derek's marriage had freed Brionney in a way the divorce hadn't. While Derek remained single, there had always been the chance he would wake up one morning and realize his terrible mistake. Brionney had learned enough about him to not have taken him back easily, but she would have given it another try if he had been willing to do so on her terms. After all, she had vowed to love him for the rest of eternity. Now that obligation was over.

"I kinda understand," Talia said when Brionney tried to explain it. "It's like you were still bound, even though he had broken his half."

"Yeah, something like that."

"And now you're free to pursue someone else—like Jesse," she said pointedly.

"He's very good with Savannah."

Her eyes narrowed. "But how do *you* feel about him? You can't marry someone just because he's good with Savannah."

"It's not like we're getting married. We're just friends."

Talia laughed. "That's what you're telling yourself, is it? Well, I don't buy it. I've seen him come over practically every night, and it's not for Savannah. He's fallen for you like a rock over a cliff. I can see it in his eyes. Now I've known for a long time that you've been worried about getting hurt again, but you'd better think about Jesse. He doesn't deserve to be hurt either."

"I'm not going to hurt him!" Brionney started to get mad. Talia sounded like she cared more about Jesse than her own sister.

"You are if you're leading him on."

"It's our first date! How could I be leading him on?"

She shook her head. "No, your first date is long past. Way long past. He's been here nearly every night for three weeks—don't think I haven't noticed—and you two are thicker than tar, sitting there with your heads together, talking and laughing. And it's not because he has nothing to do, what with work and school. No, you need to wake up, Brionney, and either put the brakes on or go after him full-heartedly. Jesse certainly knows what he wants, and he's going after it."

Brionney made some excuse and escaped from Talia's. *I'm not leading Jesse on. I'm not!*

But deep inside, she knew Talia was right. Jesse knew what he wanted. Excitement ate at her insides, and a sliver of happiness formed. Could it really be that he wanted her? Both as a person and as a woman? She let herself hope, just a little, that they could find something important together.

Saturday morning dawned bright and clear. The late June morning already showed signs of the heat that would come with the afternoon; a perfect day for water sliding. Brionney grimaced in the mirror at her figure, clad in a new blue swimsuit. She still hadn't lost that extra five pounds, but there was nothing she could do about it now. She turned from the mirror and began to pack towels, a picnic lunch, diapers, and plenty of sunscreen. With their fair skin, she and Savannah would be targets for the hot rays of the summer sun.

Jesse appeared promptly at ten forty-five with three funny hats in hand. They were made of straw and had wide brims with large pink and blue bows. One was noticeably smaller than the other two. He presented them with a flourish and a bow. "To protect your delicate skin," he said, putting one with a blue ribbon on his own head.

Brionney giggled and placed one on her head and the other on Savannah, who stared with wide-eyed surprise. She promptly took it off to see what it was, and then put it in her mouth. With a grimace of disgust, she tried to put it back on her head.

With a big smile, Jesse scooped up Savannah and carried her toward the front where his car waited. Halfway there, he stopped and returned for the car seat. "Leave the cooler," he directed. "I'll come back for it when you two are settled."

The Fiesta wasn't as bad on the inside as the rusty paint indicated. The seat had new covers and the dashboard was uncracked. Everything looked clean, if worn. "It gets good gas mileage," Jesse said, noting her interest. "And I've had it long enough to know that it heats up well in the summer and cools nicely in the winter."

Brionney laughed. "I take it that means a heating problem and no air conditioning."

"What? No air conditioning?" Jesse was affronted. "Of course we have air conditioning! Just roll down the window like this, and voilá! Automatic air conditioning. It's free, too. And all natural. No ugly Freon to ruin the ozone."

Over her laughter, he added more seriously, "At least it's paid for, and it's not as if I'll be a student forever. I'll have a real car one day."

"I like the car, Jesse."

"Even if it's a rattletrap?"

Brionney remembered Derek's fancy sports car, the one he had never let her drive. "No, *because* it's a rattletrap," she said firmly.

Jesse raised his eyebrows, but said nothing. "You know what's good to me?" he asked.

"No, what?"

"To hear you laugh." The tenderness in his voice was unmistakable. Before she could reply, he kissed her cheek and turned back to get the cooler. Smiling, Brionney belted Savannah into her seat.

All day they slid and played in the water. There were large wave pools, a varied assortment of slides, and plenty of pools for the hoards of laughing children. To Brionney's surprise, there was still no underlying tension between them, even though it was officially their first date. She didn't feel as if she were under constant observation and unable to measure up. Jesse's eyes didn't wander after the too-thin women in skimpy bikinis at the park, but stayed with her and Savannah. His chest was white compared with his arms and face, but covered with enough dark hair to fascinate the baby. With innocent abandon she pulled on the unfamiliar hairs, to Jesse's torment and Brionney's amusement.

They were indistinguishable from the many other families at the park. Dad, mom, and baby. Never had Brionney felt so relaxed and at peace. Not even in the beginning with Derek.

Near dinnertime Savannah grew tired, and nothing Brionney or Jesse did would make her happy. She repeatedly tried to put her hand into the top of Brionney's suit. "Not now, Savannah," Brionney whispered, pushing her hand firmly away. Savannah looked at her with tears in her big eyes, and promptly tried again.

Brionney felt her face color. She had nursed Savannah several times in the rest room during the day, mostly so she wouldn't become engorged and start leaking, and had also given her a variety of other foods. The baby could eat almost anything, though she didn't seem ready to give up nursing, especially when she was tired. She refused any attempts to give her a bottle, but would occasionally drink from a cup.

"I think she's not giving up," Jesse said, sounding amused.

Brionney glanced at him. "I guess not. And don't think I don't see that smile you're trying to hide. You think this is funny!"

"Well, why don't I take this stuff out to the car while you feed her?" He concentrated on gathering the towels and the cooler, not meeting her eyes. Brionney had the feeling he was trying desperately not to collapse to the grass and laugh himself silly. "Or better yet, why don't you go out to the car where you can sit comfortably? It should be cool enough now. I'll join you in a while." He straightened and proffered the keys.

"Thanks." Brionney snatched the keys from his hands and hurried away. Since they had never talked about nursing, she almost believed he didn't know about it. So much for that idea. "That is it," she said to Savannah. "You are going to be weaned—and soon!"

Despite the awkwardness of the situation, Brionney found herself smiling. Years from now, she would probably find the situation funny. Jesse certainly had.

In the car, Savannah was quickly satisfied and fell asleep. Jesse must have noted how long it usually took to nurse her, because shortly after he arrived with their things. He was still smiling, but to Brionney's relief he didn't bring up the subject. They rode home in comfortable silence.

"Did you have a good day?" Jesse asked as he carried the cooler into Brionney's kitchen.

"I did."

"You sound surprised."

She was. Not once during the day had she been self-conscious about her figure, her face, or her problems. The future seemed to burst with possibilities. "It was a great day. Thank you, Jesse."

"So will you go out with me again?"

He stood close to her in the small kitchen, still in his swimming trunks and funny hat. Their eyes met and held like they had in the movie theater in Phoenix, and Brionney knew he was going to kiss her.

But he pulled away and said gruffly, "I think I'd better be going."

"You could stay, and we could watch TV or something." She didn't want him to leave. Savannah snored softly in her bed, and Brionney would be alone.

"I don't know if that's a good idea," he said, sounding like he was out of breath. "Being here alone with you right now is too tempting. I don't want to rush anything."

Brionney understood what he was saying. She put her arms around his neck. "You're not rushing me."

His arms came around her and their lips met. For a brief moment, the emotion shocked her with its intensity and threatened to overwhelm her senses. Now Brionney understood what people meant when they said the earth stopped moving. At that moment, even time seemed to stand still.

They drew back in the same instant, arms still entwined. Jesse smiled. "We have something here, Brionney. Do you feel it?"

She nodded dumbly.

"And I want nothing more at this moment than to stay here with you. Nothing. But there's no way I want to risk what we have between us. So I'd better go. I've found that it's best to stay out of trouble before you get in so deep that you can't get out."

Fleetingly, Brionney wondered if that was what had happened to Derek. "You're right," she said. "And thank you."

He lifted her chin with his hand. This time his kiss was soft and chaste. Holding hands, they walked to the door. "Good-bye, Brionney. I'll see you tomorrow."

"Good-bye." She watched him until he rounded Talia's house and disappeared. Her heart still danced, and her chest seemed too small to contain it.

Talia came out of her back door and crossed the small lawn to her porch. "The boys saw you come home, and I couldn't wait to come out here and see if you had a good time. So did you? You look red . . . did you get burnt?"

Brionney was flushed, but it wasn't from the sun. Warm chills started in her spine and spread to her arms, legs, and neck. She knew then that Jesse wasn't just a friend, and she was already in too deep to avoid pain if things didn't work out. All she could do now was trust in him and pray.

"I'm fine, Talia."

Jesse cared for her, and she was oh, so much better than fine!

* * * * *

As Jesse's school schedule became more rigorous, Brionney saw him less. Even so, he was around when she needed reassurance, and he called often when he couldn't visit. Sundays they always spent together, either at church and at her parents' or at Talia's. By unspoken agreement they avoided being alone in her apartment, though they kissed occasionally on the porch, in plain sight of Joe Jr. and his three interested brothers, who peered out their windows every time they wanted to be alone.

July came and went and, as Savannah's birthday approached in late August, Brionney found it harder and harder to keep the toddler under control at the office. As a result, Brionney began to leave her more often with her mother or with Talia. Though Savannah didn't seem to mind, Brionney felt guilty. She had enrolled in two more evening courses for the fall, which meant two more nights she would have to leave Savannah. Brionney longed for a change—one that would let her stay home and mother her baby properly.

Her sisters, Lauren and Mickelle, both had their babies in August, four days apart. Lauren's baby was a girl and Mickelle had her second boy. The newborns were adorable, and Brionney spent long minutes staring down at them and remembering Savannah's birth the year before. A desire to have another child sprang from nowhere, surprising her with its intensity. She could almost imagine a baby with dark hair and eyes like Jesse's, staring up at her from a face shaped like Savannah's.

Eyes like Jesse's. The thought both frightened and exhilarated her.

For Savannah's birthday, Brionney held an outdoor party in Talia's backyard. "Are you ready, Savannah?" Jesse said as they brought out the cake. "This is it, baby. The cameras are rolling. Show us how you blow out that candle!" Jesse had been practicing candle-blowing with her for the past few weeks.

The relatives all gathered around as Savannah took a deep breath and blew. "Yes!" Jesse cheered. "I knew you could do it!" Everyone clapped, and Savannah took that as her cue to grab a handful of cake.

After the party, everyone except Jesse left for home. He took Brionney's hand and they ambled to her porch. As they settled in the chairs, she glanced up to make sure no little eyes watched from Talia's windows. Jesse's gaze followed. "They won't be there tonight," he said. "I asked Talia to keep them away."

"Oh?" Brionney held her breath, waiting for what would come next. When he didn't plunge right in with an explanation, tiny stars appeared in front of her eyes, reminding her to breathe.

"Brionney," he began finally. She lifted her eyes from where Savannah played in the grass with her new toys. Jesse slipped off his chair to kneel in front of her. "I know it's only been four months since your divorce, and I've tried to be patient. But I really love you! And I want us to be together as a family." His hand held tightly to hers, his face flushing that endearing red Brionney so adored. "Will you marry me?"

"Oh, Jesse." She had waited so long to hear those words. "I can't imagine life without you. I really can't. And I love you so much."

His face drew closer to hers, so hopeful and so incredibly dear. Brionney hated to say the next words. "But what about Savannah? How will you feel about her when you have children of your own?" It was a question that had preyed upon her mind.

"Savannah *is* mine!" he protested, staring intently into her eyes. "I was there when she took her first steps, remember? I'm here at her first birthday, and it was me who took her on her first water slide. I want to be her father as much as I want to marry you. I want to be there at all her firsts, seconds, and thirds—and forever. I don't know how I'll feel about any other children we may have, but I know I can't love them more than I love Savannah. I want to take care of her, to be there when she needs a father, and not just part-time as I have been these last months. And I love you. Please, Brionney, marry me. I haven't much to offer you yet, except my whole heart. Please!" His entire manner was urgent, compelling, and Brionney believed him. But there was something more.

"We've never really talked about it. Doesn't my having been married before bother you?"

Jesse looked down at the redwood planks that made up the base of the porch, a frown covering his face. "About that," he said. "It could be my fault."

"What!" Brionney had expected any answer but this one.

"I was eighteen when I first took the missionary discussions. I knew the Church was true, but I didn't join until three years later."

"Because of your parents' objections."

"Yes, but I knew it was true from the very first. You know, it says in my patriarchal blessing that I am blessed with discernment. And it's true, because I knew from my first reading that the Book of Mormon was true. I knew it. Just as I knew you that day at Debbie's." He paused, swallowing hard. "And lately, I've been thinking that if I had joined the Church at eighteen, served a mission at nineteen, and then come to BYU, it could have been me you met at that dance instead of Derek. We were meant to be together! I know that. Maybe if I hadn't been so afraid, we could have found each other years ago and spared you all of the pain."

Brionney thought a moment. How wonderful his dream sounded! But she shook her head. There was still Savannah. "We can't change that," she said. "No matter how much we want to."

"But do you forgive me?"

She leaned forward and hugged him. "There is nothing to forgive. You're forgetting Savannah. She is who she is because of my relationship with Derek, and I could never wish her away or have her be any different than she is. Would you?"

His eyes went to the little girl, still playing with her toys, oblivious to the strong emotions around her. A single tear rolled down his cheek. "No," he whispered. "I wouldn't change her for anything." They hugged a long time without speaking.

"So will you marry me?" he asked again.

"In the temple?"

"Of course. You know I'd never marry anywhere else."

"For forever?" Brionney's voice shook.

His hand caressed her cheek. "I promise."

"Yes," she said softly.

"I want you to pray about it. I want you to be sure."

"Even if the answer is no?"

He grinned. "It won't be. I've never had any doubts."

He pulled a box out of his pocket and opened it. Inside was a large diamond set in a thick but simple band. "Talia told me the size," he said, "but if you don't like it we can pick out something else." He slid it on her finger as she marveled at the beauty. Though not as large and expensive as the ring Derek had given her, it was far more tasteful.

"It's perfect," she said. "So . . . when do you want to get married?"

"How about at the Thanksgiving break?"

"That would be great." She kissed him fervently, not caring who might be watching. After a while, he groaned and rose from his knees. He turned and left her on the porch.

"Where are you going?"

"To get Savannah, before I forget myself. I've got to start teaching her to say Daddy instead of Jesse."

Brionney laughed as he picked up Savannah and whirled her around. Her new ring sparkled in the fading light, and the delighted cries of the baby seemed far away. Jesse was so good for them! In him Brionney had found both the friendship she had shared with Marc and the passion that had blinded her with Derek.

Silently she prayed, and a feeling of well-being spread through her body. She knew without a doubt that her relationship with Jesse was right as she had never known with Derek. One thing still loomed in their path. To be married in the temple, Brionney first had to obtain a cancellation of her sealing to Derek. She had no idea how long it would take or what she had to do, except that she had heard she would need a letter from Derek.

What if he wouldn't write it? What if she and Jesse were kept waiting for months? Now that Brionney knew they were meant to be together, every moment seemed too long to be apart. She stood quickly and went into the house to call her bishop. He would know what to do.

And she would make Derek write the letter if she had to go to Arizona herself.

CHAPTER EIGHTEEN

As Brionney had heard, the sealing cancellation request included not only a letter from Brionney and one from Jesse, but also a letter from Derek. Brionney and Jesse wrote theirs quickly and then waited for Derek. Weeks passed, and the letter never arrived. Brionney knew he had received it because she had sent a registered letter to the address Derek's lawyer had given Max.

"I can't believe he won't send it," Brionney said to Jesse.

"Maybe he doesn't want to break the sealing."

"Well, he'll have to."

In desperation, Brionney called Debbie. "Don't worry, I'm on it," she said. "I'll just take a little trip out to his house."

Debbie called back the next day. "I've got the letter! I stayed at the fancy new condo he and Melinda live in until he wrote it. He didn't want to be bothered, but when Melinda learned that it was so you could get remarried and he could stop paying alimony, she invited me to dinner. And I stayed. In fact, I was there until nearly eleven o'clock. I think Derek wrote the letter simply to get rid of me. To tell you the truth, I had to practically tell him what to write."

"I love you, Debbie!" Brionney said.

"Hey, what are friends for? Just don't forget to invite me to the wedding."

The hard part taken care of, Brionney settled back to wait for her bishop to send the papers to Salt Lake and for them to grant the cancellation. She eagerly planned her wedding and reception with her mother and sisters. The remaining months passed by quickly.

Two weeks before their wedding, the bishop called them into his office. "I'm sorry, but I have bad news. The papers just aren't here yet.

I called Salt Lake to see what was going on, and they can't find them. In fact, no one has any record that we even sent them. I don't know what else to tell you."

Brionney was stunned. "But I thought you said we'd have plenty of time."

"I thought so," he said, "given the circumstances of your divorce. I've never seen it take this long. I guess it just got hung up on someone's desk and misfiled. I'm really sorry. We can re-file the request, but you know what that entails. We'll have to get another letter from your ex-husband."

"But we've got the invitations, the flowers, the dresses, everything is planned." Brionney felt close to tears.

"The only option would be to get married civilly and then be sealed later," the bishop said kindly. "But would it be so terrible to wait until, say, February? I know how much this means to you both to start things off right."

"It took so much for us to get Derek to write a letter in the first place. I don't know if I can get him to do it again."

"I'll call and have a talk with him, if you think it will help," the bishop said. "And then we'll try to hurry it through."

"Okay, I'll get his number from my lawyer. Thanks." Brionney felt Jesse's arms around her, leading her from the office. Outside in the gold Fiesta, Brionney muttered, "I can't believe this is happening!"

"Neither can I," Jesse said.

She met his gaze. "So what do you want to do?"

"Get married. But in February."

"February!" Whoever thought it would take so long to separate herself from a man who had long gone on his way?

"I love you, Bri," Jesse continued, "and I don't want to wait, but I will. I only want to do this once."

He looked so anxious that Brionney smiled despite her rotten mood. "It's not going to be easy."

"I know, but I knew that since the moment I met you. I have to keep reminding myself that we have eternity." He paused. "But I have a plan that you might like."

"What?"

"We'll go see my parents during Thanksgiving break. They've been wanting to meet you. It won't be the same as a honeymoon, but we'll be together. And Savannah will have a chance to meet her new grand-parents and cousins. What do you say? It'll give us something to look forward to."

Brionney wasn't sure she wanted to meet his parents. She hadn't had much luck with Derek's family. At least not with his father.

"My parents are going to love you," he said, as though reading her thoughts. "They're not members, but they're good people."

"Okay," Brionney said. "I'll go. But I'm a little worried about what they'll say about you marrying into a ready-made family."

Jesse shrugged. "I'm more concerned about the fact that you're a Mormon. Remember, they don't approve of my being a member. But we've got to face them sometime, and it might as well be now. Besides, Savannah will win them over in a minute."

Over the next few days, Brionney half-heartedly planned what she would take for the trip. "What if they hate me?" she asked Talia.

"They're not going to hate you."

Brionney sighed. "Maybe it's just going back to Arizona I'm worried about. I haven't had much luck there."

"What do you mean? That's where you met Jesse."

"I guess you're right."

"Of course I am. Now stop worrying. And while you're there, maybe you can get Derek to sign another letter for the cancellation."

The day of Thanksgiving found Brionney, Jesse, and Savannah in the Fiesta. The late November weather was abnormally warm this year, and it grew even warmer as they approached Arizona, especially inside the car as the sun shone through the glass. The wind from Jesse's "air conditioning" beat at Brionney's face through the half-open window. She knew her hair suffered and would have to be untangled later.

As the miles passed, a tickling sensation grew in Brionney's stom-ach until she was on the verge of nausea. What if his parents didn't approve? Suddenly, she remembered all too vividly how he had wait-ed three years to join the Church out of respect for them. As much as she loved Jesse, Brionney didn't know if she could wait three years to become his wife. Waiting for the cancellation to come through was torture enough.

A psychology book from one of her classes at BYU lay on her lap. She couldn't concentrate on the words. Instead, she twisted in the bucket seat to see Savannah, who was sound asleep, clutching a tiny stuffed kitten Jesse had bought for the trip. At fifteen months, she was long weaned; and though she seemed content with that fact, Brionney found herself missing the closeness that had been theirs alone. The baby's white hair had grown slightly longer, and it streamed back in the gentle breeze, fanning out over the top part of the car seat.

Satisfied, Brionney settled back in her seat to do some serious studying, despite the weariness that tugged on her eyelids. Sometime later, a voice came to her from far away. "Wake up, honey. We're here."

She forced open her eyes. "Already? Oh, I fell asleep. I'm sorry."

"You were tired. Too much studying." Jesse took the book from her lap and closed it with a snap. "Come on. Don't worry about the luggage. I'll come back for it after dinner."

The house where Jesse's parents lived was typical of the older homes in Arizona, a touch of Mexico modernized. Its stucco exterior was freshly painted white, except for the large porch supports, which were a reddish color. On the porch stood a white swing and many potted plants, most of which were full of bright flowers of nearly every color. The yard was shaded by mature palm trees, and a waterfall bird-bath graced the right corner. On that same side of the house there was a stone walkway, lined with vine-covered lattices leading to the back. It was picturesque and more than a little daunting.

Jesse took Savannah from her seat. Wide awake now, she was ready for exploring. "Not yet," he told her as she kicked to get down.

The house was no longer quiet. People inside had noticed their arrival and began pouring out the front door. A middle-aged couple were the first down the steps. Both had dark hair, but the man was as tall as the woman was petite. He had hazel eyes and a pale complexion, while her eyes were brown and her face an attractive olive tone. They were followed by two old ladies with pasty-white faces and two darting children. Bringing up the rear was a woman near Talia's age who had bleached hair and a toddler in her arms. Brionney knew this woman must be Jesse's sister.

The children may have been slow out the door, but they were the first ones to reach the driveway. Both boys had dark blond hair and large brown eyes. "Uncle Jesse, Uncle Jesse!" they chorused. He bent to hug them, rather awkwardly with Savannah in his arms. Savannah watched the children with interest, but drew back when they touched her arm, burying her face in Jesse's shoulder.

"Easy," Jesse said. "She doesn't know you guys yet." The others had arrived, and he made introductions. "Everyone, this is Brionney Fields, my fiancée, and this is my future daughter, Savannah." He turned to Brionney. "These two beautiful ladies are my grandmothers. This is Great-grandma Hergarter and this is Great-grandma Burvon. We call them that to keep the great-grandkids from getting confused. And here are my parents, Janet and Robert, and my sister, Cathie. These three busy kids are hers." Jesse named them, but Brionney was still trying to remember his parents' names. She nodded, smiling, until her mouth felt frozen. So far everyone had been courteous, but Brionney thought his mother's greeting had been rather cool.

Janet Hergarter's dark hair was unmarred by streaks of gray, but there were fine lines around her eyes. "Come on in," she said, motioning to the house. "I'm glad we can finally meet you. Jesse's told us so much over the phone." But her brown eyes didn't agree with her words. They seemed hard and calculating. Brionney shivered despite the warmth of the day.

The rest of the relatives surrounded Jesse and talked nonstop to him as he entered the house. Brionney felt like an outsider. Then her eyes caught Jesse's sister's over the crowd and she gave Brionney a smile, wide and sincere and full of sympathy. Brionney smiled back, thinking that at least in Cathie she had found an ally.

In a short time, Savannah felt comfortable enough to get down and play. She and Cathie's little daughter, who was nearly two, played well together in the spacious family room, while the great-grandmothers watched with benevolent smiles. Both ladies were thin from the waist up, but one, who Brionney finally identified as Great-grandma Burvon, had a decidedly thick lower torso, and her loose, pasty skin was covered with dark age spots. The other lady appeared frail and her white skin paper-thin.

"She doesn't look much like Jesse," Great-grandma Burvon said loudly over the hum of the children's voices.

"That's because she's not really Jesse's," Great-grandma Hergarter replied with equal volume.

"I know, but it'd help if she looked a little like him."

How dare they! Brionney was stung by their words and glanced around for Jesse, who had disappeared into the kitchen with his parents.

"They don't mean to be rude," Cathie said, leaning forward conspiratorially. She sat on the chair next to the sofa where Brionney huddled. "They don't even know we can hear them. Both won't admit to being hard of hearing. Don't take offense. They just want what's best for Jesse. He's always been a favorite with them."

"I heard you were taking the missionary discussions," Brionney said, trying to change the subject. "Jesse told me."

"Yeah, the little weasel. Told me he'd baby-sit if I'd listen. You'd think a little brother would be good at least for some unconditional baby-sitting, wouldn't you?" She grinned.

"So how'd it go?"

Her tanned face burned with excitement. She scanned the living room, as if searching the elegant furnishings for spies. Only the old grandmothers and children were in sight. "Promise you won't tell Jesse?" she whispered. "At least until I tell him myself?" When Brionney nodded, she continued, "Well, I'm getting baptized on Saturday. Before you go back to Utah. Just me, not Phil, though I still have hopes that by the time the children are old enough to be baptized, he'll have . . . anyway, I've waited since July for Phil to decide, and I'm not waiting any more. When Jesse told us two weeks ago that you were coming, I set up a special baptismal meeting. I'm going to ask Jesse to baptize me."

"He'll be so happy!"

"I know. I can't believe I've waited so long. I mean, I should have taken the discussions years ago. But my parents . . . well, never mind. I'm just so glad that Jesse listened when I wouldn't."

"What does your husband say?"

"He didn't want me to at first. He thought it was a cult, but he's softened up. He goes to church almost every Sunday with me now. He says it's to make sure they're not brainwashing me, but I think he secretly enjoys it." She laughed.

"Where is he now?"

"Working." She made a face. "Lousy, isn't it? He's a police officer and it's his turn to take the holiday shift. But we'll have another dinner later with just us and the kids."

"Time for dinner," Janet announced, coming into the living room.

"Yeah!" Cathie's two boys shouted, appearing from nowhere.

"What'd she say?" asked Great-grandma Burvon.

"A fine swimmer," replied Great-grandma Hergarter, leaning forward to speak in her ear.

"Who's a fine swimmer? I thought they drained the pool already." The wrinkles in Great-grandma Burvon's face grew deeper as she frowned in confusion.

"No, it's time for dinner. To eat," Cathie said loudly, gesturing as if putting a spoon to her mouth.

"Oh, well, why didn't she say so?" They struggled to their feet and shuffled into the kitchen. Brionney hid a smile in Savannah hair; she was beginning to like these old ladies, in spite of themselves.

Dinner was a considerably less-noisy affair than Brionney was accustomed to at Thanksgiving. Everyone sat around a long table covered with a hand-embroidered tablecloth topped with clear plastic. The dishes were of fine china, and Janet and Cathie kept a close eye on the children. The only concession to their age was that they were given glasses instead of the crystal champagne goblets the adults used.

"Sure you don't want any wine, son?" Robert said as he filled his goblet with a red substance. A ray of light danced in his eyes.

"No, thank you," Jesse replied. "What about you? Want some milk?"

"I'm long weaned," Robert replied.

Jesse chuckled and winked in Brionney's direction.

"What's weaned, Grandpa?" asked one of the boys.

"It's when you get too old to drink milk or juice."

"Oh, hush now, Robert. You'll make them think you're serious," Janet said.

He laughed. "I am serious."

Cathie explained what weaned really meant to the curious youngsters, which led to family memories. "When Grandma took Uncle Jesse's bottle away from him, you should have seen the tantrum he threw," she recalled. "He cried nonstop for a week, unless she put some honey on a cracker for him."

"I knew what I wanted even then," Jesse said with a grin.

Brionney could tell the family loved each other. There was plenty of teasing, but no rude or discourteous comments. Only when the approaching wedding came up did tension enter the dining room, creeping in almost unexpectedly.

"So you have to wait until February, do you?" Cathie said. "That's too bad."

There was silence before Janet spoke. "Well, I'm not sorry you have to wait a few more months." Her smile had vanished and the lines around her eyes seemed to stand out. "It's good not to rush into things. And getting married before graduating and having a steady job is always risky. A family takes a lot of work and money." She looked at Savannah pointedly.

"Nothing we're not ready for," Jesse said immediately. His voice was polite, but Brionney sensed a warning directed toward his mother. "And we've known each other since April, about seven months now."

"I don't like the idea that we can't be at the wedding," Robert said. "I know that your church is important to you, but we're your family. We should be able to see our son married."

"I wrote you about this," Jesse said. "When we get married, I want it to be for forever."

"The place isn't going to change that," Janet protested. "Why, even in your church people get divorced." She didn't glance in Brionney's direction, but the implication stabbed coldly into her heart.

"Please, Mom," Jesse pleaded. Brionney expected him to say more, but he seemed daunted by his parents. They glared at him, and he looked away, flushing. "It means a lot to me," he finished lamely.

This was a side of Jesse that Brionney had never seen before. He actually seemed afraid to confront his parents, to tell them why the temple was important to him. Why wouldn't he stand up to them?

"Jesse's right," Cathie said when the lull in the conversation threatened to plunge into conspicuous silence. "I hope to get married in the temple someday and have the children sealed to us." She paused only a second before dropping the rest of the bombshell. "On Saturday, I want Jesse to baptize me."

"What?" The faces around the table all turned in her direction. The children showed surprise, while the expressions plastered on Jesse's parents' faces were more akin to horror.

"I'm getting baptized on Saturday. I want to be a Mormon."

"That's great!" Jesse jumped up and ran around the table to hug his sister. "I'd be honored to baptize you." Out of the corner of his eye, he darted a nervous glance at his parents.

"Will you come?" Cathie asked Janet and Robert. The nervousness in her voice told Brionney all too plainly that Cathie had waited to tell her parents about her impending baptism precisely so that Jesse would be there to support her.

The Hergarters stared at their daughter. Robert's face was red, and he appeared ready to burst. The silence was thick, unnoticed only by the great-grandmothers who ate as if nothing had happened. Occasionally Robert and Janet moved their stares to Brionney, as if she were to blame.

"Well?" Cathie asked.

"No!" Robert sent his clenched fist crashing down onto the table. The china clattered, and Cathie's daughter spilled her milk. Her mother and grandmother rushed to clean it up. Robert stood and left the room.

"I said I was getting baptized," Cathie murmured, "not planning to kill someone." She met Jesse's gaze helplessly, then both stared after their father.

Janet also stood from the table. "Dinner's ruined," she said. There were tears in her eyes and pain on her face. "Why did you do this today, of all days? Couldn't we for once have some peace without that stupid church getting in the way?" Without excusing herself she ran from the table, sobbing. Muttering, the great-grandmothers arose and followed her.

Cathie bit her lip and stared into space. Jesse did the same. The silence was so thick that Brionney wanted to scream. So this was what Jesse had been up against when he had decided to be baptized. No wonder it had taken him three years!

This family loved each other dearly, but they were falling apart. Not only did they not approve of Jesse's marriage, they blamed it all on the Church. And Cathie's baptism was apparently the last straw. The pain Brionney saw in Jesse's face was almost too much to bear. She arose and went to stand by his chair, placing her hands on his shoulders. He covered one of her hands with his.

Cathie focused on them abruptly, tears sliding slowly down her cheeks. "I can't do it. I know it's true, but I can't be baptized. I can't see them go through this again! Oh, why did I think it would be different? Come on, children, we're going home." She picked up her daughter and left the room. Her sons stared after her for a moment before grabbing a piece of turkey and making their escape.

"Maybe we should go, too," Jesse said.

Brionney shook her head. The situation wasn't pretty, but it had to be faced. But how could they get Robert and Janet to listen? How could they get them to accept their relationship and their religion?

CHAPTER NINETEEN

Jesse's appetite had suddenly deserted him. He had hoped the months of preparing his parents for his marriage would have softened their opposition to his continuing activity in the Church. The fact that Brionney had been married before and had a child made them look with even more suspicion upon their union.

"Come on," he said, standing.

"We can't leave." She looked at him steadily. Jesse knew she was right, but he was already weary of the battle. How many years had he fought them on this issue? Never once had they listened. "Jesse. They care about you."

"I know," he said. "Let's walk." Lifting Savannah from the high chair his mother normally used for Cathie's youngest, he led Brionney outside the double doors onto a covered redwood patio with ornate iron chairs. They continued on, descending three steps to a cobblestone path that led through the grass past the rock work that surrounded the empty swimming pool. Brionney looked around with interest at the spacious yard, almost completely lined with trees and bushes.

"It's beautiful," she said as the path skirted one of the raised flowerbeds.

Despite his mood, Jesse relaxed. "Mom grew up where there were a lot of trees and open spaces. After they were married, she missed it. She and Dad bought this house because of the big backyard. It's her haven. There at the end is my favorite place."

They fell into a comfortable silence until they arrived at the far end of the yard where a wooden bench nestled under an old lilac tree. Setting Savannah on the bench between them, Jesse leaned back.

Brionney stared at a tree to their right. "If I didn't know better, I'd say your grapefruit tree has oranges and lemons . . . naw, can't be."

Jesse grinned. "Yes it can. We could never eat all the fruit each tree had to give, so my grandfather came up with this a few years before he died. He grafted the different branches onto one tree, and it began to bear all three fruits. I don't even remember what this original tree was. After the first frost in October or November, the fruits begin to ripen and become really noticeable. That's probably why it drew your attention."

"That's incredible."

Savannah jumped off the bench and walked over to the tree, trying to reach a yellow grapefruit. Jesse lifted her up to pluck the fruit. She laughed and threw it to the ground. "Ball," she announced.

Jesse felt his heart lighten further. If only his parents would give Brionney and Savannah a chance! They meant so much to him!

"It kind of reminds me of your family," Brionney said.

"What?"

"The tree. They're all so different, yet alike enough to flourish together."

Jesse's frown returned. "Not if my father has his way," he said bitterly. "He has been an inactive Catholic his whole life. As his parents were before him. He likes tradition and he hates the Church. He hates everything about it."

"It doesn't make sense. I mean, the gospel doesn't have anything in it to make him so angry." She studied him for a few moments before coming up with one of the insights he so loved her for. "Jesse, you've never really talked to your parents about the gospel, have you?"

He shook his head ruefully. "They get so angry, especially my father. He just blows up. It makes me feel like I did as a kid when I stole some money once from my mother's purse." He gave a snort. "You can bet I never did that again. But the gospel isn't something bad, and I can't live without it. I keep thinking the years will soften them, but things only go well when I don't mention the Church at all. I don't know what to do. Sometimes I wish I could just tie them up, put on a gag, and talk to them until I'm blue in the face."

"Maybe that's what we should do. Or something like it. There has to be some way."

"There isn't. I've tried everything."

Brionney stared at him. "What? This doesn't sound like the Jesse I know. You never gave up on me."

He gave her a sheepish smile. "I guess I love you more than I love them. Don't worry, Bri. I'm not going to let them break us up, if that's what's worrying you. If they don't want to be a part of the life I choose, I can't make them, but I won't give you and Savannah up."

Brionney hugged him. "I'm sorry."

"No, I'm sorry. I know this isn't easy for you. That's one of the reasons I wanted you to meet my parents. I didn't feel it was fair for you to marry me not knowing what to expect. But I really hoped things would be different this time. I thought maybe they would have changed. I'm sorry to have put you in the middle." Jesse knew now that coming to Arizona had been a big mistake. His love for Brionney had him walking on clouds. He had hoped the miracle of their love would extend to his family.

"Maybe things *will* be different." Brionney took the grapefruit Savannah handed her. "I mean, we really haven't tried."

"You saw how they reacted to Cathie's announcement. It would probably be better if we leave. Or maybe we can go to Debbie's."

"I would like nothing better, Jesse. But we can't. Cathie needs your support. She needs it now. We can't desert her."

Jesse remembered only too well the torture he had endured alone when he had struggled to accept the gospel against his parents' wishes. Even Cathie had been against him then. Brionney was right. He couldn't leave his sister to face the same fight alone. There was always the chance she wouldn't be up to it—he hadn't been, not for years. "They'd never agree to see the missionaries."

"Well, you were a missionary. You could do it."

"They wouldn't listen."

They stared at each other in silence. "I think you're afraid," Brionney said.

Jesse felt his face flush. Oh, how he hated that telltale sign! "I'm not!"

"Aren't you? Tell me, what would you do if they weren't your parents, but people you met on your mission? Would you give up so easily?"

He glared at her. "That's different. I'll have to deal with my parents forever."

"Exactly." She touched his arm. "Jesse, when I was married to Derek, I was always afraid to go against his wishes. I never wanted to make him angry. But you know what? It didn't do any good. I gave everything I could to keep my marriage, but the only time he showed me any respect was when I stood up for what I believed—even though that meant excluding him from my life. Don't you see, Jesse? You have to tell your parents about what's important to you and why."

Jesse made a fist and hit it into his other palm repeatedly, thinking of his father's angry face. "What if he doesn't listen?"

"Speak louder. Hold him down. I don't know. But you have to really try—like it's your last shot."

Jesse felt his anger ebb. As it did, he realized that he was angry at himself, not at Brionney. She loved him enough to tell him the truth.

"On my mission," he said more calmly, "I would often work the discussions into the conversations. That way the investigators would still hear them, but not realize they were being taught until they felt the Spirit."

"Have you ever tried it with your parents?"

"No, not exactly. I mean I've tried, but I never got very far. Maybe I need a mixture of techniques." He paused, thinking. "I guess I am afraid—just like I was afraid to go against their wishes and be baptized in the first place."

"That was a long time ago. You've changed."

He appreciated her faith, but still doubted. "Have I?"

"Yes, you have." She grabbed his hand. "And I'll be right there with you in case you need me. After all, these are Savannah's grandparents we're talking about."

Jesse smiled and kissed her. "Now I know why I love you so much."

She clung to him. "Oh, Jesse. I doubt you'll ever know how much you've given back to me by loving me."

Despite her sincerity, Jesse knew that she was the one who had given him the most wonderful things in life—love, courage, and hope. She was his life, and he would spend the rest of his trying to make her happy.

They walked back to the house in comfortable silence, Savannah toddling between them. As they arrived on the porch, the sound of raised voices shook Jesse's newly gained serenity.

"You can't disown her!" his mother was saying. "You saw that it did no good with Jesse. It just made things worse!"

"I can and I will. This sort of rebellion I expect from a son, but not from a daughter."

"She's a grown woman. She can make her own decisions."

"That doesn't seem very apparent. I can't believe either of them are our children!"

"They've always been good!" Janet protested.

"Well, I don't like the idea of Jesse getting married in a place we aren't invited. The next thing you know, they won't let us see the grandchildren because we'll corrupt them. Well, I won't stand for it!"

Jesse felt his heart begin pounding. Anger and fear settled in his gut. Brionney grabbed his hand and kept walking into the house. His parents stopped as they heard the door. His father met Jesse's gaze, then looked away.

"I'm going to take our mothers home," Robert said. He whirled on his heel and left. Jesse started to follow, but Janet put a hand on his arm.

"He needs to cool down first," she said. Jesse nodded, but stared in the direction his father had taken. *Dad, stop!* his heart cried out. Of course there was no response. What could Jesse say to make him listen?

As Jesse stood there, he saw Brionney cross into the adjoining dining room and collect a stack of dishes from the table, carefully, as though remembering they were fine china. Janet smiled at her, a real smile, if a bit thin and watery, and began filling up the sink. Ignoring the dishwasher as she always did with these special dishes, she lovingly cleaned the plates with a soft sponge. Jesse sighed as the tension faded from the room. He helped Brionney bring the plates to the sink.

"It isn't good to let the food dry on them," Janet said.

Brionney admired a plate. "They're beautiful."

"Thank you. They were my grandmother's."

They worked on in silence, with Janet washing, Brionney and Jesse rinsing and drying. Janet began to loosen up. As if it was the only safe subject, she chattered away about her grandmother, with no sign of animosity toward them. Jesse wondered if she was embarrassed at the whole situation and if she was trying to make up for his father's anger. She was a good woman, wife, and mother. Why couldn't she listen to the truth?

During the cleanup, Savannah toddled near Brionney's legs and kept getting in the way. "Are you a little pest?" Brionney asked, picking her up and tickling her. Savannah grinned and nodded.

"Momma," she gurgled. Then she did a strange thing. She pointed at Janet, who had turned to watch them. "Ga'ma," she said.

Janet's eyebrows rose. "Did she say Grandma?"

"Yes. She's been saying it for a long time because of my mom, but I didn't realize she connected the word with you."

Jesse couldn't help but smile. Just as he had practiced with Savannah, teaching her to blow out the birthday candles, he had shown Savannah pictures of his parents and taught her to say Ga'ma and Ga'pa.

"Yes, I'm going to be your grandma," Janet said, seeming pleased. She smiled at Savannah, who reached up to touch her mouth. Janet kissed the little hand.

"Ga'ma," Savannah said again more clearly.

Jesse laughed and Savannah held out her arms to him. "Daddy." He grabbed the baby from Brionney and whirled her around in a circle.

"Isn't she the smartest baby?" he said

"I can't believe she called me Grandma." Janet gazed at Jesse with a new expression. He hoped she could see the love he had for Savannah, and her return love for him. *I may not be her biological father,* he wanted to say to his mother, *but I am her father.*

Janet said nothing, but tentatively held out her arms. Savannah went to her, and in that instant won Janet over and cut Jesse's problems in half. He felt love from heaven shower down on them, drawing them together and making them a real family. It was a beginning.

He didn't know how he would face his father, or what he would say. But Brionney was right: it was now or never. *Dear Father,* he prayed, *please soften his heart.*

How many times had he said that exact prayer? Too many to count. Perhaps now it was time for the prayer to be answered.

CHAPTER TWENTY

Jesse didn't hear his father return until late that night. He heard voices, but this time they weren't angry. Jesse slipped out of bed and added one extra prayer, pleading for the courage and strength that had always failed him every time he had faced his father.

Friday morning came, and he awoke to the smell of pancakes. He changed his clothes, splashed water on his face, and walked toward the kitchen. Robert stood at the stove, while Janet set dishes on the small kitchen table. Brionney was there, too, with Savannah, and for a moment Jesse watched them all from the hall.

"Did we wake you?" Janet was saying to Brionney.

"No, Savannah did. Is Jesse up?"

"He hasn't come down yet." Janet pulled back a chair from the table. "Have a seat."

"Thank you. It smells good. May I help?"

"No, this is Robert's specialty," Janet said. "He likes to make them."

"It's a secret recipe," Robert said. "A little of this and a little of that. It takes a master cook."

Janet laughed. "Yeah, right," she said dryly. "It's the only thing he knows how to make."

"I'm a specialist, that's all."

As they all laughed, Jesse noticed how relaxed his father was. Why couldn't he be that way when Jesse tried to talk to him about the things that really mattered?

"You two remind me of my parents," Brionney said. "I think you'll like them when you meet them."

Robert's smile dimmed slightly. "Are they members of your

church?" His voice was deceptively calm, and Jesse knew too well what storm raged underneath.

"Robert," Janet warned.

Brionney looked at them sadly, and Jesse knew it was time to interfere. He wouldn't let her face them alone.

"Yes, they are members," he said from the doorway. Brionney smiled at him in relief. He went to her and kissed both her and Savannah on the cheek. "Good morning."

"So they'll be going to your wedding?" Robert held the spatula in mid-air, as if conducting a symphony.

Jesse turned back to his father, nodding. Brionney squeezed his hand and urged him to speak. He took a deep breath. "I know you both are upset about my decision, but I feel I deserve a chance to explain why I feel the way I do, why it is so important to me."

"We know that you've gone against our will and are doing it again," Robert said tightly. "You are going against our traditions." The spatula clattered to the counter top.

Jesse knew his face was turning red. He wished he could leave, but Brionney's presence kept him in the room. In that instant he was transported back to his youth, and he felt frozen in fear. As if sensing this, Brionney stood next to him. "Jesse loves you both so much," she said. "If what he's doing is so important to him that he's willing to go against your wishes, shouldn't you at least understand why?"

Robert glared at her, but Brionney met his gaze evenly. Jesse wondered how many times she had faced Derek and pleaded with him. So much courage! So much love! Could he do any less?

Robert's eyes flashed now. The storm was about to break.

"Dad!" Jesse said in an agonized voice. "Dad!" He didn't say anything else, but tears filled his eyes.

Robert stared at him. "I don't want to hear your nonsense. I want my son back. The man I raised him to be!"

In another minute Jesse knew something would crash to the ground, and Robert would begin to rant in earnest. Then he would leave or Jesse would. It had always ended that way.

Not today! his soul cried.

He couldn't win his father in a word fight. He couldn't *make* him listen. The only option left was an appeal to his heart.

Jesse took a step toward his father, then fell to his knees. "Dad," he cried again. "Please." Tears were flowing now. "Please, Dad, I beg you to hear me! I love you so much. I've always tried to be a good son, but this is ripping me apart. Can't you see? It's ripping our whole family apart. If you ever loved me enough to call me your son, please hear me! Please love me!"

Jesse let his head drop, unwilling to see the anger and hatred in his father's gaze. He couldn't bear to watch him turn his back and walk out the door. He knew it would be the last time he would see his father's face. The silence was thick and deep. Jesse's heart wanted to explode. He prayed silently with all his being.

There was a gentle touch on his shoulder. He thought for a moment it was Brionney or his mother, trying to tell him that Robert had gone. He looked up and stared into . . . his father's face. "Son," Robert said in a choked voice, "I do love you." He took Jesse's hand and helped him to his feet, pulling him close in an embrace Jesse had long craved.

My father loves me!

"Okay," Robert said quietly. "I may not like it, but I'll listen to what you have to say."

Jesse hugged his father tightly. "Thank you, Dad. That's all I ask."

* * * * *

"So you believe that by marrying in the temple," Robert said to Jesse in the car on the way to the stake center, "you will be married for eternity."

Brionney smiled. Since Jesse and Robert had spent hours talking yesterday after the near disaster at breakfast, Robert had been asking many questions. At times he was irritated at Jesse's answers, but the anger he had displayed before had vanished. With his growing understanding of the Church, he had even withdrawn his objection to Cathie's baptism, albeit somewhat reluctantly.

"Exactly," Jesse said. "I love Brionney and want to promise her that love forever. We want to start out with an eternal commitment, not until death do us part. You and Mom both believe in life after death, so what kind of promise is it to stay together only until you die? Can you understand that I want more than that?"

"Well, I don't see what getting married in a certain building has to do with it. I believe your mother and I will always be together, regardless."

"It's the authority that's important," Jesse explained. "And it's not something to be left to chance."

Brionney listened with the others as Jesse launched into an involved explanation about the priesthood and its restoration. *I'll bet you were a good missionary,* she thought. She was proud of Jesse. His heartfelt plea to his father had been unexpected, but exactly what was needed. When it really mattered, Jesse hadn't been afraid to risk his heart. This was the man she would be marrying. Love swelled in her breast, and also thankfulness to a Father in Heaven who had given them so much.

They arrived at the stake center well before the special baptismal service where Cathie and two other ladies the missionaries had been teaching were to be baptized. As her father came into the room, Cathie, dressed all in white, looked at him anxiously. Brionney and Jesse had told her about Robert's change of heart—which was why she decided to go through with the baptism—but fear still lurked on her face. Brionney understood her feelings. Jesse had been struggling with Robert for over five years because of the gospel, and it was hard to believe that he had finally found some degree of acceptance in Robert's heart.

Robert walked up to Cathie. Phil, Cathie's husband, stood by her firmly, holding her hand. Robert nodded in greeting, but his eyes didn't leave his daughter's face. "Cathie, you are old enough to make up your own mind. I don't understand the appeal this church has for you—well, maybe I'm beginning to, a little—but I am your father and I will support you. That's why I'm here."

Cathie let go of her husband's hand and hugged her father. "Thank you, Daddy," she said. "That means so much to me."

The opening music began and everyone took their seats. Brionney and Savannah sat next to Debbie and Max, who had been invited to the service. Jesse gave a wonderful talk on baptism, and afterwards they filed into the room with the baptismal font. Cathie appeared radiant as she waded into the water where Jesse stood waiting. Her children crowded close to the font, threatening to fall into the warm water. Phil tried to restrain them, but their excitement was catching, and the feeling permeated everyone. Cathie emerged from the water, smiling as shining droplets fell from her face and body. She hugged Jesse tightly in thanks. With surprise, Brionney noticed Janet had tears in her eyes, and even Robert was smiling.

To celebrate Cathie's baptism, they went out to dinner at a nice restaurant on the fourth floor of a hotel. One entire side of the restaurant had huge glass windows overlooking the city. The lights shone brightly and reflected off the glass, adding to the festive atmosphere. With Debbie once more the center of attention, there was a lot of laughter at the table. Robert and Janet seemed to get along wonderfully with both Debbie and Max.

"I think it helps my dad to see that there are older, intelligent people who believe in the gospel as well as us youngsters," Jesse whispered to Brionney.

"I'm just wondering when Debbie'll offer your mom some quilts—or maybe even recruit her to help distribute them." They giggled together.

"Hey," Jesse said, "let's take Savannah out on the patio there to see the lights while we're waiting for the food to come."

Brionney followed him through a door that led to an outside patio where, during the warmer months, people dined under the light of the moon. A few other couples were outside, but they were far enough away that Brionney felt she and Jesse were alone. He put his arms around her as they stood facing the railing, Brionney's back cuddled against his chest. In Brionney's arms, Savannah's eyes were wide as her chubby hands pointed at one new miracle after another. "We're going to be so happy," Jesse murmured in Brionney's ear.

"I know." She turned to let him kiss her. Looking up, Brionney could see the stars, glittering with promise. It was good to be in Arizona with Jesse, making pleasant memories instead of those that brought pain.

Then a familiar smell broke the mood. "Ah-oh, one of us has to go change Savannah."

Jesse sighed. "I'll do it. When do we start potty-training her, anyway?"

"I'll ask Talia when we get home. But I don't think it's for a while yet; she's only fifteen months."

He kissed her again before carrying Savannah inside. A breeze wafted from somewhere below, carrying the delicious smell of freshly baked bread. Brionney breathed in deeply, for a moment transported back to her childhood and her mother's kitchen. Who ever thought she could be this happy now, when just a year before she had been living in insecurity and pain, not knowing where the future would lead?

"It almost makes me like the city," a soft voice said behind her. "The lights, I mean."

Brionney turned her head and smiled at Janet. "Yes. It does."

Janet breathed in the smell of the bread. "Mmm. Reminds me of my mother."

Brionney chuckled. "Me too."

"You know, Brionney," she said, looking out into the night. She paused as if not knowing how to continue, then hurried on in a rush. "I didn't like the idea of Jesse marrying someone with a child. And I didn't approve of him getting married before finishing college, either. I still don't."

Fear at what she would say next curled up Brionney's spine. And just when she thought the battle was over! Brionney turned to face Janet, her hands gripping the metal railing, determined to fight for Jesse, for what they meant to each other.

"But I really like you," Janet went on, staring at the darkness, unaware of Brionney's turmoil. "You know, yesterday was the first time Jesse and his father talked about his religion. I know it took a lot of courage for Jesse to stand up to his father that way. As a result, I think both Robert and I are finally beginning to understand him. And I think we have you to thank for that. You seem to give him courage."

"In the end, Jesse will always do what is right."

She laughed. "I can see what he loves about you. You have made him happy, as I always wanted him to be. Perhaps I've been a fool, unwilling to lose my little boy, but I do think that you two will be happy. And Savannah." Her gaze became tender. "I couldn't ask for a more adorable granddaughter. I can see how much Jesse loves her, and you."

"I'd like him to adopt her someday. He'll be a good father."

She nodded, taking another deep breath. "That's what I wanted to talk to you about. Children. I'm learning that your church holds families very sacred, and I admire that, but I worry that you and Jesse may jump into having more children without giving him time to adjust to the responsibility of a wife and a child. It will be a struggle for him, mentally and financially, no matter how prepared you think he might be."

"What are you saying—that we shouldn't have children?"

"No, not that. Just wait for a few years. Let him get his feet on the ground. I know there's no stopping your marriage, and I don't want to, but children could wait a little while, don't you think? It's really best for you, too."

Brionney bit her lip as the faces of her sisters' new babies came to her mind. They were so small and innocent, straight from heaven. Oh, how much Brionney longed for Jesse's baby! She could almost see the infant, with brown eyes and dark hair framing its face, looking much like the baby pictures of Jesse that Janet had shown her. No matter how much Brionney loved Savannah, she wanted that baby, as if it would somehow complete their family. Sharp words of rebuke came to her mind. What right did Janet have to tell them when to have children? Her words reminded Brionney distinctly of how Kris had warned her to put off having children until she knew the marriage with Derek would last.

As if reading Brionney's mind, Janet spoke, "I know the decision is yours and Jesse's, but he'll listen to you. He wants to make you happy. But will an extra burden bring him down? You never know for sure, but it might, and I just want you both to be happy. Can't you see how giving him time will be to your advantage in the long run?"

Doubt reared its ugly head. Brionney had been so certain Jesse wanted a baby right away, but now she wondered if Janet was right. Maybe another child was a lot to ask of him so soon. Maybe they needed time to grow together. Brionney loved Jesse enough to have patience.

She met Janet's stare. "Don't worry. I'll give him time. When we both decide we're ready, we'll have more children."

Janet smiled. "Thank you, Brionney." Without another word, she turned and strode into the inner restaurant.

Brionney sighed, having lost the joy in night lights and the enticing smells from below. Would she ever be allowed to live a normal life? To forget about the past and forge on ahead, unhindered? How she wished it had been Jesse instead of Derek she had met three years earlier! Then she remembered Savannah and took the wish back. Savannah was worth everything she had to go through.

"All clean and new," Jesse said. Brionney turned from the railing, reaching for Savannah. Cuddling her close, she breathed in her baby smell, stifling the visions of newborns that flashed in her mind.

"Hey, I want some of that," Jesse said. He leaned over from behind, encircling them again in his arms. His breath was warm on Brionney's neck. "I missed you."

Her smile returned. "You were gone five minutes."

"It was too long." Sometimes he was so corny—and romantic. Brionney turned to tease him, but stiffened. "What's wrong?" Jesse asked.

Brionney's jaw clenched as she stared over Jesse's shoulder. *Him.* No, not here, not like this. She did need to contact him, but had hoped to do it through Debbie. She blinked, trying to clear her vision, but he was still there, flawlessly groomed, face tanned, exquisitely dressed. *She* was there with him, her brown hair sprayed to perfection and her green dress plunging daringly in the front. They walked languidly in Brionney's direction, heading toward a vacant part of the railing. Courtesy would require Brionney to say something if they saw her. Maybe she and Jesse could slip away. Or maybe if she could turn back to the railing, they would walk past without—

"Who is it?" Jesse turned before Brionney could stop him, drawing the couple's attention. Recognition washed over their faces.

"Derek," Brionney whispered. Jesse said nothing, but put his arm more firmly around her.

"Hello, Brionney," Derek said, pausing in his stride. He seemed so familiar, yet different somehow.

"Yes, hello," drawled Melinda. "So nice to see you again. I suppose you heard about our marriage?" She waved her hand near Brionney and a large diamond flashed in the lights.

"Yes, I heard," Brionney said stiffly. "Congratulations."

Melinda was no longer paying attention to her. "Oh," she cooed, "is this little Savannah? Derek, she looks just like you! All that blonde hair and blue eyes. Come here, honey. Come see your daddy's new wife." She held out her slender arms, but Savannah turned away, shaking her head. Melinda appeared frustrated, and glanced at Derek for support.

"Hi, Savannah, remember me?" Derek said. Once again, Savannah turned away, bringing an angry scowl to Derek's face.

"You haven't seen her for a year," Brionney said. "Since she was two and a half months. You can't expect her to remember."

"So what are you doing in Arizona?" Melinda asked, still staring at Savannah.

"I came to meet my new in-laws. I'm getting married again. This is my fiancé, Jesse Hergarter."

"Oh, that's right. That's why Derek had to write that letter."

"They lost it," Brionney said, looking at Derek. "That's why I asked you for another one. Did you send it yet?"

Melinda's head swiveled toward Derek. "You didn't tell me that."

"I forgot," Derek said, but Brionney knew he lied. He hadn't written another letter because he hadn't wanted to.

"It'll take longer without your letter," Jesse said pointedly, "but eventually they will still grant the cancellation. We'd rather get married right away."

Derek's gaze was mocking. "There's nothing stopping you."

"We want to be sealed in the temple. We consider that important." The men stared at each other, and for a moment Brionney thought they might come to blows. "We'd appreciate it," Jesse added tightly. Brionney could tell how much it cost him to be polite.

"Daddy," Savannah said, seemingly puzzled at the odd note in Jesse's voice. She held out her arms to him. Brionney studied Derek, but this time there was no visible reaction except the tensing of his jaw muscles.

"Derek will get it taken care of right away, I'm sure," Melinda said. "And how wonderful for you. You'll be a complete little family now. Will you be trying for more children soon?"

As if it were any of her business! "Oh, in a year or so, right Jesse?" Brionney said. "We don't want to rush things." She almost wished Jesse would deny her statement, but he nodded in agreement.

"Derek and I are trying to have a baby of our own, you know," Melinda rushed on, patting her flat stomach. The hand on her tight dress called to attention the slender elegance that left Brionney feeling so awkward and overweight. Suddenly, it was too much for her to bear.

"So soon? Up for any more promotions, Derek?" Brionney said with false sweetness.

Anger flashed in Melinda's eyes. "We *want* a baby," she retorted. "And we've known each other a long time." Then her eyes grew soft as they rested once again on Savannah, making Brionney wonder how long she had been trying to get pregnant. "But since you're in town, maybe Savannah would like to spend a little time with her daddy and me. Just a day or so. How about tomorrow?" As she finished speaking, she stared hard at Derek, eyes pleading. He shrugged.

Panic attacked Brionney's heart. *What does this woman want with my child?* Savannah didn't know these people, and Brionney certainly didn't trust their lifestyle; there was no way she would let her baby go with them. The request made Brionney so angry and afraid that she couldn't speak. She jerked her head toward Jesse, looking for support. Jesse didn't see her desperation, but was already shaking his head.

"I'm sorry, but we're leaving for Utah tomorrow morning after sacrament meeting. We're both in school and have to get back by Monday. There's no time for Savannah to get used to you before we go, and we don't leave her with people she doesn't know." Jesse's chin went up in the air slightly, as if daring them to challenge his right to make such a decision. Derek glared down at him from his taller vantage point.

Brionney wanted to yell out that the divorce settlement had not included visitation rights, but prudence stilled her tongue. No use in getting Derek mad. That might cause Savannah problems in the long run. Besides, she needed his cooperation.

Derek finally looked away from Jesse's stare, and Brionney felt as though she and Jesse had won a small battle. "So, should I have Debbie stop by for the letter?" she asked.

Derek shook his head and again flashed her that mocking smile. "I'll send it."

Brionney knew he lied again. She couldn't understand why he wouldn't give her what she needed without dragging it out. He had remarried and gone on with his life. Why couldn't he allow her to do the same?

"I'm sure it'll be nice for you not to have to pay alimony anymore." There was no mistaking the irony in Jesse's voice. Derek's smiled faded. Jesse appeared not to notice the effect of his words, but his jaw twitched as though he might start laughing at Derek's reaction. Instead, he motioned to the door with his chin. "We'd better get back to our table, honey. Our order must be nearly ready. Besides, it's getting a little cold out here for the baby, don't you think?"

Without another word they walked away, but Brionney could feel eyes boring into her back, fierce with hatred. The stare came from

Melinda, she was sure, not Derek, who had never really cared about Savannah. Brionney didn't know which bothered her more.

"You were great, Jesse." Brionney hugged him with feeling. She would be on Jesse's side against Derek any day.

They settled back at their table with the others just as their meal arrived. Brionney tried to enjoy herself, but all the while the echo repeated in her head: *What does that woman want with my baby?*

CHAPTER TWENTY-ONE

Two days later, Brionney sat next to Talia on her back porch. "He'll never write another letter. I just know it. For some reason, he doesn't want me to be sealed."

"Maybe he believes in the gospel enough to know that he can't get to heaven unless he's sealed."

"Ha! Like he'd go to heaven anyway. No. I think he's doing it just for spite. You should have seen his face when Savannah called Jesse daddy."

"That doesn't make sense. He gave up visitation, after all."

"He was just mad that someone else came out on top." Brionney sighed. "Oh, how could I have ever loved that man? He's so irritating!"

Talia patted her shoulder. "Everything's going to be all right. Try not to worry so much. You've said yourself that he's caught up about money. Eventually he'll write the letter. He'll make you suffer, but he'll write it."

Jesse had told Brionney the same thing. He had also asked everyone close to them to pray for their case. On Tuesday they attended the temple and put their own names on the prayer roll.

Wednesday morning, the bishop called with wonderful news. Brionney could hardly wait to get off work that afternoon to tell Jesse and Savannah, though the baby would hardly understand.

Thinking of Savannah brought feelings of guilt to Brionney's heart. She had become too rambunctious to take to work and now spent those hours at Talia's or with her grandmother. Every time Brionney looked at her daughter, it seemed she had grown another inch. And though Brionney only worked part-time, it was always Talia or Irene who was around when Savannah did something new. Brionney felt she was missing out.

The phone rang and Brionney grabbed it, hoping it was Jesse instead of a client. Maybe he would have time to come by so she could tell him the news. At least something was finally going right.

But it was Talia, calling from home. "Savannah fell, and it looks like she will have to have stitches. On her head. I'm taking her to the doctor now, and I thought you'd probably want to meet us there."

"Is she okay?"

"Besides the cut, yes. But she's crying for you. It's so hard at this age. They don't understand."

"I'll be right there. Tell them to wait for me. I want to be with her." Without waiting for an answer, Brionney hung up, grabbing for her purse. She nearly flew into her father's office. Quickly, she explained the situation.

"She'll be fine," he said. "These things happen."

"I know, but I should have been there."

"Do you want me to come with you?"

"No, Talia's there."

"Shall I call Jesse?"

Brionney paused. She could handle it herself, but it would be good to have him with her to face Savannah's first emergency doctor visit since the accident with Derek. Besides, he would want to know. She checked her watch. "Yes, but he's at work right now. I don't know if he can get away. And I'm not sure what time he has his next class."

"Well, you go ahead and I'll find the number at your desk. Then Jesse can decide what to do."

She flashed a smile. "Thanks, Dad."

On the way to the doctor's office, Brionney couldn't help her tears. She had been around children enough to know Talia hadn't been negligent, and that accidents happened, but her guilt increased. Even if she couldn't have prevented it, she should have been there to comfort Savannah and to take her to the doctor. Brionney felt miserable. Savannah was growing up too fast. *And I'm just a part-time mother.*

In ten minutes, Brionney arrived at the doctor's office in the car she was still borrowing from her mother. Talia was already in the parking lot, waiting for her. "So how'd it happen?" Brionney asked, scooping Savannah out of her car seat and holding her close. The little girl whimpered and clung to Brionney as she peeked under the cloth Talia had tied around her head. The inch-long gash was deep and still bleeding.

"Put a little pressure on it," Talia said. She bent to release Roger from his car seat. "She fell up the back stairs."

"*Up* the stairs?"

"Yes, she was trying to carry an armload of toys and fell. If she hadn't been carrying anything, it wouldn't have happened. I was in the yard and saw her going up, but I didn't reach her in time. I have told her a million times not to climb those stairs while she's carrying stuff. It would be different if they weren't cement."

Brionney had told Savannah a million times, too, so she felt sympathy for Talia. "Well, you couldn't have stopped it. It's not your fault."

Talia opened the door to the doctor's office. "I know, but it doesn't make me feel any better."

They signed in and waited to be admitted. After a long time, a nurse led them to an examination room. The door had barely shut when Jesse burst in, his expression worried.

"What happened?" he asked, eyes going to Savannah. She smiled at him and held out her arms, but Brionney laid her on the examination table.

"Just stay still, Savannah," she said. Jesse crossed the short space and reached out for her hand. "She fell up the cement stairs at Talia's. The ones in the back."

Talia explained again to Jesse and then excused herself. "I'll be in the waiting room," she said. "The doctor won't have room to move with all of us here."

Jesse stroked Savannah's arm. "It's going to be okay, Savvy. We're right here with you." He glanced at Brionney. "Are you all right? You look pretty upset."

"I just feel guilty. I should have been there."

"It might have happened anyway."

"I know that! It's just that—" Brionney sighed loudly, looking down at Savannah's face. "With school and work, I feel like I'm missing out on her life. I should be with her more."

Jesse's eyes held hers, and Brionney was suddenly afraid of what he might say. Derek had wanted her to work, to bring in more money for his dreams instead of wasting time at home. She had learned that Jesse was nothing like Derek, but they had never talked about this before. "Maybe you should quit."

"School?"

"No, of course not. I know how important that is to you. I meant work."

"But—"

"I've been meaning to talk to you about this," he hurried on. "I mean, I admire you for how you can do it all, but I can't help thinking that Savannah needs you."

"I was only doing it to pay the rent," she said defensively.

"I know that. But I've worried about us depending on your income at all. So many of my friends have done that, saying their wives will work just until they get started, and ten years later they're still working and wanting to be home with their babies. Oh, Brionney, I believe in education, and I believe in a woman's self-esteem, but I also believe that being a mother is so much more important than money." He paused and looked thoughtful. "I remember when I was growing up. So many times I came home from school and no one was there to say hi or ask about my day. For many years I believed that my mother's job was more important than I was. I don't want any of our children to feel that way.

"I also feel that if you want to work part time because you need to get out of the house, or because you want to, then that's something we can work around. But if you're working because you feel you have to, that's quite another story. If you want to quit, I'm behind you completely. I'd rather scrape by for a few months than become dependent on your income. Like you said, Savannah will only be little once. She'll soon be in school, and maybe then you'll want to work again—or not. But for right now, your apartment's cheap enough that we can somehow make the payments. It certainly wouldn't pay to give it up, and I know how you feel about moving back with your parents. Maybe I could get another school loan or something. It's only until April when I graduate and get a good job. The important thing is that if you want to be with Savannah, you should be. The Lord has counseled women to be at home when their children are, and I believe He will provide a way for us to do that."

"You're willing to get a loan?" Brionney knew how important not getting deeper in debt was to him. Of course, she didn't think she could bring herself to take his money before they were married. She liked depending on herself.

"Yes. I'll get a loan, if that's what it takes. And this semester I've arranged to have one of the nights you are at school off, so I can watch Savannah. Or maybe take her to work after hours." He grinned at Brionney sheepishly. "When a dad baby-sits, it doesn't count as baby-sitting, right? That means she'll only be baby-sat one night a week by someone other than us—if you stop working. So how about it? Shall I get a loan?"

"No!"

Jesse didn't hide his surprise. "Why not?"

"I couldn't take your money."

"It would be our money."

Brionney shook her head. "I have some money," she said hesitantly. She had never mentioned the divorce settlement simply because it had never come up. Half of it Brionney had put into a savings bond for Savannah, and much of the rest had gone for tuition and books; but she still had enough for a few months' worth of rent and expenses. "In the divorce settlement, I got half the savings. I've been using it for school."

"Well, that's it then!" Jesse snapped his fingers. "Use that money and we'll pay for your schooling as we go. You've already paid for next semester, haven't you? And when I get a steady job next April, it'll be easy. The starting wage at most companies is about four times what I make now. Computer programmers are in demand."

Brionney didn't like the idea of using all her money; it was the only security she had. Having some back-up in the bank had given her great feeling of independence. "I don't know," she said.

Jesse watched Brionney, genuinely confused. "I don't understand, Brionney. You said you wanted to be at home. If you don't, that's fine. I don't want to push you into doing what I think is right. Just help me understand."

"I do want to be home. It's just that I'm . . ."

"Afraid."

Brionney nodded. "Of losing my independence. Of having to depend on someone else for my food and shelter and—"

"You're afraid of trusting me." His expression was sad.

"I do trust you." But Brionney knew he was right. Giving her trust to the wrong man had been one of the most painful lessons she had learned with Derek.

"I'll always take care of you." He put a hand on her arm and looked at her earnestly. "Everything I have will be yours, I promise. If it makes you feel better, you can keep charge of the checkbook after we're married. As long as we pay tithing and the bills, I don't care what you do with it. You've got to trust me. I need you to believe in me." His eyes pleaded for understanding and acceptance.

Before Brionney could reply, the door opened and Dr. Cotton walked in with a nurse. "Hello, Brionney." The doctor was thin and short, with sparse dark blond hair. His body moved slowly, deliberately, as if each movement had been preplanned for the least amount of waste. "What seems to be the matter? The chart here says that Savannah fell?"

"Up the stairs," Jesse supplied.

Dr. Cotton smiled. "That happens a lot. Now Savannah, I'm just going to take a look." Brionney and Jesse held Savannah's hands as the doctor examined the cut. "Not bad at all. It will have to have stitches, though."

Savannah cried when he gave her a shot, and Brionney felt even more guilty at her daughter's pain. She wished Savannah could understand why she let the doctor hurt her.

"It gets easier," Doctor Cotton said, glancing at Brionney. "By the time you've had five or six accidents like these, you'll not feel so guilty. There's nothing you can do to stop children from growing pains."

Placing the stitches was easy compared to the shot. Savannah lay perfectly still, tears drying on her flushed cheeks. Afterward the nurse presented her with a sucker, and she was all smiles again. Jesse carried her out to the waiting room where Talia played with Roger in the little toy room.

"How'd it go?" she asked.

Jesse hugged Savannah. "She was a brave girl," he said, more to Savannah than Talia. "Of course, she had to be in front of her dad." Savannah laid her head on his shoulder and Jesse gently kissed her cheek. As he sauntered to the door ahead of them, Brionney's eyes watered at a reason other than Savannah's suffering. Jesse was such a good man. Though he might not be perfect, he was hers and she loved him. Brionney bid Talia farewell and hurried after Jesse. They had unfinished words between them.

She opened the car door and Jesse put Savannah in her seat. As he straightened, Brionney hugged him. He had never let her down, and there was no reason to suspect he would ever do so. He should not have to pay for Derek's sins. "I'm sorry," she said. "I do believe in you. I really do. Sometimes I'm just afraid of what could happen."

He held her face in his hands. "Our future is going to be great. And as for Savannah, the decision is yours."

Brionney swallowed the lump of fear in her throat and took the plunge. "I'm going to quit."

"Okay." His voice was noncommittal, but Brionney knew he was content. And so was she. More than anything, she was grateful he understood how much she needed to be with Savannah right now. No longer would she have to feel guilty for not being a full-time mother. Her dream was coming true. She thought of all the things she would have time to do in the apartment, ways to save money and things to make their lives more comfortable after their marriage. "I might even have time to wax the kitchen floor," she murmured. "Not that I like doing it, mind you."

Jesse kissed her and they grinned at each other. "I can't wait to marry you."

"Oh, but you don't have to," she said, suddenly remembering. "With this whole thing, I almost forgot. The bishop called me this morning. They found our original papers, and we have the approval now! It came while we were in Arizona, if you can believe it. We can get married whenever we want!"

Jesse hugged her. "You almost forgot that? " he teased. "How could you? So when do you want to get married?"

"I don't know. It will take a while to get things planned."

"What do you mean? We have the dresses, the silk flowers, most of the decorations. The only thing we have to do is change the date on the invitations, and I'm sure your sisters will help write that in."

Brionney felt joy burst through her soul. "Okay, how about at Christmas break? That's less than three weeks away."

"Perfect!"

"Well, I don't know. It's a big time for weddings. I hope they have an opening at the temple."

"They will. Even if I have to call every temple in Utah!" His arms came around her again, and their lips met in a long kiss. Jesse chuckled as he pulled away. "You know, it's strange that they found the papers now, isn't it? After we went to Arizona."

"I don't think it's so strange. Cathie needed us. Your parents needed us."

"Yeah. You're right. The Lord knew exactly what He was doing." They hugged for a long moment.

Then Brionney laughed. "And now we don't need Derek to write the letter! I'd love to see his face if he knew that his little delay didn't make a difference after all."

"He's lost out on the best thing he ever had," Jesse said. His voice was soft, his face tender. "I almost feel sorry for him."

"You always know the right thing to make me happy." She kissed him again, wishing he didn't have to go to school. "See you tonight." He stood in the parking lot and waved as he watched her drive away.

Glancing back at Savannah, Brionney saw that the little girl was sound asleep. Lying there, she looked so much like Derek that the memories came back and threatened Brionney's peace. Their trip to Arizona had obviously been orchestrated by the Lord, but where did meeting up with Derek and Melinda fit into the plan? Brionney remembered only too well the interest Melinda had taken in Savannah. Was she reading too much into the encounter? Or was it a time bomb waiting to explode?

CHAPTER TWENTY-TWO

The December weather turned very cold as though to make up for November's warmth, but Brionney was so excited about getting married to Jesse that she barely noticed. Everything was set for their wedding and their four-day honeymoon in Long Beach, California. Jesse had worked overtime to get the funds for their trip. Seeing his stress, Brionney suggested delaying their honeymoon or going somewhere for only a night or two, but he wouldn't hear of it.

"You want a honeymoon by the ocean and that's what I'm giving you," he said with a grin. "I've been scrimping, and my parents have pitched in for our present. You're going to have the honeymoon you always dreamed of—even if for only four days."

Four blessed days out of the cold, and all alone with Jesse! It was a dream come true. Savannah would stay with Talia, and while it would be their first overnight separation, Brionney felt she and Jesse needed at least that much.

To Brionney's delight, Zack called to say he and Josette and their two boys, Emery and Preston, would be coming for the wedding. They arrived at the Salt Lake airport the day after a big snowstorm. Zack gave Brionney a huge bear hug. "I've been wanting to do that for some time."

Brionney grinned. "Me too." Then Josette pushed him out of the way, handed him seven-month-old Preston, and threw her arms around Brionney, kissing her soundly on both cheeks. In a short time they were talking together like the great friends they had been during Josette's time in America.

Three-year-old Emery was fascinated with the snow, and begged to go out to play the minute the car stopped at the Fields' home. He and Brionney's other nephews dragged Zack and Jesse outside with them, where they romped until Irene insisted they come in to eat.

Zack sidled up to Brionney. He looked at Jesse across the room. "For what it's worth, I think he's great. I get a good feeling about him."

Brionney was glad. Though he had also come for her marriage to Derek, Zack had never told her he approved of him. "It must be all the snowballs he threw at you," she said with a snort. "Male bonding, or something."

Emery barreled into Zack's legs, jabbering something in French. "Now, now," Zack said, picking him up. "You must speak in English here. I know French is easier, but you can do it. That's why we practice English at home."

"Don't like that food," Emery said, glancing self-consciously at Brionney.

Zack chuckled. "It's good, you'll see. I know it's different, but Daddy has been waiting a long time for it. Come on, I'll give you a taste."

Jesse came to stand beside Brionney. "He's a great guy, your brother."

"He likes you, too."

"Whew, I passed the test then."

Brionney hugged him. "Yes, with flying colors."

Jesse kissed her cheek and whispered, "Only two days left."

She leaned into him and sighed.

* * * * *

Friends and family gathered at the Provo Temple. Even Debbie and Max had come from Arizona. "It was me who introduced them," Debbie told anyone who would listen, a self-satisfied expression plastered on her face. "I knew they would get married."

Those who could not enter the temple, mainly Jesse's family, waited on the temple grounds or in the waiting room. Brionney was nervous as the ceremony began, but she knew that she and Jesse were meant for each other. Every time Jesse stared into her eyes, she saw the promise there.

Joy filled Brionney's heart. *Thank you, Father,* she prayed silently. *Thank you for giving me a second chance, for helping me to find Jesse.*

After they pledged their eternal love, Jesse hugged her. In his face, Brionney saw the happiness she knew was reflected in her own eyes.

"You know what I would like?" he whispered.

"What?"

"I'd like to adopt Savannah."

His desire was the crowning triumph of the day, a sign of complete acceptance and love. Brionney couldn't ask for more. During the past months, she had often dreamed about asking Max to approach Derek about adoption, but one thing held her back: Melinda. Brionney was terrified that if she brought up the idea of adoption, Melinda would urge Derek to seek partial custody. The fear paralyzed Brionney; Derek was her biological father, but a stranger all the same.

She kissed Jesse. "One day, I hope. But she is yours already."

They floated out of the temple doors together, as if in a dream, and immediately friends and family enveloped them with hugs, kisses, and cameras. At that moment, Brionney felt that at last she had begun a family no one could destroy.

The rest of the day passed quickly. At the reception, it seemed everyone Brionney had ever met was there to offer congratulations. To her surprise, Derek's mother, Kris, appeared at the church. "Congratulations," she said. "I hope you'll be happy this time."

Brionney could hear the sincerity in her voice. "Thank you. And thanks for coming."

"Well, I've put off coming to see Savannah for too long. But that's over now. I'm moving to Utah, to Orem, and now I can be a real grandma."

Brionney didn't know how she felt about that, especially since Jesse wanted to adopt Savannah, but could one more person loving Savannah hurt? "That's good," she murmured uncertainly.

Before the last guests left, Brionney and Jesse gave Savannah a week's worth of kisses and stole away. Outside, Jesse's Fiesta was packed with balloons, and a cluster of aluminum cans had been tied to the bumper. Proclamations of their new status were scrawled over the entire car in shaving cream and lipstick. Cathie's husband, who was Jesse's best man, had done his job well.

"For once I'm glad I drive a rattletrap," Jesse said, clearing out enough balloons so they could get in the car.

From the church they drove to a hotel in Salt Lake, and in the morning boarded a plane for California. The next four days they spent walking on the beach, watching the sunsets, shopping, discovering each other. Every night they called Savannah.

Brionney was perfectly content being with Jesse, except that her desire to have another child seemed to grow instead of diminish. Janet's words came back to her more forcefully. Several times, Brionney tried to bring up the issue with Jesse, but never got very far. *Stop being so selfish,* she told herself.

When they arrived home, Savannah was up and waiting despite the late hour. "Mommy!" she shouted and ran into Brionney's arms.

"I missed you so much!" Brionney said.

"Miss you," Savannah said.

Jesse picked her up and tickled her. They said good night to Talia and headed for their apartment.

"Wait," Jesse said, stopping Brionney on the porch. He placed Savannah in her arms and picked up Brionney and carried them both over the threshold.

"You are so—" Brionney began, but he stopped the words with a kiss. Savannah giggled and held up her face for a kiss, too.

"It's good to be home," Jesse said with a grin. "Finally, I get to sleep here."

Later, when Savannah was asleep and they cuddled in bed together, Brionney asked, "Do you mind waiting a year to have another child?" It wasn't what she really wanted to say.

"That's probably a good idea," he said slowly. "But whatever you want."

Brionney frowned in the darkness. What she wanted was a baby now, but how could she tell him that when he seemed so content to wait? She sighed.

"Is something wrong?" he asked.

"No. Nothing."

"Are you sure? You can tell me anything. I love you, you know. And I'm always going to be here for you."

Shame washed over Brionney. If she told him what was bothering her, she knew he would give her what she wanted. But as it was, he struggled at work and school to support them. After the next rent payment, her money would be gone. To make funds stretch until Jesse graduated at the end of April would be more than a challenge.

She stifled the longings inside her. A few months' wait would make no difference in the long run. If Jesse could do his part, so could she.

Brionney turned to Jesse, snuggling closer to the warmth of his body. "I love you, too. And everything is just fine."

* * * * *

The next month was filled with work and school for Jesse. He knew he was gone too much, but he also knew that in April it would be over. In his few moments of spare time, he began applying for computer programming jobs with the idea of starting right after graduation, but had not yet found anything promising. Though he and Brionney hadn't wanted to leave Utah, he felt forced to send several applications out of state.

Pressure steadily mounted, and at times he would arrive home at nearly two o'clock in the morning, too worn out to eat. He would check on Savannah and then tumble into bed next to Brionney, who always waited up for him. Then they would snuggle and talk until he fell asleep. Those precious moments were what he lived for.

When he arose in the mornings, Brionney was often still sleeping. He would watch her for a few moments and caress her cheek gently before dragging himself to the shower. When he came out, she would be awake for their morning prayer and brief scripture study.

At the end of January, he kissed Brionney good-bye and went out to the Fiesta. Two flat tires awaited him. "Oh, no," he groaned. He had already gone weeks with putting air in them each day, having no time to take them to the shop, but that wasn't going to work any longer.

He went back to tell Brionney the bad news. "They need to be replaced completely." He sighed wearily. For a moment frustration ruled his tongue. "It's just one more thing. Why can't something go smoothly for once? Just until I graduate and get a job?"

Brionney put her arms around him. "I'll get them fixed today. You just take them off, and Talia and I will take them in. Meanwhile, I'll ask Mom to let you use her car."

He smiled gratefully. "Thanks. I appreciate you taking care of it. I don't know if I can handle one more thing right now. It's just so overwhelming."

"You'll find a job," she said, pinpointing the true root of his frustration. "It's just a matter of time. Even if you don't find one before graduation, you'll have plenty of time to find one after. It's only three more months now."

He held her. "I know. But thanks for reminding me."

"I love you," she said, kissing him as he went out the door.

He knew. Her love was the thing that kept him going. He walked back to her side and gathered her in his arms for a proper kiss. "I love you, too."

* * * * *

Brionney watched Jesse drive off in her mother's car, wishing for the millionth time she could alleviate his burdens. She had thought about going back to work at her father's office, but the additional money wasn't their real problem. If they became desperate, her parents had already offered to help. Brionney knew that if only Jesse could find a job, he would be more content.

Aside from all the pressure, their marriage was all she had dreamed. Jesse was loving and considerate, and if he didn't have time to help much at home, he knew where his priorities were. He called when he couldn't make it home, and often surprised Brionney with a single flower or an inexpensive card. On Sundays he never did homework, but spent the whole day with Brionney and Savannah, turning it into an even more special day.

It'll be over soon, Brionney thought. *And at least we're facing this together.* She said her morning prayers, but afterward, instead of calling Talia about the tires, she fell back into bed. *Just for a moment,* she told herself.

The moment stretched into an hour. Light filtered in from the curtained window, announcing that the day was well underway, but Brionney didn't want to leave the bed. She felt tired and queasy. Savannah woke up and climbed into bed with her. "Hungry, Mommy."

Brionney moaned and pulled herself into a sitting position. "I think Mommy's sick, Savannah." Maybe she was beginning her monthly cycle. The thought brought a mixture of relief and disappointment. She and Jesse had been very careful so they wouldn't have a baby just yet. As Brionney's cycle was irregular, they had taken even more care.

Abruptly bile rose in her throat, and she barely made it to the toilet in time. Stomach flu, perhaps? She didn't think so. She remembered this feeling all too well. "I must be pregnant." She sat on the bathroom rug as Savannah stared at her with uncomprehending eyes. "How can I be pregnant? Oh, how am I going to tell Jesse?"

She thought of the stress in his voice as he told her about the tires, the weariness in his face as he came home each night, the disappointment of each new failure to obtain a job. Would this one thing more cause him to crack, as his mother had suggested?

Maybe it would be better not to tell him until life had calmed down. He had given her so much, and this was a burden she could bear alone for a time. But even as she worried about Jesse, joy sprang up inside her heart. She wanted this baby as intensely as she had ever wanted anything.

Later that morning, she felt perfectly well and told herself she wasn't pregnant at all. When she had been pregnant with Savannah, it had been an all-day feeling. Many nights, she had awakened and thrown up. *I'm probably not pregnant at all,* she said to herself through the sharp disappointment. *Something I ate last night must have made me sick. It really is for the best.*

In the afternoon, Brionney and Talia went to the tire shop to have the tires replaced. Afterwards, Brionney settled contentedly on the sofa with a book, planning to read a while before making dinner. Savannah played with her toys on the floor. But before Brionney knew it, she was fast asleep.

Jesse came in the door at seven, early for him. "Are you sick?" he asked with genuine concern.

"No, no. I didn't feel really great today, but I just lay down and before I knew it, I was asleep."

He sat on the couch and put an arm around her. "I know what you mean. I find myself starting to fall asleep all the time. But it's almost over. Only three months left of school. And I put in three more applications today. One of them was in Washington. It looks promising. One of these just has to be it. If not, well, I'll put in more."

Brionney clucked sympathetically, but a deep worry rooted in her breast. What if she was pregnant? No. She pushed the thought away, burying it deep in her mind. There was nothing she could do about it now.

Savannah left her toys on the floor and climbed up on the couch, settling into Jesse's lap, babbling words that seemed to make perfect sense to her. "I missed you, Savannah." Jesse tickled her stomach until she was helpless with laughter.

"Play," she said, pulling him down to her mound of toys.

"What you need is a brother or sister," Jesse said, not looking at Brionney. "Maybe in a couple years, we could arrange that. Would you like that?" Savannah nodded as if she really understood, and Brionney felt sick to her stomach again.

"What's wrong?" Jesse asked. "You look kind of pale."

Brionney wanted to confide in him, but she couldn't; he had so much on his mind already. "Nothing. I was wondering what to make for dinner."

"Need a hand?"

"Have you finished your homework?"

His face wrinkled in a frown. "I wish."

"Then you can do it while I make dinner." Brionney went into the kitchen. When she peeked in later, Jesse was deep into a book, scribbling furiously with a pencil. She picked up her own book and went to join him while dinner cooked. Studying together was better than nothing.

The morning found Brionney again hugging the toilet. Once more she tried to dismiss it, while at the same time feeling an all-consuming hope. After nearly a week of morning sickness, all doubts were gone. She was definitely pregnant.

She felt guilty hiding the news from Jesse. Sometimes she would be so elated at the idea of a baby, his baby, that she could hardly contain herself. But she yearned for it to be a happy thing for both of them. How different it would be if Jesse could share her joy!

Each morning she waited until Jesse was in the shower before eating the saltine crackers she now kept under the bed. This usually tided her over until he left the house. On mornings the crackers weren't enough, she ran for the kitchen garbage can, hoping he would stay in the shower until she was finished. During the day she would rest, and if Jesse noticed the house being any messier than usual, he didn't comment.

On Saturday morning, Talia came to the house early to ask if she wanted to go to some garage sales. Normally Brionney jumped at the offer, but today she had scarcely finished her morning ritual in the bathroom and wanted nothing more than to lie down. Jesse had long since gone to the BYU computer lab to finish a program for a class.

"I don't have any money," she told Talia. "Besides, I don't feel well."

"You do look kind of green. What is it?" Then her expression changed. "Could you be pregnant?"

Brionney looked at her with a grimace. "Maybe."

"But you want a baby. That's wonderful!"

"No, it's not." Brionney slumped onto the sofa and sighed. "Jesse's under too much stress. I just can't tell him. We agreed to wait for a while to have children. I'm afraid this one more straw would break the camel's back."

"But Jesse loves kids! He'd be thrilled."

"One more mouth to feed. One more to worry about. I can't do that to him now. He's so beat."

"He has been looking kind of bad lately."

"I'll tell him in a few months. Or when he's out of school. That's not long now."

"But babies take nine months," Talia said. "By the time it comes, these hard times will be nothing but a memory."

"We won't have insurance. That's a big worry on its own."

"Well, neither did I for my first two. You'll make it."

"But what if he changes now that I'm pregnant? And what if we drift apart?"

"He's not Derek," she said. "That's the real problem, isn't it? You're afraid that having Savannah is what put a wedge between you and eventually caused him to leave. I'm not saying it isn't so. Pregnancy and children sure do put pressure on a marriage. Every time I'm pregnant, I don't want to be touched, I don't want to go anywhere, and I don't cook or clean. All I want to do is sleep and eat. It's hard on both of us. But pregnancy won't ruin a real commitment, only reinforce it. And when it's all over, nothing could be more worth the months of torture."

Brionney groaned. "Torture. You said it. And I've already gained weight, though I don't know how since I've been throwing up so much. It's probably all the lasagne I've been eating. It seems to be the only thing I can keep down."

"What you need to do is take a pregnancy test."

"But then I'll know for sure."

"And you don't now?"

"Okay, I'll think about it."

"Good." Talia patted Brionney's leg. "Well, the yard sales aren't going to wait. I hope to find some of those big plastic toys for the kids to play with outside."

"They'll like that," Brionney said. "But, Talia, please, not a word to anyone about this."

"Okay. But I think you're making a mistake. Jesse deserves to know he's going to be a father."

"He already is a father."

"I know. But as much as he loves Savannah, this is different. He's never been through pregnancy and childbirth with anyone before."

Scowling, Brionney watched her sister leave. She knew Jesse had a right to know, but what was another three months? Abruptly, she felt sick again and headed for the bathroom. From her vantage point, she could see the bathroom floor was dirty and the toilet tank desperately needed cleaning. When had the house work gotten away from her? And she had only felt sick less than a week! She groaned, feeling helpless, frustrated, and alone.

CHAPTER TWENTY-THREE

Jesse loaded his books in his backpack and headed out of the BYU library. He yawned as he glanced at his watch. He still had time to go to work and put together a computer or two. Or repair one someone had brought in. He could use the extra hours, and since the owner of the company had given him a key, he could work whenever he had the time. He examined the new tires on the Fiesta. For two weeks now he hadn't had to put air in them. One less thing to worry about.

At work he called Brionney. "I should be home before midnight." As the ward clerk, he had to get up early for bishopric meetings tomorrow, but the rest of the day he would be able to relax with Brionney and Savannah.

"Thanks for telling me." Her voice sounded groggy. "I love you. Be careful driving home."

"I will, and I love you, too. But don't wait up for me, okay? You need your sleep."

"You're the one who needs sleep," she said, a teasing note entering her voice.

Jesse waited for her to bring up the idea of him quitting work and studying at home with Savannah while she worked for her dad. She had brought it up once or twice the past month. But Jesse knew how much it bothered her to be separated from Savannah, and with all the pressures of motherhood, he didn't want her to have the additional stress of earning a living. That was his job.

But this time, Brionney didn't suggest returning to work. "I like waiting up for you."

"Okay, I'll see you then." He said good-bye, knowing she would wait up, and though it was selfish, he was glad. But the feeling was not without guilt. Brionney looked so pale lately, so fragile. He wondered if she was getting sick. She'd had a slight cold the previous week, but insisted it was nothing. Yet he noticed the house wasn't as clean as she normally kept it, and their meals were more simple. Neither of these facts bothered him, but he wondered at the difference.

One change did bother him. In the evenings when he arrived home, Brionney had always been full of news about her day and the cute things Savannah had done. With her vivid descriptions, he felt he had missed little. In the past few weeks, however, this had gradually changed. Now she would cuddle up to him and by the time he had finished a brief synopsis of his day, she was asleep. He tried to tell himself she needed the rest after dealing with Savannah all day, but his yearning for her made him sad and his sleep more troubled.

He missed Brionney, and worried that there was something seriously wrong with their relationship. When he asked, Brionney would deny it. What was she hiding? He thought he had known her so well, but apparently there was more to her than he knew. Or maybe it was the stress he was under that was making him depressed and his imagination run overtime. *I have to get a good job quickly,* he said to himself. *And get through these last months. Then everything will be all right.*

Jesse turned back to his work, feeling a heavy burden on his shoulders. When would this pressure ease? April seemed like an eternity away.

When he arrived home at midnight, Brionney was in bed, but awake, reading a school book. She put it down and smiled as he came in from his nightly trip to Savannah's room. "Hi, honey." He lay down beside her, holding her to him. "Ahhh," he sighed. "It feels so good to hold you."

Brionney looked breathtaking in her nightgown, and he kissed her passionately. She kissed him back, but pulled away too soon. He wondered if it was the light, or if she really looked like she was going to throw up. Didn't she want to kiss him? After being away from her all day, he just wanted to be with her. Didn't she feel the same? She had once.

Jesse lumbered to his feet and changed into his pajamas, keeping his face averted so she wouldn't guess his thoughts and how much they hurt him.

"Are you hungry?" she asked.

"No, I grabbed a hamburger earlier."

"Well, I made some lasagne."

He laughed at that.

"What are you laughing for?"

"You've been making lasagne a lot lately, that's all."

Brionney frowned. "I thought you liked lasagne."

"I do. A lot. I'll have some tomorrow. Right now I just want to snuggle with you. I missed you today."

A shadow passed over her face—or was that his imagination? Jesse got into bed, and she cuddled up to him. He held her tightly, wondering what was wrong and how to tell her his feelings. For a long time he simply held her, stroking her hair. She didn't speak. The pressure inside him built instead of easing.

"Brionney," he said. "We have to talk."

No answer. "Brionney?"

She was asleep.

Jesse stroked her cheek, wanting to wake her, but not knowing what to say. He moved quietly away from her body and knelt to pray, hoping that would fill the emptiness. *Please help me to find out what's wrong,* he begged. Obviously, he was getting nowhere on his own.

Then he went into the kitchen, heated some lasagne in the microwave, and watched a late movie until he fell asleep on the couch.

* * * * *

Early the next morning, Jesse went to the church. To his surprise, no one was there. He called the bishop but there was no answer. Next, he tried the first counselor. "I'm sorry," Brother Richie said. "Didn't someone call you? The bishop is out of town, so we're not having any meetings today."

Jesse thanked him and immediately drove home. He wished someone had told him beforehand, because he could have used the morning hours to catch up on his sleep. *Or talk to Brionney.*

At the apartment, she wasn't in their bedroom. He went into Savannah's room. The little girl was awake and held out her arms for Jesse to pick her up. "Where's Mama?" he asked.

"Mama sick."

It was then Jesse heard Brionney in the bathroom, heaving. "Brionney?" he said through the closed door. "Are you okay?"

"Yes," came a weak voice. He heard the toilet flush and the water run. She opened the door and looked at him warily.

"Do you have the flu? Why don't you get back in bed and let me get breakfast?" He took her arm and led her to the bedroom. Tears rolled down her cheeks. He put Savannah on the bed and put his arms around her. "Honey, what's wrong?"

"Nothing. I'm fine."

"Then why are you crying?"

"I—I—"

"Tell me," he urged. Fear grew inside him. What was she hiding? Didn't she love him anymore? Had she discovered that she was still hung up on Derek? No, that couldn't be it, could it? "Please tell me."

"I can't. You already have too much on your mind."

He pushed back her hair so he could see her face. "Brionney, we promised when we married to be honest with each other. To be there for each other. If something's wrong, you have to tell me."

Brionney didn't look at him. "I think I might be pregnant." Her voice wasn't more than a whisper.

"Pregnant?" It took a full moment for the shock to settle in, and then he smiled. "Are you sure? Why didn't you tell me? Oh, this is wonderful!"

Her eyes flew to his. "But I thought you wanted to wait to have more children."

"What? I thought *you* wanted to wait. I figured you were still recovering from the first one. I read somewhere that it takes two and a half years for a woman's body to recover completely. I didn't want to rush you." He sat on the bed and added softly, "Besides, I thought you needed time for me to prove I would be a good husband and not leave you. I wanted to give you time to trust me."

"I didn't want to put more pressure on you," she said. "I mean, I've been wanting a baby. I have since Lauren and Mickelle had theirs last year, but I worried . . . I mean, when your mom said we should wait—"

"What? What does she have to do with this?" he demanded.

"Well, in Arizona, she said she thought we should wait. And you seemed to agree."

Jesse shook his head. "I love my family, Brionney, but they don't share my values, except for Cathie. My parents are good people, but they haven't a clue as to what is really important. Children, family, that's what's eternal. The rest just fills in the time before you die."

"Why didn't you ever tell me you felt like that?"

"Well, you kept saying in a year or so, and I wasn't going to push you. You didn't have an easy time before we met. I thought you wanted to make sure it would work out."

"Well, that's a relief."

"I'll say! I've been feeling pretty lonely. I thought you were acting strange."

She groaned. "Oh, I am! My whole life is different now. I seem to spend more time in the bathroom than anywhere else. And all that lasagne. I'm so sick of lasagne I could die. But it makes me feel better."

"I'll be here to help you now. But don't you ever keep a secret like this again, okay? You should have told me!"

"I know. I'm sorry."

He kissed her soundly. "I can't believe it!"

"Believe it," she said with a laugh. "We have a saying in my family that we're so fertile we just have to wash our underwear together, and presto, nine months later there's a baby."

"I'm glad." Jesse looked at Savannah, who watched them intently, her shock of white hair sticking out in every direction. "Did you hear? We're going to have a baby! You'll finally have someone smaller than you to pick on." He stood up and danced her around the room, chanting, "We're gonna have a baby. We're gonna have a baby, a baby, a baby!"

"Baby?" asked Savannah when she had stopped giggling enough to form the word. "Savannah." She pointed at her chest.

"No, not baby Savannah. Another baby," he explained. Savannah smiled without understanding.

"Let's not tell your mother for a while, though, okay?" Brionney said.

He laughed. "Whatever you want."

"Jesse, I don't know if you're ready for this. I mean, I won't be easy to live with. I'll throw up, be cranky all the time, want my back rubbed, and won't want to go anywhere or do anything. If you think I'm a bad housekeeper now, just wait. It's hard for me to even kiss you without starting to feel, well, sick." She looked at him apologetically and added, "Sorry."

So she *had* been going to throw up last night! "It's only nine months," he said, putting his arms around her.

"That's what you say now."

His arms tightened. "Whatever it takes, I'm going to be here."

For the next few days, Jesse was euphoric. Brionney was going to have his baby! He went out and bought a pregnancy book so they could see how big the baby was at each stage of development. The whole process fascinated him, and he spent precious hours reading the book when he should have been sleeping or studying. His homework piled up, and just looking at all he had to do made him want to scream.

Then things became worse. Brionney got so sick that she couldn't get out of bed without throwing up repeatedly. She had to drop her school classes because she couldn't attend them. Jesse awoke early each morning, brought her something to eat, dressed Savannah, made sure Brionney had plenty of snacks nearby, then hurried off to school. He came home for lunch to see if Brionney was all right. He had to shop for food and tried to clean a house that already had weeks of build-up. For two days in a row, he had to wear a shirt out of the dirty clothes basket. Because of the extra load at home, he began to fulfill his hours at work during the night while his family slept. A constant headache battered at him; before the week was over, he was trembling and his vision occasionally blanked out with the pain.

He stopped by the doctor one Friday afternoon in February to ask about his vision loss. "You need to take it easy," Dr. Cotton said after the examination. "You're working too hard, and not sleeping enough."

"I can't stop," Jesse said. "Not yet. I have a family to support."

Dr. Cotton looked at him gravely. "Well, perhaps you need to re-think your priorities. What if your vision blacks out while you're driv-ing? What will your family do then?"

Jesse stifled a quip about his life insurance, but the thought sobered him. One more thing to worry about.

He thought about his friends whose wives had worked to put them through school. Now he understood why they had done so. He still didn't agree, but his understanding was much greater. Why had he judged them so harshly? He had to admit that if Brionney had been capable of working until April, he would probably want her to do it. Of course, with her pregnancy and constant sickness, that was out of the question.

How hypocritical he felt! When things grew tough, he was ready to break God's counsel. No! He wouldn't! For a brief moment, he was almost glad Brionney was so sick and couldn't work. That would protect her from his weakness. He would make it through somehow. Wouldn't the Lord provide a way, as he had with Nephi?

Later that night Jesse was still at work at four in the morning. His head ached, and all he could think about was how much he'd rather be in bed next to Brionney. His head slumped to his hands. *Father, I can't do this anymore!*

Maybe his mother was right. The thought came suddenly and shocked him to his core. Maybe this baby was too much additional pressure. After all, it was the reason Brionney couldn't help out at home or go back to work in her father's office. Jesse hated himself even as he thought it. Already he loved the baby, and wanted it. But he had to admit that the timing was terrible.

Three more months, he told himself. *No, less than that now. Just over two.* But he still had no job offer, and if he didn't finish school because of the stress . . .

The pressure in his head mounted. Tears sprang from his tired eyes. He felt completely and utterly helpless. Worse was the knowledge that by wishing Brionney wasn't pregnant, he was betraying her. He had promised to love and support her through anything, and now he couldn't. Was he any better than Derek who at least had the decency to show her that he couldn't be trusted?

Oh, Brionney, I love you so much. But I'm failing you!

He knew he should pray, but he was too tired and devoid of hope. Then he felt a voice urging him to his knees. At once, Jesse let go of his pride and begged for relief. *Dear Father, please hear me. I need thy help. It's just over two months. Help me make it through—and find a job and do everything else . . .*

His despair increased, as did the pain in his head. He knew that if he opened his eyes, he wouldn't be able to see at all. He kept them closed. Then he heard a distinct voice in his head. It was his father-in-law, Terrell. "I'd be happy to give you a loan so that you don't have to work these last few months. It wouldn't be a problem at all. In fact, you can just have the money. Consider it a gift. If you feel you have to pay me back, then do it whenever you can. If you can't, then don't worry about it. I'd be happy to help out."

"We're fine," Jesse had said.

Then another voice came to him, that of a sister in the ward. "We'd love to bring in some dinners to help out until you finish school or until Brionney is feeling better." That, too, he had refused.

Talia's voice came next. "I could check in on Brionney and Savannah at lunchtime and clean up a bit. Really, it's no problem."

"Don't worry about it," he had said. "You watch Savannah too much as it is."

Jesse begged for the voices to go away. Was he having a nervous breakdown? The pain . . . his head . . . Why wasn't there anyone to help him? . . .

Then he understood. The Lord had sent many, but he had refused them all. "Idiot," he said to himself. "I'm the one who's been putting unnecessary stress on myself, not the baby."

The pressure eased from Jesse's head, taking with it much of his despair. He would accept Terrell's loan and take the last two months off work or limit it to a few hours on the weekends. That would leave him time to study and seriously look for a job. Tomorrow, he would even call Talia and the others to let them help as well. He wasn't alone. The Lord had already prepared the way for them to be obedient and to succeed. Jesse had only to take the right path.

Thank you, Father, he prayed. *And thank you so much for this new little life that Brionney's carrying. I know it'll be worth all the effort.*

The next morning, Jesse carried out his plan. His boss was understanding and had plenty of college students lined up to take his place. For the first Saturday in almost a year, Jesse didn't work. He asked the bishop to excuse him from one week of meetings and called Talia to take her up on her offer. Then he took a long nap before studying for his tests. His headache disappeared completely.

Brionney and Savannah were happy to have him home more. And Jesse found himself actually enjoying school again. He still worried about finding a job. He had two offers that were very low in compensation, and he didn't feel he should accept either of them.

"You'll find something better soon," Brionney told him. She patted her slightly rounded stomach. "We're doing everything the Lord has asked us—even multiplying and replenishing the earth. The Lord has given us this child and he will give us a way to take care of it, don't you think?" The love on Brionney's face was apparent, and an equal love surged in Jesse's heart. He was so grateful for his family! And he was grateful for the lesson the Lord had taught him. He wasn't alone in the world, but part of a huge and loving family.

Six weeks passed. Jesse was still under pressure, but it was manageable. His vision hadn't blacked out since he had stopped working. In the last few days Brionney had begun to feel better, and his load lightened even more. He still hadn't found an adequate job, but was buoyed by Brionney's positive attitude.

Then he came home from school at the first of April to find Brionney near tears. "What is it?" he said, rushing to her side. "Is it the baby?"

She shook her head. "No. Debbie called; she said Derek's lawyer has contacted Max. They're testing the waters to see how firm we are on visitation rights. He—he wants a picture of Savannah. Oh, Jesse, what are we going to do?"

CHAPTER TWENTY-FOUR

The first week in April slipped by slowly for Brionney as she worried about what Derek was planning. All traces of her morning sickness had vanished. With Savannah, Brionney had been nauseous for six months, and she felt sure the Lord was blessing her now.

"Look here," Jesse called excitedly as he came in the door from school. He waved the mail in his hands. "Remember that job I sent a resume to in Washington? Well, apparently the business moved back here to Utah over three years ago, and my letter was somehow forwarded. Can you believe it? After three years!"

Brionney put down the photo album she held in her hands. "So do they want to interview you?"

"Well, not exactly. The owner has been downsizing lately, but he says he has a friend whose business has just taken off, and he could probably use the help. He asked me to call if I was still interested, and he'd set up an interview with the guy."

"Wow! That really is a miracle!" Brionney jumped up from the couch and hugged him.

Jesse laughed. "Yeah, who would have ever thought that I'd have to send a resume to Washington to get a job in Utah!"

"Well, call, already," Brionney said, handing him the phone.

Jesse sat on the couch, preparing to dial. His eyes fell on the photo album. "What are you doing?"

The joy went out of Brionney's heart. "I'm trying to see what picture I should send Derek. How about this one?"

"You can hardly see her face."

"Exactly."

Jesse rubbed her back. "I'm sorry this has happened, Brionney. But maybe the picture will be the end of it."

"I called Debbie today," Brionney said. "She sent one of the investigators Max uses to check up on Derek and Melinda. He found out that Melinda has been trying to get pregnant for a long time. They've gone to fertility doctors and everything."

Jesse's face looked as anguished as Brionney felt. If Melinda couldn't have children, Derek's desire to see Savannah might increase. The idea of Savannah staying at a house where people smoked and didn't care for gospel values terrified Brionney. She had seen first-hand what that life had done to Derek.

Jesse held her. "I'd just about forgotten Derek was her father," he said. There was pain in his voice. "I want to be that so badly."

* * * * *

In the next two weeks, Jesse was offered three jobs. The highest paying was out of state, but after careful thought and prayer, Jesse took the job found by the resume he had sent to Washington. "It's got to be the right one, coming as it did," he said to Brionney.

She smiled, grateful the decision was made. With the pressure of finding a job behind him, Jesse was able to focus on his finals. When the last one was finished, he took two days off to spend time with Brionney before starting his new job. During the time off, he and Talia's husband dug a huge sandbox in the backyard for the children to play in. Brionney helped a little with the shoveling, careful not to overexert herself.

She had finally sent a recent family picture to Debbie to pass on to Derek, hoping he would understand that Savannah was content and happy with two stable parents. Since weeks had gone by with no further request, Brionney tried to put the whole incident from her mind.

Happiness was becoming a way of life. Deep inside, a little whisper seemed to caution her exuberance, but Brionney refused to listen. Worrying wouldn't help her avoid future problems.

The next weeks passed slowly, with the world awakening to new shoots of green everywhere. The heat of summer was still distant, but the cold had long since disappeared. May was Brionney's favorite month of the year.

Jesse loved his new job and came home each day shortly after five, happy and excited. Savannah was undergoing a big change as well, and at nearly twenty months was learning to use her potty chair. She had grown taller and more slender, losing much of her baby fat.

"Now the fat's on me," Brionney complained. She had gained fifteen pounds already. "I can't believe it. I'm so fat, I feel like a cow!"

"You're not fat," Jesse said, pulling her close. "You're pregnant." He laughed. "Besides, I like you this way. I think you're beautiful."

How different from Derek!

Brionney smiled and hugged him back. "I love you, Jesse Hergarter. Even if you do have a funny name."

"What! I didn't know you didn't like my name!" He tickled her until she fell on the couch, begging for mercy.

"I love your name! Stop. I promise, I love it!"

Jesse put his face next to her stomach. "Hey, you in there. You like my name, don't you? You gotta hurry and come out here so your mom can see how beautiful the Hergarter babies are."

He tickled Brionney until she kissed him into submission. "Okay, you win," he said. "It is a funny name. But you're stuck with it."

* * * * *

The second week in May, Jesse was sent to Colorado for a four-day training seminar on a new computer system they were installing. It was the first time they had been separated for more than two days since he had come to Utah the year before, and Brionney wasn't looking forward to being without him.

"I'll call every night," he promised early Tuesday morning, kissing her good-bye before leaving for the airport with a colleague. "Take care of yourself and don't work too hard."

As Brionney watched him go, she couldn't help but worry. She knew people flew in planes every day. It was safer than driving, but still she worried. If she lost Jesse, it would be too much to bear. She went inside and dropped to her knees, praying that all would be well with him. The uneasiness didn't leave.

That night he called her from his hotel, safe and sound. "Is everything all right?"

"Yes, everything." Brionney was relieved to hear his voice.

"I miss you already."

"I miss you, too. And I don't know if I'll be able to sleep tonight." She had grown accustomed to sleeping with someone again.

"Me either. But try. I'll be home soon."

After their conversation, Brionney did sleep surprisingly well, feeling more tired than usual. When she awoke, the apprehensive feeling awoke with her, refusing to be put aside. Her eyes fell on the phone. Was Jesse all right? Or did her uneasiness have anything to do with him? Could Derek be planning something terrible?

"Oh, stop it," she finally told herself in the bathroom mirror. "You're just missing Jesse. Everything will be all right once he's back home."

Early Wednesday evening, Brionney decided to go shopping for baby items. Jesse had received his first paycheck at the beginning of the week, and for once she had a little money. K-Mart was having a big baby sale, and she wanted to pick up a few generic items—little diapers, T-shirts, and sleepers. Soon she would have an ultrasound and be able to pick out more gender-specific items, but at least she would have something new right now for the baby. Brionney touched her stomach, feeling the small bulge. In a few weeks she would be halfway through! The next month the baby would really begin to grow. She couldn't wait to hold the infant in her arms, or even to feel it move inside her. According to the doctor, that should be any day now.

"Come on, Savannah," Brionney said, coming out of the apartment. "Let's go to the store." Savannah was outside in the new sandbox, playing with her cousins under Talia's watchful eye. She and little Roger were best friends and played together every minute they could.

Savannah shook her head and picked up her shovel. "No wanna. Stay wif Roger."

Talia glanced up from the other side of the box, where she was planting a new cherry tree that would one day shade the sandbox. "I'll watch her. I'm about done here, then I'll go in and fix dinner. You two can join us."

This was one invitation Brionney was not about to pass up. "Thanks. I wasn't looking forward to eating without Jesse. The apartment seems kind of lonely."

Talia looked at her sympathetically. "I figured as much. Go ahead, have a good time. Savannah will be fine."

"Thanks," Brionney repeated. She bent down to kiss Savannah before leaving. When she slipped behind the wheel of the old Fiesta, she felt oddly free and young without her daughter tagging along.

K-Mart had all of the promised bargains and more. Brionney picked out several outfits, both boy and girl, rationalizing that she would need some to give away for baby showers during the year. Then a baby girl outfit attracted her attention, and she reached up to the top rack to get it. Abruptly, she felt a rush of fluid between her legs. Time seemed to freeze. Her heart pounded in her ears, one loud, slow beat at a time.

It's nothing, she told herself. *Just my imagination.* But it seemed too real to be nothing. Self-consciously, Brionney took her light jacket from the shopping cart and tied it around her waist. Slowly, she made her way to the checkout. *Everything's fine. I'll just buy these clothes and be on my way. My baby's fine. That rush was all in my imagination.*

Time resumed, and Brionney noticed the rapid hammering of her heart. Part of her wanted to throw the baby items to the floor and flee, to make sure everything was all right. But she stayed in the line. As long as she actually bought the clothes, her baby would certainly be okay. The clerk chattered happily, but Brionney didn't hear what the woman said. She wrote her check mechanically.

She went from the checkout to the car, walking very slowly as though that would prevent disaster. Inside the privacy of the Fiesta, she looked down, expecting to see nothing, as she had told herself so many times in the store. But dark red stained the inside thighs of her jeans. Brionney stared for a long time, uncomprehending.

Dear Father, no! It can't be!

Panic overwhelmed her senses, and all she could think about was getting home as quickly as possible. The old Fiesta started on the first try, for once, and she soon pulled up in front of Talia's, remembering nothing of the drive home. The steps across the grass in front seemed to stretch for eternity, but at last she rounded the house and could see her apartment. Her heart again beat loudly in her ears. Her breath also came rapidly, sounding harsh and desperate.

"Please, dear Lord," she begged aloud. "Don't let my baby die!"

CHAPTER TWENTY-FIVE

In the tiny bathroom all alone, Brionney cried with deep, heartrending sobs that shook her whole body. Would the tears ever stop, and if they did, would she ever be the same again? For long minutes she sobbed out her grief and fear, feeling all alone and wishing Jesse was there to hold her and tell her it would be okay.

"Brionney? Are you all right?" Talia's voice came from the front room.

Brionney drew a shuddering breath and called through the closed door. "I'm in the bathroom."

Talia's voice came closer. "The children saw you come home. They said you were crying. I knocked, but no one answered. Savannah's with me. Are you sick?" She sounded worried, as though wondering what was so serious that Brionney would come home first before checking on Savannah.

"Just give me a minute," Brionney managed.

"I'll wait in the front room."

Brionney wiped her face and set about changing her clothes. After the initial rush, the flow of blood seemed to stop and hope flared in her breast. *It was just a fluke,* she thought. *Everything's okay.*

Brionney walked slowly down the hall. Once in the front room, she sank to the sofa, gathering Savannah in her arms and nestling her face in her hair. Savannah felt so good, so alive.

"What's wrong? You've been crying."

"I'm bleeding," Brionney said dully, the tears coming once again. "At least I was. It started at the store. I'm so afraid." Her hand went to her stomach. "I don't want to lose this baby!"

Talia was beside her in an instant, putting an arm around her and pulling her close. Brionney's tears came more rapidly as she clung to her sister. "You're a nurse," she said between sobs. "What should I do?"

"How much blood? What color is it? Is it still coming? Did you ever bleed before with Savannah?"

"Enough to soak through my jeans, but I think it's stopped now. It was bright red. I did spot a little with Savannah, just a drop or two a couple of times. But this was so much!" Brionney closed her eyes, seeing the red again. *So much! Could her baby be all right?*

"There's nothing you can do, really, except to stay down." Talia's eyes took on a faraway look. "But many people bleed some during pregnancy, so unless it's heavy, you shouldn't worry yet. Let's call your doctor, but since it's stopped, he'll say the same thing."

Brionney was comforted by her words. But there was a question she had to ask. "Was this how it began with your miscarriage?" She knew Talia had suffered a miscarriage before Roger.

"Which one?" Talia asked dryly. Her face was blank.

"How many did you have?"

"Four. One at four months, one at three, the others at about two and a half."

Brionney reeled with the information. The idea of losing her baby terrified her. How could Talia have endured it so many times? "I never knew you had so many."

"Well, you were really young and I didn't go around talking about it. But that's why there's that six-year gap before Roger. Two began with a rush like you describe, the other two with spotting. But I also bled with two of the boys and they were just fine. Have you been feeling sick at all lately? Before my miscarriages, I always stopped feeling sick."

Her words sent chills down Brionney's spine. "I haven't been sick for the past month," she said. "But isn't that normal? Don't most people stop being sick around three months?"

"A lot of people," Talia agreed. "But I'm always sick until about six months, and so are Lauren and Mickelle. What about with Savannah? When did you start feeling better with her?"

"Six months." Brionney could barely get out the words. The Lord was blessing her, that's all. Or was He? "But don't you think that's because the second one is easier?"

Talia didn't meet her stare. "I don't know. Maybe you just need to rest."

"Did they ever find out why you miscarried?"

"No. Never. Just told me it was a genetic defect. They didn't know what caused it. Just one of those things."

Brionney tried to stifle her panic. "Maybe we should call my doctor."

"He'll send you to the emergency room. They always do that if you're bleeding. But at least they'll see if they can find a heartbeat. That would make you feel better."

"What if they can't find it?"

"They'll do an ultrasound."

"No, I don't want to go. Not yet." Brionney was suddenly afraid of going to the emergency room and being told her child was dead. For now, she wanted to wait and hope. "There's nothing I can do, and I'm afraid to move. Besides, Jesse should be there. I'll go in if I start bleeding again. But it's probably nothing. You said so yourself."

"I hope so," Talia said softly. Her face filled with sorrow. "I really hope so. Miscarrying is an experience you never completely get over. It's . . . oh, I hope you're not—" She shook herself and climbed to her feet. "I'm going to get Joe and someone else to give you a blessing. Don't get off the couch if you can help it, though they say that won't really help. I'll be back to help you with Savannah."

While Talia was gone, the phone rang. Brionney knew from the hour on the clock that it was Jesse. "Hello?" she said, tears sliding silently down her cheeks.

"Hi, honey. It's me. How are things?"

For a moment Brionney couldn't reply. Closing her eyes, she tried to picture his face. "I—I started bleeding today. It's stopped now, I think."

She heard him swallow and start to speak several times before he succeeded. "What does that mean?"

"I don't know. Maybe nothing. But it might mean that I'm having a miscarriage."

"But I thought after three months you didn't miscarry."

"Talia miscarried at four."

"Are you lying down? Oh, I wish I could be there to help you!" The frustration in his voice was obvious. Brionney could hear something more as well. Jesse was crying.

"Talia will help."

"I'll see if I can come home early, although I don't know how I can. But Friday seems a long way from now."

"No, it'll be okay. Just pray."

"Have you had a blessing?"

"Not yet. Talia went to get Joe." Brionney's voice cracked on the last word.

"Blast it! I should be there! I'm so sorry, Brionney."

"I'll be okay. Really. Talia will be with me."

"Call me if there's any change at all, okay? Otherwise I'll call you tomorrow night as planned. I miss you. I love you."

"I love you, too. Good-bye." Brionney hung up before she broke down again. She clutched Savannah to her chest and sobbed.

"Mommy awright?"

With a hand on her stomach, Brionney tried to answer Savannah. She couldn't speak past the lump in her throat, so she hugged the baby until she struggled uncomfortably. *Everything's going to be all right,* Brionney thought fiercely. *Please, Father. Oh, please!*

Joe and Terrell gave Brionney a blessing, and she went to bed clinging to the hope it gave her. They had not promised she would keep the baby, but that the Lord's will would be done, just as she had asked when Savannah was missing. She knew the Lord loved her and had faith that He would help her through.

All day Thursday Brionney stayed on the couch, watching TV and videos. Talia brought over some herbs from the local herb shop that were supposed to relax her uterus. The bleeding didn't return, and Brionney grew more hopeful. By evening, she was more confident when Jesse called. She even made dinner.

Friday morning, her hopes were dashed when she began to spot. She again told herself it was nothing, as if saying so would make it true. When Jesse arrived home in the afternoon, she was in bed reading, trying not to think serious thoughts. Savannah took advantage of her indisposition and decorated the entire apartment with her toys and a roll of pink toilet paper, laughing all the while as if nothing were wrong.

Jesse said little, but lay next to Brionney, his arms cuddling her body. Having him back was her best comfort. The bleeding increased during the day, until it was like having a regular period. Talia shook her head sadly each time she came to check on Brionney, her face locked in memories only she could see. Still, Brionney clung to the slight hope that her baby would survive.

"I think we'd better go in to the doctor," Jesse said. Brionney agreed. Jesse called the doctor and, as Talia had foretold, he suggested they go to the emergency room.

At the Utah Valley Regional Medical Center, the emergency room doctor found no heartbeat. "I'm sorry," he said. "We'll need to do an ultrasound. The machine is in use just now, so it'll be a little wait."

Brionney clung to Jesse's hand. She felt like she was in a nightmare and couldn't wake up. *Please, dear Father. Please, dear Father. Please, dear Father.* She mumbled the words so many times they no longer held any meaning.

After a two-hour wait, Brionney was finally given the ultrasound. On the screen she saw a black mass. There was no life or movement. "Well?" she asked desperately.

"I'm sorry." The doctor didn't look at her. The nurse also avoided her gaze.

"Why? What happened?" Brionney's voice verged on the hysterical.

"A genetic defect. A fluke. There's nothing anyone could have done."

"But everything was fine at my three-month checkup. I heard the heartbeat!"

"Must have happened right after. No one can predict these things. They just happen. But the good news is that you aren't in danger of your uterus rupturing or anything. You can go home and let nature take its course, or we can take it out now. I warn you, it won't be pleasant."

Brionney gasped and Jesse squeezed her hand. "Isn't there any chance at all?" he asked.

The doctor looked at him pityingly. "There's about a point-zero-zero-one percent chance that the ultrasound is wrong. I have heard of cases where other pregnancies have occurred meanwhile, but it's very rare, and I see nothing to indicate that at all. I'm sorry. I know it sounds cruel, but at this point you either have it removed or you go home and rest and let the miscarriage happen on its own."

It. Brionney noticed that not once had the doctor assigned her baby a gender. *It* wasn't human anymore. She shut her eyes against the pain. "I want to go home."

The doctor gave Jesse some cautionary signs of hemorrhaging, but Talia was already aware of this danger and would keep a close eye on Brionney. "Give her Advil for the pain," he said. "Or if you change your mind, you can come back here if the contractions become too painful." Jesse thanked the doctor and took Brionney home.

Saturday dragged by with no change. But in the middle of the night, Brionney awoke with thundering pains in her abdomen. She felt as though she were in labor again with Savannah, except the area was much smaller. Brionney panted with the pain, willing it to stop, mumbling prayers with every breath. "Hold on, baby," she cried. "Just hold on!"

Jesse gave her more of the uterus-relaxing herbs and another blessing, then held her hand, looking on helplessly with tears on his cheeks. He called their doctor again, and he told them the same thing he had before: go to the emergency room.

Miraculously, the contractions stopped and Brionney lapsed into a grateful slumber. The frail hope that had been dashed by the contractions was born anew, fastening onto her heart and giving her courage to continue on.

Sunday, she stayed in bed. She was still bleeding. Jesse walked around silently with a dejected face. He spoke in low tones to Brionney's family when they came or called, and to the bishop when he told him he wouldn't be at church or any of the leadership meetings.

Afternoon came, and so did new contractions. Brionney cried out and couldn't help wishing the baby was out of her body so the torturous pain would cease. Guilt and sorrow immediately followed that thought. Jesse called Talia, and she came over to help. Savannah stayed with Joe at their house.

"I never knew miscarrying was like labor," Brionney said in the midst of the gut-wrenching pain. "Why didn't you tell me?"

"It isn't for everyone," Talia said. "It depends on when it happens. And each person is different."

Only this was worse than having a baby. With full-term labor there was a short span between contractions, but these were continuous. In desperation Brionney took the Advil, but it seemed to do nothing for the pain. Talia put her in a warm bath, and only then were the contractions bearable. Shortly, the water in the bathtub was pink with blood.

Pink water. Brionney looked at the water that cradled her body, the obvious sign of her baby's death. Convulsive tears flooded her eyes.

"I need to get out. I can't stand this water on me. Get it off! Give me the towel! Oh, Father, help me!"

"Maybe we should go to the emergency room," Talia said.

Brionney grunted and shook her head. That black form on the ultrasound monitor was still too vivid in her mind. The doctor had said there was some chance, even though it was next to nothing, and she still wanted to believe that her baby would live.

Sitting on the edge of the bathtub, she let Jesse help her put on a nightgown. In the next minute all hope died. With an agonizing pain, Brionney felt something come out, followed by a relief so intense that she would have collapsed if Jesse hadn't been holding on to her. She turned and saw it there in the draining bathtub: a small red sac.

With tears streaming down her face, she scooped it up with both hands. It was warm and heavy for something barely longer than her hand. She held it to her heart and looked up at Jesse. Tears wet his face as he knelt beside her.

"I have to know what's inside," she said. The doctor had told them to bring in the tissues so they could be sure it was all out, but Brionney couldn't turn her baby over like that without knowing. "I need to see. I need to hold our baby. Will you help me?"

Jesse gave a shuddering breath and nodded. Brionney's hand shook as he ripped open the thick tissue. Water spurted out and fell into the tub. Inside, still attached by a cord thinner than a piece of yarn, was a tiny baby boy. He had two eyes, a mouth, ten miniature fingers and toes, and looked perfect to Brionney in every way.

She stroked his thin body, feeling a desperate urge to wake him. She wanted to bring his impossibly small mouth to her breast and give him life. What had gone so terribly wrong?

But there was something missing. The feeling was too overwhelming to be dismissed. Brionney looked into the tub where the amniotic fluid had mixed in with the pink water. Floating there, she saw another miniature baby, who must have fallen from the sac when she opened it. He was slightly less developed than his brother, but no less perfect-looking. Jesse picked up the baby in the palm of his hand and laid him next to his brother.

"Ohhh." Brionney gave an agonized cry as she stared at her sons. Identical twins. Ever since she was a little girl, she had dreamed of having twins. Now she had, but they would never take a breath. She would never dress them in matching clothes, play with them at the park, or kiss them good night. The pain was too much and she had to close her eyes and cry, holding her tiny babies to her chest. Jesse sat next to her and held her silently, his tears mingling with hers.

Even with her eyes closed Brionney could see them, staring sightlessly. The one still attached to the placenta especially tore at her heart. He had clung on, as though still trusting her to give him life. He had believed in her, they both had, and somehow she had failed them. *No! No!*

A long time passed as she sat there holding the babies, wondering what came next. Could there be anything after such a loss? She felt dizzy and was grateful for Jesse's arms around her.

"Come on, Brionney. You need to lie down," Jesse said. He tried to take the babies from her, but she didn't want to let them go.

"It's just for a moment." Talia wrapped them in a receiving blanket. They looked so small. Perfect tiny dolls.

Brionney was crying again, feeling a deep despair. There was nothing she could do. She let Jesse help her to the bed. His face was whiter than Brionney had ever seen it.

For the next hour the house was quiet as Brionney's parents and Talia tried to comfort them. Brionney's body ached as it had after having Savannah, a sharp and constant reminder of what she had lost. She welcomed the feeling, as it seemed to take the edge off her emotional pain.

Brionney didn't want to take the babies to the hospital. "I want them close, not in some lab. I'd like to bury them under the new cherry tree." She added brokenly, "But I—I can't watch."

Jesse nodded his agreement. "I'll do it."

He left her with Talia and Irene to go in search of a small box.

"I'm so sorry," Talia said. "I want you to know that I'm here, if you need me."

In a flash of memory, Brionney recalled that Debbie had once said the same thing to her regarding her relationship with Derek. Brionney closed her eyes. "Thank you. I appreciate it. But do you think I could be alone now?"

Talia nodded. Irene patted Brionney's hand. "Just let us know," she murmured.

They left, and Brionney was finally alone to shed her tears. Deep, heartrending sobs shook her body.

* * * * *

Jesse found a small cookie box the right size. He was glad Brionney's family had gone home, leaving him to do this utterly personal thing alone.

He went into the bedroom and dressed in his church clothes, even his tie. Brionney watched him with haunted red eyes and a pale face. Jesse wished he could take away her pain. The agony in his own heart was fierce.

"Are you going to church?" she asked in amazement.

He shook his head, excusing her for the thought. "I'm not going to leave you. It's for the babies."

Jesse sat next to her on the bed, and they said a final farewell to their sons. Brionney leaned down and kissed each tiny forehead. The effort weakened her, and she lay back on the bed, exhausted. He kissed her cheek. "I'll be back."

In the backyard by the cherry tree, he dug a hole and placed the small box in it. Then he knelt and said a short prayer. "Watch over them, Father." He covered the box with dirt and pounded two stones on top to mark the spot, feeling as he did that a piece of himself was also buried there. During the trial of the last months of school, hadn't he wished that Brionney hadn't been pregnant? That it could have waited until his own burdens were lighter? He felt so guilty for that now. Oh, how he wanted them! He wanted to take them camping, he wanted to tuck them in at night as he did Savannah. He wanted to ordain them to the priesthood. How could he have been so blind to the miracle of a child, even if temporarily? Now they were gone.

He turned his back and went into the apartment. Questions assaulted him. The babies had never breathed and wouldn't be blessed or put on the records of the Church. So would they one day be a part of their family? The gospel had always answered all of Jesse's questions. But this time there was no answer.

CHAPTER TWENTY-SIX

The next day Brionney sat on the couch and watched Jesse leave for work. "I wish I didn't have to go," he said solemnly. As a new employee, he had no choice. He couldn't afford to lose his job. Brionney was left alone with Savannah. She envied Jesse his release, and wished she had somewhere to go, something else to focus on. She hadn't signed up for summer classes because she had been too ill, and the money hadn't been available.

When her mother came to visit that morning, Brionney was relieved. Irene sat next to her on the couch. "I'm sorry it happened, honey. I had one, you know."

Brionney looked at her. "You did?"

"Yes. When you were three. It's a hard thing. I kept blaming myself, thinking that if I'd taken things easy, it wouldn't have happened."

"I keep wondering that myself. If I had slept more, or eaten better, or something. Maybe I shoveled too much sand when they made the sandbox."

"No," Irene said. "You can't think that way. You have to let it go. Just forget it, and go on with your life. You're young. You can have more children."

Tears filled Brionney's eyes. "Just forget it and go on? How? They didn't even have a chance to live! I can't forget it just like that." The idea of more children also hurt. Another baby couldn't replace those she had lost.

"It'll take time," Irene said. "I wish I could help you better."

"I'm really tired, Mom." Brionney suddenly wanted to be alone. Her mother's words had only brought her more pain.

"Okay, I'm leaving. Do you want me to take care of Savannah?"

"No. I need her here."

"Well, call me if you want anything."

"I'll be all right."

"Shall I make a dinner?"

"No. My visiting teachers are bringing it. They called when I wasn't at church yesterday, and Jesse told them about . . . about it."

Irene left, and Brionney held tightly to Savannah. She began to sob again.

* * * * *

The days dragged on. The pain in Brionney's body was gone, but the mental torment didn't dim, though occasionally she was given relief in numbness. On Wednesday, the bishop brought a potted flower and a condolence card. The flower was yellow with bright green leaves, full of life and color. Brionney took it with tears in her eyes.

"Thank you," she said, staring up at the tall, slightly stooped man. He had light brown hair, thinning on top, and faded hazel eyes banded with heavy wrinkles, the kind of eyes that encouraged trust.

"It's hard to understand," he said quietly, "when good people try to have children and can't, while throughout the world people are aborting babies."

"It doesn't make sense," Jesse agreed. "And so many young, unmarried girls who are having babies as easily as if it were nothing. And then not taking care of them." His jaw quivered as he fought tears.

"What I really want to know," Brionney said, pushing this new thought aside, "is—is—" Tears slid down her cheeks. "Is if they are mine. If I'll see them again. Or was that all for—for nothing?"

"I don't know." The bishop's kind eyes conveyed sadness. Brionney knew he wanted to help, but couldn't. "The Brethren haven't come out and said what happens in these situations, but I'll try to find out any information that might help."

"Thank you," Jesse said. He walked the bishop to the door.

Afterward, they sat in silence, staring at the TV. There seemed to be a gulf between them, one that in their grief they didn't have the energy to broach. Brionney went into the kitchen. The flower the bishop had brought and another bouquet from her visiting teachers caught her gaze; they were bittersweet reminders. She started to cry. Gathering the flowers, she tossed them into the trash. Jesse came into the kitchen and held her as she cried.

The week after the miscarriage, Brionney went to church. She made it halfway through the service before the sight of so many mothers cradling their new babies brought her to tears. Clutching Savannah to her, she abruptly left the building and walked home. Jesse was on the stand where he took notes and counted the people. He didn't see her leave.

The following Sunday, Brionney kept her emotions under control until the mother of a baby born two months premature stood and bore testimony of how the Lord had saved her son's life. Brionney went into a rest room stall and wept. A miracle was what she had needed, but it hadn't been granted. What had happened to her babies must have been the Lord's will. Why was it so hard to take?

"Mommy hurt?" Savannah asked. The little girl put her arms around Brionney and kissed her on the cheek.

Brionney hugged her daughter gratefully. How lucky she was to have this special spirit!

Savannah kissed her again. "All better, Mommy." Brionney wished it were true.

Talia waited outside the rest room for her. "I saw you leave. Are you okay?"

"Not really," Brionney said.

Talia put an arm around her shoulders. "I know. And you have to let yourself grieve. It'll take time before the hurt heals a bit, before you stop blaming yourself and searching for the reasons. I used to cry on the anniversary of the days I miscarried and when the babies were due. But things do get better. The hurt does go away."

"Do you think those babies will be yours?"

Talia looked thoughtful. "I really feel the one I lost at four months will be. The others . . ." She shrugged. "I just don't know. Sometimes I think the last three were all Roger, trying to come down. Maybe you'll have the babies again. We don't really know about those things. Maybe they'll get another chance at life."

Since no twins ran in either Jesse or Brionney's family, another such occurrence would certainly be a miracle. "Well, if I ever have twins, I guess we'll know."

"They wouldn't have to come together."

"But being twins is special," Brionney protested. She thought about how close Marc and Josette were. "If they were meant to be, they should be twins."

"Maybe. I wish we knew."

That was it. The not knowing was the thing that hurt. Were they her babies? If they were, when would she have them again? And if they weren't destined to be hers, then the pain of a miscarriage and those tiny bodies had been for nothing. Brionney knew that somehow she had to come to a peace within herself. She needed to know or at least have faith in what was to come. She had to stop seeing the pink water and those small bodies every time she closed her eyes.

"We'd better get to class," Brionney said. "Thanks for being here."

"Do you want me to take Savannah to the nursery?" Talia had been teaching there for the past month.

"No. I want her to stay with me."

Talia nodded in understanding. "See you later then."

Brionney walked down the hall toward her class, glad that her job as a visiting teaching supervisor didn't require her to teach. Jesse was probably in the office filling out forms and things for the members. Brionney missed sitting with him in class, but when he was able to finish the work during Sunday School, he could usually come home with her instead of staying after church.

A giggle flashed through the air. Brionney thought she saw something and turned. Two dark-haired toddlers, holding hands, were running around the corner. Brionney's heart lurched. Who were those children? She didn't recognize them. She dodged past the people trying to enter the Sunday School room, but when she turned the corner, no children were in sight. Again she heard the laughter. From the corner of her eye, she thought she saw the boys again. When she turned, the hall was empty.

She shakily leaned up against the wall. *My babies!* she thought. Tears blocked her vision. How much she wanted to hold them, to know that they were hers!

"Are you all right?" asked the Sunday School teacher, Brother Luckfield. He looked at her kindly.

Brionney breathed deeply. "Yes, I'm getting by, thank you."

"I heard about your loss. Have you had a priesthood blessing?" The words stung, inferring that if she had, the priesthood would immediately heal her heart and completely take away her pain.

Brionney had received a blessing from her father, as had Jesse, and though it had comforted her, she still needed to grieve. She had learned too well with Derek that going to church, receiving priesthood blessings, and obeying the commandments wouldn't spare her from all trials or growing pains. The gospel wasn't an abrupt cure, but a help, a comfort, a guiding light. The way home.

Why weren't people content to let her mourn her loss? Why did they think it meant so little?

That night, Brionney tried to broach the subject with Jesse. "Do you think the babies will be ours?"

"I want them to be. But I don't know." He sighed. "I just wish it had never happened. I wish they were still here." Though his words were polite, Brionney felt the distance between them grow. What was happening to their relationship?

His put his arms around her, and for a long moment they stood without talking. Then Jesse lowered his face and kissed her gently. Brionney pulled away and started to cry. "I can't," she said. Again, she saw the toddlers from the corner of her eye. She couldn't be happy—not yet.

Jesse withdrew immediately into the bedroom and dressed for bed. The house was utterly quiet.

Brionney's heart ached. She needed Jesse, needed his laughter and his love, his understanding, but she felt only coldness and silence from him. Somehow, they had to break through the surrounding barriers and find what they had lost before it progressed beyond repair. Like it had with Derek. Brionney's apprehension increased. How could she help Jesse, when she didn't seem to be able to help herself?

* * * * *

Jesse threw himself into his work with a vengeance. For the first time in his life, he felt completely alone. Brionney was immersed in her own grief, and he didn't know how to bridge the gap between them. She had tried several times to talk about the babies, but his own guilt was too heavy for him to look at or share. The emptiness in his heart seemed to grow. Each night he would pray, but he felt faithless. Why couldn't he just pick up and go on?

* * * * *

The second week in June, nearly a month after the miscarriage, Brionney was beginning to feel a little better. The sun sent bright rays from the sky, as though trying to warm her heart. Her visiting teachers had called to come over and Brionney put extra chairs on the porch, anticipating a nice visit.

One was an older woman named Emma Stillman. The other, Angela Philips, was about Brionney's age and was expecting her third child. "What a good idea, sitting out here on the porch," Angela said. "It's in the shade so we're not too hot, but we also don't have to be cooped up inside. I've been thinking all week that we need to build a covered front porch onto our house." She settled down in her chair with a sigh. "Only a month pregnant and I'm getting fat. And I've been so sick. I can't believe this pregnancy!"

Brionney smiled sympathetically, but her heart felt empty. When Emma brought out her *Ensign* to give the lesson, Brionney tried to listen, but she secretly watched Angela. What she wouldn't give to be sick and pregnant with the twins!

"So how do you feel about that?" Emma asked.

"What? Oh, I'm sorry. I didn't hear you. I—" Brionney suddenly wanted to cry. Since the miscarriage, the urge to weep came often and without warning.

Emma touched her shoulder. "I know you've had a rough time, dear. I'm so sorry you have to go through this."

"At least you have Savannah," Angela said. "And you know you are able to have more. I have a friend who miscarried with her first. She just feels terrible, not knowing if she's able to have children or not."

Brionney knew she was lucky to have Savannah, but she didn't feel it made losing the babies any easier.

"I don't know," Emma said. "I miscarried with my first baby. It was very painful at the time, but since I've had children, I have often thought how much harder it would have been for me to miscarry after knowing what I was missing. After having a child, I knew what it was like to feel their chubby arms around my neck. I knew how much I loved them. I felt the sacrifices and the joys. And had I then lost a child, I would have known that I was missing out on so much with that little baby. But I didn't know any of that before I had children, or at least not in the same way, because I hadn't learned what having and loving a child was all about. I guess that at any time miscarriage is a very difficult thing to deal with."

That was exactly how Brionney felt. She loved and missed her little boys so much! Emma's understanding comforted her.

"Well, I tried to tell her it was just tissue gone bad," Angela said. "And that she was lucky not to be burdened with a disabled child."

"Well that's not so bad," Emma said. "My little Michael has been a joy."

"And you do so well with him," Angela said. "But it is a lot of work, you have to admit."

Angela's comments, though said with good intent, made Brionney's grief even sharper because they denied her the right to have loved her babies as babies at all, suggesting that she was grieving for nothing. Did "tissue gone bad" have a soul?

"Oh, but it is getting warm, even out here," Angela said, not noticing the silence. She fanned herself with her hand. "Summer is just such a bad time to be pregnant. It makes you so much sicker. Oh, I wish I could feel good for a change. It just goes on and on."

"At least you have your baby." Brionney said the words before she knew they were coming.

Angela looked surprised. "Yes, I guess you're right. I never thought of it that way. I should be thankful." She stood, fanning her face with her hand. "Could I go inside and get a glass of water? I'm really getting hot."

As soon as she was gone, Emma leaned forward. "Don't be too hard on her. She hasn't had to go through many trials. Her turn will come. It always does. It's the refining fire."

"Thank you," Brionney said. "Thank you for coming and for understanding. It helps." She stared over the sandbox at the cherry tree. Not a whisper of a breeze played in the green leaves. She thought she heard laughter.

* * * * *

June continued, hot and sweltering. "July's heat in June" was everyone's favorite saying. The heat only added to Brionney's grief, listlessness, and growing unease with Jesse. She felt adrift in a sea of despair, with no direction in mind or compass to steer by. She prayed for relief, and the strength to hold on until it would come. "Hanging on" became her new motto. Talia had gone on from her miscarriages to find happiness, as had Emma and countless others. So would she . . . somehow.

One late afternoon, Brionney sat on her porch, watching Savannah in her wading pool. She and Roger held the hose, spraying water at the fish covering the inside of the sturdy plastic, seeming to get more water on the grass than inside the pool.

"Hi, Brionney."

She looked up to see Kris, her ex-mother-in-law, coming across the lawn. Her dark blonde hair had new highlights, and her makeup was subtly enhancing. Kris had visited several times since moving to Utah, but in the last month she had been scarce. Brionney had begun wondering if she had moved back to California.

"Hello, Kris," Brionney said, standing. "Come sit down."

Kris paused for a moment to talk to Savannah. "Look, Savvy, I brought you a present. It's a boat and people." Savannah accepted the present and promptly turned her back on Kris. She put the boat in the pool, and Roger tried to sink it with water. Both children laughed as if it was the funniest thing they had ever seen.

"Well, I'm good for something," Kris muttered as she came onto the porch. "I knew she'd like the boat since she's always in the pool, but I thought she'd at least look at me."

"She ignores me, too, when she's playing. It must be the age."

"Ahh." Kris settled on the top stair, closing her eyes. "It's better here in the shade."

"You look really good. You changed your hair."

Her lids fluttered open, and the blue eyes seemed more alive than Brionney had ever seen them. "I've just come from the beauty parlor. I've got a special date tonight."

"Oh, yeah? Who?"

"Name's Gary. He's a widower. I really like him."

"How'd you meet?"

She smiled. "He's my bishop. His wife died about six months ago, before I moved up from California. He's really nice."

"I didn't know you even went to church," Brionney said, nearly biting her tongue at the words.

Kris only laughed. "I didn't. But when I moved here, I decided it was time to get my life in order. I'm tired of being unhappy."

"I'm glad. You certainly look happy now."

"I'm getting there. And you? How's that new baby coming along?"

Brionney's breath was taken away by the unexpected question. "I . . . uh—" Unbidden, the tears came to her eyes. "I miscarried last month, about five weeks ago. Twins."

Her expression showed surprise. "Twins? Oh, I'm so sorry, Brionney. And me asking about it so unfeelingly. I'm sorry."

"It's okay. At least, I think it will be."

"Do you know—were they boys or girls?"

"Boys."

"Identical or fraternal?"

Pain shot through Brionney's heart. *My babies! My babies!* She took a deep breath. "Identical. They were in the same sac. Talia looked it up, and it's called monoamniotic twins."

Kris' face drew in puzzlement. "Is that bad? Sharing the same sac?"

"Well, it happens in less than two percent of all twins. It means a higher death rate, fifty to sixty-two percent." Talia had uncovered a varied array of information on monoamniotic twins, most of it unencouraging. Brionney had read all of the information in her quest for answers, but she didn't feel like talking about it now with Kris.

"I'm sorry, Brionney," Kris said again.

Brionney didn't reply. She let the pain in her heart fade into the afternoon as they sat in silence, watching the children play. In her mind, Brionney could almost see her other two splashing with them, a glimpse of dark hair and eyes before they slipped away.

"It always gets me how much Savvy reminds me of Derek when he was little," Kris said. "All that white hair and blue eyes. Of course, you have them, too. But when I see her, it reminds me of him when he was little and all mine."

"I can't imagine Savannah growing up and leaving me."

"Well, it will happen, but she'll remain close. Your family members are close, aren't they?"

"Yes, I'm very lucky."

"I often wonder how Derek would have turned out if his father had been around more. He was always leaving us, then coming back. It really hurt Derek, especially as he grew and began to understand more. It wasn't a life for a child." She paused and sighed. "I'm glad Savannah has a stable home. At first I wasn't too happy about Derek not exercising visiting rights, but it's better this way. Much as I don't like to admit it, Jesse's a better father for Savannah."

"He asked for a picture of her." Until now, Brionney had put that from her mind.

"He did? That's odd. But maybe he's growing up. I hope he doesn't cause problems for you."

"Me too."

"Well, I'll stick up for you if need be. I think Jesse's doing a great job." She paused, looking at Brionney worriedly. "What's wrong? Did I say something?"

"No. It's not you. It's Jesse. Ever since the miscarriage, things haven't been the same. At first I thought it was because he was tired of me moping around, but now I'm not too sure. I want him back the way he was before I lost the babies."

"He's probably having problems adjusting. Talk about it with him. You'll see."

"I'm scared to lose him," Brionney confessed. The remote feeling reminded her too much of her life with Derek. "I mean, he's never rude to me, and he comes home on time, but it's just not the same."

"I've seen how much he cares for you and Savannah. But don't be afraid to be the one to try to make things better. Maybe Jesse's feeling the same way you are. Maybe he doesn't know what to do about it."

Brionney thought about what she said. It was true; she had been waiting for Jesse to approach her, as he always had when something was wrong. The day she had told him she was pregnant was a prime example. Maybe this time he needed her to open the discussion.

"Thanks, Kris. Maybe I do need to get this out in the open."

"Better than worrying about it, that's for sure."

Their conversation moved on. They talked until Jesse came home from work. He sauntered across the grass, stopping to kiss Savannah and splash Roger.

Kris stood. "Well, I'd better get going. You let me know if you need anything. In fact, I'd love to baby-sit for you to go out with Jesse. How about on Friday?"

"Thanks, Kris. I'll let you know."

Kris stopped to greet Jesse and say good-bye to Savannah. After she left, Brionney joined Jesse near the pool. Together they emptied the water before going inside the house. Savannah pouted, but was quick to show Jesse her new boat. Jesse nodded and smiled, though he seemed far away. Brionney turned on the stove to heat up the casserole she had made earlier, all the while wondering how to broach the subject. While she paced in the kitchen, Jesse sat on the couch to read the paper.

"We're just coping," she said, loud enough for the words to carry. She didn't care how awkward they sounded. She wasn't about to live through another lonely night.

"What?" he said.

Words deserted her. "Nothing." But Brionney began to cry. She ran into the bathroom, sobbing, and Jesse put down his paper and followed. She was frustrated at her own tears, wondering why she couldn't simply talk to Jesse without such intense emotion. Talia had told her that depression and roller-coaster emotions were common after a miscarriage, but Brionney hated feeling out of control.

"What's wrong?" Jesse asked.

"What's wrong?" she repeated. "What's wrong? You're here, but you're not here. I need you, but I feel you slipping away. I've been in a marriage like that before, and I won't repeat the experience. *You* tell *me* what's wrong! Do you want to just give up, is that it? Are you tired of me?"

"No, no." He shook his head vigorously. "Not that. I love you! Oh, Brionney, don't ever think that! I will always be here for you. Forever, no matter what." He reached out but she backed away from him, sitting on the closed toilet seat.

"Well, you're not here for me! And I don't know why. Is it the babies? I can understand that." She motioned to the bathtub. "I feel it, too. I can't close my eyes or come in here without seeing that tub filled with blood, or seeing our tiny babies who trusted me. I failed them, don't you see?" The tears slid down her cheeks unchecked. "And now I feel that I'm failing you somehow. We need to talk about it. We need to stand together." Brionney wiped furiously at her eyes so she could see Jesse's expression, not knowing what to expect. She only wanted him back the way he had been.

He sat on the edge of the bathtub and took her hands. This time she didn't pull away, wanting so desperately for him to hold her. "It just doesn't seem real," he said. "The baby—babies—being gone. And I thought if I could just work it out in my mind, then things would be okay."

Brionney gulped, trying to stop the flood of tears. "I know. I know. I need to understand about the babies, to know if and when they will be ours. But no one knows. Everyone believes something different, even among the members."

"I talked to the bishop today. He called me at work. He did some research, but all he could say is that the Church doesn't have a policy on babies who die before they are born, even full-term babies. None are recorded on the official records of the Church. He did find a quote saying that every loss in this life will be compensated for, somehow."

"But how? And when? And how can you and I go back to what was before? I want us to be happy!"

"I want that, too—more than anything. But there's something I didn't tell you, Brionney. Back when I was in school and you got so sick, I started to wish you hadn't been pregnant at all. I thought if we had waited, it wouldn't have been so hard. And even though I realized I was wrong, and that I was the one who was being too proud to accept any help, I wished the pregnancy away. And now the babies are gone. It just hurts. How could I be so blind and stupid?"

"It was just a thought," Brionney said, looking at him earnestly. "In the end, you did what was right. You supported me, let others help, and loved those babies! Why, if a woman miscarried every time she wished she wasn't sick and pregnant, there wouldn't be any babies at all! Don't you see? You don't have to feel guilty! I love you so much, and I know you would do anything to have our babies back again. Let's just face this together."

He hugged her tightly. "I wonder why us?" he asked softly. "I mean, we've been trying to do what's right. And we want children. We haven't even waited years before having them like some people. And then this happens to us, when there are so many people out there aborting their babies, giving them away, or abusing them. It's hard for me to understand. It's almost like the Lord doesn't care about how hard we've been trying."

"I don't know," she said. "And I didn't know why Derek left me, either. But now there's you, and I can't live without you. I just couldn't see that then, when I was suffering."

"But how can this be good for us? There seems to be no purpose."

Brionney wished she had an answer. "Maybe someday we'll know."

"So this is what growing feels like," he said with a groan. "I'm afraid I haven't passed this test very well. It's hard to lose so much."

"We have each other."

He put a hand on either side of her face, and in his eyes she could see all of the love he had in his heart. "And I won't give you up. You are the best thing that ever happened to me."

"You too," she agreed. "But do you think we'll see the babies again? I want so much to know."

"I believe so," he said. "I feel it in my heart. But I don't know how or where. And all I can think of is for us to pray with all our hearts to be able to come to some understanding, and to ask the Lord to bless our marriage, so that we can be there for each other. I meant what I said before. I love you, and I promise that will never change, but we need some help getting through this."

Brionney tightened her grip on his hands, more grateful than she could express for a man who could turn to the Lord to solve problems, instead of running away. "Okay, let's do it." They hugged again, more tightly, and Brionney felt the tension between them evaporating.

But Jesse wasn't finished. "You have to stop blaming yourself, too. Promise you'll try? There was nothing you could do. You tried to give them life. What happened wasn't your fault."

His words eased the guilt she felt more than anything she could have told herself. "I promise," she said. "But there's a lot of promising going on here."

He laughed and drew her to her feet. "Oh, Brionney, we are just beginning with the promises. The best is yet ahead. We'll have a wonderful future!"

That night they lay in bed after a fervent joint prayer, with only the moonlight coming through the thin curtains to light the darkness. Holding each other, they calmly discussed the possibilities of seeing the twins again. Brionney felt a peace come into her heart. She didn't know if her babies would come down to her again in the form of infants, or if she would have them in the millennium or beyond, but she knew they were hers. She knew the Lord loved her and Jesse and the babies, and at last that seemed to be enough.

Brionney heard laughter, and she looked toward the source. Even in the dark she caught a glimpse of the twins. This time there was no sadness, only a promise. The Lord had been sending reassurance all along, only she hadn't recognized it as such. Maybe it was time to try again.

CHAPTER TWENTY-SEVEN

"I want another baby," Brionney said a few weeks later. Her cycle had returned the week before, and she would be ovulating soon. As the days had passed, she had stopped seeing the pink water, and only occasional sadness marked her days. She felt closer than ever to Jesse as they had made a practice of sharing their deepest thoughts each night in earnest prayers to the Lord. This strengthening of their marriage because of the miscarriage was a blessing Brionney hadn't counted on, but for which she was profoundly grateful.

"But we're supposed to wait three months," Jesse said. Brionney had visited the doctor following the miscarriage, and he had been very firm about waiting. "I'm worried about your health."

"But I can't wait anymore, Jesse. I need another baby. Please can we try? I feel fine. I'm strong and rested."

"If you're sure that's what you want," he conceded reluctantly after several of her heartfelt pleas.

Brionney jumped in the air with a shout. "Oh, I am."

The next month went by and she didn't get pregnant. She was depressed, desperately wanting a baby more than before. "What if we can't ever have another child?"

"Don't worry," Jesse said, holding her close. "Remember how fertile your family is? We forgot to wash our underwear together, that's all. It'll happen next month."

But August came, and again Brionney felt cramps signaling the onset of her menstrual cycle. In frustration, she left the house as soon as Jesse arrived from work, taking the Fiesta for a long drive. She cried and begged the Lord to give her a child to replace those she had lost.

A calming feeling spread over her, but she refused to be comforted. When she returned to the apartment, dinner was long cold and Savannah already in bed.

Jesse met her at the door. "Are you okay?"

She nearly fell into his arms. "I guess. I thought for sure I'd be pregnant this time."

"Maybe you are."

"But the cramps . . ."

"I called your mother when you were gone. I was worried about you, and I thought maybe you went there. She asked if you had left Savannah. I said yes and she said I shouldn't worry, that you'd be back real soon. You'd never leave Savannah for long. She said you were acting so crabby that you must be pregnant!"

Brionney laughed despite her depression. Jesse turned from her and picked up the car keys where she had thrown them on the coffee table. "Where are you going?" she asked.

"To buy a pregnancy test. You can take it tomorrow, can't you?"

She nodded. "They say the test is best in the morning, when there's a higher concentration of the hormones. It's more accurate."

"I'll be right back." He kissed her and disappeared into the night.

The next morning they eagerly awaited the result. Negative. Brionney was too upset to even cry, and Jesse held her, stroking her hair. "It's okay. We should have waited three months anyway. Remember what the doctor said? This merely proves that your body needs time to heal." His words were comforting, but it was heartbreaking for her to want a child so desperately. Maybe the miscarriage had messed something up inside, and she would never be able to conceive again. There was always that possibility. Brionney had known people who hadn't been able to have children, and for the first time, she began to have a very small understanding of what they had been through.

"It sometimes takes time," Talia said to her later that afternoon. She had come to pick up Roger after running errands in the heat of the day. Her face was streaked with perspiration. "I've heard of people not getting pregnant again for six months or more after a miscarriage. Some have to wait over a year before their bodies are ready."

"You never had any problem." Brionney helped Savannah add a block to the tower she was building next to the couch.

"No, but that doesn't mean much. People are different. For instance, we come from the same family, but I have dirty dishwater hair and you have pure blonde locks that people would die for."

"Yeah, right. But I'm tired of waiting! Each day seems like an eternity. Logically, I know it's not yet been three months, but it seems more like three years."

Talia sighed and slumped onto a chair. She accidentally kicked Savannah's block tower over with her foot. "Oh, don't cry. Aunt Talia will help fix it."

"I can do it," Roger said importantly. He was three and a half and mothered Savannah at every opportunity.

"I do it myself!" Savannah insisted, her words blurred but recognizable.

Brionney smiled. "She'll be two this month. Can you tell?"

"Oh, what joys are in store!" Talia said. "Maybe it's just as well you aren't pregnant." Ignoring Brionney's frown, she added, "Well, I guess I'd better get up to the house. The other children will be wondering where I am. Joe Jr. is a good baby-sitter, but his patience with his brothers doesn't last very long."

"I haven't heard anything from them. They would have come over if they had a problem."

"Well, I told them you were in charge, but you never know. Thanks for watching Roger. Come on, buddy, let's go."

"No. I want to stay and play!"

"Come on. Now." Talia's voice was firm, and Roger stood up obediently. Brionney made a mental note to practice that tone. Perhaps it would work with Savannah.

The phone rang and she hurried to answer it. Sometimes Jesse called from work, just to say hi. "Hello?" Brionney said, waving to Talia.

"Hi, Brionney, this is Derek."

"Derek?" Her heart seemed to stop beating. She had hoped never to hear his voice again.

"Come on, Mom," Roger said when his mother stopped in midstride. "Let's go."

Talia shook her head. "We're going to stay for a little longer."

"Yeah!" Roger was on the floor in a second, reaching for a block.

Brionney closed her eyes, and the scene before her vanished. There was only Derek and the phone. "How are you?" he asked.

"I'm fine. And you?" Her voice was dull and mechanical. "Why are you calling?"

"Well, I wanted to see how you and Savannah are doing."

Brionney knew him too well to believe that. "What do you want, Derek?"

"Just to see Savannah."

A flurry of emotions ran over Brionney—rage, curiosity, and fear. "Why? Why now?"

"Do I need a reason to see my daughter?"

Rage won, and she let it come through in her voice. "Yes, I think you do. You've never showed any interest before, then suddenly you ask for a picture, and now you want to see her. Why? Tell me the truth."

"I just want to see her."

"I don't buy that," Brionney said through gritted teeth. "What's the real reason?"

"It's Melinda," he said after a long pause. "We've been trying to have a baby and it's not working. I thought maybe if she could spend some time with Savannah—"

"You want to see my daughter so your wife will feel better? You have got to be kidding! You call after this long and don't want to see her for yourself, but because of Melinda?"

"Easy, Brionney. You wouldn't know what it is like not to be able to have a child."

His words made her fume. "I will not take it easy! I'm not interested in Melinda's feelings. I don't care if she ever has a child, and I won't share Savannah with her!"

"I am Savannah's father." Derek's voice was still calm, but Brionney could hear the controlled anger. "She needs a father, and just because I gave you guardianship at the divorce doesn't mean I don't have the right to at least see her."

"She has a father," Brionney said. "One who loves her more than you ever did, one who has been here for her every day that you weren't."

"I just want to see her for a few days a month, not take her away."

"But she doesn't even know you from a stranger on the street!" She wished she could pound the words into his brain. "You can't expect to come back into her life so easily. And what if you do? Once she loves you, are you going to promise never to leave her again? I've seen your mother a few times these last few months, and I know that's what you went through as a child with your father constantly leaving. Is that what you want for Savannah? Well, I don't want her hurt. She deserves stability. And what about the gospel? Will you teach her how important it is? Surely you still believe it's important."

"I see I'm going to have to go through our lawyers," he said tightly. "I thought we could work out something amicably, but—"

"And I'm not saying we can't," Brionney said. "But I want what's best for Savannah, not for Melinda."

"Well, I've got to run. I have a meeting. Think about what I said. I'll be in touch." Derek hung up before she could say anything more.

Brionney stared at the receiver in her hand, not believing what had happened. "Not now," she murmured, sinking to the couch. First she had lost the twins, and now Derek wanted Savannah.

A vision came into her mind of that terrible day when she had found a tiny Savannah hanging from the bars in Derek's bedroom, pressed against the blankets. Her face had been so dark. A minute or so longer, and Savannah wouldn't be alive today. And this was the man who wanted to see her daughter? *Dear Father, please, no!*

"Brionney?" A tentative voice called her back from the agonizing memories. Talia took the receiver from her hand and returned it to the cradle.

"It was Derek. He wants to see Savannah." Brionney looked at her daughter, playing so innocently on the floor with her tower of blocks. "Melinda wants to see her. She stole my husband, and now she wants my baby."

CHAPTER TWENTY-EIGHT

Pacing the small space between the kitchen and the front room, Brionney waited for Jesse to come home. Too upset to make dinner, she continued her rotations, stopping occasionally to help Savannah with her blocks. The little girl's face was filled with delighted abandon at each new addition, and her laughter resounded through the small apartment when the blocks toppled and fell to the ground.

How could Brionney share even a minute of Savannah's time with Derek? What kind of things might happen to her when Brionney was far away? Her last time alone with Derek had nearly killed her. Even putting that aside, what kind of health risk would the second-hand smoke have for her? And was Derek still into pornography? Would Savannah cry herself to sleep without Brionney or Jesse to read to her? What kind of morals would she learn? There was no end to the questions.

Sunlight fell through the open mini-blinds and onto the floor near Savannah, and she left the blocks to examine the pattern, unconcerned and trusting. Brionney sighed and walked back to the kitchen, picking up several discarded crayon wrappers from Savannah's earlier play. As she put them in the garbage under the sink, her eyes fell on the remains of the pregnancy test Jesse had bought the night before. She shut her eyes to soothe the sudden burning sensation. Everything seemed to be rapidly falling apart.

A banging door made her whirl and take the few steps back into the living room. There, Jesse was hugging Savannah with one arm, and holding in the other a large bouquet of red roses. He straightened and grinned as Brionney came into the room, then presented the bouquet to her with a flourish. "Beautiful flowers for the most beautiful woman in the world."

Her mouth curved in a tight smile. She knew he was trying to tell her it didn't matter that she wasn't yet pregnant, but at the moment that was the least of her concerns. Jesse looked so young, open, and loving, and she wished she could simply throw her arms around him instead of telling him the terrible news.

"What's wrong?"

She buried her nose in the heady fragrance of the flowers just once before setting them to the side and taking his hand. "We'd better sit."

Jesse's face wrinkled in worry, but he complied without comment.

"Derek called. He wants to see Savannah."

Jesse paled. "He can't! I thought he gave up all custody rights."

At the mention of her name, Savannah walked over and climbed onto Jesse's lap. He smiled at her absently, stroking her hair.

"He did. But it doesn't exclude visits, though I'm not sure exactly how it's worded. He didn't seem interested in Savannah at all at the time, except to teach me a lesson about fighting him. At first, I actually hoped he'd change and want to see her. But now things are different. She has you, and Derek is so unstable. He and Melinda both smoke, and I don't want Savannah in that kind of environment, even temporarily. And who knows what Melinda will teach her?" Brionney was becoming agitated again, wringing her hands and biting her lip between words. "Besides, she needs her mommy!"

Jesse grabbed her hands and held them tightly. "It's going to be okay. We always knew this could happen one day. No matter what, we won't let him take Savannah from us. That's not even an option."

"I had decided to ask Max to approach Derek about your adopting Savannah. I thought Derek would agree, especially since he and Melinda had their own life now. Since they asked for the picture, we haven't heard anything. And that was months ago, before the miscarr–" She broke off, unable to continue.

"Well, the first thing we need to do is call Max and see exactly where we stand."

"But we can't let her go. She doesn't even know them!"

Jesse's eyes were red from emotion, and she knew he didn't want to let Derek see Savannah either, but his expression showed there was something more to his feelings—something Brionney might not like. "Brionney," he said slowly, "I know Derek may not be the best father, but he is Savannah's father."

"You're Savannah's father!" she cried. "He gave up rights to her. What kind of a father would do that?"

His eyes pleaded for her to understand. "It came to me just now, in a flash. What if he misses her? What if seeing her brings him back to the Church? What if he loves her? I know it would destroy me if I couldn't at least see Savannah. Do you remember when I wished you hadn't been pregnant? Like I blamed my troubles on the baby—that if it didn't exist, I would be able to make it all work the way I wanted it to? Well, I know now how wrong I was. But at the time, it seemed so logical. I started thinking just now: what if that's what happened to Derek? What if at the time Savannah was born, it was just too much? What if now he feels he could handle the responsibility?" Jesse's voice broke. "I don't want him in Savannah's life any more than you do. It tears me up inside to think of her calling him Daddy. Like you said, *I'm* her daddy. But maybe like with the miscarriage, we can't see the whole picture now."

Brionney shook her head, furious at him for giving Derek attributes she knew he didn't possess. She had never imagined he might feel sorry for Derek. "No! You don't know him like I do. He wants Savannah simply because Melinda can't get pregnant. He told me so himself."

"He said that?"

"Yes."

Jesse's eyes narrowed. "If he doesn't really want her, then that changes things. We can't let him disrupt our daughter's life simply because of Melinda. She has no say in this."

"I'm calling Max," Brionney said, grateful to hear him call Savannah "our daughter." Grabbing the phone off the side table, she dialed the number from memory. Debbie answered.

"Hi, this is Brionney."

"Well, how wonderful to hear from you! How are things?"

"I need to talk with Max. Is he there?"

"No, but I can have him call you when he gets home. What's up? It sounds serious."

"Derek called and wants to see Savannah," Brionney said brokenly. "She's so little, and she doesn't even know him. I'm afraid!"

"Well, don't you do anything until Max calls you, okay? He'll know what to do. Just sit tight. I'll call him at the office. He'll still be there for another hour or so."

"Thanks, Debbie," Brionney managed. "You're always saving me, aren't you?"

"Hey, it puts interest into my life. Hang up now, okay? Max will call as soon as he can."

Brionney let the phone drop. Next to her, Jesse held Savannah with a wistful expression. "I wish she were mine," he said softly. The torment in his voice made Brionney forgive him completely for his earlier comments.

"In every way that means anything, she is yours."

He nodded, his jaw clenched. "We'll get through this somehow. We will." His voice was determined and his arms tightened about Savannah. She squirmed uncomfortably until Jesse stood and put her on his shoulders. "Let's see about dinner, huh, Savannah? Your mom's too upset to figure it out. Come on." With Savannah squealing in laughter, Jesse galloped into the kitchen.

Men! How can they think of food at a time like this!

Max didn't return Brionney's call until three hours later. Savannah was already asleep in her bed after hearing four bedtime stories from Jesse. Lying there so still, she looked sweeter than any angel Brionney could imagine. The thought of being separated from her daughter, if only for a few days each month, made Brionney's heart freeze. Visions of Savannah alone on an airplane were particularly torturous. And the long days she would spend with strangers. How could Brionney protect Savannah if she couldn't be with her? Derek certainly didn't know how.

Brionney picked up the phone on the first ring. "Max?" she asked without saying hello.

"Yes. I'm sorry I've taken so long in getting back to you. I was with a client."

"Did Debbie tell you what's going on?"

"Yes, and I've been reviewing your divorce papers. It says here that Derek can have day visits, but only in the state in which you reside."

Relief swept through her. "So I don't have to let him see her in Arizona?"

"No. He'd have to come to Utah."

"Is there any chance he could get that changed?"

"He could go back to court, but given Savannah's age at the separation and the fact that you reside in Utah, I doubt he'd accomplish anything but squander a lot of money. His lawyer will tell him the same thing. In fact, his lawyer probably did. I'll bet that's why he called you directly."

"But if he does come here, I have to let him see her?"

"Yes."

"But she doesn't even know him!"

"In that case I can make sure there is an adjustment period, or perhaps a third-party person who could go along on the visits. But he does have the right to see her. Of course, exercising those rights could mean that he has to pay child support, if you insist."

"Oh, I would." The pocketbook was one place Brionney knew Derek was sensitive. "But I'd rather have Jesse adopt her."

"I can draw up that request. But given Derek's phone call, he probably won't agree. At least not right now."

"I don't know what to do."

"Well, sleep on it and let me know what you decide. He said he'd call you again, but maybe he won't. Meanwhile, I'll make sure his lawyer knows that in order to see her, Derek will have to pay child support."

"I think I need a miracle," Brionney said.

"Well, pray hard. Good luck."

Brionney hung up the phone and repeated the conversation to Jesse. He put his arms around her. "We can fight this," he said. "We can make it so miserable for Derek that he gives up. If that's what you want."

"Or?"

He heaved a long sigh. "Or we can pray and decide what's right. But I don't think any decision we make is going to be easy."

"It never is, is it?"

"No. But we still have each other."

* * * * *

The next week they both spent a lot of time on their knees. On Sunday they fasted and finally came to a decision. As much as they disliked the idea, if Derek wanted a relationship with Savannah, they couldn't deny it to her. She had the right to know her biological father. At least it would only be for a day at a time and in Utah, so safety would not be as big an issue.

"But what if he kidnaps her?" Brionney hadn't wanted to bring it up, but it was something they had to discuss. "He did it once before."

"But then he would have to give up his whole life. And from what you tell me, he's rather selfish in that respect. Besides, our answer came from the Lord, didn't it?"

Brionney knew he was right. "I'm so glad you're here facing this with me. I couldn't do it alone."

Derek called on a Monday morning. Brionney wondered if he chose that time because he knew she would be alone, and perhaps more vulnerable. Brionney didn't feel vulnerable. She was like a tigress protecting her young, and Derek was fresh meat.

Phone in hand, Brionney sat on the sofa with Savannah on her lap. She could see their reflections in the glass of the entertainment center, and a sudden picture of herself when Derek had left her came to mind. The woman she saw now no longer resembled that other Brionney. She was strong and sure of herself and of her standing before the Lord. She had faced great trials and had won.

As calmly as possible, Brionney told Derek what Max had told her. "So if you are serious about seeing Savannah, you will have to come here."

"You couldn't just send her on a plane?"

"No. I won't. And you'll have to pay child support."

"For just a couple days a month?"

"Either you are her father, or you aren't. You can't have it both ways."

"Whatever," he grumbled. "You'll get your money."

"And you'll have to make the first visits here or somewhere with us until she is used to you. I won't let her go unless she wants to be with you. Convincing her will be your job—yours and Melinda's." The name tasted sour on her lips, but she forced herself to continue. "Now it's up to you. And, Derek, Savannah's a special little girl. I love her more than life itself. If you start this, there's no going back. You can't hurt her like that. I want you to be sure *you* want this, that you're not doing it for Melinda. Think about how your wife will feel about Savannah when she does finally get pregnant or you adopt a child. Or if you break up and you remarry again. How will that affect our daughter?"

Derek grunted, but other than that gave no sign of having heard.

"Please, Derek. Once she meant something to you. We both did. Please think about it."

"Okay," he said gruffly. "Look, I'll get back to you about the first visit. I think we could drive down in a couple of weeks. Maybe stay with my mom."

"It's her birthday this week. Savannah's, I mean."

"It is?"

"Yes, on Friday. She'll be two."

"I'll send her a present." It wasn't quite the reaction Brionney had hoped for. Not once had Derek said he wanted to see Savannah for himself. Still, perhaps it was a start.

* * * * *

The week flew by as Brionney made preparations for Savannah's birthday. She decided to have a family barbecue in the evening, when the August heat would have cooled a bit. Brionney invited her parents, her sisters and their families, and Kris, Derek's mother. Talia volunteered to help with the food, and Jesse decorated the tall shade trees and the picnic table with balloons and streamers.

As the people gathered, Savannah was excited to see the growing pile of presents on the table, not quite understanding about turning two, but knowing they were for her. She clapped her hands and laughed loudly, running about the yard in a fevered excitement.

The cousins piled in the huge sandbox, filling the air with laughter. They made everything from castles to bridges, the older children ordering the younger ones about as if they were contractors on a job. "Hey, what about a moat," Jesse said, looking as though he would like to join the children.

The sandbox was unshaded since the cherry tree had not grown very tall or bushy in the three months since its planting. The children didn't seem to mind. The two flat stones still marked the base of the tree, leaving Brionney with the feeling that her other children were there in spirit.

"Is everyone here?" Talia asked, coming out of her house with a plateful of raw hamburgers.

Brionney scanned the small crowd. "Everyone but Kris. I think she'll be here soon. We should start the hamburgers cooking now and say the prayer when she gets here."

Talia nodded, but she seemed distracted. "Hey, Joe," she called, "here are the burgers." Joe ran across the lawn and took the plate from her. With his free hand he opened the gas grill and deftly slapped the meat on.

"Did you tell her?" he asked, glancing at Brionney.

Talia shook her head. "I'm going to right now."

"Tell me what?"

She sighed and walked away from Joe, motioning for Brionney to follow. "I'm pregnant. I wanted to tell you before Joe announces it tonight."

The news hit Brionney hard, but she loved her sister enough to be happy for her. "But that's wonderful! At least I think it is. Do you want another child?"

"Yes, we do. But I think this is the last one."

"I don't blame you. Five children and four miscarriages are enough for anyone to go through. How far along are you?"

Her face reddened slightly. "Three and a half months. I—I found out right after you miscarried, and I was afraid to tell you. At first I thought you'd notice how sick I've been, but you've had your own troubles. And the more time passed, the harder it grew, especially since you've been trying to get pregnant. I didn't want to hurt you."

"I'm happy for you, I really am."

She seemed relieved. "Well, let's just hope I'll keep it."

"Have you been to the doctor?"

"Yes. He gave me an ultrasound last week, and everything is okay so far."

"That's good."

"Yes, and don't you worry, your time will come." She patted Brionney's arm and went off to help Joe with the hamburgers. Brionney sighed. Finding out that Talia was pregnant wasn't as hard to take as her last patronizing words.

Kris's arrival drove these thoughts from Brionney's mind. She came from the front, accompanied by a distinguished older gentleman, and looking happier than Brionney had ever remembered. They both staggered slightly under the weight of an enormous box wrapped in gold foil paper.

"That's some present!" Brionney crossed the lawn to meet them.

Kris' smile dimmed slightly. "It weighs a ton."

"Hey, we need some help over here!" Brionney called. Jesse and one of her brothers-in-law came running. The children spied the box and began yelling excited guesses at one another.

"I'm glad you could make it," Brionney said to Kris when they had relieved the older couple of the monstrous box. "We've been wondering when you'd show up. We're about ready for the prayer."

"I got a phone call just before we left. It took longer than expected." The way she said it made Brionney feel that somehow the phone call concerned Savannah.

"What—"

"I'll tell you later," Kris said. "But first let me introduce my date. This is Gary Winston, my bishop." She smiled at him, winking.

"It's nice to meet you. I'm Brionney."

Gary was tall and good-looking, with graying hair and a kind smile. His eyes held a sad wisdom as if he had seen many trials, yet they were also full of new hope. "And it's very nice to finally meet you," he said. "Kris has told me all about you."

Kris introduced Gary around, then Jesse called for a prayer. In the following rush for food, Brionney nearly forgot about Kris and her phone call until Savannah opened her presents. For the first time, Brionney noticed that Kris had brought another small package, wrapped in different paper than the gold foil-wrapped box. As though of its own will, Brionney's hand reached out to the giant box and removed the unsealed card. A small stack of pictures slipped out, and immediately she understood. Her heart stilled further as she read the card. *From Dad and Mom-Melinda*, it read, written in a woman's flowing script. The audacity of the wording made Brionney's blood boil. *Whatever you are to Derek*, Brionney told the absent Melinda, *you will never be a mother to my daughter.*

"The utter gall of that woman!" Kris said. "I would have removed the card, but I felt you should see it."

"The phone call was from Derek, wasn't it?"

"Yes. He called to ask me if I would go with him and Melinda on their outing with Savannah. I didn't realize he'd decided to see her."

"Well, he has. But it's not him who wants Savannah, it's Melinda."

"That much I guessed. I talked to her on the phone, too. That's what took me so long. She went on about how we'd take Savannah to Lagoon, and how she hoped these visits could eventually last for a few days. On and on she went about how she and Derek would be such good parents. It positively made me sick."

Hearing her say it, Brionney's own stomach became queasy. "She doesn't care about Savannah, does she?"

"How can she? She doesn't know her. I think she just has a dream of being the perfect wife and mother—no matter what it does to Savannah. It's purely selfish."

"What can I do, Kris?"

She shook her head slowly. "Nothing. Except pray for a miracle." The words sounded strange coming from her lips, but she had changed a lot in the last year. "But I'll take good care of Savannah, don't you worry. And I'm going to come by every other day in the next week so Savannah will feel more comfortable with me."

"Thanks, Kris. Who would ever have thought you could be so great, when Derek is so—"

"So stupid," she finished. "But even stupid people can change." She took Melinda's card and ripped it into shreds. "Whatever happens, we won't let Savannah suffer." She turned into the melee of gift givers, pushing the present nearer the birthday girl. "Here's one more, sweetie." She didn't mention who it was from.

Savannah had the eager help of cousins as she tore the paper to reveal a Little Tikes plastic castle. There were whistles of amazement among the adults and shouts of glee from the children.

Brionney sighed. This extravagant present was as presumptuous as its giver.

* * * * *

Later that evening, when Jesse heard about Derek's phone call and Melinda's card, he was worried. He had tried to be fair where Derek was concerned, but he didn't like the way things had begun to look.

His own guilt over not wanting and then losing the babies obviously had no relationship to Derek's nonexistent feelings for Savannah. Jesse wished he could fight the man for paternity. He knew he would win.

Jesse gazed at Savannah, who had fallen asleep in his arms. "I think it's time you and I went to Lagoon," he said to Brionney.

She turned to him in surprise. "You too?"

"For the first time at least. We have to feel good about it. If this is what the Lord wants, we need to comply. But that doesn't mean we trust them completely."

"That's just it. Derek's not trustworthy. And even with Kris along . . . I don't know. I'm really scared."

"Heavenly Father loves Savannah," Jesse said. The confusion he felt was endless. Derek was Savannah's biological father, but Jesse was there for her every day. In the Lord's eyes, when did Derek's rights end and his begin? He wished the situation were more simple. "Let's pray as hard as we can."

A miracle was all they needed, yet Jesse prayed not for it, but for Savannah. If it was best for her to see Derek, then that's what he wanted—no matter how fiercely he detested the idea. He would do anything for her, even though it pierced his heart to let another man into her life.

In their joint prayer, Brionney finished by saying, "We pray that Thy will be done." Jesse added his silent petition to hers.

CHAPTER TWENTY-NINE

The visitation was set for the first week in September, just over a week after Savannah's birthday party. The days passed more quickly than they should have, and each day Jesse's anxiety grew. "Did you tell them we were going with them?" he asked.

"Not yet." Brionney's eyes had deep shadows around them, as though she had slept little. "But I'm still going."

"Me too." He sat down on the couch with the pictures Melinda had sent. "Come here, Savannah. I have something to show you." Savannah came willingly. "See this man here?"

"Man," Savannah said.

"Yes. He's coming to take you to a really fun place."

"Go bye-bye?"

"Yes, exactly. His name is Derek, but he's also your dad. Your other dad."

Savannah pointed to Jesse's chest. "You Daddy."

"Yes, I'm your dad, but his name is Daddy Derek. Can you say that?"

The little girl's eyebrows scrunched together. "You Daddy."

"I know. And this is Daddy Derek."

"Daddy Derek?" Savannah giggled.

Jesse's heart filled with pain. "Yes, that's his name. And this is Melinda."

"Linda," Savannah repeated obediently.

"Good, now who's this?" Jesse pointed to Derek.

"Him," she said.

"Daddy Derek."

"Daddy Derek." Savannah lost interest in the pictures. "Ride, Daddy. Want ride. Give ride me?"

"Sure." Jesse arose and put her on his shoulders.

"Yee-ha!" Savannah shouted.

Jesse played with her until she tired of the game, then he went back to the pictures. "Do you really have to do that?" Brionney asked. The pain in her face matched the torment in his heart.

"We don't want her to be scared. It's the only way I know. It worked with my mom. I just wish—" But there was no use in wishing. He turned to Savannah. "Who's that?"

"Daddy, you!" she said. "No him."

* * * * *

The dreaded day arrived. The brief rap at the door was strangely familiar, and Brionney went to open it with a heavy heart. Derek stood outside, as handsome as ever, but obviously nervous. Behind him was Kris and also Melinda, who looked ravishing but slightly overdressed in a tight-fitting gold pantsuit.

"Come in." Brionney opened the door wider. Kris flashed her a sympathetic grin. "We'll be ready in a minute," Brionney said. She called down the hall, "Jesse, they're here."

Jesse came out with Savannah, who was dressed in Levis, her favorite pink-striped shirt, and white tennis shoes. "Hey, Savannah. Look who's here. Do you remember those pictures?"

Savannah gazed curiously at the strangers, but made no move toward them. Melinda approached and said in a bright tone, "Well, hello there, sweetie. I'm Melinda. Can you say Melinda?"

Savannah ducked behind Jesse.

"Look what I brought you," Melinda continued in the same falsetto. She shook the sack in her hands. "It's a present. I thought you could wear it on our outing today." Melinda pulled out a designer-label toddler outfit, full of ruffles and lace.

Savannah peeked at the party outfit, but shook her head. "No way." She pointed to her pink top. "Shirt pretty."

Melinda looked frustrated, but she didn't push the issue. She turned to Brionney. "Would you put this on her?"

"For Lagoon? Are you kidding?" Brionney glanced at Derek, who was studying the couch. Kris' face showed amusement.

"I don't know if you've heard about the terrible twos," Jesse said. "But part of that means picking out her own clothes. These here are her favorites. Brionney has to coax her out of them at bedtime as it is. I really don't see the purpose of making her cry just to wear something else, do you? It's really not important, and this is her first impression of you. Besides, they match. You should see some of her other choices."

"Very well." Melinda gave a frustrated sigh and shoved the elaborate outfit back into the bag. She didn't give it to Savannah or Brionney. No doubt she would try to make Savannah wear it on some future outing.

Derek glanced at his watch. Brionney noticed that it wasn't the one she had given him for their wedding. "We should get going."

"Do you have six seat belts?" Brionney asked. "Or should we take separate cars?"

Derek looked surprised. "Six?"

"We're going too. It's her first time. You can't expect me just to let her go."

Melinda glared darkly at Brionney. "But that's what Kris is here for!"

"She's never been away all day, even with Kris," Brionney retorted. She met Melinda's gaze without flinching.

"Well, there are enough belts," Kris said. "They have a new car."

Now Melinda glared at her. Even her glares were attractive. She turned to Derek. "How are we ever going to get to know her if they're with us?"

Brionney frowned. "Time. It takes time. We've known her two years, you've known her two minutes. If you're serious about being part of her life, you need to have patience. Or you can turn right around and go back to Arizona."

"We're not going to hurt her," Derek said. His voice inferred that Brionney was an idiot to even think such a thing.

Brionney didn't flinch. "That's what I thought the last time you took her."

They stared at each other for a full minute. "Okay, let's go," Derek said finally.

Melinda started to say something, but Derek's eyebrows furrowed in warning. She clenched her fists and fumed silently.

Kris turned to Savannah. "Come on, Savvy. Let's go bye-bye." Savannah smiled and held out her arms to her grandmother.

As they passed Derek by the door, Savannah pointed at him. "Derek, you."

Derek smiled. "That's right. I'm Derek."

"Daddy," Melinda corrected.

Savannah glanced at Jesse. "Daddy Derek?" Then she laughed.

Brionney thought she saw a flicker of pleasure in Derek's face. Jesse looked sick, and Brionney took his hand, squeezing it in reassurance.

The long drive was tense and silent. Only Melinda felt the need to chatter, and Brionney wondered if it was because she wanted a cigarette. The car certainly smelled like tobacco, but she had made Derek promise not to smoke in a closed space with Savannah. Once in the Lagoon parking lot, Melinda immediately jumped out of the car and lit up.

Savannah was filled with excitement at the rides and noise, but after a few hours she was cranky and tired. Melinda constantly talked to her in bright tones and a wide smile, while Derek merely watched from a distance. They stopped for lunch, and Savannah fell asleep in Brionney's arms.

"May I hold her?" Derek asked.

Fighting the urge to say no, Brionney let him take Savannah in his arms. The contented look on his face was one she had never seen before, and even the satisfaction in Melinda's eyes didn't make Brionney regret letting Derek hold Savannah. After all, it was Derek who was Savannah's father, not Melinda. He was the one who needed to know his daughter, if either of them did.

The whole morning Brionney had tried to stay in the background, to let Savannah get to know Derek and Melinda. Jesse had done the same. "But that woman makes me so angry," Brionney whispered to him privately. She glanced at Melinda at the next table, who sat as close to Derek and Savannah as she could possibly get without sitting on his lap. "I want to strangle her or something!"

"She is irritating," Jesse agreed. "I keep trying to see her as a woman who can't have children. But I keep thinking maybe that's a blessing for those who should have come to her."

Savannah awoke then and struggled from Derek's arms. "Need potty," she said.

Kris stood from the table. "I'll take her."

"Can't it wait?" Melinda looked upset. "We're getting along so well with her."

"Not unless you want her soaked," Kris said cheerfully.

"Well, I'll go with you." Melinda stood and arched her back. "I need to check my makeup." Her makeup looked fine—if the stares the men gave her were any indication.

Brionney and Jesse waited on a nearby bench while Derek walked them to the rest room. Melinda hugged him and seemed to whisper something in his ear. As she left, Derek watched her.

"I'm surprised he's still with her," Brionney said. She wondered what it was that Derek saw in Melinda.

"Well, you said Derek is into status, and Melinda certainly catches the eye."

"Well, he can have her. I think she's obnoxious." She gave a long sigh. "Boy, my feet are hurting."

Jesse put an arm around her. "You should have worn your tennis shoes."

"I know." Brionney didn't want to admit that she hadn't wanted to feel insecure around Melinda and had dressed up a bit more than usual. Now she wished she had worn jeans and a T-shirt instead of the casual pants that had already gained a greasy stain from the metal on one of the rides. Brionney doubted it would ever come out.

"Why are they taking so long?" Jesse asked. "It's hot out here in the sun."

"The lines are terrible. Especially in the women's rest room."

"Where'd Derek go? He was standing there a minute ago."

"Maybe to the rest room himself. Probably wants to check his hair."

Jesse laughed and put an arm around her. "I love you, you know."

"I know." Brionney leaned against him, smiling her first real smile of the day. It was short-lived.

Kris came running out of the rest room. Her head darted from one side to the other. "Where are they?"

Brionney sat up. "Who? Where's Savannah?"

"With Melinda. She was combing Savannah's hair after I took her potty. I was washing my hands. There were a lot of people in there, and I turned for just a second, and then they were gone. I was sure they were waiting out here. Maybe they went out the other entrance."

Brionney felt the blood drain from her face. "Derek's gone, too."

She looked at Jesse. "They wouldn't take her like that, would they?"

"I'm checking on the other side." Jesse sprang to his feet. Brionney went with him, yelling at Kris to stay there in case Melinda or Derek showed up.

At the other entrance to the rest room, they found no trace of the other couple. "I'm looking inside," Brionney said. She went into the crowded facility and began peeking at the shoes beneath the stalls. "Melinda?" she called. There was no answer, and no shoes resembling those Melinda had worn. Ignoring the curious stares, Brionney left the bathroom at a run. Jesse was coming out of the men's side.

"Nothing," he said.

"We've got to find them!"

"I'm going to the car," he said grimly. "This is probably just another one of Melinda's tricks. But if they try to leave, they'll have to go through me."

Brionney ran back to Kris. "Jesse went out to the car."

"They wouldn't take her like that. They wouldn't!"

Brionney was no longer sure. "He did once before."

"I'm going to have them paged."

"Maybe you should call the police."

Kris wrung her hands. "And what are you going to do?"

"I'm going to find them!" Brionney took off at a run, ignoring the blisters on her feet. She had to find Savannah! A vision of the day she had discovered her baby in Derek's apartment two years earlier filled her mind. She had almost been too late then. Would she make it in time now?

Brionney began to pray.

* * * * *

"I'd like to see the look on their faces," Melinda said with a laugh.

Derek didn't join her. "Melinda, it's already been a long day. Don't you think it's time to go home?"

Melinda held on to Savannah more tightly. "I just want to have a chance with her, don't you? Think about it, Derek: this may be the only child you'll ever have."

"Derek?" Savannah said, turning her gaze to him. Her face reminded him of Brionney, who seemed as pure and untouched as when he had first met her at that dance so long ago. He wondered if she ever thought of him with regret instead of hatred. For some reason it suddenly mattered.

"She's so adorable. She looks just like you. Don't you, sweetie? You look just like your daddy."

"Where Daddy?" Savannah asked, looking around at the swarm of people. Her face paled and she began to look frightened.

"Your daddy's right here," Melinda said, pointing at Derek. "And he loves you so much."

"No Daddy. Where Daddy?" Tears gathered in Savannah's eyes.

"Will you stop that?" Derek said. "You're upsetting her."

"It's a shame she doesn't know her own father. Well, all that's going to change." She bounced Savannah in her arms. "Wanna go on another ride?"

"Mommy," Savannah said with a soft sob. "Mommy?"

The whine irritated Derek. It brought back that night when Savannah had cried alone in his bedroom. If the police had ever known he had left her there and gone out to eat with Melinda, he could have been charged with negligence—or worse. And if Brionney had come a minute later, none of them would be standing here now. Derek suddenly felt ill with guilt. He wished he were back in Arizona.

"You know what?" Melinda's excited voice shook him from the memories. Her cheeks were flushed and her eyes glittered. He loved it when she looked like that. "We could take her. Just up and leave. Then she would be ours without any problems."

"What are you saying?"

"We could go to a new state, get new jobs. We'd be a family!"

This was not going as Derek had planned. He'd agreed to come to Utah and visit Savannah because Melinda was so desperate to have a child, but what she was suggesting was too much. "I'm not giving up my career for a child."

"But she's yours! Don't you want her?"

Derek hesitated. Savannah was a beautiful child, and part of him felt some bond with her. But she also reminded him of Brionney and his own failures.

"She might be the only chance we'll have for a child," Melinda pressed, sensing his weakness.

Savannah began to cry in earnest. In her face, Derek now saw himself as a child. How many times had he stared out the window, crying, as he watched his father leave?

"No," he said shortly.

"For just a few days then, until they catch up with us. Maybe in Arizona we can get a fair trial for custody."

"And what if you get pregnant?"

There were angry tears in Melinda's eyes. "What if I don't?"

"And what if we don't stay together, then what?"

Melinda gasped. "Are you seeing that new secretary? I won't put up with it, I swear I won't!"

"Shut up. Can't you see you're making her cry even more? Let's get her back to Brionney."

"No! Just for a few days, or even a few more hours. She'll grow to like us. And I'll make it up to you. You'll see. I'll make you so happy, you won't regret it."

What Derek wanted was a drink, but he didn't know where to get one. "Look, did you ever think that a move like that would just make it worse for us? What judge would let us see her again if we took off with her?"

"They couldn't do anything if they couldn't find us." Melinda put her hand over Savannah's mouth, trying to quiet her. Savannah cried harder.

"But I'm not a criminal. And I've worked hard to get where I'm at." The words fell on deaf ears, but Derek knew how to reach her. "Look, honey." He put his arm around her slender shoulders. "We haven't been trying that long for a child. And I love you. What I want is a baby with your eyes. Savannah is cute, but think what your baby will look like. Beautiful. Like you. There is no other woman in the world like you." Part of him even meant it. He wondered if loving her was his penance for leaving Brionney and the Church.

Melinda softened under the words. "I guess we could always wait to see what happens. I mean, Savannah will always be around if we can't have our own child."

Derek tightened his hold and kissed her warm lips. Emotion stirred in his breast as it always did when he touched her. "Come on, let's go back to the car. Brionney is probably waiting there."

"Couldn't we just take her on a few rides first?"

Savannah's cry grew louder. "Mommy. Want Mommy!"

"Shut up!" Derek said, annoyed more by the looks from the people around him than by her crying. "We're going to find her." Savannah wasn't comforted. She continued to cry. Derek reached out and flicked her hard on the cheek. Savannah abruptly cut off, her eyes wide with surprise. She put her hand on her cheek, her lips quivering.

"What are you doing?" Melinda questioned.

"Teaching her to obey." Derek frowned as he heard his father in the words. He touched his own cheek in remembrance. "Come on, let's try that ride over there."

* * * * *

Brionney ran the whole length of the amusement park, going from one ride to the next. Savannah's age precluded many of the rides, but Lagoon was so big, they could be anywhere. *If they are still in the park at all.* Brionney didn't want to dwell on that scenario. "I'll never let him near her again," she vowed. "Never! And if I get my hands on Melinda, I'll strangle her!"

Several times, Brionney saw little blonde girls who looked like Savannah. Each time her heart leapt with joy, and each mistake hurt worse than the last. Would she ever see Savannah again?

A couple strolled by with a group of children, including twins in a side-by-side stroller. Brionney's heart grew heavy as her own losses came to the forefront. First the twins, and now Savannah. The grief was swift and crushing. *Oh, dear Father, help me find my baby!*

When she could walk no more, she decided to limp out to the car. At the front gates she spied Derek walking with Melinda, who had Savannah in her arms. The little girl looked as though she had been crying. "Savannah!" Brionney shouted. In a few seconds she overtook them, and grabbed her baby from Melinda's arms.

"Mommy!" Savannah clung to her, burying her face in Brionney's neck.

Brionney faced Derek. "Where on earth have you been?"

"We got separated, that's all."

"And Savannah was a little unhappy about it, so we took her on a few rides," Melinda added. "Really, she's just fine."

Brionney didn't believe them for a second. She turned on Melinda. "You planned this, I know you did! You just aren't happy to let things go slowly, are you? Savannah is my only child! Can you imagine what I've been going through these past hours? How dare you!"

"She's fine. I just wanted to get to know her."

"Well, I know you," Brionney said. "And apparently your stealing isn't limited to husbands!"

"Well, at least I'm woman enough to keep my man!"

Brionney looked at Derek in disgust. If anything, he seemed amused by the whole incident. She snorted. "You left me for this? Well, you're welcome to her. But keep her away from *my* daughter!"

"Really, Brionney. I'm sorry," Melinda said in her silky voice. "I didn't know you'd be so upset. It won't happen again."

Brionney left them, walking as quickly as her blistered feet allowed. By the time she arrived at the car where Jesse and Kris waited with several police officers, her anger had abated slightly. The warmth of Savannah in her arms was a great comfort. "I'll never let her near you again, baby. I promise." Brionney didn't know how she would keep that promise, but she would try.

Jesse ran to her and hugged them both. "I was beginning to think—where did you find them?" He looked over her shoulder at Derek and Melinda, who were following at a short distance.

"At the front gates. They were coming out to the car. They claim they got separated from us."

"And you don't think so?"

Brionney blinked away tears. "I honestly don't know. Maybe I just hate her because of Derek."

"What happened to her cheek?" He gingerly touched the red mark on Savannah's face.

"I don't know. I didn't see it." Brionney examined Savannah. Underneath the red, she could see a tiny bruise forming.

"What happened, Savvy?" Kris asked, her face paling.

"Hit me. Hurt." Savannah sniffed and buried her face in Brionney's neck.

"She fell, that's all," Derek said, coming up beside them.

"Is everything okay then?" a police officer asked. "Is anyone pressing charges?"

Brionney looked at Melinda's face, wishing she could put the woman behind bars. "No," she said. "But thank you for coming."

The ride home was filled with silence. Even Melinda was quiet. Derek drove up in front of Talia's well before dark. Savannah, her crisis forgotten, immediately ran to the sandbox where Roger was building what appeared to be a volcano.

"I guess we'll see you in three weeks," Derek said.

"We'll see." Brionney wanted to talk to Max again and see if there was anything she could do to prevent further visits. Perhaps move to Alaska? She had always wanted to see Alaska.

Melinda smiled at her sweetly, as though nothing out of the ordinary had happened. "I hope someday you'll let Savannah visit us. It's such a long drive to make once or twice a month. And you can see now how much we love her."

Brionney hadn't seen anything of the sort.

"I promise that when you're not around I'll be a good mother to her," Melinda added.

Brionney's rage returned instantly. "*I'm* her mother."

"Of course, but when we start sharing custody—" Melinda broke off as if she had made an error, but her dark eyes were calculating. The woman knew only too well what she was saying. "Well, I'm going to go say good-bye to her. Coming, Derek?"

Derek's eyes met Brionney's, but she couldn't read their expression. Questions ran through her mind. Did he want partial custody? Was he willing to go to court and shake up Savannah's whole life? Why did he care now when he never did before? Did he love Savannah as a father? Or was he here only for Melinda?

They walked over to the sandbox and tried to get Savannah's attention. She refused kisses or hugs, but waved to them willingly. *Glad to see them go,* Brionney thought.

When their visitors finally left, Brionney sagged against the porch railing. "I wish I never had to see her again. Or him. Either of them."

"Me too." Jesse stared in the direction they had gone.

"Did you ever consider moving to Alaska?"

He shook his head. "Africa is farther away." He rubbed Brionney's shoulders, and she sighed.

A miracle. All they needed was a miracle.

* * * * *

Kris held her anger in until they arrived at her apartment. Melinda was taking a bath, and Kris was alone with Derek. "What a stupid trick," she said. "Can you just once think about Savvy and Brionney instead of yourself?"

"I don't know what you're talking about, Mother." Derek used the same tone of voice with her as Logan had—as though she were a backwards child.

"Don't play innocent with me. I saw that mark on Savannah's cheek. Did you think I didn't recognize it, even if her parents didn't? How many times did your father do that to you?"

"I don't want to talk about it."

"Well, I do. And for once you're going to listen! Or you can get out and never come back."

"Get it over with, then."

Kris paced the floor. "Savannah is the most loving and open child I have ever known. If you had given her a chance, she would have come to love you. Instead, you took her away from her mother, and then you hit her. I saw how she reacted to you after that. She doesn't want anything to do with you! Anything! Just like you didn't want anything to do with your father."

"I love my father," Derek growled.

"No, you fear your father and you crave his love. But he doesn't love you, not really. You're just a showpiece to him, like Melinda is to you. Your father doesn't care about you any more than you care about Savannah. But you don't see it. Your father is too selfish to love anyone but himself. And you know what? If I had to do it all again, I would take you and run so fast and far that he could never have any influence on you." She looked at him with pleading eyes. "Derek, there is good in you. And if you want to be a father to Savannah, do it. Love her. Give it your best shot. Brionney and Jesse would support that. But if you are just letting Melinda mess with her life until her own baby comes along, then love Savannah enough to let her go!" Tears ran down Kris' cheeks. "Please! I love Savannah, and I can't bear to see her go through what you went through."

"Are you finished?" he asked, his voice cold.

She stared at him sadly. "Yes."

"Then I think it's time I got Melinda and left. It's obvious whose side you're on."

"Leave then." Her heart ached at the little boy only she could see in his eyes. "But I want you to remember that I love you. As much as Brionney loves Savannah. I've always loved you." Kris turned from him and went into the bedroom. She lay on the bed and didn't move until she heard the apartment door close.

CHAPTER THIRTY

"Short of moving farther away or going back to court, there's nothing you can do," Max said when Brionney called him. "And going to court could always mean that he'll end up with more rights, not less."

"What about Melinda? Do I have to let her come with him?"

"That's not your call to make. I'm sorry, but that's all I can tell you. The best I can do is require Kris to be there. She'll still go, won't she?"

"Yes. She's mad at Derek, but she loves Savannah. You know, I don't think Derek really wants Savannah at all. Couldn't you approach him about adoption? Just put out some feelers. Please?" Brionney had no real hopes, but she had to try.

"Look, I'll do everything I can. Try not to worry too much."

Brionney did worry. She usually enjoyed September, but this time she barely went through the motions of living. During the days after Derek's visit, she and Jesse spent every minute they could with Savannah. They went camping, hiking, and swimming as a family. Every night she and Jesse prayed fervently, and their whole family held a special fast. Brionney fought despair. She knew Melinda's pain and determination. No matter what Derek wanted, Melinda would never stop trying for custody.

* * * * *

A few days before Derek's next planned visit, Brionney received a phone call from one of her visiting teachers. "Hi, Emma. What's up?" Emma and Angela had visited earlier in the month, so she couldn't be calling to make an appointment.

"It's Angela," Emma said. "She had a miscarriage yesterday and needs some support. Her husband is out of the country on business, and she has no way to contact him. Her mother is out of state, but is on her way. I'm with her now."

Brionney's heart lurched. She knew only too well how Angela would be feeling. "Would you like me to come over?"

"Yes, if you would. My miscarriage was so long ago, and I've really come to terms with it. I don't know how to help her."

"I'll be right there."

Brionney left Savannah with Talia and walked to Angela's house. She found Angela sobbing on the couch, her two children looking on anxiously. Brionney looked at Emma. "Why don't you take the children for a walk while I stay with Angela?" She focused on the children. "Wouldn't that be fun? You guys go take a walk with Sister Stillman, and I'll stay and help your mommy. She's going to be fine."

"Yes, go on kids," Angela said. "I'll be okay." She managed to hold her sobs back until they were outside. Then Brionney held her as she cried. "I just can't stop crying," she said. "It hurts so bad!"

"I'm so sorry," Brionney said. Those words were the ones that had helped her the most when she had lost the twins.

"I keep wondering what I did, and I feel so guilty."

"I did too, but you couldn't have done anything. Just as I couldn't. It's not your fault."

"I guess I know that, but it still hurts. I need to know if I'm going to see my baby again." More tears cascaded down Angela's cheeks, and her voice turned hoarse and despairing. "They couldn't even tell if it was a boy or a girl. It was so small. It had been dead for a long time. Inside me. That brings such a horrible picture to my mind." She gave a moaning cry. "I don't even know what to mourn!"

Brionney held her for a long time. "I know it hurts. It hurts a lot. But you know what else? I know you'll see your baby again. One way or the other."

"I want my baby!" Angela sobbed. Her shoulders shook uncontrollably.

Brionney's heart filled with compassion. "I know you do. I know it so well! But do you think that just for a little time, you can trust the Lord? He'll take care of your baby. He's taking care of mine."

Angela wiped at her wet cheeks with both hands. "Oh, Brionney, I want to believe that!"

"Well, I do."

"People say things. They're trying to help, but they don't understand. They make it worse!"

"I remember." In fact, Angela had been one of those people who had unknowingly added to Brionney's pain.

Angela began to cry again, harder. "I feel so empty."

Brionney knew there was nothing she could do but love and listen to her friend. She called Jesse at work and let him know to pick up Savannah at Talia's. Then she stayed with Angela, talking until late in the night. She shared her feelings about her own miscarriage. The pain in her own heart was born anew, and she wept with Angela.

Mourning with those who mourn. The phrase now held new meaning for Brionney.

Angela's mother finally arrived, and Brionney knew it was time to leave. "Thank you so much for being here," Angela whispered. The agony still showed in her eyes, but she faced it with new strength. "I don't know what I would have done without you tonight. You're the only one who knows how I feel."

"I'll come back tomorrow," Brionney promised. "You're not alone."

Angela hugged her. "I know that now."

Brionney walked home in peaceful silence. The stars in the heavens lit her way, and a calm pervaded her senses. The renewed ache of losing her babies was once more lifted from her shoulders, as though by a loving Father. Their presence and their memory was still strong, but she didn't feel the need to cry.

Jesse waited up for her. "Well?" he asked. He touched her face. "You've been crying."

"It was just so close, reliving it all with Angela. The pain of losing them. You know, sometimes days will go by and I won't think about them at all. But tonight, I missed them so badly. We cried together."

He held her close. "Are you all right?"

"Yes, that's the strange thing. It helped both of us to talk about it. And then on the way home, the pain went away. And it was worth missing them so much, Jesse, because my experience actually helped someone tonight. Like Talia and others helped me. There's no way I could have helped Angela if I hadn't lost the babies. Maybe that's another reason why we went through that trial—not only to be strong ourselves, but to help others. And I know this might sound really stupid, but if I can help someone deal with the anguish of losing a baby, then maybe all that pain we suffered was worth even more than we knew."

His arms tightened around her. "That doesn't sound stupid. We're all here to help each other, after all."

"I thought of Melinda, too," Brionney said more slowly. "I realized that she is also a daughter of God, and she's hurting inside. I still don't want to have anything to do with her—the idea makes me want to run away to Africa or wherever—but for Savannah's sake, I'm going to try to become her friend. I'm going to try to see the good in her. It's got to be there somewhere, because she's a daughter of God. I'm going to love her and forgive her as I already have Derek. Maybe that will make this whole situation better. The Savior always loved his enemies. I think it's time I began loving mine as well."

* * * * *

The Saturday morning of Derek's visit dawned early, despite Brionney's desire to hold on to the night. She knew Derek and Melinda were somewhere in Orem, preparing to come for Savannah, to play parents for the day. The thought made her sick, and she nearly threw up. The fact that Melinda wanted to mother her baby hurt terribly. Her new resolve to befriend Melinda weakened.

"Maybe Derek and Kris can go with Savannah," she said, mostly to convince herself. "And maybe Melinda and I can go somewhere and get to know each other."

"Good luck," Jesse said. His expression darkened. "But I'm still going to warn him about Savannah falling. She'd better not have one tiny bruise when she comes home."

The doorbell rang, and Brionney tried to put on a happy face. She knew she looked awful with her eyes puffy from crying. "It's for Savannah's good," she whispered. "It has to be." With Savannah in her arms, she opened the door and stood blinking in stunned surprise.

"Aren't you going to invite us in?" Debbie asked. "Hello, Savvy. How are you?" Debbie pushed her way into the house, Max trailing behind.

"What are you doing here? I mean, come on in. What a surprise!"

Debbie sank onto the flowered sofa with the countenance of a neighbor who had just stopped in for a brief visit, instead of someone who had driven hundreds of miles. In contrast, Max appeared weary, with lines of stress accentuated around his eyes. His hair seemed grayer than Brionney remembered. She had no doubt who had driven most of the way from Arizona.

"Well this is a surprise," Jesse said. "To what do we owe this visit?"

"Oh, we just couldn't wait," Debbie began in a rush. "We had to come up and see you. You won't believe what has happened!"

"Is everything okay?" In Brionney's mind, surprises were just as often bad news as good.

"The letter," Max said. "Show her the letter."

Debbie's bottom lip jutted out in disappointment. "But I wanted to tell her."

"What letter? What's going on?"

"It's from Derek," Debbie said.

"But he's supposed to be here any minute to pick up Savannah."

Debbie shook her head. "He's not coming. That's why we're here."

Joy surged in Brionney's heart. "He's not?"

"You came all the way from Arizona to tell us Derek's not coming?" Jesse asked.

"No, no, no," Max said. "Debbie, give them the letter."

Debbie pulled out her purse and reached for a sealed envelope. Brionney let Savannah slide to the floor, then she opened the letter, hastily jerking out a single piece of paper and unfolding it with unsteady hands. Both the letter and the envelope were an undecorated white, and sure enough, Derek's familiar script covered the page. Her eyes quickly went to the first words, written with black ink that was slightly smeared in some places. In others, a few words had been crossed out, as if perhaps the phrases had been thought over a great deal. Jesse came to her side, studying the letter over her shoulder.

Dear Brionney,

By now you know that I'm not coming to Utah to visit Savannah. It has been a difficult and soul-searching few weeks for me. When we began with the idea to visit Savannah, I admit I was reluctant, pushed on by Melinda's desire to have a child. But things changed when I spent that day with her. Savannah began to be real to me, a person, not a thing, and I realized I wasn't part of her life, and that she was doing fine without me. In fact, better without me. I'm not ready to be her father. And I find I want the best for her. I don't want her growing up with a father like I had.

Melinda is pregnant, barely six weeks along. Funny, but she was already pregnant when we went to Lagoon that day. She's in the hospital now because of some complications with her smoking and because she can't keep anything down, but she's happier than I've ever seen her. She's lost interest in Savannah, which is just as well, I suppose, given my feelings. I won't try to say that her pregnancy hasn't affected my decision to let Jesse adopt Savannah—

Brionney stopped reading, her eyes wide with disbelief. He was going to let Jesse adopt Savannah! She blinked rapidly, trying to read the rest through sudden tears.

—I won't try to say that her pregnancy hasn't affected my decision to let Jesse adopt Savannah. It has. And money is particularly tight now, especially with the doctor bills we'll be having and the new house we are planning to buy. I know that sounds bad, and you'll think money is the real issue. Maybe it is. But I like to think that I don't want my daughter to suffer what I did as a child. I don't want to see her torn between us, and I know that was what Melinda intended. Regardless, I can't give Savannah what she needs. And now that Melinda's expecting, she's completely against my seeing Savannah again.

I know you'll be happy about my decision. You don't feel that Melinda and I are a good influence, and you're probably right. I don't think I'd like to see Savannah smoking or doing the things I've done. I hope Melinda and I can do better with our new baby.

Good luck and have a good life. You deserve it.

Derek

"He's giving her up," Brionney said, dropping the letter into Jesse's hands. She began to cry. "Oh, I can't believe it. It's a miracle!" She knew that only the Lord could have caused it to happen. In some small way, perhaps Derek *had* finally come to love Savannah; and with that love, he had no choice but to let her go.

"We'll never have to worry about losing her again," Jesse said, barely containing his tears.

"I feel a little sorry for their baby," Debbie said. "But motherhood changes people. Maybe it'll do Melinda good."

Brionney met Jesse's gaze. "It just might bring out the good in her heart," she said. "I believe she has some." *Maybe that's the lesson I was supposed to learn from all this.*

Brionney hugged Jesse and then Debbie and Max in turn. Happiness surged over her like a wave. She picked up Savannah and held her tightly. "You're all ours," she whispered. "I love you so much." Brionney kissed her face all over until the little girl laughed.

All at once, Brionney's wave of happiness became something else. Blood drained from her face and bile rose in her throat. Shoving Savannah into Jesse's arms, she ran to the bathroom, heaving and bringing up nothing since she hadn't yet eaten breakfast. Jesse followed her worriedly. After what seemed like a long time, the urge passed, and Brionney made her way slowly back to the front room.

"Are you okay?" Debbie asked.

"I think so . . . it must be all the excitement."

"I don't know. If I didn't know better, I'd think you were pregnant. Remember, I went through it with you when you were expecting Savannah."

Pregnant? Brionney ran to the kitchen and the calendar, her hands trembling with eagerness. *Am I late? I must really be losing it if I don't even know.*

She had been so distressed about Derek and Melinda's visit that she hadn't thought to worry about anything else. The last time she had taken a pregnancy test had been before Savannah's birthday, when Derek had first called and upset their lives, and she hadn't had a cycle since that week. "I am late! But I'm always late, so it means nothing. Of course, I don't usually throw up."

Jesse gawked at her. He shook his head, smiled, danced a little with Savannah, then practically fell on top of Brionney with a bear hug. "I love you so much!" he said. "I knew it would happen. I knew it! A father twice in one day. Can any man be so lucky?"

Before the reality could set in Brionney's mind, Jesse turned to leave the kitchen. "Where are you going?" she demanded.

"We've got guests," he said. "I'm going to the store to get some videos for tonight, or some steaks, or treats, or something." His face cracked into a wide grin. "And a pregnancy test. Savvy and I'll be back in a minute." He ran out of the room.

Brionney looked at Debbie and Max, who were both smiling. "Don't worry," she said, picking up the car keys and swinging them on her finger. "He'll be back. He can't go anywhere without the keys."

EPILOGUE

"Are you disappointed?" Jesse asked. They were in the car, coming home from a prenatal visit where she had had her first ultrasound halfway into her pregnancy.

She lifted her eyes from the ultrasound picture the doctor had given them. "No. Well, I guess I was at first. I had hoped we'd have the twins again."

"So did I. But then I realized we're having a healthy little girl, and that's what's important. And it doesn't mean that we won't have them someday."

"You're right. That's exactly how I feel."

"Did I tell you that you look beautiful today?"

She smiled. "About a million times. Thank you—again."

"Well," Jesse said, stopping the car in front of Talia's and leaning over next to her, "you are beautiful. And I love you." He kissed her to prove his point. Brionney thought life couldn't get any better.

That night she wrote in her journal:

> We are having another precious little girl. Savannah doesn't really understand yet, but I know she'll be so excited to be a big sister once the baby is here! As for us, Jesse and I still firmly believe that the twins will one day be a part of our family. And each day the ache of losing them dims a bit more, though there will always be some portion of my heart reserved for them.
>
> Time heals all wounds, they say, but I've learned that only in the Savior can the scarred tissue be made new. He will do the same for me; He has promised it. Until then, I will find happi-

ness in all the other blessings He has bestowed. Life is beautiful, and I plan to live it to the fullest. Whatever challenges life demands, Jesse and I will conquer, learning and growing together. We will keep the promise.

ABOUT THE AUTHOR

Rachel Ann Nunes (pronounced *noon-esh*) is a homemaker, student, and Church worker who lists writing as one of her favorite pursuits. *To Love and to Promise* is her seventh novel to be published by Covenant. Her *Ariana* series has been very popular in the LDS market.

In addition to writing and family activities, Rachel enjoys reading, camping, volleyball, softball, and traveling to or reading about foreign countries. She served an LDS mission to Portugal. Rachel and her husband, TJ, are the parents of five children.

Rachel enjoys hearing from her readers. You can write to her at P.O. Box 353, American Fork, UT 84003-0353, send e-mail to rachel@ranunes.com, or visit her web site at http://www.ranunes.com.